SOULBOUND

A.J. Hanna

For My Children

My three living threads of fate,
woven into my soul across every world.
My proof that love transcends time and death.

Trigger Warning:

This book contains themes and scenes that may be disturbing or triggering to some readers. Please read with care and prioritize your well-being.

Content Warnings include:

- Torture (physical, psychological, magical)
- Abduction/kidnapping
- Mental illness (e.g., depression, anxiety, PTSD)
- Panic attacks
- Drug use
- Graphic violence
- Blood/ Gore/ Death/ Murder
- Sexual content (consensual and intense)
- Emotional abuse and manipulation
- Transformation scenes
- Ritualistic elements
- Strong language

If you are sensitive to any of these topics, please proceed with caution or skip sections as needed. Your safety and comfort matter.

Title: SOULBOUND

First Edition
Cover design by A.J. Hanna
Published by "Independently published"
Printed/Published in the United States of America

Chapter 1

I didn't hear Andrew enter, but I felt him. His warmth brushed against my awareness like sunlight breaking through storm clouds, pulling me back from the edge of another waking nightmare and into the quiet hum of machines and the too-still air of the hospital room.

"Astrid," he said softly. His voice was low and careful. Like if he spoke too loudly, something fragile might shatter.

I turned toward him slowly, my hand still wrapped tight around Trovi's. Her skin was cool beneath my fingers, her breaths shallow and mechanical, each one measured by the steady beeping of the machines beside her.

"She hasn't woken up," I said, my voice distant. "Not once."

Andrew moved closer, the dim light catching in his eyes, the green turned molten, like fire trapped behind glass. He knelt beside me, close enough that I could feel the heat of him, grounding in a way nothing else had been.

"You've been here every day," he said gently. "Every night for a month."

A month. The word echoed in my head, heavy and hollow. A month since the attack. A month of watching her lie there, unmoving. A month of wondering if I had saved her… or only delayed losing her.

"I should have done more," I whispered.

"You did," he said immediately. "She's alive because of you."

My throat tightened. "Her body is. But she's not… here." My grip on her hand tightened without thinking. "She's stuck somewhere in between. And no one knows if she's coming back."

Andrew didn't answer right away, but his hand found mine warm and steady against my shaking fingers.

"She will," he said finally. "Trovi doesn't give up."

I wanted to believe that.

I really did.

But the quiet in the room felt wrong, too heavy and watchful. Like the air itself was holding its breath. And the nightmares never let me forget why.

Even now, they clung to the edges of my vision the shadows curling where they shouldn't, stretching just a little too far. Sometimes, when I blinked, I swore I saw movement. A shape. A presence that is just watching and waiting. Sometimes it was Trovi that stood among them, silent but reaching towards me.

Other times… Something else answered instead. My chest tightened, and I forced the images back before they could take hold. Something had changed that night. I could feel it.

Not in my thoughts, but deeper. Beneath skin and bone, coiled in my marrow itself. It was quiet and patient. It didn't speak. It didn't need to. And that was the worst part.

"It's not just what happened to her," I said, my voice lower now. "Something's wrong with me too."

Andrew's attention sharpened. "What do you mean?"

I hesitated, my hand tightening into a fist before I could stop it. "When it stirs… I feel it," I admitted quietly. "It's not just the power anymore, Andrew… it's something else. It's calling for more blood, more life. There are whispers… things I

don't want to feel." My fingers twitched as I clenched them tighter. "And a part of me… wants to listen."

His hand tightened slightly as it was over mine. "Then we'll learn to control it. Together. No matter what, we face it side by side."

Silence settled between us, heavy but not empty. His thumb brushed slowly over my knuckles before he continued.

"I feel it too," he said quietly.

That made me look at him.

"There's something bleeding through our bond," he continued. "Something dangerous. But that doesn't make you a monster, Astrid."

'He sounds like Trovi,' Mani whispered, and the ache in my chest deepened.

"And what if I do lose my direction?" I asked, glancing at Trovi's motionless form.

"Then I'll be there to remind you who you are."

I swallowed hard, fighting the rising tide of desperation. His words broke something loose inside me. I wanted to believe him. I *needed* to. This power was a living thing inside me now; it didn't want belief. It wanted release. It wanted to tear and burn and *feed*. And the truth was... I had tasted the darkness. And a part of me liked it.

"I'm scared," I breathed. "Scared I'll hurt the people I love."

"I know." His voice softened as he pulled me into his arms. "But you're not alone in this. You don't get to be alone in it."

We stayed like that for a long while, wrapped in the quiet hum of machines and the soft shimmer of moonlight spilling across the floor. The weight of everything pressed down like stone, yet in his steady presence, a fragile ember of hope flickered to life within me.

I let myself lean into him, just for a moment, felt the warmth of him, the quiet strength, the rhythm of his heartbeat grounding mine. For a second, the shadows felt farther away. When he finally pulled back, his hand didn't leave mine.

"Come on," he said softly, giving a gentle tug toward the door.

I hesitated, my gaze drifting back to Trovi.

What if she woke up and I wasn't there?

'Then we rush our asses back here' Mani said

The thought twisted tight in my chest, but the room already felt suffocating, thick with memory, with fear, with everything I couldn't fix. Even the air itself seemed too heavy to breathe.

My fingers tightened around his.

And then, quietly, I let him lead me out.

Back in our room, the fire had already been lit. Its glow painted the walls in shifting gold and shadow, chasing away the worst of the cold, but not all of it. Some of it had settled too deep.

I sat on the edge of the bed, staring at the floor while Andrew knelt beside the hearth, adjusting the logs.

"You've barely slept since she's been admitted," Andrew said, kneeling to stir the fire. "Even wolves need to rest, you know."

"I can't," I murmured. "Every time I close my eyes…" I trailed off. "And what if she wakes up and I'm not there?"

"She won't want you destroying yourself for her," he said, glancing back at me. "You've done more than enough."

"Have I?" My voice cracked. "It's just… the room… it feels like it's holding its breath. Like something's… *watching.*"

Andrew crossed the room and sat beside me, his hand brushing over my shoulder as he pulled me into his side.

"Yeah," he said. "I felt it too."

That made my stomach twist.

"So, it wasn't just me."

"No." His gaze flicked briefly to the fire, the flames shifting, just slightly, before settling again. "It wasn't."

Silence fell, heavier this time.

"You're safe here," he said quietly.

A small, tired laugh slipped out of me. "You sound very sure of yourself."

"I'm not sure of much lately," he admitted, resting his forehead lightly against mine. "But I know that when you're with me… everything, all the chaos, gets quieter."

The chaos. He didn't need to name it. The same chaos I feel each night, when my dreams burn red. We both feel it, the Garmr's hunger thrummed at the edges of our minds, a call to rage and ruin. It is stronger with Mani and me; we have pushed back against it with bared teeth. And beyond it, the shadow of something larger, a wolf-shape that is crowned with dragon wings, circling the edges of my sleep, waiting for the night it would find me.

"I need that," I whispered.

"I know."

"You make me feel... safe," I admitted. "Even when it feels like the shadows are breathing down my neck."

He cupped my face, his thumb brushing over my cheek gently. “And you make me feel like I can be more than all this… all that’s going on around…and with us.”

The fire’s crackle was the only sound between us, a fragile song of warmth. The nightmares, the rage pressing at the door, they felt far away, muted by his presence.

“Ready for some rest?” he murmured, but he didn’t wait for my answer, as he guided me down gently, like he was afraid I might shatter if he moved too fast. His arms came around me, firm and protective, his warmth chasing away the chill that had lingered since the night everything fell apart. My head found its place beneath his collarbone, where his scent, pine and the damp forest after a storm, lingered in the quiet between heartbeats. Each steady thud beneath my cheek grounded me, reminding me he was real, and that we were both still here.

I pressed closer, my head settling beneath his collarbone, listening to the steady rhythm of his heartbeat.

For the first time in days, the tight pressure in my chest eased.

Not gone.

But bearable.

The darkness could wait.

Tonight, there was only warmth, the slow fade of the fire, and the fragile illusion of peace.

Chapter 2

The next morning, golden sunlight spilled through the windows, too bright and after the weight of the night. For a moment, I didn't move. Andrew was still beside me, his warmth still clinging to my skin, his arm draped heavy and familiar around my waist.

For the first time in a month, I'd slept deeply. There weren't any shadows at my heels and no nightmares clawing me awake. Just breath, warmth, and the steady rise and fall of his chest against my back. I shifted slightly, and his arm tightened instinctively, like even in sleep he didn't want to let me go.

"Astrid," he murmured, half-asleep.

"I'm here," I whispered.

We stretched together, slowly and lazily, savoring the fragile moment of the morning. He finally loosened his grip, and I slipped out of bed to dress, the cool air brushing over me, and felt his gaze before I ever turned. Andrew remained Lying there in the sheets, still rumpled from sleep, eyes half-lidded, but focused. Like I was the only thing in the room that mattered, like he was memorizing every piece of me before the day could take me away.

"Staring is rude," I murmured, though my smile gave me away.

"Not staring," he said, his voice still thick with sleep. "Just admiring what is mine."

Heat curled through my chest despite the eyeroll I gave him. A soft laugh escaped me before I could stop it.

"Debatable," I said.

"Not from where I'm lying." He stretched again, the sheet slipping dangerously low on his hips. "Come back to bed."

"I thought you liked it when I got dressed." I turned toward him, catching him staring for a moment at the scar marring my chest, a permanent reminder of Alastor. His eyes returned to mine, that familiar, teasing grin brushing his lips, and my chest clenched with something I couldn't name. I pulled my shirt on deliberately slow, savoring the reaction I knew I'd provoke.

"I just like it when you're close to me," he said simply. "Clothes are optional." He shrugged.

"We need food," I replied, pulling my shorts up into place. "And coffee. Preferably before you start talking like that again."

"I like how I'm talking," he said.

"Of course you do."

He made a low hum, one that vibrated like approval and protest all at once. "Fine. But only if you let me have you later." The words sent a quiet thrill through me, as soft as it was possessive. I crossed the room and brushed my fingers along his jaw, feeling him lean into the touch.

"Later," I promised, and he caught my hand, pressing a kiss to my palm before letting me go.

'It has been a month, you know,' Mani said, whining

'I know,' I said quietly, a twinge of guilt in my voice.

'He hasn't pushed you for anything. You should give him more attention... I'm pretty sure he's struggling not to tear our

clothes off this very second,' Mani added, and I couldn't help the small, guilty smile that tugged at my lips.

He finally rose, tugging on his pants with a sigh like he was being forced out of paradise. When he reached me, his fingers threaded through mine without a second thought.

With our fingers laced, we wandered toward the kitchen, guided by the bright scent of herbs and the soft promise of fresh bread lingering in the air. It felt as though the world itself had shifted overnight from shadow into something almost gentle.

The kitchen pulsed with life. Pots clanged, steam curled from simmering pots, voices rose in soft laughter and conversation. Rosemary, warm dough, spiced meats, all the scents that should have comforted me, but it didn't, not fully.

A prickle slid up my spine that was cold and certain. The shadows seemed to cling too tightly, too thickly, at the edges of the room. Rippling with a slow, liquid-like movement, as if they breathed on their own. The runes on my hand thrummed in answer, their glow stubborn against the daylight, refusing to dim, as if trying to warn me.

"Astrid?" Andrew's fingers tightened around mine.

But dread was already closing in, pressing against my ribs, sharp and suffocating.

"Let me go get you some water…stay here." He said, letting go of my hand and walking away.

I tried to respond, but the world shifted. Then, in a heartbeat, the kitchen dissolved and everything went black around me. Tile turned to frozen black sand, the biting cold cutting through my knees as I fell. The air thickened into shadow, stretching into trees that breathed, their bark shifting like skin. A cliff rose before me, jagged, then dropped into nothing. On the cliffs edge was a bone-white tree, its branches clawed at a bruised sky. The cliffs edge unraveling into nothingness. Far below, silver flickered in a vast, churning dark.

Then, a presence that was familiar, and immense, but just out of sight, leaned toward me. I knew this figure, somehow. A figure I seemed to fear...no not fear, longed for? Its outline wavered, stretching like smoke caught in a storm.
I reached for it, but it vanished.
My breath tore out of me, as the light rushed back so fast it hurt my eyes that I had to cover them.

I blinked hard, gasping, and the kitchen snapped into place again, the warmth, the noise, the smells. I grabbed the edge of the table to steady myself, breathing sharp and uneven. But the cold from that other place clung to me like frost, sinking deep into my bones, refusing to let go.

'You saw him,' Mani said.

'I...saw... something,' I whispered back. *'It was like he was right there, but I couldn't touch him. The tree... the lake...'*

'Between worlds,' Mani murmured.

"Astrid." This voice was familiar, but different at the same time. A shiver ran down my spine as a hand brushed my arm.

"Hey..." I turned, expecting it to be Andrew.

When I turned Andrew was not there. Instead, I made eye contact with Naomi. She stood half-veiled in the shadows beneath a rack of hanging herbs. Her silver hair hung loose around her face, and her amethyst eyes, usually bright with smug mischief, were fractured, their light dull and uneven. She didn't blink.

Before I could speak, she inclined her head toward a narrow door hidden between the spice shelves and dry pantry.

"We need to talk," she said, her voice brittle, charred at the edges. She didn't wait for an answer. She just turned and walked through, never looking back.

'We shouldn't go,' Mani murmured, low and tense.

'But we are,' I answered, my feet already moving, my pulse pounding in my ears like a warning drum. This wasn't the Naomi I knew; she thrived on spectacle, always made an entrance when she knew she could control the room.

'Maybe she's finally realized she's no match for us?' Mani offered a thread of sharp amusement in her voice.

'No,' I replied, my eyes locked on Naomi's retreating figure. *'That's what makes this worse. She isn't playing her normal game. Not this time.'*

I stepped into a narrow office. The air cooled. Ledgers lined the walls. Herbs hung in bunches overhead, their scent too sharp in such a small space. The door shut behind me, and the world hushed. Shadows leaned closer, thick and aware, clinging like damp breath against my skin.

Naomi stood in the center of the room, unmoving. Her posture was too still, too rigid. Her fingers twitched like marionette strings held too tight.

"Astrid," she said, but it wasn't just her voice. It came layered, guttural and warped, like something inhuman was wearing her words.

'She's not...Naomi...,' Mani warned. *'Not fully.'*

I didn't respond. The light behind Naomi's eyes wasn't hers. It was like someone had cracked the mirror of her soul and tried to hold her together with shadows.

"What happened to you?" My voice barely a breath.

Her lips curved into a hollow smile. Her eyes flickered, not to black but to an ember-yellow glow. “I’m not who I was. Not anymore.”

“What do you mean?” I took a step forward, every instinct screaming at me to stop. “What's…who’s… is someone controlling you?”

Her gaze caught mine, fractured light shimmering in her pupils. “Not yet little wolf. For it circles, it waits, the wolf, the dragon.”

I took another step towards her.

Her gaze didn’t leave mine. “He’s in me. I’ve been chosen as a vessel. But not for long. He’s not here for me.”

My heart clenched, “Then who?”

Her smile twisted into something venomous. “You… it’s always you. Your blood. His fire. That bond you share…that you cling to,” Her head tilted, almost birdlike and unnatural. “But not for long. We will fracture it, make you vulnerable, and rip it apart for the unraveling. Then the rage will hollow you out. And when it does, he’ll claim what’s left.”

My fingers twitched at my sides, the runes blazing with a sudden surge.

“I’m going to tear you open,” she whispered. Shadows crawled over her skin. “Rip everything you love to shreds. And you’ll watch it happen.”

I stumbled back, my pulse thundering.

“This is my warning to you,” she said. Her mixed voice, sharp and icy. “Trust no one… not even Mani.”

The sound of her name ripped through me. Pain flared behind my eyes, sudden and sharp, like fingers digging into a place no one was ever meant to touch. My breath stuttered, my

skin prickling as if something had reached *inside* me—past bone, past blood—into the place where Mani lived.

'How does that bitch know my name?' Mani snarled, her anger edged with unease. *'She shouldn't know my name.'*

"But… how?" I whispered, my throat tight.

'Don't believe her,' Mani said fiercely. '*You know me, Astrid. You know me,'* but I could feel her trembling. The words had cut her deeply.

That was the part that scared me most. Because this wasn't a distant threat anymore. It wasn't just lurking in the shadows. It was here in my home now, wearing Naomi's skin.

"Astrid?" Andrew's voice cut through, and the door burst open behind me.

I turned, startled. "Andrew…what are you…?"

"I should ask you that. What are you doing in here all alone?" His gaze searched mine, concern etched into every line of his face.

I spun back toward Naomi.

She was gone.

'What?!' Mani snapped. *'There's no other door! No window...how did she...?'*

I stood frozen, staring at the empty space she had filled only seconds ago.

Andrew stepped closer, gently pulling me into his arms. "Hey, hey. Breathe, love. You're shaking. What happened?"

"I thought… Naomi…she wanted to talk. She was right here. She told me…she said I couldn't trust anyone…Not even Mani." My voice cracked on her name, and I felt Mani go very still inside me.

Andrew's jaw clenched. "She didn't come out. I would've seen her. Astrid, what did she *mean*?"

"I don't know," I whispered. "But it felt like she wasn't alone… like something else was speaking *through* her. Her eyes…they flashed the same color of the dark völva's."

He held me tighter, his warmth keeping me on solid ground. "Then we'll figure this out. Come on. Let's get something to eat."

I let him guide me back through the doorway, but I didn't look over my shoulder.

Because I already knew what I'd see.

Nothing, just an empty room that felt too quiet and still.

The silence behind us was too heavy, and the fear in my chest throbbed with the sharp certainty of something, or someone was tracking me, watching and waiting. Even in full daylight, I couldn't shake the feeling that unseen eyes were fixed on me.

Chapter 3

Andrew and Red had finally managed to coax me into eating something. It wasn't much, just a few bites, barely enough to count as a meal, but it was enough to ease the worry etched into both their faces. Afterward, Andrew guided me back to our room, his hand warm at the small of my back, the quiet between us soft and steady.

After a while of quiet stillness, it hit. A sudden shift in the air, as if the world exhaled all at once… and forgot how to breathe back in.

It wasn't weather. It was magic.

It struck with no warning, no sound, only a bone-deep tremor shuddered through me, so sharp it felt surgical, like invisible wires were being tightened inside my chest and then snapped all at once. My fingers went weak around the book I was holding; it slipped from my hand and hit the floor with a dull thud.

My heart lurched hard, painful, and staggering. Something was wrong. Terribly and impossibly wrong. Not with me. I snapped my gaze to Andrew, expecting to see the same shock, the same jolt of pain, the same recognition of danger. But his expression didn't change. He didn't flinch. Didn't tense. He didn't feel it at all.

'Andrew seems okay... so...' Mani murmured, her voice low and uncertain.

I winced, as another wave passed over me. '*It's not Andrew.'*

“Trovi.” Her name ripped from my throat at the same moment Mani hissed it.

A violent wave of nausea surged through me, curling hot and cold in my gut. A freezing spike shot down my spine. The runes carved along my hands flickered to life, bright and frantic, before dimming again like a failing heartbeat. The scent of parchment in our room turned sour in my nose, thick and wrong. The silence around me tightened until it felt like a hand around my throat.

“Love?” Andrew’s voice cut through the suffocating stillness, soft but edged with rising concern as he crossed the room. “Everything ok?”

“Yes…No.” My voice cracked. I pushed to my feet so fast the world tilted. “I’m fine, but we need to go. Now.”

I didn’t wait for his answer. I was already halfway out the door before the words finished leaving my mouth. His voice called after me, muffled beneath the thunder of my pulse as I tore down the stairs, through the halls, and out onto the street. I barely felt the stone beneath my feet. My vision tunneled, narrowed to a single need so fierce it swallowed everything else.

I had to get to her.

I just needed to get to her.

Crowds blurring into streaks of color as I tore through them. People stepped aside at the last second, startled shouts trailing behind me, but I barely heard them. Every step drove the same truth deeper into my bones…she was pulling me. Not with magic, not with anything mortal. But with something older, something woven into me before I ever understood its shape. A thread, frayed to its last fibers, yanking tight with desperation.

By the time I burst into the hospital room, my lungs were on fire, and my runes were glowing faintly. The sharp bite of antiseptic slammed into me first, then the unmistakable metallic sting of blood. But my gaze snapped instantly to the far bed.

Trovi.

A cluster of nurses surrounded her; their palms lit with trembling healing magic. The air around them crackled with frantic energy. Panic threaded their whispered incantations, their movements jerky, and uncertain. One looked up as I stumbled in, his eyes widening, panic reflecting back at me like a mirror.

"She started seizing less than five minutes ago," he stammered. "Then she just… stopped. We can't get her to respond."

I didn't react at first, then I moved straight to her bedside and sank onto the edge of the mattress. Her face, usually so full of life and awe, was slack and pale, drained of everything that made her Trovi.

"Trovi…" My voice cracked, barely a whisper, as I reached for her wrist. Her pulse fluttered weakly under my fingertips, and her skin was cold.

I willed the runes to ignite. They answered with a violent heat that wasn't comforting. It was a warning, a demand, and a plea all at once. They surged like a living thing, rising along my hands in jagged pulses.

I grabbed her hand with one of mine and pressed the other firmly against her sternum, channeling everything I could.

"Come on," I whispered, my breath trembling. "You're not done. You don't get to be done yet."

'Astrid!' Mani's voice rang sharp, brittle with fear. *'We don't know what happens when we use this power!'*

'It heals…!' I snapped back, desperation drowning all reason. *'We have to get it to work. That's what we need...what she needs, and we need her!'* I struggled to concentrate on the runes.

I drew a shaking breath and forced my focus inward—toward the runes, toward the power coiled beneath my skin, toward whatever answer waited in the space between life and death, and I pushed further.

Magic flared between us, wild and unsteady. Then the air rippled, the bed beneath Trovi shuddered, and my runes blazed so brightly I could see their reflection in the metal cabinets around us. I felt Andrew, his presence flooded into me like a second pulse. Like his heartbeat slipped into the rhythm of mine, until they beat as one, steadying what should have shattered me.

I didn't know how and I didn't have time to ask, but he was there, lending me strength through the bond we never fully understood. Our bond tightened, raw and bright, our magic threading together, mine and his, sharp and raw, the Garmr's bloodlust pressing at the edges, intoxicating and terrifying.

The runes on my skin blazed hotter, fed not only by me, but by him.

I focused, pushing power through our bond into her, precise and desperate, threading life into the fragile threshold where she hovered. Then again. I gritted my teeth, fighting to keep the edges of *us* intact while power surged between our bodies, threading into Trovi with desperate precision.

And as the power leapt toward her, something stirred in Trovi. Not death, but a crossing. A threshold so thin it felt like

ice beneath bare feet. She was hovering on it, she was too still too quiet, as if choosing which side to fall toward.

Then Trovi's chest lifted once, shallow and fragile, like a breath borrowed from another world. But it was enough. Then I pushed again.

The connection between us trembled, a silver wire pulled taut between here and somewhere impossibly far.

"Hold on." I whispered, brushing damp hair from her forehead with trembling fingers. "I'm here. I'm with you. You're not going anywhere without me."

Andrew wrapped around me, grounding me, lending his magic, holding me as I poured everything into her. When the last threads slipped from my hands, my body gave out. His arms were already there, catching me, gathering me in. Hot tears traced my cheeks, and his thumb brushed them away with gentle precision.

Exhaustion hit heavy and mercilessly. The runes across my skin flickered weakly, dimming to a restless glow.

"I can't leave her…" The words broke raw against his chest.

"Astrid," Andrew murmured, his voice low but firm, in that way that meant he was terrified but holding steady for me, "there's nothing more you can do without tearing yourself apart."

"She's…she's not fighting her way back," I gasped, choking on the weight in my throat. "She's heading toward something…I felt it."

He didn't argue. He didn't try to feed me an empty comfort. He just held me tighter, his arms locked around me as if he could keep me from breaking apart completely. I sobbed against him until my lungs ached, until my tears soaked the fabric of his shirt, until there was nothing left inside me but the hollow fear of losing someone I should have been able to save.

Andrew never let go. Not even for a second.

“Come on,” he whispered after a while, his hand smoothing over my spine like he was coaxing me back into my body. “ Let’s get some rest. We’ll figure out our next move.”

I nodded, weakly. My gaze drifting back at Trovi. The room had quieted. Finally, the heart monitor’s slow, steady beep marked the fragile return of life.

“I want to stay.” I murmured. “I just…I just want to be here tonight…Is that ok?” I asked him softly.

His fingers threaded through my hair tenderly, as he kissed the top of my head. “You don’t need my permission, love. I just don’t want you forgetting to take care of yourself.” As he looked into my eyes, his thumb brushing my cheek. “I’ll get us some blankets and something to sleep on.”

I sank into the chair beside Trovi’s bed, tracing faint, meaningless shapes against the cold metal frame. Every inhale she took felt like a coin flipped in the dark. The dark völva’s eyes flashed in my mind, they were knowing, hungry, and sparkled with triumphant. Then bile tightened my throat.

“Here,” Andrew said when he returned, arms full of blankets as nurses wheeled in spare cots. “Lay down and get some rest.”

I exhaled shakily, grateful for anything softer than a chair. The moment my body hit the thin mattress, exhaustion swallowed me whole, but sleep offered no mercy.

The nightmare came again. Endless rivers of blood flowed, but it wasn’t mine. Faces flickered, broken memories

that didn't belong to me. Hunger gnawed at me, wild and relentless, twisting into rage, desperate to tear everything open.

Then the trees bled shadow. Smoke curling and shaping itself into a creature, a wolf rippling into the shape of a dragon. Its eyes like molten ambers rimmed with dying moonlight. The serpentine slits glowed alive with rivers of red. They burned with the patience of something that had seen worlds wither and gods decay. Within their depths, stars seemed to collapse, each one a light swallowed, each one a life undone. Its gaze did not simply look, but consumed, peeling back flesh, fate, and time itself.

It didn't lunge.

It didn't speak.

It simply *watched*, as if memorizing the shape of my soul.

I jerked awake with a gasp, drenched in cold sweat, heart battering my ribs. The room hummed quietly around me, machines steady and oblivious. But the shadow of that gaze clung to me like a bruise, throbbing with every breath. I stared at the ceiling, wishing for silence, real silence, one without blood or whispers.

Faint light pressed through the window, night bleeding slowly into dawn. I looked over to Trovi, not expecting movement. But her eyelids fluttered, then they slowly opened, clouded, but aware.

"Trovi?" I whispered.

Her lips parted, a breath rasping out like dry leaves crushed underfoot. "Astrid…" she croaked.

I ripped the blanket away and rushed to her side. "I'm here," I whispered, cupping her cheek. "You're safe."

Her gaze drifted past me, over my shoulder, through the walls, into some place I could not see. "Be careful," she breathed, her voice trembling. "The dark völva … and… he's watching. Not just you…" Her throat worked, struggling. "But your power."

My throat tightened. "My power? He? He who?"

Trovi's fingers twitched weakly. Her gaze drifted to the glow of the runes on my hands, her voice barely a breath. "Your power." She murmured. "It's different now. It's not just your magic. The bond…your souls…" Her eyes fluttered, struggling to stay open. "They're trying to break it. If it twists you… it twists him. The darkness won't just take you… it will take both of you."

A cold shiver ran down my spine. "We won't let it control us. I swear it."

Her expression softened, exhaustion overtaking her. "Promise… be cautious…my study…go…"

Her voice dissolved, her eyelids falling shut again. The moment slipped away like mist through my fingers. I stayed frozen, clutching her hand, pressing my forehead to her knuckles as her warning pulsed through me like a curse with a heartbeat.

Finally, I tore myself away and hurried to the nurses' station, giving them only what they needed to continue care. They rushed past me toward her room, and I stayed in the hallway, finding a small bench and sinking onto it. The silence pressed down on me like a shroud.

Andrew found me minutes later, woken by the nurses' sudden commotion. His steps softened when he saw me hunched forward.

"Hey," he said gently, crouching in front of me. "What happened? Is she okay?"

"She woke up," I whispered. "Only for a moment."

His brows furrowed. "What did she say?"

I hesitated, *'Do we...'*

'Tell Him!' Mani urged sharply. *'He is just as much a part of this as you are...tell him.'*

I let out a slow breath, "She said... they are watching my power. That it's not just my magic...our bond...our souls... could... consume us if twisted?"

Andrew's expression hardened. "The bond?" he repeated quietly. "Your power, our bond...it's got to be tied to something deeper."

I nodded. "She said if it twist me... it twist you. It's... something they want to control."

His jaw tightened, his hand closing around mine, strong and sure. "Then we don't have time to waste. We have to learn to control it...whatever this is... before it controls either of us."

My chest tightened. "I'm scared. It's growing in us. And the Garmr's rage...Andrew, it wants more than magic...Trovi just proved what we feared!"

He leaned forward, pressing his forehead gently against mine, the heat of his breath soft against my skin. "We'll face it together," he whispered, voice low and steady. "I won't let you fall. Not now. Not ever."

For a moment, that fragile flicker of hope stirred in my chest, a small but defiant glow in the shadows like a dying ember refusing to be snuffed out. But I still felt the echo of the wolf-dragon's eyes in the back of my mind.

Then I remembered the last thing Trovi said, "Her study..."

Andrew looked up, "What about it?"

"I don't know, that was the last thing she said, my study, go." I said, looking up at Andrew.

"Okay. Well, it's something." He stood and offered me his hand. "Let's get some real rest. Then we'll head to her house."

I nodded, letting him pull me to my feet. We stepped out into the early morning air, cold and still, and the silence felt too deep.

'We aren't alone in this; we have Andrew and Atius.' Mani reminded me. *'Don't push him away from us now when we need him now more than ever,'*

'I know...but even still, with all this? The weight of what we'd uncovered...I don't want to add to his stress.' I say back.

'And you think that not telling him will fix that?'

'Ok, ok, I get it.' I rolled my eyes.

"What are you two arguing about?" Andrew asks with a smirk.

I huffed. "She's lecturing me about not pushing you away. I just… I don't want to add to your stress. But we said we were in this together."

"Yes," he said, lifting my hand and threading our fingers. "Together."

The gesture tugged a smile from me despite everything.

"Hey Mani, don't let her forget that" he says looking deep into my eyes. I feel Mani straighten and I roll my eyes again at her smug satisfaction.

I groaned, "Ok, are we done picking on me?"

He laughed soft and warm, the sound grounding me in a way nothing else ever could.

"Come on," I said, quieter than I meant to. "Let's stop by the library first. Maybe there's something there… something that can point us in the right direction."

Because the thought of going to her house… of stepping inside without her there, it settled heavy in my chest. Everything about it felt wrong. Like the world had shifted out of place.

Her life was still hanging in the balance, caught somewhere between life and death, and no one knew if she would ever fully come back.

Andrew's hand tightened gently around mine, pulling me back before I could sink too far into my thoughts. "Yeah," he said softly. "We'll start there."

I nodded, even though the dread hadn't loosened its grip. Because the library felt safer than her house. Safer than the silence her absence would leave behind.

Then together, we turned and headed toward the library, toward shelves lined with answers… or at least something that might keep me from breaking under the weight of not knowing.

Chapter 4

Since Trovi had awoken briefly, the nightmares eased slightly, but only the way a storm eases, pulling back just far enough to make you hope, before slamming into you again. Even after days of rest, I can still feel them, clinging to me like smoke, it feels impossible to scrub from the corners of my mind. Every time sleep dragged me under, the same silhouette waited at the treeline of my dreams, its shape stitched from wolf and dragon. It never stepped fully into the light, but it knew that it didn't need to. It hunted me from the shadows, content to let dread do its stalking.

Each morning, I woke with its presence lingering in my bones, a cold breath trailing my spine, and the metallic bite of iron on my tongue. So, I buried myself in the library, deep stacks, the quiet halls, dust and parchment, anything to avoid the silence waiting in Trovi's house. I was finally ready to admit what I'd been running from: Trovi might not come back. The truth sat in my chest like a hot coal, burning through every excuse I'd made.

But accepting that didn't mean I could walk through her doorway and feel the weight of her absence crush me all over again. I wasn't ready for that. I wasn't ready to see her chair empty. Her tools untouched. Her life paused mid-breath, waiting for someone who might never return.

So, I stayed here instead, in the only place that didn't demand I look grief in the eye, half-searching for answers and half-hiding from the whispers I wasn't ready to hear.

Warm lamplight flickered over shelves warped by age, shadows dancing across spines of cracked leather and vellum turned brittle with centuries. The scent of parchment, dried herbs, dust, and something older, magic soaked into stone, wrapped around me like a cloak. I leaned over a long table littered with scrolls and grimoires; their pages spread open like offerings and let the scrape of ink and the weight of real paper anchor me to the world.

Hours bled into days, all of it blurring into a quiet ache.

And then, buried between forgotten histories and half-rotted rune compendiums… something finally shifted. I wasn't searching with purpose anymore, flipping absently through brittle vellum pages, letting the weight of ink and age keep my hands occupied while my mind spun circles around everything, and anything else.

But on a page warped with moisture and time, a sketch caught my eye. A pattern I knew, because it was etched into me.

My breath stilled. Slowly, I lowered the book into the lamplight.

The Helm of Awe glowed faintly from the page, staring back at me.

My breath caught, not because the symbol was unfamiliar, but because it was *mine*. The eight-armed compass etched into the vellum mirrored the one etched into my skin. Something stirred in my hands. A low thrum pulsed beneath my palms, like a distant drumbeat answering its own name.

Along each finger, two smaller runes, eight total, four pairs, rested like sleeping embers waiting for breath.

I read the first two: Uruz and Fehu.

My fingers twitched before I consciously moved them. Heat flared along my index finger, sharp and raw, and for a heartbeat I wasn't in the library anymore, I was straining against invisible restraints, my muscles screaming.

'Uruz,' I repeated. Strength born of refusal.

Beside it, *'Fehu'* flickered warmer, steadier. Not destruction, but transformation. Fire that can be *changed* instead of just devouring.

'Careful,' Mani murmured.

I swallowed and forced myself to breathe.

The next two I read was Perthro and Algiz.

The air thickened as my middle fingers brushed the page. A ripple passed through my skull, half-memory, half-premonition. Claws clattering on stone. Paths branching and collapsing.

'Algiz' answered as I read with a sharper note, like a shield snapping into place. My shoulders loosened an inch without me meaning them to.

Then I read Laguz and Sowilo.

Cool washed up my arms, a deep, tidal pull that dragged at my ribs. Water in moonlight. Dreams slipping through fingers. Then, light. Sudden and blinding, a flash of clarity so clean it hurt.

Truth whispered the rune. Whether I wanted it or not.

The last two I read were Kenaz and Tiwaz.

The moment my eyes reached the last pair, my pulse spiked.

Kenaz burned hungry and bright, a flame that wanted, needed, to be fed. But it was Tiwaz that stole the breath from my lungs.

Sacrifice.

The word didn't read so much as *strike.*

White-blue light detonated across my palm, heat flaring hard enough that I hissed and nearly dropped the book. The rune blazed like a wound ripped open, and suddenly I understood, in my bones.

Justice that demanded loss.

My hands trembled as I traced each meaning, each purpose. Dust drifted through the lamplight in slow, spiraling threads, like secrets trying to rise and escape before I could read them aloud.

The book read:

"The Helm of Awe, or Aegishjalmr (EYE-gis-hiowlm-er), is a sacred ward of gods and giants, a circle of eight runes forged to instill fear, fortify the spirit, and bend the will of battle. Warriors painted it before war to strike terror in their foes and steel their own hearts. It resists corruption... but only when the bearer's will remains unyielding."

I stared down at my palms, at the helm etched into my skin.

'So... is it... a gift? A curse? Or a brand from gods I'd never prayed to?' I whispered. *'Do you think it really works like that?'*

'I fucking hope so,' Mani muttered, low and sharp. *'But there's nothing here that says how it works.'*

'Maybe...' My fingers trembled as I turned my hands in the lamplight. *'Maybe it's not about casting a spell. Maybe it's about how I choose to use it. About... will-power?'*

'That makes sense," Mani said thoughtfully. *'Thinking back, when you used it, you didn't invoke anything. You forced it. Or rather... willed it into being.'*

The runes pulsed beneath my skin in answer, soft at first, then growing deeper. Even the mark on my forehead, silent since Niflheim, stirred faintly. All of it humming together, as if I'd become an instrument being tuned by unseen hands.

Andrew was a few shelves away, thumbing through dusty council records, but his presence felt like a distant echo. The silence buzzed in my ears.

"Astrid?" Andrew's voice cut through the silence, startling me. I hadn't heard him approach. When I looked up, he was closer than I remembered, his gaze was locked on my hand where Tiwaz still burned, reflected sharp and bright in his eyes.

The runes weren't passive. They weren't symbols waiting to be interpreted.

They were *listening*.

The next page of the grimoire caught my eye. A page that was unlike the others, it wasn't bound into the spine, it was brittle, and older than the others. Its script was a blood-red, handwritten with ink that hadn't faded. A sketch spread across it, a ritual with the same eight runes, an ancient slab of stone. And beneath it, three lines written, each one darker than the last.

Blood of the Forgotten.
Key of the Bound.
Forge of the Final Rite.

My throat closed, the chill in my chest spreading like frost under my skin. The lamplight dimmed at the edges of my vision, shadows pressing closer as if the words themselves had weight.

Andrew leaned closer. "What else did you find?" His eyes tracked the page, tension pulling at the corners of his mouth.

"I don't think they're just symbols." I murmured, "It's some… kind of a process."

"To what?" His voice was low and wary.

My fingertip traced the shape of the Helm, "The Final Rite." I whispered. "These three lines, they look like… steps. A ritual. Something that forges or binds blood…and maybe soul." Andrew's jaw clenched. "And this? A Völundr?"

"I don't know." Frustration and fear tangled in my voice. "Maybe it's the beginning of it. Or maybe it's a person. A title. A thing that's made, or a thing that makes."

The silence between us was heavy and charged. Then Andrew slowly reached for my hand. The runes flared beneath his touch, pale blue at first, then flickering toward white-hot, like they recognized him.

He swallowed. "You've been different lately." His voice was quiet but steady. "Your power feels stronger… but also hungrier."

I flinched, pulling my hand away, "Because it is." The words came raw. "I keep dreaming of blood that isn't mine. Of memories that aren't mine. And sometimes…" my breath shuddered out, "…sometimes I want to tear things open just to make the noise stop."

Andrew stilled. "Astrid…"

"I feel like I'm losing control," I snapped, my panic rising. "And the worst part? I don't know if I care anymore."

The runes pulsed hard. Heat flooded my palms. The table beneath them hissed and smoked, darkening as the marks etched into my skin burned their reflection into the wood, like the magic wanted to prove the lie of my words.

Andrew moved fast, one of his hands caught my arm, and the other caught my chin, forcing me to meet his gaze. "Look at me." His voice was low and fierce. "You *do* care. That's why you're afraid."

I shook my head as tears blurred my vision. "What if I'm not scared of losing control? What if I'm scared that I will like who I'll become when I *have lost* it?"

He didn't answer. Instead, he reached into his pocket and pulled out his mother's journal. He flipped to a page that he had earmarked and set the journal down on top of the ancient book. My breath faltered, the sight hit me like a blow.

It was the same runes. The same phrase. But there was more lines that had been added, scrawled in black ink:

The one who bears the mark must choose:
Bind the soul...or be lost to it.

My stomach hollowed. "It's not a gift." I whispered, "It's…it's a trap."

Mani's voice ripped through me like a growl. *'I won't let anything happen to you.'* Her anger shook at the edges but fear trembled underneath. *'How long has he known?'*
The thought hit me like a strike.

My head snapped toward Andrew. "How long have you known this?" I demanded, stabbing a finger at the journal.

He froze for half a second too long. A flicker of guilt, quick, but unmistakable crossed his face. "I… found it a few days ago."

"A few days?" My voice rose, sharper than I intended, heat spiking in my chest. "And you didn't think to tell me?"

His jaw worked as if he was choosing each word with care. "I wanted to. But I wasn't sure what it meant yet."

"I thought we were in this together?" I stepped closer, the runes on my hands glowing in my periphery like coiled warning. "If it's about me, about us, I have a right to know."

His gaze flicked to my hand, watching the pale-blue glow spill between my fingers. “I know. But I didn’t want to bring you something half-formed.”

“Keeping me in the dark doesn’t protect me.” I snapped. “It just means I’m fighting blind.”

He inhaled slowly, his chest rising with tension. “I thought… if I could figure it out first, I could shield you from the worst of it.” He stepped closer, tension rippling through him.

I shook my head, closing the last inches between us. “If one of us falls, we both do.”

Neither of us moved as we stood inches apart, our breath mingling. The air between us vibrated with the hum of runes and heartbeat. Andrew lifted a hand, cupping my cheek with a gentleness, making his touch warmer and steady.

“We can agree that it’s some kind of ritual. And you’re the only one who can decide what the outcome will be,” he said, his eyes locking with mine. “I just want to keep you safe, Astrid. Whatever this thing is that’s hunting you, we will face it together...it won’t take you away from me.”

Without thinking, I fell into him, and he wrapped his arms around me as if stabilizing both of us, holding me fiercely. We clung to each other, the world outside dissolving into nothing but the press of his arms and the rhythm of our breathing. For a moment the chaos softened, edges blurring.

I wanted to believe him. Gods, I wanted to. But as his arms held me, the chill returned, sliding down my spine like cold steel. Somewhere beyond the flicker of lamplight and the scent of parchment, I could feel it: that wolf-dragon shape that’s haunting my dreams.

When I stepped back, I looked down at my hands again. The runes shimmered faintly, not burning as before, but thrumming with a low, ceaseless pulse. The hunger lingered beneath my skin like a second heartbeat. Was this the Garmr's gift, or its curse?

'You feel it too,' Mani murmured, her voice taut and agitated. *'It's not just power. It's rage. Bloodlust. Like it wants to drown us.'*

My throat tightened. The Garmr, the guardian of Hel's gates, the devourer of gods, protector forged in shadow and blood. It had always been on my side, a sentinel against the world's worst. But now… if I didn't master it, if I didn't bend its rage to my will, it wouldn't just defend me. It would consume me.

'What if it's...bad?' I whispered. *'Evil?'*

'It could be,' Mani admitted, unflinching. *'But not everything that's monstrous is evil. Sometimes rage is just… rage.'*

The truth stung like truth usually does. I closed the book and exhaled a shaky breath. *'Then we'd better figure this out.'*

"Should we finally head to Trovi's house?" Andrew asked gently, pulling my attention back. "She might have other books that might help."

The question settled heavy in my chest. I nodded anyway, forcing a small, fragile smile. "Yeah… we should." My voice wavered just slightly. "Hopefully she won't mind if we make a mess while we look."

The words felt thin, like they didn't quite hold.

Because the thought of walking into her house without her there, of feeling that absence in every room, made something in me twist tight.

But we needed answers. And I wasn't going to run from that.

He offered his hand and I took it. "Come on…don't look so glum. You made progress." Andrew's hand tightened around mine. "Hey," he murmured, stepping closer until his chest brushed mine. His thumb traced the inside of my wrist, slow and deliberate. "Look at me."

My eyes slowly lifted to his, and the worry lining his face softened into something warmer. "You're not alone in this, Astrid," he said, his voice barely more than a breath.

My throat tightened. "I know." I whispered. "I just… I feel like I'm walking into something I'm not ready for."

A beat passed, my grip tightening slightly in his.

"But I'm going," I added, quieter but firmer. "I'm not leaving her behind—not like this."

The dread didn't ease. But it didn't stop me either.

"Then let me hold all the pieces." He whispered, pulling me closer.

I don't know who moved first. Maybe it was me. Maybe it was him. Maybe it was just our bond humming between us. But in the next heartbeat, Andrew cupped my face with both hands, and my lips crashed into his.

Heat surged through me, raw, wild, consuming, and there was nothing gentle about it. His fingers slid into my hair, pulling me closer, like he was afraid I'd vanish. I pressed back with equal hunger, clutching at his shirt. The world narrowed to the warmth of his mouth, the press of his body against mine, the steady, frantic rhythm of our breathing tangling together. The runes along my fingers flared faintly where they brushed his skin.

He broke the kiss only to rest his forehead against mine, both of our breaths shaking.

"Astrid…" His voice was rough. "I'm right here."

"I know," I whispered, leaning into him. "That's what scares me the most…I can't lose you."

His thumb brushed my cheek, tender in a way that made my chest ache. "You won't."

I wanted to believe him. But even as our fingers intertwined, I knew that something or someone was watching. I felt it in the edges of my vision.

As we turned to leave, perched on a nearby table, a raven watched us. Its beady black eyes followed our every movement, head tilting in that unnerving, intelligent way.

I froze mid-step, my cheeks heating. "Great," I muttered under my breath.

Andrew glanced down at me, lips twitching with amusement. "It's just a raven"

"I… it's not just a raven!" I hissed.

Then, in my mind, sharp, impatient, and unmistakably the raven's voice, a warning hissed: *"Do not... get hot and heavy in the library. Why are humans so foolish."* then it flapped its wings before disappearing into the shadows above.

I groaned, burying my face in my hands. "Perfect. Magical, terrifying, judgmental ravens. Just what I needed to top off my day."

Andrew laughed softly, brushing my hair back from my face. "Don't worry. It's not judging you… much."

I shot him a glare, but it was hard to keep it fierce when his warmth pressed close. Still, I couldn't shake the heat creeping up my neck from being caught like that, by a damn bird, of all things.

'Really, Astrid?' Mani's voice was sharp with amusement. *'You got caught... making out... by a raven? This is what we're worried about?'*

I stayed silent, cheeks burning hotter with every word.

'How do you expect me to take anything else seriously?' Her voice dripped with amusement.

I rolled my eyes, but the corners of my mouth twitched. *'Yeah, ok, thanks. Really helpful.'*

'Always,' she replied, smug as ever. *'Now let's focus. We've got bigger problems than library embarrassment.'*

I huffed, shaking my head, but even as I did, a small smile threatened to break through. *'Yea, ok fine... focus. I got it.'*

Chapter 5

The next morning, the dread was already there, low and constant, like a weight I couldn't shake. Trovi was stable. That's what they kept saying. Stable, but still not awake. Still not here.

And now we were walking into her house without her. The thought sat heavy in my chest as we made our way there, each step forward feeling like I was leaving her behind all over again.

When I finally stepped inside, the air clung to me as if I'd walked straight into a memory that refused to loosen. Dust, old parchment, dried herbs… and something faintly floral—lavender, worn thin by time.

It should have been comforting.

Trovi always smelled like this.

Instead, it pressed against my chest, sour and wrong, like the house itself knew something was missing.

Everything was exactly as she had left it before the attack, untouched and unfinished. Her worn forest-green cloak, still hanging from a peg by the door, the hem stained with mud. A book lay open on the coffee table beside a cup of tea gone gray with mold. The whole house felt… paused, as if it had been holding its breath ever since.

I lingered in the doorway, my fingers brushing over the carved runes framing the entrance. Each sigil whispered faint traces of warding, of protection meant to keep some kind of evil at bay. But it hadn't been enough.

"She's kept everything," I murmured, my voice dry and brittle. "Like she was preparing for this day."

Andrew stepped beside me, his broad shoulders casting a shadow across the runes. His eyes swept the room, sharp and alert. "Or" he murmured, "like she was preparing for someone else to finish it."

I didn't answer. His words hit harder than I expected. My throat ached too much to speak.

We moved carefully into the living room, disturbing as little as possible. Every step made the floorboards sigh, as if the house remembered us. Remembered her. Somewhere in the wood and dust, it grieved too, begging us not to forget. I tried not to touch too much at once; some irrational fear whispered that the room might snap awake if I disturbed it, might remember everything that had been lost. So, I started with what was the easiest, sifting through the surface clutter piece by piece.

Towers of weathered books leaned in precarious stacks, one tremor from collapse, their spines cracked and flaking. Scrolls peeked from carved wall niches, their wax seals still intact, Trovi's sigil pressed deep into each one, her signature, as if she never imagined she wouldn't be here to explain them. I pulled a few loose, running my fingers over the frayed parchment edges.

Diagrams stitched with colored thread were pinned to sheets of vellum: ward circles, spell matrices, and constellation maps I half-recognized from meditations she guided me through. Some were stained with old wax, smudged with soot, or marked by the ghost of an old teacup. Trovi's sharp, relentless notes filled every margin, annotations that felt like her voice muttering over my shoulder.

I recognized most of it. Healing formulas I'd seen her use on pack members after skirmishes. Bundles of herbs hung from ceiling beams: mullein, yarrow, mugwort… and darker things too. Ones not used for healing but protection… or restraint. Charms against possession. Powders for breaking enchantments. Binding chants scribbled across open journals, full of warnings and crossed-out alternatives.

Still, none of it explained the fire running through my veins, the occasional pulse in my blood that made my teeth ache. Or the way Mani and I both felt the Garmr's rage and bloodlust flickering against us, not seeking to control, but testing, feeding its fury into our own.

Andrew bent over the table, brushing a hand across a disordered stack of parchment. His fingers stilled on a page marked with Trovi's unmistakable, jagged notes. "Astrid," he said, voice low. He pulled a sheet free.

Dense writing covered both sides, but one phrase sat in the center, circled three times:

Foreign magic cannot be destroyed.
Only integrated.
To resist is to fracture.
To accept is to transform.

My stomach twisted. "Integrated?" I whispered, the word sour on my tongue.

Mani stirred, her voice a low growl. *'She can't mean surrender... We've seen how that goes. Naomi? Yeah—hard pass. Not our aesthetic.'*

"Surrender," I repeated aloud.

A strangled sound escaped me, half laugh, half panic.

"No," Andrew said, tapped the margin where Trovi had written more. "Not surrender. Look, she says that resisting only

feeds the invader. Creating friction gives the magic a place to spark against you." his finger traced the underline. "But acceptance, deliberate acceptance… forces it to change shape, to bend. It becomes yours. Claimed instead of borrowed."

I swallowed against the heat crawling up my throat. "So… to control the Garmr…"

"You don't fight it," Andrew said gently. "You stop thinking of it as something separate from you, having its own identity."

The words turned to ash on my tongue. The memory of the void, its silence, its teeth, its endless wanting, pressed in until my lungs tightened painfully. Mani squared her stance in the back of my mind, ready to face the monster again. Still, beneath her bravado, I felt a tremor of hesitation, it was small but unmistakable.

"It's dangerous," Mani said, her tone clipped. *"But that thing's already running through your veins. Push it off, and it'll break the leash just to amuse itself."*

My hand trembled as I traced the ink. Trovi's notes spread out across the page, half warnings, half desperate attempts at an answer. Diagrams of bodies threaded with light and shadow. Chains drawn and then broken. A wolf's skull, its jaw unhinged, filled with runes.

Andrew's hand closed over mine. "You already faced it once," he said, steady. "You didn't bend. This… this could mean you never have to fear it… but control it."

The room felt too still, the lavender scent suddenly suffocating. I stared at the words again, *acceptance, integration, transformation.* Each word on the page weighed heavier than the last—a promise of power edged with ruin.

My jaw tightened. “Then I’ll have to learn how to own it. Not cage it. Not run from it... Own it.”

Mani hummed, low and approving. *‘Whether we fall or rise...you know I’m with you. Might as well kick some ass along the way.’*

Andrew exhaled slowly, his thumb brushing against mine. “Then we do this together. No matter how deep it goes.”

He began clearing the table, sweeping aside the stacks of parchment and half-burned candles until only Trovi’s notes remained between us. The room seemed to dim, as if the house itself understood what we were about to attempt.

“Here?” I asked, my voice tight. “Now?”

“Where else?” His jaw was set, but his eyes never left mine. “Better to face it when you choose...”

“Am I choosing…or are you?” I asked, not breaking eye contact, and I see his shoulders drop slightly.

“Astrid,” he said, stepping closer. “It’s been months since Hel gave you this power…its already starting to fester…”

I knew he was right, I let out a sighed, “I know…I need to accept…this…I just wasn’t expecting to do it today.”

Mani chimed in, unhelpfully blunt. *‘He’s got a point. You’ll just keep making excuses if we wait... Or worse, until someone pisses us off hard enough and we go full berserker mode and accidentally kill everything.’*

I let out a slow breath. “Okay, Okay…let’s just…get it over with.”

‘You know...’ Mani warned. *‘Once we open that door...’*

‘I know.’

I pressed my palms flat against the wooden table, the runes glowing faintly on my skin. They thrummed in rhythm with my pulse.

"Alright," I whispered. "Let's try."

I closed my eyes and focused on my breathing, shutting everything else out. The first breath came easy. The second was fire as it surged. The Garmr's rage rose like floodwaters behind a cracked dam. My bones vibrated under the weight of it, the hunger swelling until my teeth ached and my throat burned for blood. Shadows rippled at the edges of the room, thickening, bending toward me as though pulled by gravity.

My hands trembled against the wood, claws threatening to break through my fingertips. I felt myself slipping, like I was being pulled down into its jaws.

Then Andrew, his presence flared hot against my back, his hands on my shoulders, our bond burning through the cracks. I didn't fight the darkness, but tempered it, like steel plunged into flame.

"Breathe, Astrid." His voice was low. "Fight it. Hold it. I've got you."

Mani's growl rumbled deep inside, circling the beast. *'We are not prey. We are hunters. Accept it, but we kneel for no one!'*

The Garmr's pressed harder, snarling and biting at the edges. Its rage, hunger, and violence surged, hot and blinding, a blinding tide ready to swallow me whole. My vision blurred, the table warped, the runes on my hands burned until I thought they'd sear through my bones.

"No!" I gasped, though the word came out strangled. Then the world ripped apart around me.

Blood soaked the stone beneath my feet, spreading in endless rivers. The sky churned red above, lightning slicing through clouds that bled smoke. A howl rose in the distance, my voice, yet deeper, something feral.

The Garmr stepped from the mist. It was vast, fur black as grave ash, matted with blood, and eyes glowing blood red, with a bottomless hunger. Its breath steamed with every exhale, as if walking in the dead of winter. Every exhale a gust of death. Smoke warped around its paws, even the ground seemed to recoil from its weight.

"You dare call me," it thundered, vibrating the very air. "And yet you think to bind me."

Terror clawed at my throat, but I could still feel Andrew's hands were still on me, his warmth steadying me.

My pulse thundered, but I planted my feet. "You are rage. You are bloodlust." I lifted my chin. "But you are not free." My voice wavered, but it held. "I don't think to bind you. I *am* your binding. By Hel's decree."

The beast laughed, a low snarl, sharp as broken glass. "Bound?" It echoed. "No. I am the truth inside you. The slaughter you hide. The hunger you deny." Its jaws opened wide enough to swallow me whole, teeth dripping with fresh blood. "Give in," it whispered. "And we will never be weak again."

Then images struck me like blades, Naomi torn apart at my feet, enemies falling like wheat under a scythe, Andrew's enemies gutted before they could touch him. For one heartbeat, the fire of it burned so sweet, so intoxicating, I almost reached for it.

Almost.

Andrew's voice cut through, his hands steady on mine, the warmth of his voice when I broke, the fear I'd see in his

eyes from the visions if I ever surrendered. Not afraid *of* me, but afraid *for* me.

I dragged a breath. "No."

The Garmr lunged, all claws and jaws, a nightmare made flesh. It crashed into me with the force of a collapsing mountain, slamming me back into the bloody earth. Its weight crushed the breath from my lungs; it's hot, rancid breath blasted across my face, smelling of iron and death. The world narrowed to its jaws that were gnashing, unhinged, and eager to tear me into the pieces and remake me as something monstrous.

But the runes carved into my skin ignited.

A crackling surge exploded outward, blue-white light flaring from my hands. They didn't just glow; they howled, answering some command I wasn't sure I had spoken.

I willed them to listen.

To obey.

To stay with me.

And they did.

Light erupted from me, chains forged from starlight, lashing outward with the scream of metal tearing open the sky. They snapped into existence around the beast's colossal frame, spiraling around its ribs, its throat, its gaping jaws. The impact shook the world.

The Garmr roared, an earth-splitting sound that made the blood-soaked ground tremble and the air shiver. It thrashed against the chains, its body searing where the light struck it. Shards of darkness breaking off like glass and dissolving into the void.

"I am not your prey!" The words ripped from me, raw, fed by its own fury crashing inside my veins.

“You are not my master!” it shrieked back, voice a hurricane of hate and hunger. “You are to be a weapon!”

The chains tightened with a groan that sounded like the world grinding its teeth. They dragged the beast down, inch by brutal inch, until its massive knees struck the ground. My runes burned fiercely, casting fractures of white-blue light through the crimson landscape, as though my heartbeat was splitting reality open. The Garmr writhed, snarling and snapping, its eyes twin furnaces of rage… and then, slowly, something flickers behind the fury. A silver of hesitation, question, then recognition.

My legs shook as I stepped toward it, every instinct screaming to run, to hide, to be small, but I refused. I stood taller than I’d ever stood and I advanced. Its breath hit me in ragged bursts. Its hatred radiated off its body in waves, but beneath it was something else.

I lifted my hand and pressed my palm to its muzzle. Its skin radiated heat through its thick, matted fur, it was hotter than flame. It seared my flesh instantly, blistering, but I didn’t pull away. Beneath that hellish warmth was a deep, thundering heartbeat pounding against its own ribs.

My runes reacted. A flare of light burst from my palms, ripping into the Garmr’s flesh. Runes of my name blazed across its hide like a divine brand. The beast snarled, jerked, then shuddered violently as the mark took hold.

A claim, my claim, a bond forged in blood and will. And the beast trembled, not in fear, but in acknowledgment.

I gasped awake… still at the table. Drenched in sweat, and my lungs burning like in inhaled fire. The runes still glowed faintly, pulsing with power.

The Garmr wasn't tamed.
It was not silenced.
But bound, because I willed it.

Andrew's hands were still on my shoulders. "You… did it?" he whispered, searching my face as if checking what parts of me remained. Or which ones I'd brought back with me. I managed a nod, exhaustion knotting with something sharper, relief.

Mani purred deep inside me, the sound a low, rolling rumble of satisfaction laced with cautious pride. *'You did good, but don't get cocky now. But yeah… you did damn good.'*

The house remained still. The shadows loosened their grip. The air seemed to settled into quiet affirmation. And for the first time since inheriting the Garmr, I felt its presence shift. It no longer was a devouring monster, not as my enemy, not a curse gnawing at my bone, but as something I could command, a weapon tempered by will, a force I could call forth on my terms. Not fully mastered and not tamed entirely either, but it was leashed at the least.

And for now… that was enough.

The silence stretched around us, but it wasn't heavy anymore. It felt… expectant. As if the walls themselves knew we had taken the first step, and now we were ready for the next.

Chapter 6

The air in Trovi's house felt lighter, even if only slightly. There was a low hum that thrummed faintly from the walls. Inside me, the Garmr had gone quiet, too quiet, but the echo of its fury rattled through my bones, leaving my pulse stuttering in an uneven, trembling rhythm I couldn't quite steady.

Andrew noticed before I even had a chance to pretend otherwise. Without a word, he swept me into his arms in one smooth motion, his hold careful but unyielding, as if I weighed nothing. He smelled of pine and the damp forest clung to him, tethering me to the present. He carried me to the couch near the hearth, its worn cushions steeped in Trovi's familiar, dried herbs and earthy scent. I sank into them, the weight of exhaustion pulling me down.

Andrew knelt in front of me, close enough that the fire's heat mingled with the warmth radiating off him. His hands closed around mine, steadier than I deserved.

"You're shaking," he murmured, his thumb tracing slow, deliberate circles on the back of my hand.

My throat tightened. I tried to answer, tried to reassure him, but the only sound that came out was a thin, tired laugh that cracked halfway through.

He didn't push. He rose and crossed the room in two quiet strides, grabbing the thick wool blanket draped over Trovi's reading chair. He shook it out gently, then returned to me and wrapped it around my shoulders with a tenderness so deliberate it made heat bloom behind my ribs. Something inside me tightened unmistakable, love.

It hurt in the way only something real can, steady enough to feel undeniably real, and impossible to hide as he tucked the blanket in with careful hands like I was something precious.

"There," he said softly, smoothing the blanket's edge over my arm as though to shield me from the memory of everything I had just endured. His fingers lingered near my jaw, then he sat back down on the floor holding my hand.

"I'll be here," he promised. "Right next to you until you wake up." His gaze caught mine, his green-orange eyes burning, as if nothing in the world could break his promise.

The warmth of his touch, the low burn of the fire, the steadiness of his presence… it all sank into me. The trembling finally eased, the knot in my chest loosening just enough that I could breathe without strain.

My eyes fluttered shut, heavy with exhaustion. Andrew brushed a strand of hair from my face and whispered, "Just rest for now. I love you."

Time slipped away, measured only by the soft crackle of embers and the rise and fall of my breathing. My body finally stilled, sinking into the familiar sag of the old couch, the blanket cocooning me in warmth.

When I woke, the quiet rustle of pages stirred me. I blinked into the dim glow of the hearth. Across the room, Andrew stood before one of Trovi's bookshelves, shoulders bent in concentration. The lamplight traced along him, a soft gold along the edges of his hair, warmth across the line of his jaw, as he leaned forward to study the shelves. His fingers skimmed lightly over spines, pausing with instinctive care before pulling a single volume free. He flipped through it slowly, reverently, as though even dust and parchment deserved gentleness.

For a moment, I just watched him. The way he filled the room so completely. Even rifling through dust and parchment, he seemed like he belonged here. As though he were sifting through the remnants of someone else's secrets to guard mine.

Then, as he slid the book into place, his boot pressed against the rug and a thin, abrupt squeak split the stillness, making him freeze.

Another step, another faint sound, but this time from beneath the faded rug, almost like a sigh caught in wood. Andrew crouched, his fingertips tracing along the floorboards until he found an edge hidden beneath the fringe.

"Strange," he murmured, tugging gently. "This one… doesn't sound… right."

Curiosity pushed me to get up from the couch and join him, kneeling beside the rug. The board resisted when he pulled, then gave a soft hum, wards sparking across its surface like fireflies disturbed from sleep.

Andrew's gaze flicked to me. "Trovi didn't want just anyone finding this. Whatever she hid under here… she went to great lengths to protect it."

I pressed my palm to the sigil that appeared on top of the wood. The air stirred, a subtle current that prickled along my skin. The ward didn't reject me. It responded instead, as though it had been waiting.

'Did we just unlock that?' Mani asked in awe.

I exchanged a look with Andrew, and I could see the same question written across his face, but we didn't say anything, and together, we lifted the plank.

Beneath it lay a long, narrow trunk wrapped in old wolf pelts and ringed with dried wolfsbane. I recognized the protective symbols burned into the wood, old ones. My heart pounded as I undid the pelt and opened the latch on the box.

When I opened the lid, a slow surge of dormant energy curled into the air, it was neither warm nor cold, just aware, like something waking up. Inside, scrolls and small journals lay bundled with meticulous care, untouched by time or hands.

I reached inside and drew out the first journal. It was bound in dark leather, the edges singed, as though someone tried to destroy it. I opened it, and inside the pages were scrawled with names, coordinates, and different symbols. Some pages mapped intersecting ley lines, lines of raw power, some crossing through places that no longer existed on any modern maps.

Andrew leaned in over my shoulder, eyes narrowing. “These aren’t notes… they’re names. And whoever wrote this wasn’t documenting them… they were following them.”
And then I saw it, circled in red ink: The Odinsráð.

My breath caught. “What… is that?”

‘Never heard of it,’ Mani murmured, her voice curious but cautious. *‘Sounds like trouble.’*

‘It’s always trouble with us,’ I admitted, tracing the letters as if they might rearrange themselves into something familiar.

‘Feels… old,’ Mani added.

“I thought they were a myth,” Andrew’s brow furrowed. “Some secret ancient cult wiped out during Ragnarök.”

“Not completely wiped out, apparently,” I murmured, lifting the journal. “Scattered and hiding but not gone.”

Beneath the name, in Trovi’s unmistakable handwriting:

Thought lost in Ragnarök. Possibly surviving through fractured bloodlines. Seek the VÖLUNDR. Seek the Flame.

I stared at the words. "She was tracking this order of… magic-users? Ones that were never meant to survive?"

"They weren't just spellcasters," Andrew murmured, taking the journal and flipping through more pages with a growing intensity. "According to this, they were something else. Guardians of some kind. Keepers of old magic… as old as the first gods? Maybe older than the realms?"

My fingers trembled as I traced the edge of a diagram. Trovi's handwriting here had changed. It was more frantic, almost desperate:

One remains. A Keeper of the Flame. Hidden but walks among them, veiled in plain sight. Presence unnoticed, Purpose unchanged.

A chill crept up my spine. "Is that supposed to be me? She wasn't just studying us. She was *preparing* us. Trying to find someone who could help before our bond completed?"

Andrew went still, his gaze halting on the next page. "Astrid," he said, voice tight.

There, hastily scrawled between two paragraphs, was a symbol I recognized from my dreams: a twisting black shadow entwined with tree roots. Beneath it, written in crimson ink:

The wolf-dragon will rise again… but only if the wolf survives the fire.

Andrew looked up, face pale. "That can only mean you."

"And you." I whispered. "If this Order kept bloodlines alive, then maybe that's what she was tracking. What's in me. What's in you."

His jaw clenched. "Then this Völundr isn't just a ritual. It's more of a forge. A test. Maybe to make us into a weapon."

I turned to the final page.
The ink was newer, darker, as if written only days ago:

The dark völva is watching. Naomi is the window. But the wolf… is the door.

Everything inside me stilled as the silence settled between us.

'So, they're watching us,' Mani growled softly. *'But we're not prey.'*

"I'm not just being hunted," I said, rising from the floor. Mani's fury surged in tandem with mine, raw and echoing, meeting the Garmr's fire instead of yielding to it.

Andrew rose with me, stepping closer. "You're being *used…* and I think it's Trovi."

'Used!' Mani snarled. *'That is worse than being hunted. Hunted means they fear you. Used means they think they own you.'*

A painful knot tightened in my throat. *'That can't be right…'*

Andrew's eyes hardened. "We find this Odinsráð, we find our answers. And we find that damn door… and kick it in."

I glanced down at my hands. The runes pulsed faintly under my skin, like something knocking from the other side. "I think it's already opening," I whispered.

'Then, like Andrew said…' Mani hissed fiercely. *'We go and tear it off its fucking hinges!'*

Andrew leaned back against the table, his eyes scanning the rows of brittle scrolls and stacked folios like a hawk hunting movement in the shadows. I let my fingers drift across the spines of ancient tomes, tracing worn grooves and faded sigils. The room smelled of cedar, dust, and ink, a scent that felt alive, almost breathing, carrying the weight of secrets waiting to be uncovered.

Hours blurred into parchment and muttered theories. My eyes burned, my fingers numb from turning brittle pages, while the runes on my skin echoed the rhythm of my heartbeat, restless and insistent. Eventually I slumped back into the chair, every muscle heavy, as though gravity had doubled just to keep me from unraveling.

"Astrid… love." Andrew's voice drifted from behind me, soft as warmth on winter air. I felt him lean close, the brush of his fingers sweeping a loose strand of hair from my cheek. "We've been at this for a while. Come on… let me get you onto the couch. You need to rest."

Before I could argue, a blanket settled around my shoulders, the soft, warmth seeping into me like a quiet promise. Then, with a gentle laugh, he scooped me up bridal style, holding me close as he carried me over to the couch. Every brush of his body against mine, every careful step, grounded me, anchoring me amid the swirl of thoughts and magic that had me spinning.

"Just… breathe," he murmured against my hair, his lips a whisper at my temple. "Her archives aren't going anywhere. The answers will wait. You don't have to hold it all by yourself right now."

I blinked up at him, exhaustion pressing down harder. When he guided me toward the couch and eased me down, his hand never left mine, his fingers curling around mine with a quiet, grounding insistence.

Andrew sat first, settling into the corner of the couch with deliberate care. I shifted onto my side, sliding closer until my head rested in his lap. The solid warmth of his body was immediate, steady, real, anchoring beneath my cheek. I let

myself sink fully into the cushions, letting the heaviness drag through me, a slow surrender I was too tired to fight.

He adjusted instinctively, as if he'd been waiting for me to lean on him. One hand stayed woven with mine, steady and sure, while his other drifted into my hair, combing through the strands in slow, tender motions. His fingers traced a soft, steady rhythm—protective, reassuring, a silent promise that I wasn't facing any of this alone. With every touch, another thread of tension loosened, drawing me closer to rest… and closer to him.

"Rest," he murmured again, voice warm, his thumb brushing my cheek as he leaned in slightly. "I've got you. Everything else… can wait."

The blanket draped across our laps, wrapping us in quiet comfort. The faint hum of papers and lingering magic faded to the background, leaving only him, the steady warmth beneath my cheek, the quiet cadence of his fingers through my hair, the heartbeat that held steady even as mine stumbled.

I let go. For the first time in a long time, I let myself relax fully, eyes fluttering closed, letting the world shrink to him and the safety he radiated. For the first time that day, I surrendered completely, drifting into sleep with Andrew beside me, a steady, comforting anchor in the midst of everything.

There was a ripple across frozen water. I stood in a forest drowned in frost, where skeletal trees loomed like lifeless, silent sentinels beneath a mourning, gray sky. A cold wind whispered through their skeletal branches, carrying voices I couldn't place, old, mournful, and half-forgotten.

Beneath me, the ground trembled faintly. I looked down and saw runes glowing in the frozen soil, jagged, deliberate, serpentine lines entwining with lupine marks. They pulsed in a rhythm that echoed the wild and relentless inside me.

Mani surfaced within me, her form bleeding into the space beside mine, fur bristling with a readiness that wasn't fear at all, just instinct.

Then I saw it, a shadow. Not fully wolf, not fully dragon, but a writhing amalgam of fang, claw, and scale. Black as midnight, somehow darker than the surrounding night, slithering and prowling through the trees, moving with impossible grace. Its eyes like molten ambers rimmed with dying moonlight. The serpentine slits glowed alive with rivers of red. Every time I blinked, it was closer, yet always at the edges, as though restricted to some boundary it had no reason to honor. I wanted to run, but the blackened snow beneath my feet rooted me in place.

The wind carried the voices again, whispering names: *Hati... Hati...* and the ground shivered beneath the weight of something immense. My pulse raced, and I could feel fury and strength bolstering me, daring me to meet the shadow on its own terms.

Through the ice and snow, the shadow stretched and yawned like a nightmare awakening, but never fully approaching. And in the distance, a pillar of faint, golden light rose from the forest floor, a sigil of runes spinning around each other: wolf and serpent entwined, drawn in fire that never burned. The vision was fleeting, but it imprinted itself into my mind.

Mani growled low. '*It will come for us. One day.*'

I woke with a gasp, my heart racing, the echo of that dream still thrumming through me. And beneath it, lingering like a shadow clinging to the edge of consciousness, was the certainty that somewhere just beyond sleep, it watched, endlessly patient.

'Was that a nightmare... or a vision?' Mani asked.

'They're starting to feel like the same thing' I muttered back, though the truth sent a shiver that crawled beneath my skin, they didn't feel like dreams at all, not anymore.

The days that followed felt sharpened, every moment stretched thin beneath an invisible weight. It was as if the dream had never truly ended, only spilled over into the waking of day.

And I could feel Mani closer now, near the surface, like she was already bracing for whatever waited the next time I closed my eyes.

Chapter 7

Morning came slow and gray, the light barely pushing through the thin curtains of Trovi's living room. I woke still curled against Andrew, his arm heavy around my waist, our breaths fogging the cool air between us. For a moment, everything was still, just the quiet thrum of his heart beneath my cheek, and the distant groan of the old house settling. Andrew must have felt me stir; his hand softly brushed a strand of hair from my forehead, his eyes searching mine with the same unspoken worry that had followed us for days.

"Library?" he murmured, voice rough with sleep.

I nodded, then glanced down at his legs and the awkward angle of his spine, a small ache of guilt threading through my still-sleepy thoughts. "You couldn't have gotten any sleep… sleeping like that."

He huffed a tired laugh, rubbing a hand across his face as if trying to chase the night from his eyes. I could still feel the warmth of his thigh where my cheek had rested for… I wasn't even sure how long. Hours, maybe. Long enough that his leg must have gone numb.

"You should've moved me," I murmured, softer this time. "I basically used you as a pillow."

His gaze met mine, warm and a little bleary, like I was the last thing he wanted to let go of. "I wasn't going to wake you," he said, voice graveled with sleep. "You needed it more."

I pushed up from the couch, blankets slipping from my shoulders. “Come on,” I said quietly. “Let’s get some fresh air… and maybe a change of scenery.”

Andrew stretched, shook out his numb leg, and reached for my hand without seeming to think about it. We moved through Trovi’s creaking halls barefoot, our footsteps soft against ancient wood. Somewhere beyond the walls, thunder rumbled across the mountains—low, distant, coming closer.

By the time we reached the upper floor of the library, the storm was already gathering, wind clawing at the glass as if demanding to be let in. Candlelight sputtered in iron sconces, casting trembling shadows across bookshelves and a table cluttered with ancient vellums, cracked leather tomes, and half-drained cups of coffee that had long grown cold.

I sat cross-legged on the rug, my fingers idly tracing the faded ink of Trovi’s notes. The scent of dust, ink, and something that was electric clung to the air, like the breath before a lightning strike.

Andrew sat across from me, rigid in a high-backed chair, his mother’s journal balanced on his knees. His jaw had been locked for the better part of an hour, his lips drawn tight, and his brows furrowed. His eyes were fixed on a single illustration as though staring hard enough might make it yield its secrets.

I rose from the floor and walked over to him, the floorboards creaking beneath my steps. When I placed my hands on his shoulders, I felt the tension knot deep beneath his skin. I worked my thumbs along the muscle, hoping to ease even a fraction of whatever storm he was holding inside. Leaning forward, I glanced at the open page before him.

It was an inked image of the coiled Jörmungandr, the World Serpent, jaws locked upon its own tail, its endless body threading through the deep roots of Yggdrasil. A crown of thorns circled it, carved with runes so old, so sharp with warning, that no voice had dared speak them in generations. Especially not now, not in this age.

"Is this something forgotten?" I murmured, almost to myself.

'Or was it hidden?' Mani replied, her voice low. Her question made my stomach drop.

My gaze lingered on the serpent's coils. For a heartbeat, under the candlelight, I could have sworn the lines themselves shifted, as if the ink moved. "It almost seemed to pulse…" My voice came out low, caught between fascination and unease. "Not with life…with intent."

Andrew tilted his head, meeting my eyes in the dim light. "So, you feel it too?" His voice was quiet, but I could hear the strange blend of relief and dread beneath it.

His fingers tightened against the edges of the page. "It's old… Who drew this? And why?"

"Do you think it's a warning?" I asked, my thumbs still pressing into his shoulders, though my hands had gone still.

'Or a summons,' Mani murmured.

"A summons?" I echoed under my breath.

Andrew's gaze snapped to mine. "A summons for what? For who?"

I studied the runes etched around the serpent. "The serpent… maybe. Or whatever bound it."

'Nothing binds Jörmungandr, not forever,' Mani said, sharper now, impatient. *'It is the end beneath the sea, the hunger that waits. Chains rust. Stones crack.'*

"Jörmungandr?"

Andrew leaned back slightly, his jaw tightening. "But this…" he tapped the image. "This isn't just Jörmungandr. Look at the roots, it's tangled in Yggdrasil roots, not rising above it. That's… it's… wrong."

'Maybe it's not the wrongness you should fear,' Mani said.

I exhaled slowly. "I don't think it's a truth…. more like a mislead?"

"Meaning?" Andrew asked, his eyes narrowing.

"It could be to throw us off. You know right away that this is wrong. Given your heritage, Nidhogg is in the roots." I said.

Andrew nodded in agreement. "So?"

"So…" the words faltered, heavy in my mouth, "I don't know what comes after that,"

"It's ok," Andrew says, pulling me from behind him and placing me in his lap. "It's a start," he says, pressing a lingering kiss on my lips.

When we parted I searched his face. "If this is wrong… then what does it mean for the Nine Realms?"

Andrew didn't answer. His eyes searched mine, weighing whether to speak the thought forming behind them. "It means… something is shifting."

Mani's tone dropped low and dangerous. *'And if it stirs, the tree will tremble ... probably crush a few realms on the way. No pressure.'*

I swallowed hard, the weight of her warning settling deep inside me. "Let's not force it tonight," I murmured, eyes still on Andrew. "Whatever's in there… it'll wait."

"No," Andrew said, his voice low and frayed. "It *won't*."

He turned a page in his mother's journal, the paper crackling softly. The ink shimmered, partly with age, mostly with old enchantments that hadn't faded. Some words writhed in draconic script beneath his fingertips.

"She left this for after my bond awakened," he said, almost to himself. "She knew something would happen. She knew it before I was even born."

My breath stilled, and I turned to the journal, still sitting in his lap. "The Soulbound?"

Andrew nodded slowly, still staring at the page.

When the old blood stirs, the Lindwyrm will wake but not alone, tethered.

The dragon's mate will be at the threshold, caught between light and shadow.

She must choose and not be unmade.

A cold pulse spread through my chest, sinking into my bones. The runes on my hands tingled as if reacting to the words.

"She meant me?" I whispered.

"No," Andrew shook his head, finally lifting his gaze. "She meant *us.* She wasn't just warning us about magic. She was warning about what it *could be.*"

He turned the journal toward me. The next page held a diagram; hand-drawn in precise lines. A figure caught between forms: neither fully human, nor fully dragon. Muscles elongated, ribs warped, a jagged spine arched, smoke etched into bone. Beside it, runes scrawled like veins. Binding symbols I recognized from Trovi's house. Not containment, but a fusion. It looked… painful.

"She thought the bond could... rewrite us, I guess?" Andrew said, his voice barely above a breath. "Not just connect us, but *combine* us?"

I stared down at my palms. The runes beneath my skin pulsed once, slow and deliberate. They were no longer passive, and they were alive, shifting and waiting.

"I keep... feeling something," I whispered. "Not in me. Outside of me. Like a thread pulling tight. It's subtle, but constant. Like I'm being drawn somewhere."

Andrew's expression sharpened. "Drawn where?"

I pushed gently off his lap and walked toward the balcony doors. Rain traced frantic paths down the glass, the wind hurling itself against the world beyond.

"I don't know." My voice came softer, more unsure. "Sometimes it feels like you. Sometimes it's Trovi. Sometimes its Naomi. But other times… it's distant. Familiar in a way I can't explain."

Andrew rose sharply. "Could it be someone you know?"

I swallowed hard. "Something wants me to believe it is… Every dream lately, I sense someone. Not clearly... but like a presence at the edge of things, watching and waiting."

Andrew's expression darkened, a mix of anger and unease flashing across his features. "He? *Who*?" Andrew demanded. "How could someone like that be tied to all of this?"

He closed the distance between us, taking my hands in his. The runes on my skin responded to his touch, as if recognizing their counterpart.

He exhaled sharply, a shadow crossing his features. "Then we find him," he muttered, almost as if saying the words aloud made them worse. "Whoever… this 'he' is."

I nodded, though dread knotted low in my stomach. "Because if he's reaching for me… it might mean he knows what's coming."

We walked back over to the table and Andrew 's eyes lingered on the journal. At the bottom of the diagram, a final note sprawled across the page, almost violently:

Beware the echo. The dragon's life is not his alone. When fire burns black without restraint, the gate will open—from within.

He closed the book slowly, each movement pressing the words into the air between us.

"We're not just waking up to our magic," he said, his voice low, and threaded with unease.

The pause that followed was thick, and alive with meaning. Outside, the storm tore at the mountains, but beneath its roar I felt another truth stirring, rooted deep in my marrow, entwined with the fire burning in Andrew's blood. It was patient and it was inevitable.

We carried the weight of what we'd learned, unsure where, or how, to move forward. We walked out though the dim corridors, past flickering lamps and shuttered windows, until the great doors of the library shut behind us. The storm still raged beyond the walls, but inside, a quieter, darker tempest had taken root.

By the time we reached our room, the night had thickened, softened only at the edges. The hearth fire glowed steady and warm. But in my dreams, the shadow endured, patient, watchful, and waiting.

Chapter 8

We lay tangled together in silence, letting the world fall away around us. The only sound was the fire snapping softly across the room and the rhythm of our breathing. His ragged against my shoulder, while mine stayed slow and measured, like I was savoring the moment instead of collapsing into it.

The runes on my hands pulsed faintly, their ghost-blue glow tracing the sharp line of his jaw, the curve of his throat, the rise and fall of his chest. The Garmr's bloodlust and rage throbbed within me, tethered, chained, alive but bound. It wasn't possession. It was part of me now, intertwined with my strength, a power Mani and I could wield without losing ourselves.

'Finally,' Mani purred, low and approving. *'About time you let some of that tension out. You've been holding... a whole month of it.'*

'Thank you for the reminder,' I murmured, heat softening every word.

I smiled faintly and leaned down, pressing soft, lingering kisses to his chest. Not out of desperation, but out of something quieter and stronger. A warmth blooming in my chest that I hadn't felt since Trovi's demise. My lips traced the firm plane of him, feeling the way his body reacted beneath me.

His hand rose to my jaw, his fingers brushing my skin with a gentleness that wasn't about fearing that I might break, but the kind of touch you give something you can't bear to lose. His eyes searched mine for a moment, then he pulled me up to his lips, closer, until there was nothing, but our breath left between us.

And then even *that* disappeared.

The kiss wasn't gentle this time. It deepened quickly—our breath stolen and our tongues sliding in a slow claiming that made my pulse spike. My hands slid beneath the hem of his shirt, seeking the familiar heat of him. My fingertips lightly traced the hollow just beneath his ribs, his body responding to me, he had been waiting for this, for *us*.

He rolled, shifting above me, and the weight of him settled between my thighs, solid and grounding. My back arched instinctively, drawn with the need to feel him, craving the contact.

His mouth moved down my throat, slower now. I felt every drag of his lips, every rough scrape of stubble against my skin. When his hand slid lower, steady and sure, a sharp sound escaped me before I could stop it.

It was not delicate. Not controlled. Just a hungry sound.

My fingers tangled in his hair and held. "Don't stop," I breathed.

His answering groan vibrated through my skin. We moved together with unhurried care, meant to be lingered in, savored, not spent too quickly. His touch pulled away. A small, involuntary whimper escaped my lips. Then, he cupped my cheek, his thumb stroking it slowly, while the other gripped my waist like letting go wasn't an option.

Every kiss he gave felt like a vow*, you, and only you,* and I answered without words, arching into him, offering myself like flame bending towards its own source. Our bond between us ignited, my runes flaring like starlight scattered across my skin, drawn to him, answering him. His aura

expanded outward, wrapping around us like silk and smoke, not a cage, but a shield, our sanctuary. A promise that here, in this space, we were untouchable.

I pressed my mouth to his shoulder, my sharp canines grazed his skin before sinking in just enough to draw a sharp breath from him. He went still, then unraveled completely. Then I trailed kisses upward, leaving faint love bites along the curve towards his collarbone. His muscles tensed beneath my lips, and when I reached the soft, shuddering spot just below his throat where my mark lies, his breath caught entirely. It was the collapse of every restraint he'd held, every thought of control unraveling beneath the weight of need. His hands gripped me with a fierce urgency, as if the world itself would vanish if he let go. I felt the pulse of his blood, racing beneath my lips, the heat of him pressing into me, demanding to reclaim me.

His lips left mine only to trail a path down the hollow of my throat. I shivered under him, the arch of my spine answering him instinctively, my fingers threading into the thick of his hair, anchoring us together. Every brush of his skin against mine, every groan that slipped from him, spoke of a desire so raw it could have burned the room around us.

His hands roamed without care, each touch igniting a flare beneath my skin. A wild pulse of desire surged within me, in rhythm with his own, a shared current of heat and hunger, weaving our bodies and magic into one.

I gasped as he pressed into me fully, slow at first, deliberate, stretching the moment until I thought I might break from the anticipation. Then he moved.

He wasn't gentle.

He wasn't cautious.

This was a reclaiming.

The rhythm built between us, sharp and breathless. His forehead pressed to mine, our breaths tangling. Every thrust dragged a sound from me I couldn't swallow down. My nails raked lightly down his back. His mouth found mine again, swallowing my moans like they belonged to him.

The world narrowed to skin and heat and the relentless glide of him. I swear that I saw magic spark between us, responding to every shift, every tightening pulse.

When our release hit, it didn't crash.

It detonated.

My body locked around him, I wanted him to feel it. To know exactly what he did to me. Pleasure tearing through me in waves that felt almost violent in their intensity. He followed with a broken sound against my throat, hands gripping hard enough to leave marks.

We collapsed together, trembling and breath shattered. We lay in each other's arms for a moment trying to catch our breath. As the waves of our climax ebbed, we just held each other, our breathing and pulse intertwining then evening out. And in that silence, I knew, without doubt, that he was utterly mine—and I, his.

'Mine,' Mani purred. *'I do enjoy it when he reminds you who you belong to.'*

Heat crept up my throat. *'We belong to each other,'* I corrected.

She gave a low, amused huff. *'Of course.'* A pause. Then, her voice sounded like silk over steel: *'Still… I appreciate the demonstration.'*

He rolled to the side, and I rested my head against his chest, listening to the steady drum of his heart. "You… you're incredible," I whispered with a smile.

Andrew chuckled, low and ragged, his fingers tracing patterns across my back. "You have no idea what you do to me," he murmured. "I… I've never wanted anyone like this… never like I want you."

I lifted my gaze to meet his, the faint glow of my runes still flickering across our skin. "I don't want you to ever feel like you're not wanted," I said softly, cupping his face. "Every part of you… every part of *us*… it's all mine. I've been waiting for this as much as you have."

His jaw softened, a small smile tugging at the corner of his lips. He pulled me closer, as if the moment could never end. "Astrid… I love you," he said, low and fervent.

I smiled, my heart swelling. "I love you too, Andrew."

We lay like that for a long moment, letting the warmth and the quiet aftermath settle around us, the world outside forgotten, our bond between us absolute. Only this moment. Only us.

No matter what the world demanded.

No matter how close the darkness crept.

No matter what this power was, coiling hot and ancient in our veins, or what monsters we might become to survive it.

Here, in this room, in this bed, with his heart beating wild against mine.

We were whole.

We had each other.

And for now, that's all we need.

Just before dawn, pale light crept through the window, soft, silver, and quiet. It was a dreamless night, no shadows creeping through the cracks, no whispers in my thoughts, and no claws dragging memories back to the surface. Only warmth. Only him. The sunlight spilled slowly across the room, brushing the bed, the floor, the walls, touching everything within the room.

I lay still, listening to the quiet. Beneath the calm, my pulse still simmered, what remained of the Garmr lingered faintly, different now, quieter. Mani shifted uneasily inside me.

'I don't like this,' she said softly, a low growl threading through her words. *'It's different... too quiet.'*

I exhaled softly. *'I feel it too,'*

Andrew stirred beside me, eyes still heavy with sleep. "Are you ok?" he asked, voice rough.

"Yes," I said, turning to him. "But… I feel…Mani and I… we've been having dreams. Visions? A shadow, it's a wolf and dragon twisted together. It was subtle, at first, but I always feel it there. Like it was tracking me."

Andrew propped himself on his elbow, fingers rasping through his hair, suddenly wide awake. "A shadow?"

I let Mani surface, Andrew watching my eyes change,. As Mani's voice came through. "It's patient. It doesn't want to strike… yet. But I feel like it's learning while it's watching and waiting... I don't know that we can…should handle it on our own."

Mani receded and I took control again, looked down at my hands, the runes pulsing faintly. I rubbed them softly. "That's why… I think we need to talk to Bo. He'll know what to do. He always does."

Andrew's jaw tightened. "Dad… you really think he can help with this? With the bond?"

"We need help," I said firmly. "If anyone can help us right now, it's him…at least he can provide an outside perspective."

Mani growled low, I could feel her tension coiling like a spring. *'Then quit stalling. Go. Now. Before the shadow decides it wants a cameo in your waking life too.'*

I exhaled, chest tightening with resolve. "Okay."

Andrew nodded, brushing the last of sleep from his eyes. "Together," he said, his hand finding mine. "Let's find dad. Let's see if he can help figure out what is going on."

'Good. And Astrid… don't let all this turn you into a drama queen.' Mani said.

I rolled my eyes *'Got it.'*

We got ready and headed towards Bo's office, the storm outside softened to a persistent drizzle. Each step felt weighed, as we edged closer to find the truth. I could sense that the wolf-dragon shadow lingered at the edge of awareness, tugging subtly at the corners of my vision, but I didn't look back. If I looked, nothing would be there.

When we reached Bo's office, the door swung open before we could knock, as if he'd been expecting us. The familiar scent of polished wood, ink, and old books greeted us. His sharp eyes softened slightly at the sight of Andrew and me.

"Sit," he said, voice calm but cautious. "What's going on?"

I swallowed, fingers tugging at the hem of my sleeve before I lifted my gaze to Bo. "It's… the bond," I said slowly. "It's shifting. The Garmr, its pulse isn't wild anymore. I can feel it, but it's not overwhelming me. It's… listening. It knows I can carry it now."

Mani stirred in agreement, her presence steadying me. I drew in a breath. "The rage, the bloodlust…it's still there, but I can hold it. Direct it."

I hesitated, my voice lowering. "But there's a shadow… the wolf-dragon. It watches from the edges. Every time I close my eyes, it's there, circling. Not attacking, not retreating. Just waiting."

My hands tightened in my lap. "I don't think it's the Garmr I have to fear anymore. It's whatever that thing is—because it feels like one day, it's going to step out of the shadows."

Andrew stilled next to me. His hand, which had been resting lightly in his lap, tightened into fists. When I glanced up, I saw it, the flicker in his eyes, the way his jaw clenched like he'd been carrying something unsaid.

"Astrid," he began carefully, his voice rougher than before, "you see it in your dreams?"

"Yes," I breathed. "Every night." My pulse quickened. "Why?"

His gaze locked on mine, fierce and unyielding. "Because I've seen it too."

The words slammed into me harder than I expected. I blinked, breath catching. "What? Why didn't you tell me?"

He nodded slowly, his expression grim. "The same shadow. Wolf and dragon both, never fully formed, always circling. Watching me the way you just described. I thought it was just, my blood, my bond with Nidhog." His hand raked through his hair. "But if you're seeing it too…"

A chill traced my spine, colder than it ever had been. For a long moment I could only stare at him, the silence between us heavy with the truth we'd both been holding.

"It's not just me," I whispered. "What could it want with us?"

Andrew's hand found mine, fingers curling tight. "Whatever it is, it's tied to both of us, everything comes back to the both of us."

Bo leaned back in his chair, eyes narrowing as he absorbed our words. His fingers drummed against the polished oak desk, the faint scratch of pen against paper punctuating the silence. "The bond isn't just a connection," he murmured. "Does the Garmr's power run through both of you?"

"Yes," Andrew answered without hesitation, "But since Astrid claimed it fully I haven't really felt it like before."

"But the shadow… I doubt you're imagining it." Bo said almost to himself.

I shivered, though I tried not to show it. "It's like it's waiting to hunt me… to consume me fully. I don't know if it will, or when. But I know it's coming."

Bo's gaze sharpened, steady and unyielding. "Then you don't just hold it back, you learn to wield it. The rage, the bloodlust, they're not shackles anymore, Astrid. They're weapons. But a weapon is only as strong as the one who commands it. If you keep suppressing it, you'll break under its weight. If you give it too much, it'll hollow you out. You need balance. Control. Learn when to draw on it, and when to let it rest. That's the difference between being consumed and becoming unstoppable."

Andrew's jaw clenched. "And the wolf-dragon shadow? The thing we keep seeing?"

Bo's eyes softened briefly. "Patience. Some things are meant to be glimpsed before they are confronted. You're at a threshold. The training grounds will help you understand the limits of your bond and your own resilience."

I nodded, chest tight. "We decided that we weren't going to run from it. That we will face it...together. But you think leaning into the power is the best way?"

Bo got up from behind his desk walking in front of us and leaned back onto his desk. His hand rested briefly on mine. "Together. That's the only way either of you will make it through." Bo said as he leaned back, eyes scanning us carefully. "So, you're ready to test the edges of this… bond?"

I nodded, running a hand over the faintly glowing runes on my skin. "We agreed. We need to understand what we've stumbled into. The Garmr's power… it's in both of us now, somehow."

Andrew's jaw tightened. "It seems that her time-manipulation and healing are hers alone. But my strength feels… tripled. I can feel the fury running through me, almost like it's my own, almost."

Mani's voice was sharp and impatient. *'About time you two quit babbling and started moving.'*

I shot her a glare in thought. *'Patience, Mani. We're about to push ourselves, not throw ourselves at chaos blindly.'*

Bo gave a small nod, the corners of his mouth tugging into a thin line. "Exactly. You'll need control. Testing limits isn't reckless, it's about knowing when to hold back and when to push forward. Andrew, you channel the strength, but it doesn't own you. Astrid, the Garmr's presence is tethered to you now; feel it, don't fear it. Together, you'll learn to move as one."

Andrew's hand found mine, fingers curling tight. "We'll move together. Whatever comes… we'll meet it head-on."

I exhaled slowly, letting a small weight leave my shoulders, only to feel a new tension coil in my chest, tight but purposeful. “Ready,” I said. “We won’t wait for it to break over us. We’ll face it, on our terms.”

Mani snorted softly. *‘Finally. Now let’s see if you can actually back up the talk.’*

Bo’s gaze sharpened, steady and unyielding. “Then let’s begin. Training grounds await.”

Leaving the office, I felt a small weight lift. Outside, the rain had softened to a mist, clinging to every surface. Each step toward the training grounds was an unspoken agreement that whatever was coming, we would meet it head-on.

Chapter 9

The training hall smelled of damp wood and sweat as we stepped inside. The rain pelted the slanted roof, each drop drumming a sharp, insistent warning. Mud churned beneath boots outside, but inside, the floorboards echoed with the rhythm of strikes and grunts.

Bo stood at the perimeter, his arms crossed, jaw tight, the carved silhouette of a man shaped by storms far worse than this. His gaze tracked Andrew and me with the precision of a predator, weighing every step, every shift, every flicker of magic that rippled beneath our skin.

Andrew moved opposite me as we circled each other, our boots whispering against the slick floorboards. His veins glowed faintly, his power coiled beneath his skin. Mine answered in turn, the runes warmed on my hands, pulsing in steady rhythm with my heartbeat.

The storm outside pressed against the walls. The rain became a metronome to the tension within.

"Remember what I told you." Bo barked, his voice cutting through the room, steady and sharp. "Let it guide you. Don't fight blind. Rage can sharpen the blade, but if it is left unchecked, it breaks it."

Andrew's gaze met mine as we circled again. Our bond hummed in every impact, not just strength meeting strength but a deeper convergence, as though magic itself was threaded through each muscle. I tested him, letting Mani step forward to lend speed to my strike. He sidestepped it with a fluid, and

unnerving precision. The surge of his power, now tripled, was iron-warm as it brushed past me, his green-orange eyes narrowing.

"You're rushing," Andrew said, voice low, teasing, but I felt the tension lurking beneath it.

"I'm not rushing," I shot back, ducking beneath his arm, letting my momentum carry me forward. "I'm testing the edge. Finding where control ends and my power expands."

Bo grunted, unimpressed, shifting his weight slightly. "Good. But remember, force without rhythm gets you broken."

We exchanged a series of blurred passes, breathless parries, then my shoulder slammed against the wooden floor with a sharp *thwack*. I rolled away, springing back to my feet, breath ragged, heart pounding.

Andrew smirked at me, only half controlling the heat in his veins. "You're thinking too hard again."

"I'm thinking just enough," I countered, stepping in. "Testing the line. Seeing where our power begins and ends."

I lunged. Mani rose in me like instinct, granting speed that blurred the edges of the room. Andrew twisted, barely avoiding the strike, shadows of his own power trailing the movement.

We collided, my fist to forearm, his palm to my shoulder. Sparks of heat and cold chased up my spine.

"You feel it, don't you?" I murmured, stepping back into stance, fists ready.

His breath hitched. "Yeah. Every time we touch."

Bo cut in sharply. "It's convergence. But don't mistake it for control. Harness it." His shadow loomed closer, sharper against the light.

He stepped between us, gaze shifting from Andrew to me. "Both of you…look inward." His voice softened but somehow sounded more dangerous for it. "There's a thread tying you two tighter than power or magic alone. Find it."

Andrew was still breathing heavily from the training, his breath stirring the air between us. My heartbeat still pulsed wildly at the base of my throat.

Bo pointed a finger at our chests. "The bond is the fulcrum. The bridge. Everything else, the speed, strength, magic, that's just noise if the anchor is loose."

Andrew swallowed, jaw flexing. "And… what exactly am I looking for?"

Bo stepped closer to him. "The part of you that answers her without thinking."

His eyes snapped to mine, and a fire bloomed in my chest, tight and tender, with a recognition that it was ours alone. Mani prowled forward, hungry, as if she'd been waiting for the command to move.

Bo turned to me. "And you, whatever you think you are alone, double it. Then find where he is already filling the space."

Bo stepped back, folding his arms. "Close your eyes if you must. But find the thread. The bond. The thing that pulls in both directions and forces them into one path."

His voice dropped lower. "Because if you don't learn to wield that together, then someone else will learn to break it."

The storm outside hammered harder, as if the world itself tried to underline the warning.

I inhaled, letting the sound of rain and wind fade into the background. My feet dug into the floorboards, planted and steady. I closed my eyes, knowing Andrew was standing just a

few feet away, his presence heavy and alive, pulling at something deep inside me.

The runes on my hands flared faintly, sensing him, a quiet, electric hum bridging the gap between us. Mani stirred within me, coiling and waiting, her attention fixed on him full of anticipation. I let her be, letting the energy sharpen the invisible thread that ran between us.

Andrew's voice broke the quiet, low and cautious. "Astrid…"

I opened my mind, peeling away the layers of thought and distraction, letting myself reach across the space. The bond wasn't just magic. It wasn't the Garmr's pulse, his dragon blood, or the echoes of something ancient. It was recognition, a thread of inevitability connecting us, taut and tense, alive with the weight of what we could give to each other but also what we could take.

And then, I gasped. A sudden, sharp inhale that tore through the quiet. In my mind, images flared: Atius, Andrew, shadows that intertwined them, a memory…or a possibility…I couldn't place. The thread between us pulsed violently, and I knew, before I even opened my eyes, that Andrew had seen it too.

Andrew's breath hitched, a mirrored gasp cutting through the space between us. His green-orange eyes widened, reflecting the same recognition, the same shock. The bond thrummed, wild and alive, carrying the unspoken truth that what we shared was no longer only our own, it had threads that stretched beyond the here and now, into something vast, and undeniable.

The moment it settled, I felt him in the pull, across the few feet separating us. Our breaths subtly synchronized, the gap between us charged with a quiet hum of energy. Mani purred beneath the surface, vibrating with the rhythm of the bond.

"Good," Bo said, voice cutting through the stillness. "You're feeling it now. That thread, that pull… it's your anchor, your weapon, your shield. Don't let it fray."

I opened my eyes, meeting Andrew's gaze. His green-orange depths glimmered faintly in the light, and for a heartbeat, the storm outside ceased to exist. There was only the space between us, and the thread that tied us together. It felt fragile, but unbreakable.

"Enough talk. Show me. And don't hold back."

The next few exchanges were a blur. Fists and feet wove, strikes cracking through the hall, breathless parries, the air shivering with the clash of our magic and power. Andrew swept in, faster than he'd ever been. I countered, runes flaring in time with the storm outside.

I ducked low, sweeping my leg toward him. He jumped, twisting midair, and landed behind me. "Not bad," he muttered, breathing heavy. "You're getting faster."

"You're getting cocky," I shot back, grinning tightly, though exhilaration and relief mingled at the edges.

Bo clapped sharply. "Both of you, pause… Step back… Feel it… Listen to the energy flowing between you. It's blood, the bond, and magic. Push too far, and you'll burn yourselves…or worse. Think of it like a muscle, the more you strengthen it, the stronger it will become."

The words sank into the crackling quiet, making us freeze. The storm outside erupted, thunder shaking the rafters. I glanced down at my hands; the runes pulsed faintly, in rhythm with Andrew's subtle glowing veins.

Bo's gaze softened slightly, though his voice remained firm. "This is only the beginning. This Völundr, the magic, it's waking something. If you can't stand together in the storm, you'll be torn apart when it comes…or tear into each other."

I let out a long breath, fingers still tingling with residual heat. Andrew's eyes met mine; nothing flashy, just a raw, shared understanding. The convergence pulsed between us, dangerous, alive, and not yet obedient.

Thunder rolled through the sky, shaking the hall as Andrew and I stepped back from our sparring stance. My muscles still hummed with energy, and my runes lingering warmer and pulsing stronger. Bo's gaze lingered on us, sharp but unreadable.

"Enough for today," Bo finally said. "Let it settle. Let your bodies and your bond adjust the rhythm."

I nodded, though every nerve in me still tingled. Andrew exhaled slowly, brushing his dark sweat-slicked hair from his forehead. His green-orange eyes held that same intensity. After showering and changing, I found Andrew waiting for me by the training hall doors.

We left, heading towards the courtyard. The rain had softened to a mist, clinging to our skin like cold breath. Our boots squelched through the waterlogged walkway, the steady drip from the eaves marking our rhythm. The wind had died down just enough for us to walk under an umbrella. I was glad the training had drained some of the restlessness out of me. I pulled my coat tighter around my shoulders, shivering not just from cold, but from the lack of the magic that was fading away from the sparring match. The further we walked, the more the magic faded. I missed it immediately.

By the time we reached Trovi's house, the windows were still dark, and no home-made food was being cooked. The emptiness hollowed me in that familiar way, unsettling yet strangely intimate, like a shadow I knew well. Inside, the air was still heavy with the familiar scent of cedarwood, old parchment, and a small trace of dried sage and lavender. Every step toward her study felt like a return to another kind of battle, a quieter, and deadlier one. Here, silence held the weight of secrets, and I could almost feel Trovi's presence lingering among the tomes and scrolls.

My fingers drifted along her shelves, tracing the leather spines of brittle folios, brushing away dust and time. Every book, every scroll seemed to hum faintly beneath my touch, responding to the pulse still thrumming in my veins from the sparring, echoing the subtle energy woven into her study.

'She's not gone,' Mani whispered. *'Just... resting.'*

"Yes," I murmured back. "Just resting."

Andrew moved beside me. "Take your time," he said, his voice low and calm.

But something tugged at me. This was where Trovi had worked in silence, hunting through history, tracking forgotten truths most would have left buried. And now... she was silent too.

'Only for now,' Mani added, and a small smile tugged at the corners of my mouth.

Andrew's eyes scanned the shelves with quiet precision, weighing each title, each worn spine. His presence made me feel at peace, tethering me to the present. Then my hand froze.

A thick leather-bound journal, wedged between two warped tomes, called to me. Its worn spine heavy in my hands, dark green wax seal caught the candlelight. Knotwork twisting

around the border, delicate droplets tracing the edges like falling tinctures, her signature of her mastery over potion concoctions. The moment my fingers closed around it, I felt her there, a quiet pulse threading through the leather, a whisper of the years she had poured into this work. My breath caught as I lifted it free, as if the journal itself were breathing with me.

"I feel like we shouldn't be reading this," I murmured, more to the room than to Andrew.

Andrew didn't look away from the journal. "Trovi would've wanted you to…I don't think she would have put us…you in danger. She didn't write this to bury it. She wrote it for someone who could finish what she started."

I cracked the seal, and the scent of ink and dust rose like an exhaled breath from the past. The first page was filled with a familiar script, and beneath it, a symbol drawn in dark ink. A circle of runes wrapping around two forms. One serpentine. One lupine.

"Are they fighting?" Andrew asked, looking over my shoulder.

'They aren't fighting,' Mani's voice slid through the bond—into mine, into Andrew's, into Atius's. '*More like entwined.'*

Andrew went still, clearly hearing her as sharply as I did.

"Same style," he murmured, pointing to the ink.

'The pattern matches,' Mani added coolly through the link. '*The same structure. The same hand.'*

"Same runes as your mother's journal," I said, and Andrew nodded slowly as I turned the page.

"Völundr, again." Andrew read aloud. "The Binding Rite. Designed to force the convergence of incompatible magic. Wolf with lindworm."

I stared at the runes, tracing the ink with my eyes as if willing them to move. They mirrored the ones that had appeared on my skin. Threaded with deliberate intent, as if each line had been etched centuries ago with purpose I could still feel.

"What is this?" I whispered. "Is it just... symbolic?"

Andrew's jaw tightened. "I don't think so. This look like… a ritual."

My fingers hovered over a bold passage inked deeper than the rest:

One must break to remake. Völundr *will forge. If done without clarity, the result is madness. But if forged in true bond, the power multiplies.*

A shiver ran through me, crawling along my spine and settling in my chest. My hands trembled as I whispered, "This isn't about control… It's transformation."

I turned the page, and we both went still. Fire had scorched the parchment's edge, blackening half the text, but what remained was unmistakable: a bloodline chart. Most names were illegible, but one survived, almost carved into the vellum.

HATI.

I whispered the name like a prayer. Or a curse.

"My ancestor wasn't merely a wolf," I said, voice low. "Hati… he was a jötunn-born hunter, cursed to chase the gods themselves."

Andrew stepped closer. "That still doesn't explain why your magic reacts to mine. Why my blood flares when you're

near. We're not just bonded… We're… there has to be…something more."

I stumbled back a step, dropping the book. The runes shimmered faintly, pulsing with the same rhythm as my heartbeat. For weeks, dreams started to bleed into reality, visions of a black moon, voices rising from the earth, and glimpses of a dark, twisting shadow: wolf and dragon-twisted, always at the edge of perception, watching, waiting.

"I saw him," I said suddenly, voice trembling. "Beneath the roots of a white-burned tree, in a place suspended between worlds. Darkness pressed from every side, and the air was thick with whispers of lost wolf souls, wandering and howling endlessly. There was a cloaked half-man, half-beast. It looked like he was grieving. I didn't see his face, but…"

Andrew's voice was barely a whisper. "Who?"

I swallowed, dazed. "This beast…He's not dead… well not fully. He's somewhere... in between, watching and waiting. And I think he has answers. About Völundr. About Hati. About me."

Andrew reached for my hand, his fingers threading through mine with quiet certainty. "Then we find him."

'If we find him, there's no guarantee that we will ever find him again,' Mani pleaded.

Outside, thunder split the sky wide open, sleet hammering against the windows. For the first time, I felt it, our magic merging, not clashing, a pulse of power moving in tandem. Flame and fang thrummed in harmony, calling to a rhythm older than either of us. And in that rare clarity, hope bloomed. I needed answers. That's what I needed, the truth. I had to know the story of Hati, and hoping this beast-man knew what this bond was forcing us to become.

'You think this beast is between worlds?' Mani asked.
'If he is lost, we will find what remains.'

The first step had been taken. And the path ahead would demand everything of me.

Chapter 10

The storm eased again by nightfall, leaving only the soft whisper of rain against Trovi's windows. I lay back, exhaustion pressing at me, the runes on my skin thrumming faintly, like embers buried beneath ash. The rain's rhythm was gentle, almost a lullaby, and though I fought to stay awake, my eyes slipped closed.

The silence that followed was not peaceful. It was thick and heavy. There was a predator circling just beyond my vision. A cold prickle ran over my spine, and I felt the world shift around me. The floor beneath me had turned to fragile ice. Then it broke.

I fell.

The descent ended in a cavern's clearing, carved like a wound in the earth. Smoke and iron choked the air, mingling with the coppery tang of blood and the acrid bite of burned feathers. The ground was scarred with runes, charred so deep they pulsed faintly, like a dying heartbeat trapped beneath the stone. Circles of bone and shards of obsidian marked what looked like a ritual space.

This didn't feel like a dream. It felt like a memory, just not mine. It was something borrowed, yet impossibly vivid.

'Mani... where...' I stopped. I didn't feel Mani, and my heart raced.

At the stone podium stood a cloaked figure. The dark völva. His cloak had to have been woven from shadow; a void so complete it devoured the light all around him. Slowly and deliberately, he turned toward me, as if I had arrived late to an appointment he had been expecting.

My mouth opened, but no sound came out. The air held my voice hostage.

The dark völva raised his hands. Fire licked the cavern ceiling, etching runes into the stone, runes I knew, because they were etched into my skin.

"You were born for Ragnarök," he stated, his voice sliding into my bones like a blade. "You will also be the weapon… more than you are."

'So…this is Hati's memory?' I thought, it had to be.

A shockwave of magic tore outward, splitting the ground like flesh beneath a blade. Then, in a blink, the vision shattered.

The cavern was ripped apart, replaced by a jagged peak that cut into the sky. Above, a storm churned of divine rage, clouds fat with lightning and the taste of metal in the air. Thunder shattered the heavens into jagged pieces.

Two massive figures faced each other atop the ridge. Hati, his fur matted with blood, jaws still slick with the moon's death, his pale eyes burned like blazing moons. Opposite him loomed, Níðhögg, his scales oozing black fire and the stench of rot, eyes molten with judgment. They were not here as enemies. They were bound by something, war possibly, or something else entirely.

Hati stepped forward, silver flesh dangling from his teeth. Níðhögg lowered his head until their breath mingled, wolf's moonlight and dragon's smoke.

Their claws carved into the stone, the silver flesh wrapped in black fire dripped into the cracks. The claw marks ignited. It wasn't a pure light, but wet and glistening, with a hint of darkness, as if drawn in by the fresh sacrifice.

"By fire and fang, by shadow and moon, we bind our fate," Hati growled, his voice like the grinding of frozen bones.

Níðhögg's reply rumbled deep enough to make the peak tremble. "So shall moonlight and shadow be one, for a time."

They tore into themselves, ripping flesh willingly. Hati's red blood mixing with Níðhögg's blackened blood, sinking into the earth as the mountain drank with greedy hunger. Then the sky cracked open. White-hot light ripped through the clouds, blood-soaked and blinding.

From that wound rose something impossible, something profane and holy at once, a creature of wolf and dragon, forged in shadow and flame.

A violent pull seized me, dragging me downward. As though the roots of Yggdrasil itself had coiled around me and were dragging me into its depths. I was pulled through veins of earth, roots slick with the shine of ancient offerings, stone striated with echoes of prayers carved in blood, soil heavy with the weight of forgotten ages. It wasn't a fall but a descent through memory, through the very marrow of creation, where time slowed and thickened like honey, humming with primordial power.

When at last I struck the ground, it was a frozen plain stretched beneath me, black and glittering with frost that sang with every touch. The cold seared, pure as a blade. My lungs seized.

Before me loomed a forest black and breathless, its silence so absolute it pressed into my chest, making my heartbeat seemed loud as war drums. The air reeked of frost, but beneath it lingered something older, memories, truth the realms themselves had tried to bury. And then, from between the skeletal trees, they emerged.

Wolf-spirits, pale and spectral, their bodies flickering like moonlight on broken water. They stalked forward in silence, eyes burning with a cold luminescence, their forms shifting between flesh and vapor. Slowly and deliberately, they encircled me, their movements heavy with ritual gravity, until I stood in the center of their ring of reverent stillness.

From behind me, one spirit drew nearer. Its muzzle brushed against my hand, and though its body was half-seen, the sensation was real, its fur rippling beneath my fingers, warm and alive beneath the glow. Nose to tail, I traced its shape, and it did not vanish. Instead, it turned, padding forward, its head inclining as if to beckon.

I looked to the others. They did not follow. They only watched, as their forms swayed like pale flames in the windless darkness. Waiting for me, expecting me to follow because this path was not theirs, it was mine.

My throat tightened. *'Mani... what is this?'*

Her presence rolled through me, warm and sudden. Her voice was low and reverent. '*Kin... Lucky you, you've got an audience of the dead, and they don't look like they're here for autographs.'*

I swallowed hard, glancing at the ring of waiting spirits. *'They're waiting... for me.'*

'Seems that way,' Mani muttered. *'And you think I'm the dramatic one. They'd like you to follow, Astrid. Don't keep the dead waiting, it's rude.'*

The spirit in front of me paused, looking back, luminous eyes steady and unblinking.

'If I follow, what happens?' I whispered.

'You think I know more than you?' Mani replied. *"But if we go down this path, Astrid... it cannot be unwalked."* after a brief pause. *'But hey, no pressure.'*

I let out a shaky breath and followed through mist that clung to my skin, until the forest started to thin, the trees bowing back, until the ground ended in a sheer cliff. At the cliff's edge, rooted in blackened earth as if grown from bone, stood a bleached-white tree. Its ivory bark gleamed, skeletal branches clawing at the sky. And beneath it… him.

He was barefoot, toes curled around the stone, as if he could feel the mountain's slow, patient heartbeat. A fierce, feral light burned in his eyes. It was too bright, too raw for any ordinary man. Runes were branded across his arms, throat, face, like molten lines that pulsed with the rhythm of some ancient power. His hair was a matted snarl, tangled with twigs and the faint glimmer of white. His skin rippled where bone strained to shift beneath it, his shoulders twitching, spine bowing, jaw caught halfway between a human's snarl and a beast's maw. Breath hissed between too-long teeth; the air around him reeked of iron and decay. He was caught between things, wolf and man, myth and flesh, and yet something had lodged in my bones that had recognized him, like I was remembering a song. This was my father.

He was not the man I barely remembered. He seemed more of a myth now, a warning that parents use to keep their children in line. And for a moment, he wasn't a man at all, he was only a feral wolf that was half transformed. His back hunched, lips curled, teeth bared in a soundless snarl towards me, but I did not flinch.

"Stop," I said. My voice steadier than I felt. "I know who you are."

Recognition seemed to bloom across his face, then pain. "…Astrid?" His voice came rough and unused. "You've grown," he said, his voice trembling. He tried to stand, to smooth himself into something more human. "You look like her…" he rasped, staring as though measuring me against some distant memory. "Your mother."

My throat tightened, but I didn't look away. "You left us."

He flinched as if the truth had a weight of its own. His hands trembled. "I had to." He said. "The thing inside me… it wasn't meant for me. I didn't shift. I *fractured*. I became *something else*."

I stepped forward and reached out to touch him. "What happened?"

He watched me for a long moment, then bowed his head as though to summon the story. "I was trained to hunt darkness. The dark völvas, specifically. I was good at it, too good. Then one night, I was chasing something. It wasn't quite a creature, but more like a spirit. I thought it an echo of Odin—his disciples, the Odinsráð. It bit me in retaliation." He showed me his arm; the flesh was mangled, knotted with old wounds. "It cursed me, and it never let go."

He stepped away, turning back to the edge of a silver ocean and pointed into it. It stretched to the horizon seeming endless.

"At first I thought leaving was the best way to protect you, both of you. But the truth? I ran because I was afraid of the thing I was becoming."

My jaw clenched. "What *did* you become?"

He kept his gaze on the silver water. "I am a draugr, deathless and wandering. A ghost… A warning etched into memory. The story spoken in the dark to keep children from stepping beyond the safety of home." His words were bitter and small.

I stood next to him on the bank. The silver ocean mirrored me and then did not. Three reflections swam across the silver surface, rippling and smiling back at me.

The first one was cloaked in shadow, with eyes like splinters of moonlight, cold and cutting, catching every movement as if weighing it for the kill. Her pale irises ringed in shadow, the kind of gaze that doesn't just see you, it hunts you.

The second one was cloaked in starlight, the eyes were Mani's glowing electric blue but still ringed with shadow. Across the skin, shadows pulse with moonlight and shadow, binding me in both the divine and dreadful. My claws seemed to drip with blood and starlight alike, each claw carrying the promise of ruin and renewal. That I am neither mercy nor wrath alone.

Then the third one was small and fragile in a way that made my chest ache. Weak, unremarkable, and painfully human. She was the girl I used to be, with hands that had never killed, eyes that still believed the world would not come to save her, and a heart so scarred by the weight of that house.

"What is this?" I breathed.

“The truth,” he said. “You are not one thing. As of right now you are three. You carry all of these versions of yourself and the Völundr will use that if you don’t decide.”

I met his gaze and there was pain, memory, and warning tangled in his expression.

I stared at him. “How?”

“You have to choose. Before something *else* chooses for you. You are stronger than I ever was,” he said. “But don’t mistake strength for wholeness. And don’t think your blood will protect you from what’s inside.”

“What?!” I shouted at him. “I want answers, real answers!” I sat stepping towards him. “I want to know how I’m supposed to choose when I don’t have all the answers?”

His mouth twisted into a sad, knowing smile. “You are so much like your mother.” He said making me stop in my tracks. “You will know what to do. You’re the balance. The tipping point. Don’t fear the power that will become you.”

Then the lake shimmered, and my reflections were gone. I looked behind me and the wolf spirits began to circle again.

“Wait!” I cried. “What about you? What will happen to you?”

He turned and stepped back into the mist. “I’m already gone.” He said. “But you,” he swallowed. “*You* still have a chance.”

The wolves closed ranks, nudging me toward the silver water edge. Their motion was polite but inexorable, like a tide. He shrank into the haze until he was no more than a silhouette, then a memory. I felt the world tilt as the spirits pushed; the silver surface of the lake rose to meet me, and then everything turned to smoke.

I tore back to myself with a ragged gasp, sweat slick against my skin, heart hammering as if I'd run a marathon in my sleep. The runes on my hands flared, casting the room in a jittering blue light that trembled across the walls.

Andrew was up in an instant, beside me, eyes wide. "Astrid? What—"

Words tumbled loose and raw. "I saw him," I said, my voice thin. "My father. The dark völva. Hati. Níðhögg. Pieces of the past…or a warning?"

He wrapped his hands around my shoulders gently, making me look at him. "Tell me."

I looked down at my shaking palms, the three reflections from the lake flickering through my mind—shadow, starlight, and the small, human girl. "I spoke with him," I whispered. "He said I'm stronger than he was. But if I don't choose who to be… the Völundr will choose for me."

Andrew's jaw tightened, resolve settling into his features like carved stone. "Then we get answers." He said, his voice quiet but unyielding, steel wrapped in warmth. "So, no one can decide what you or I become."

The image of what my father had become crawled up my spine like cold fingers.

Three reflections waited.

The shadow.

The Starlight.

The fragile girl.

The Völundr could offer strength. It could promise survival. It could whisper of destiny and make it sound inevitable.

But it did not get to choose for me.

That choice was mine.

And this time, when I faced my reflection—
I would not look away.

Chapter 11

The dawn bled pale and slow across the horizon, spilling through Trovi's windows, but the light did nothing to ease the pressure crushing my chest. I didn't truly sleep. I only drifted, held under by a shadow that refused to lift even with morning light.

His voice still echoed through my thoughts, cold and relentless: *"You have to choose. Before something else chooses for you."*

Inside me, the fractured pieces strained against one another. I mindlessly traced the glowing runes along my palm, feeling the restless thrum beneath. Then came a voice, whispering in the dark spaces of my mind, a voice that is both seductive and cruel.

'Let go, Astrid. Give in to the shadow. It is your birthright, the wolf of the moon. Be stronger than them all.'

My jaw tightened, nails biting into my palms as though I could anchor myself with pain. *'No,'* I hissed back. *'I won't become a mindless monster.'*

Mani groaned, exasperated. *'Great, another voice... Is it a new one, or one we've heard before? I can't keep up anymore.'*

A strained laugh scraped out of me, too thin to be real. I muttered under my breath. *'At this point, I need a damn roll call just to know who's trying to hijack my brain.'* My pulse stuttered, the air trembling with that other presence still pressing at the edges of me. *'But I know one thing. It's not me. And I'm not letting it win.'*

'What monster, I wonder?' Mani asked, her voice a warm, feral growl threading under the darker whisper. *'The gods made Hati a 'monster' when he hunted their moonlight. They will call you the same, no matter what path you choose.'*

Her words struck sharp, my heart aching against my ribs. *'I am not him,'* I whispered. *'I am not Hati.'*

'No,' Mani murmured, her voice gentler now. *'You are more than any one shape they try to force on you. You are the girl. I am your wolf. Together we are the moon.'*

She pauses.

'Shadow and light. Destruction and grace. All of it. And I will not let you forget that.'

'Now, who sounds like Trovi,' I said as a smile tugged at my lips despite the weight in my chest.

'Please,' Mani snorted. 'If I started handing out "great wisdom," Trovi would be out of a job by sunrise.'

A quiet laugh slipped from between us, easing some of the tension just enough to breathe. But it didn't last. I let it fade before I drew in a slow breath, steadying myself before the words settled into something solid.

'Mani... I just... I won't let this darkness consume me.'

'And if it is not darkness?' She pressed. *'What if it is our fate, Astrid, to be the night that devours the day?'*

I had no answer. Her words sank into me. *The night that devours the day...*

The shadows in the room seemed to thicken, shifting like they knew my name. Mani prowled closer inside me, unsettled, her hackles prickling along my spine. My pulse wouldn't settle. Restlessness coiled under my skin until it

burned. I slid out of bed and drifted to the bathroom mirror. The runes cast their eerie glow across my face, and shards of ghost fire dancing across the walls.

Then… something struck, sharp and merciless. Ice and fire were twisting together around my neck. The whisper sweetened until it hurt, until it promised ruin and ecstasy in the same breath.

"Why fight it?" The layered voice was velvet, curling from the dark between heartbeats. *"You were born for this. Let it in. Let it take you. Be what you are meant to be."*

I lifted my gaze and saw light spilling from me. My eyes burned like twin moons, tears of pure moonlight cutting down my cheeks.

'Mani?' I breathed, unsteadily.

'Not Mani…' came the reply, velvet and inexorable.

My nails sank into my palms, the sting was exquisite but grounding. Blood welled, warm and vivid, sliding across my skin in ruby streams.

Then the mirror shifted, I glimpsed her face, Naomi, standing just behind me. Her presence pressed icy sweat along my spine, venom in my marrow.

"Look at yourself," she whispered, her tone both taunt and caress. *"This is strength. This is freedom. Why chain yourself? Give in, Astrid. Give in, and nothing will touch you again. Not the gods, not the wolves, and not him…"*

The mirror rippled with shadow, and in it I saw not just ruin, not monstrosity, but me, standing tall, smiling and terrible. Light and shadow coiled around me like crowns.

For a heartbeat, I believed it. My father's warning flickered somewhere distant, smothered beneath the swell rising inside me, warm, coaxing, almost kind. "*This power could protect you. Save everyone you love. Why fear what was always yours?"*

The surge hit hard, sudden and intoxicating, as if Naomi herself were pouring it straight into my veins.

Mani screamed. "*No!*" The word snapped through me, sharp and instinctive, but the power drowned it out before I could hold on.

My runes flared, burning bright—but their rhythm wasn't mine. It was hers. And the dark völva. Their magic pressed into me, pulse for pulse, until my breath hitched.

"Just this once..." The words slipped free before I could stop them, heavy with promise and already tasting of regret.

Naomi's laughter curled through the air, low and sinuous. *"Yes. That's it. Taste it. Breathe it. You'll see. You were never meant to resist."*

Shadow and moonlight collided, rushing over me in a blinding tide. My vision fractured, blue fire caught at the edges, darkness swallowing the rest. The ecstasy was sharp and terrifying, but exquisite. It was like I was drowning and rising at once.

When I caught the reflection again, the smile staring back was not grim or weary. It was Naomi's smile, sharp and radiant, wearing my face.

And in that instant, I finally understood my father's warning: not that this power was just ruin, it wasn't something I needed to fear, but to control. It could shield Andrew. It could save everyone I loved. It could end the dark völva. With that thought, I could unmake what threatened us.

This power would protect what I loved, but only if I chose to master it. Anything else was surrender. And I would not surrender. Not like this. Not if it owned me.

I forced myself to push back, shoving their magic outward, reclaiming space inside my own skin. Naomi resisted instantly, her whispers slid softer now, velvet-wrapped and dangerous, each promise edged like broken glass.

"Let it take you," she urged. "*Let it name you."*

Her presence coiled tighter, smoke threaded with frost, seeping into every weakness I hadn't sealed. She wasn't content to linger at the edges, she was digging, trying to anchor herself in memory and dreams, reaching for my waking thoughts with greedy intent.

She didn't want to haunt me.

She wanted it to own me.

"Why resist?" she purred from the mirror, the words honeyed. *"This isn't your enemy, Astrid. It's a gift. You already feel it, don't you? The power thrumming in your veins, the way it bends to your will. All you have to do is let go…let it drown you, let it crown you. You could keep…keep them all…safe. No one would ever touch what's yours."*

The venom of her magic coated my tongue, sweet, bitter, and false. It tasted like freedom dressed in ruin.

And still, I fought. Mani's growl rumbled through my bones. Andrew's fire pressed steady at my back. Inch by inch, I tore myself free, wrenching her magic loose until her shadow finally slid away, slick and reluctant, like oil retreating from water.

I sagged, gasping. The hunger still stirred beneath my skin, but it was *mine* again.

Not hers. Not the dark völva's.

Then Mani cut through the haze. *'You should not have opened that damn door,'* she rumbled, low and steady, like thunder rolling beneath ice.

'I...I didn't mean...,' I gasped, trembling.

'Did you feel her slithering?' Mani roared. *'She will use your hesitation against you until you cannot tell which teeth are hers and which are yours.'*

'I just needed...,' I whispered. *'...just for a moment.'*

For a heartbeat, Mani was silent. I could feel her pacing, torn between instinct and devotion. Then her voice came again, low but steady.

'Being cautious is not cowardice, Astrid. But boldness doesn't always mean bravery.... idiot.' Mani let out a sigh. *'If you choose to walk the knife's edge, then I will walk it with you. You will not stand alone as long as you don't cast me aside.'*

My throat tightened, hot with relief and fear all at once. *'Then we face this together?'*

'Of course, someone needs to kick ass when you can't' Mani laughed, a vow and a promise in the sound. *'Together. You and I are forever one soul, one body, one shield. They will not claim us.'*

Before I could answer, Andrew's voice followed, fierce and unshakable. "They won't have you. Not while I breathe. Not while I can fight."

I turned toward him. His eyes smoldered red with Atius's fire, but the heat wasn't anger, it was fear. Real fear, for me. Before I could say anything he pulled me against his chest, his arms wrapping around me with a fragile desperation, as though if he didn't hold me close enough, I might slip away.

I could feel every shake of his breath against my skin. His thumb slipped under my jaw, lifting my face toward him with heartbreaking care. "You came back," he whispered, his voice splintering. "Don't scare me like that," The last part came out barely audible.

I froze. All that reckless surrender I'd almost fallen into, the temptation to give up, to stop fighting, to stop trying to understand the power twisting inside me, crashed over me in a wave of humiliation. My cheeks burned. I felt foolish and small. I'd nearly thrown away everything I'd been clawing my way toward.

"I… I didn't mean to," I breathed, barely getting the words out. "I just…everything felt so loud, and I thought maybe… maybe if I knew what I was dealing with…and I do…I understand what it means to have control over my power…"

His hands cupped the back of my neck, thumb brushing my skin with a gentleness that almost broke me.

"You don't get to just give up," he murmured, his forehead pressing softly to mine. "You're not alone, not ever again."

I swallowed hard, the weight of my almost-mistake pressing into my chest.

"I know," I whispered—but the words fractured as tears spilled over. "I'm sorry. I'm trying… gods, I'm trying so hard to understand this. To control it. But for a second, I just…"

My voice failed me.

He pulled me closer without hesitation, his arms tightening around me as his breath warmed my cheek.

"She won't take you from me, Astrid," he said, voice low and certain. "She'll have to go through me first."

A bitter laugh slipped from me. "Isn't that what she wants…just you, all to herself?"

Mani's growled, sharp and feral. *'I will kill him myself! Fuck that bitch.'* Andrew raised an eyebrow at me, hearing Mani's growl.

"Mani," he said gently, voice low but sure, "no one is taking me away. Okay?"

He pressed a soft kiss to my forehead. The effect was instant, Mani's growl dissolved into a begrudging huff.

'Fine,' she muttered, settling back but not silent. *'But I'm watching.'*

Andrew's gaze shifted past me, over my shoulder, hardening as it locked on the mirror. Irritation flashed across his face, his jaw tightened, and his eyes narrowed. I turned to look and in the mirror, Naomi's reflection still lingered, her smile gone, her eyes sharp with rage. But she no longer filled my veins. The power she dangled still pulsed in the air. The shadows quivered at the edge of my vision, reaching and testing.

I straightened, my hands were shaking, but I lifted my chin anyway. My voice was steadier than I thought it could be. "I'm not yours," I stated, steadying. "I will never be under your control."

Naomi's frown deepened in the mirror, but I did not flinch. For the first time, I believed she, and the dark völva behind her, could be beaten.

I stepped away from the counter, my breath shaky but mine again. The air felt heavy with the remnants of her poison… but lighter than moments ago.

I sank into the large chair near the fireplace, curling my knees to my chest. Letting the warmth seep through the chill of the night and the remnants of fear. The runes on my hands pulsed quietly, their light a slow, steady heartbeat against the shadows.

Andrew knelt beside me, striking the flint to the wood again, coaxing the fire to life. Flames caught and danced,

flickering across the walls and painting the room in warm gold and amber. I watched the glow, the way it licked the edges of the room, and felt the quiet tether of safety he offered.

He settled beside me, close enough that our shoulders brushed, his warmth seeping into the cold still coiled in my bones. His hand found mine, steady and sure, his thumb tracing small slow circles across my knuckles.

No words came at first, just the rhythm of the fire, the soft cadence of his breathing aligning with mine, and a fragile harmony after what happened in the bathroom. He shifted slightly, angling toward me, every line of his body attentive, patient, like he would wait all night if I needed.

I let myself lean into him, the weight of my head resting on his shoulder, and little by little… the tension inside me loosened.

Without thinking, I moved closer, then I climbed into his lap, curling into his warmth. His arms wrapped around me instantly, strong but careful.

He murmured into my hair, his voice low, but certain. "Whatever you saw, whatever waits out there… it doesn't change this. It doesn't change us."

The steady thrum of his heartbeat pressed into my ear, drowning out the echoes of my father's voice and the visions that had followed me back. Neither one of us spoke, not yet. Andrew just let me fold into him, one hand stroking slow circles along my spine, the other cradling the back of my head while he placed soft kisses into my hair. For a moment, I allowed myself to breathe, to feel, to sit in the aftermath without fighting the shadows.

Chapter 12

The gray hush of early morning clung to the windows like smoke, thick and unmoving, casting the room in a muted haze. Cold pressed against the walls as if trying to seep inside, but I barely noticed it.

I sat curled in the chair before the fireplace, sleepless and still, my mind refusing to rest.

The runes etched into my hands pulsed faintly, small warnings that the power inside me was still stirring, still waking. My thoughts circled endlessly, tightening like a noose—not just around Naomi, not just the shadows creeping into the cracks of my sanity, but around my mother. The emptiness she left behind. The unanswered questions. The silence.

A thin breath trembled out of me as I stared at the floor, trying to anchor myself. Then a soft knock pulled me from my spiral, making me jerk upright.

Mani snapped fully awake. A growl rumbled through me, though my throat made no sound.

'This isn't good,' Mani warned as I lifted my head and made eye contact with Naomi.

She was leaning against the doorway as though it belonged to her. Her silver hair spilling across her shoulders, the early morning light caught in her amethyst eyes. But something else lived behind them, merciless and wrong.

"Astrid," she purred softly, her voice curling like smoke. "Still hiding?"

Mani's rage prickled under my skin. Mani pressed against me, restless. '*Don't trust her. Just tear her throat out.*'

'*Let's see what she wants first,*' I responded, pushing to my feet, my spine stiff despite the tremor in my hands. "What do you want?" I asked

Naomi's smile was slow and deliberate, like a knife sliding out from its sheath. "You're stronger than I expected. I'll give you that. The bond that binds you… it's more tangled than even your precious Trovi realized."

My fists clenched, Mani's claws prickling beneath my skin. "Just say what you came here to say. Stop talking in riddles."

She tilted her head, eyes narrowing as she assessed me. Behind her, the shadows peeled off her back, seeming restless, and listening.

"I just came to tell you something." She stepped forward, her presence bleeding shadows as she walked into the room. "Something about your mother."

I froze as every hair raised on my arms, my instincts screaming.

Mani's snarl tore through me, feral and vicious. Naomi barely reacted, just a slight lift of her brow in faint amusement before her interest slid away entirely. '*Don't listen to her lies.*'

"You don't know anything about my mother," I said as my pulse stumbled.

Naomi's smile widened, cruel and soft all at once. "Well… I know she's alive."

The world started to spin. My breath caught; my knees nearly buckled.

Mani surged forward, a snarl tearing through my chest like thunder. '*Lies! Trickery!*' Her rage tore through me, hot and savage, and for a heartbeat I welcomed it—her certainty, her fire. Yet beneath it… something else. A flicker of doubt. A question I didn't want asked.

Mani faltered. *'...Can it be true? She doesn't smell of lies...'*

Her hesitation hit harder than Naomi's words.

I swallowed hard and forced myself to focus, to listen. Naomi's pulse drummed slow, steady… no tremor of deception, no betraying skip.

"No…" I whispered. "How…can it be…true?"

Naomi's lips curved, as she stepped closer, her voice dipping low and venomously- sweet. "She vanished because she refused to give you up. Give you to the one who believes you were the key. She went into hiding because of you, Astrid. For you."

Mani was pacing now and it was becoming frantic. '*She wants to break you. Don't believe her. We already knew all that...mostly.'*

"I know she wanted to hide me," I rasped. "But you said I was a key. A key for what? For who?"

"They call themselves the Odinsráð," Naomi murmured, her eyes gleaming. Mani growled while flattening her ears. "They are the guardians of the Allfather's secrets. Keepers of the runes' power. And in this modern age, where war is fought through shadows, code, and silence, they shape fate from the unseen places."

Mani snarled, then faltered, her ears still flat. *'How does she know this? She's not that important to know all this.'*

I echoed Mani's thought aloud. "Why tell me this? Where is she now?"

Naomi's gaze hardened, like a predator's satisfaction glint. "Because you were 'safer' not knowing. Because she didn't want you to be caught up in a war older than the Realms. But secrets always rot, Astrid. They rot, then they poison."

My breaths came fast and shallow. Mani pressed close, but her growl was hollow now, threadbare with uncertainty. *'I don't trust her... But... I feel truth in her words'*

I clenched my fists and steadied my voice. "Then what do you want from me?"

Naomi's expression sharpened. "I want you to see what's coming. You're not just a girl with a wolf in her bones. You're the tipping point. And your mother knew it. That's why she ran. That's why they want YOU." she points toward the runes pulsing on my skin.

Power surging through the panic in my mind. "And you?" I demanded, stepping closer. "Who are you? Who's inside you? Who holds you?"

For the briefest moment, something flickered behind Naomi's eyes, it was her pain, fear… her humanity. Mani tensed, torn between lunging for her throat and leaning closer. Then it was gone.

Naomi's voice dropped to a whisper. "Whether you want it or not, our fates are bound. And soon you will meet what your mother feared most…and why she wanted you left behind." She stepped back into the hallway and disappeared, like smoke merging with shadow.

Then silence fell.

I just stared at the empty doorway, my hands trembling. Mani prowled restlessly, snarling and divided. I couldn't tell where her fury ended and mine began.

'She's dangerous. Let me end her,' Mani growled.

"No," I whispered, shaking my head. *'Didn't you see it? That flicker? That was her free for a moment. Someone else has a leash around her throat.'*

Mani went still. *'You think she's still being controlled?'*

'Not controlled,' I answered bitterly. *'Used. Twisted. She thinks she has power, but she doesn't. She's a tool, and I don't think she even sees it...'*

A low growl rumbled through me, but it wasn't rage. It was grief. *'Then she's already lost.'* Mani murmured.

"Maybe," I said softly, my fingers brushing the runes still glowing faintly across my hands. *'Maybe... maybe she can still be freed.'*

Mani paced again, slower this time, her voice grim. *'Great, then it's not just her we're fighting. It's whoever holds the other end of those strings.'*

'Most likely the dark völva,' I agreed, and dropped to the floor. As everything was replaying in my head, the bond, my mother, the Odinsráð, and Naomi.

The floor creaked from the hallway and my head shot up to the door, my heart lurched until Andrew's silhouette filled the doorway. His smile faltered when he saw me on the floor, then he set our breakfast down quickly.

"Astrid," he said gently, crossing the room in quick strides. His arms slid around me, steady and warm. "What happened?" His voice was low, protective, already edged with a simmering fury on my behalf.

I pressed my face into his chest, torn between confessing what happened with Naomi or just staying quite a moment longer. Mani's growl still thrummed beneath my ribs, vibrating against his heartbeat.

His hand cupped my chin, lifting it up gently, forcing me to meet his gaze. They burned with fury, aimed at whatever hurt me, never at me. "Astrid… Tell me."

And at that moment, I didn't know if I could keep the truth from him.

'*Tell him!*' Mani urged.

I told Mani. *'He'll never see what we saw. He'll only see an enemy.'*

Mani's snarl was wounded. '*She IS an enemy. You think mercy will change the strings? After all she's done?'*

'Not mercy,' I answered, my throat tight as I leaned into Andrew's heartbeat. *'A choice, my choice. Not theirs, not the darkness.'*

Mani quieted, caught between fury and the faintest flicker of reluctant respect.

Andrew stayed quiet as his eyes searched my face. His expression softening. "Whatever it is, I'll stand between you and it. Always."

His vow rang like steel, so certain it almost broke me. I wanted to tell him everything. I wanted to unburden the secret clawing inside my chest. Before I could answer, he leaned in, pressing a slow, deliberate kiss to my forehead. His lips lingered there, not in haste, not in pity, but in promise, like he was sealing the vow into my very skin.

My eyes stung, the ache in my chest cracking open under the warmth of it. Mani went utterly silent, stilled by the rawness of the moment.

When he pulled back, his thumb brushed over my cheek, gently. "You don't have to carry this alone."

"I know," I whispered. "Just… not yet."

He nodded, even though I saw the questions burning in his eyes. Mani was not happy or wanting to forgive Naomi, but she understood my decision and respected it.

'If you're wrong,' she warned, '*We'll all pay for it.'*

'I know,' I breathed. *'But if I'm right... she doesn't need to be destroyed... She needs to be freed.'*

Andrew leaned his forehead against mine, and we stayed like that until the embers in the hearth faded, holding onto the fragile peace I bought with one small, stubborn decision.

Chapter 13

The nights bled together into a blur of half-sleep and dread. Every time I woke up, my heart was hammering against my ribs, the walls of my room swelling and shrinking, as if they breathed. Shadows stretched into forms I almost recognized, then retreated when I tried to focus on them. Voices pressed against the edges of my mind, too many of them overlapping, and none of them belonging to me. Sometimes it was Naomi's, smooth and honeyed. Other times it was the guttural rasp of the dark völva. Each carried the same stain, the same twisted mark that clawed into my skull like a brand burned too deep to fade.

I saw flashes of places I had never walked, not with my own feet, and glimpses of places I visited briefly. A shoreline that was a cliff, drenched in storm light. A cavern where creatures made their home in the darkness. None of it mine, and yet all of it pushed into me, demanding I carry their weight.

Andrew was always there. His hand found mine in the dark, his thumb tracing slow, steady circles that pulled me back from the edge. The heat of his body at my back anchored me more firmly than any dream could unravel. When the visions swelled, he drew me into his chest, his heartbeat thundering beneath my ear until it drowned out everything else. His breath warmed my hair, his voice a low murmur. "I've got you."

And I believed him. With his arms wrapped around me, the weight of the worlds I carried eased, not gone, but bearable. The weight was shared; suddenly, I wasn't holding them alone.

The firelight painted his skin in flickering gold, the room warm and enclosed. Andrew pressed closer, his body hard and steady against mine, melting the dread that had clung to my bones. His breath ghosted over my neck, slow and intimate, sending a shiver through me that had nothing to do with fear. Desire stirred in its place—warm, insistent, pooling low and sharp, chasing away the last remnants of unease.

My pulse sped, attuned to him, to the measured rise of his chest beneath my hands, the strength held carefully in check. His fingers traced my spine over my shirt, not hurried, not demanding. Each touch was a tether, coaxing me closer, daring me to let go. I didn't hesitate. I turned over and leaned in, pressing my body fully against his, letting the tension unravel as our breathing synced.

My lips sought his, desperate and hungry, brushing against his with longing threaded through need. Every press of his body against mine, every breath that tangled together, threaded me tighter into him, binding me in the fire of our bond, until the world beyond him ceased to exist. His heartbeat hammered against my ear.

Steady.

Certain.

And then… it wasn't.

The warmth curdled. His mouth went ice-cold. His hands, once steady and reassuring, pressed against me with a sharp, alien strength. The embrace twisted, rigid and unyielding, pressing and pinning me in a way that was uncomfortable and almost painful. I lifted my eyes, searching for the fierce gentleness I knew better than my own reflection.

But his eyes… they were wrong. Empty in a way that felt carved out, hollow and merciless. The green orange I knew

was gone. His irises swallowed whole by solid black. They were still as ice sealed over a frozen lake, without warmth, and without recognition.

This wasn't Andrew.

It only wore his face.

"Andrew?" My voice cracked, thin and fragile against the sudden weight pressing down.

He smiled, but it wasn't him. It was a hollow, empty carved smile that spread across his face. It was a cruel mimicry.

Before I could pull away, his hands snapped to my neck, his fingers closing with brutal strength, stealing my breath in an instant. Panic detonated in my chest, my lungs screaming as my vision blurred. Every instinct screamed fight, but because this thing wore Andrews face I hesitated.

"No breathe…" he rasped, the voice turned jagged and wrong. His eyes gleamed with a deliberate, hollow predatory hunger that sent ice racing through my veins.

Then Mani. A low, insistent rumble vibrating in my chest and spine. '*No! Stop! Wake up!*' Her growl tore through the illusion, shredding the silken threads that had bound me in its trap.

I gasped as my nails dug into his wrist, fighting the crushing pressure as his fingers digging into my skin. Ice shot down my spine, snapping me fully awake in panic. Mani surged harder, her power pouring into me, sharp and feral. '*Fight, damn it! That's not Andrew!*'

The false warmth fully collapsed into something vile. My pulse spiked, and instinct finally roared free. I drove both feet into his chest, the impact wrenching me loose. He toppled back, crashing onto the floor, and I sucked in ragged air, my throat aching, and my skin seared with phantom cold.

And then I saw it, the cracks. The illusion, thin as brittle glass, beginning to fracture. The thing that had stolen Andrew's face splintered, and what remained was hollow. Not my Andrew. Every feigned touch, every echo of intimacy reeked of corruption.

Mani's growl detonated into a savage roar inside me, ripping through every nerve like wildfire. Rage flooded my veins, hot, blinding, and merciless, dragging me fully awake.

I realized how close I'd come, how easily it had almost trapped me. I unleashed it with her.

The sound tore from my throat, feral and thunderous, slamming into the walls hard enough to make them tremble.

The illusion wavered, flickering like smoke in candlelight, but it didn't disappear. Its eyes, those hollow, predatory pits, locked onto me. I could feel the lingering warmth of the bed beneath me, the echo of the closeness, the false Andrew had tried to trap me in, and it made my blood boil.

'Now, Astrid!' Mani snarled. *'Fight!'*

I drew in a trembling breath, letting her rage intertwine with my own. The air between us vibrated, heavy with the pulse of her power, my heartbeat syncing with hers. *'He's not Andrew.'*

Then something deeper stirred, the Garmr power. It wasn't heat, but weight. A brutal gravity that was pushing my rage upward until it could no longer be contained. I let it bleed into us, slow and corrosive, the reins slipping from my grasp just enough to glimpse the ruin it promised. The world collapsed inward, all nuance stripped away, until only one truth remained: prey and predator. And I knew, without a doubt, which one I preferred.

Mani pressed closer, not resisting, not warning, only sharpening. Her fury twined with mine until I couldn't tell where she ended and I began. The world sharpened at the edges, every sound too loud, every shadow too alive. My blood felt like it was burning.

We merged completely, and the roar that ripped from our throat shook the room again. I launched myself at the false Andrew still staring at me on the floor, my runes blazing across my hands, vibrating like iron struck on an anvil. We collided with bone-jarring force, the impact driving his back into the floor so hard that the wood floor cracked beneath us.

He hit hard and then hit back harder. He moved faster than I expected. His stone-hard hands slammed into my ribs, hurling me sideways. I hit the floor hard, my breath ripping from my lungs as cracks spider-webbed through the boards beneath me. Pain flared white-hot. My grip slipped. For a heartbeat, I was pinned.

His shape rippled and warped above me, flesh sagging, stone grinding beneath skin that no longer knew what it was meant to be.

The scream that tore from him wasn't human anymore, it was high, warped, and furious, as the magic stitching his shape together began to fail. His body convulsed, flesh rippling and sagging, struggling to remember a lie it could no longer hold. He clawed at himself, desperate, dragging fingers through his own skin as if he could force Andrew's face to stay.

I scrambled up while he was distracted with his melting body. Once I was out from under him and standing, I was striking blindly, my runes flaring as I drove a blow into his shoulder. It connected, but instead of breaking him, the magic skidded, sliding off malformed stone beneath borrowed skin.

He seized my wrist, his grip crushing tight enough to make my bones scream. Pain shot up my arm as my knees buckled, and he slammed me back against the wall hard enough to rattle the frame. And for the first time in months, fear, real fear flared hot and suffocating.

Then Mani snarled at me, '*Focus! There is no place for fear here!*'

I took a ragged breath and my fingers turned into sharp scythes, and in one swipe I nearly cut off its arm. It let go, and I could fully breathe again, but my vision was swimming. I leaned against the wall to steady myself.

Then the illusion peeled back like smoke ripped apart by the wind, revealing what lay beneath.

Not flesh. Not Andrew.

Gray muck and jagged stone heaved beneath collapsing skin, a golem struggling to hold its shape. Before I could think clearly, its weight crashed into me again, slamming me against the wall, pinning me there. Cold, crushing mass pressed the air from my lungs. Panic clawed up my throat.

'Move,' Mani snarled, raw and feral. '*You're stronger than this.*'

I tried. My arms shook. The thing didn't budge. My strength alone wasn't enough. Every strike felt like punching a mountain. Until my hands were caught and started to sink into it. As if it was trying to absorb me. The golem leaned back just enough to punch me in the face causing my head to snap to the side with such force that the other side of my face slammed into the wall.

Something inside me *snapped*—not in rage, or in loss. But a decision, to let loose completely. I drew a breath and let go of the Garmr's chains. My runes burned white-hot, searing

into me like brands, as the Garmr slammed fully into the merge, a chained beast snapping its jaws, drowning me in merciless fury. The edges of my vision bled red, every movement suddenly clear, every weakness laid bare, as my heartbeat thundered like war drums in my skull.

'The core!' Mani roared. '*TEAR IT OUT! END IT,'*

The world narrowed, every false detail stripped away until I saw it: a blackened totem embedded in its chest, pulsing faintly, wet and rotting, like a heart that had never been alive. I didn't hesitate. I forced myself to be steady, to not be reckless, not wild, but calculated.

The golem loomed over me, its weight crushing, stone fingers locking me in place. I couldn't break free. Not yet.

Its massive arm drew back for another strike.

That was my only opening.

As the fist came down, I twisted beneath it, barely slipping past the blow. I seized its forearm, using the force of its own movement to wrench myself forward. Stone grated against stone as I drove both my hands into its chest with everything I had.

The cold sludge fought me, sucking and resisting, trying to swallow my arms whole. I tore through deeper, until my fingers curled around the totem's slick, pulsing surface.

The golem shrieked, and convulsed violently, as its body began to collapse. I looked into its eyes as I tighten my grip on the totem and smiled. Then with one brutal wrench, I ripped the totem free, crushing it in my hand as I watched the golem.

The effect was instant, as its body folded in on itself. The flesh turning fully into the gray muck, sloughing away in wet folds, dissolving into a shapeless pile of mud that hit the floor with a sickening slap. The totem writhed in my grip, glowing like dying coal in the dark. The glow sputtered, sizzling out, and died. Ash spilled through my fingers as the last of the magic bled away.

Silence crashed over the room.

I staggered back onto the bed, trembling, and my chest heaving. The stench of wet earth and burnt magic clung to me. Mani prowled inside me, her growl low and triumphant. *'It's gone. We ended it.'*

But beneath her satisfaction lingered Garmr's echo, heavy and violent, whispering promises of what more this power could do if I let it. My hands shook as I pressed them to my face, adrenaline still blazing in my blood.

Slowly, the world steadied. The silence of the room wrapped around me, heavy and suffocating. No flicker of Andrew's warmth beside me, no steady rhythm of his breath. Just me, completely alone.

Panic curled sharp in my throat. "Andrew?" I whispered. No answer.

'Calm down,' Mani muttered, dryly. *'He probably just went to get something to eat…the man never really stops eating, honestly… Unless, of course, he's been replaced by another mud puppet…"*

"Don't," I hissed aloud, teeth gritted.

Mani clicked her tongue. *'What? I'm just saying… if another mud puddle dressed as Andrew attacks us again, I'm biting first and asking questions later.'*

A shaky laugh slipped free. The terror dulled slightly, replaced by exhausted relief. I pushed myself up, even though every muscle screamed achingly. The floor was cold beneath

my feet as I moved toward the door, my heart still thundering in my ears.

The house groaned with its usual nighttime silence, yet it felt wrong now, emptier and hollow. I gripped the railing as I descended the stairs, the shadows below swallowing me whole.

Chapter 14

'Where could he be?' I muttered to Mani, my voice unsteady.

Before she could answer, I passed my old room—and there he was.

Shirtless, he leaned over the bed, every muscle in his back drawn tight with strain. He stood unnaturally still, frozen mid-motion, as though the world itself had paused around him.

Relief flickered in my chest as I stepped closer, fragile and uncertain after what I'd just done. My heart still pounded from the fight, but beneath it was something deeper—an aching pull, desperate and afraid this, too, might not be real.

Then something shifted.

The air felt wrong. Too heavy. Too quiet.

And I saw it all at once… he wasn't alone.

Another figure was perched on the bed in front of him, so close their mouths were nearly touching. My anger spiked sharp and sudden at the sight of her arms looped around Andrew's shoulders. Then she turned towards me, and my stomach dropped.

It was me.

Every detail, scar, freckle, the wild fall of my hair, woven into cruel perfection. Her eyes, my eyes, gazed up at him with that soft, molten warmth I reserved for him alone. Seeing it mirrored back at me, stolen and hollow, made bile rise in my throat.

A low growl vibrated through my chest. Mani's warning was feral and absolute.

'*He is… he looks frozen,'* I said. The realization landed like a bruise.

The false me leaned closer, sliding her arms around his neck with practiced ease. Her lips parted in invitation, her chest brushing his. The scent she wore was wrong… too sweet, cloying, threaded with something rotten beneath. She whispered his name, her voice thick with desire.

Heat surged through my veins, spiking sharp and volatile, fury honing itself into something merciless. Mani's claws dragged phantom trails beneath my skin, urging me to leap, to tear, to reclaim what was mine.

And beneath that, something darker stirred, something colder. A whisper coiled through the rage, silk over steel.

Break her.

End her.

Andrew's lips parted. His hands hovered, trembling between restraint and surrender. He wasn't touching her yet, but his body leaned toward the pull of the illusion, magic threading into bone and instinct alike.

"No," I hissed, my voice so sharp it cut the air.

The counterfeit Astrid's head snapped toward me, her eyes shone with hunger, then her body stuttered, before the illusion of myself dissolved in a shimmer of smoke. What remained made my stomach twist.

Naomi sat where the false version of me had been. Her silver hair spilled over her bare shoulders, glinting like liquid moonlight on a blade. Her lips curved into a smile that was all teeth and cruelty, yet her eyes burned with something desperate beneath it. She wore my skin to tempt him. To steal what was mine.

Andrew recoiled as if burned, horror dawning on him. “You…” His voice broke with disgust. “Glamoured…”

I didn’t move, my stomach twisting, betrayal curling deep in my gut, but I knew it wasn’t his fault. Mani’s claws remained, urging me towards violence, urging me to strike, to protect, to reclaim what is ours.

Yet beneath the fury, “She is being used,” I said. The words came out small, but true.

Naomi’s smile faltered, just for a heartbeat, and the room seemed to shiver. A single tear slipped free and traced down her cheek. Mani stiffened inside me, her ears flattening, tail lashing, claws digging in. She was not calm but stayed on high alert. The control over Naomi was slipping. His control, the dark völva’s leash that twisted her will, wavered for the briefest moment.

My breath came ragged, fury and nausea tangling like barbed wire inside me.

Naomi tilted her head, her smile slinking wider. “Don’t be so cold, Andrew.” She purred. “I gave you exactly what you wanted.” Her voice dripped with false sweetness, each syllable coiling like a serpent. She slid off the bed, hips swaying with deliberate provocation, her fingers brushing his bare chest as if testing his restraint. “I could be her. I could give you *everything* she won’t.”

Mani’s snarl tore out of me before I could stop it. “Touch him again and I’ll rip your arm off and shove it up your…”

“Always so violent,” Naomi interrupted, her lips curved slowly, pleased rather than threatened. “That’s exactly why they want you. Power like yours… raw, emotional, and untamed.” Her eyes darkened. “You can’t control it on your own.”

I smiled. It wasn't human. Mani's teeth flashed behind it, her voice threading through mine, low and lethal. "No," I said softly, every word edged with promise. "I *choose* not to kill you."

I stepped closer, letting her feel the weight of us. "Touch him again," we breathed together, "and I won't choose restraint twice."

For a moment, the mask slipped. Naomi's smile faltered, her hand trembling against his skin. A tear welled in her eye, glinting in the dim light before she swallowed it down. Behind the glamour, behind the hunger, something fragile broke through, fear.

Andrew's gaze snapped to mine, raw with conflict, but then his hand reached back, finding me, fingers locking tight around mine. His warmth was solid and real, grounding me.

Naomi flinched, her lips peeling back into a snarl too sharp, too feral, even for Naomi. Her eyes flickered, amethyst to shadow, shadow to amethyst, her breath hitching as if the air itself fought her lungs. And for one single, fragile second, I saw her. The girl beneath the strings. Suffocating under the dark völva's tether, but it was fraying.

Her smile wavered, trembling on her mouth, and the whole room seemed to shiver with her. A lone tear slipped down her cheek, catching the light like a shard of glass. The control binding Naomi was slipping.

For the briefest moment, I thought it would break. Then it snapped taut again, violent and merciless, then Naomi laughed. It was wrong and hollow; a sound borrowed from something darker.

The air thickened, the walls seemed to hold their breath as shadows bled across the floor like spilled ink. Naomi's body convulsed, her spine arching unnaturally, her breath tearing out of her lungs, until this terrible laugh ripped from her throat and she collapsed like a puppet whose strings had been severed. The sound hung in the room, raw and broken, and then eerie sudden silence slammed down so hard it felt like a blow.

Andrew pulled me against him, his arms tight and instinctive. His heartbeat thundered under my ear, keeping me in this moment. A lifeline of heat and pine and forest scent cutting through the cold tang of that ruined laughter. We both stared at Naomi's limp form on the floor. The hush was strangled by the echo of her breaking sound.

In that awful quiet, the truth settled heavy and sharp: killing her would be easy, but unfair. Saving her, if it was even possible, would mean stepping into the same darkness, wrestling the same shadows that gnawed inside my own veins.

Her shoulders jerked. Another tear carved down her cheek, as if whatever held her had loosened for a moment. Her hands were clenched, her knuckles blanching. Through Mani's senses I felt every tiny betrayal of control, the tremble along Naomi's spine, the stutter of her breath, the faint, foreign pulse of magic running in her veins. For a single, fragile second a girl crouched behind it: scared, small, and suffocating under the dark völva's tether.

'Do you believe me now, Mani?' I whispered. Mani's answer was a tired rumble of reluctant agreement. Andrew threaded his fingers through mine, tighter now, and stepped closer. The steady heat of him pressed against my palm and anchored me. Each breath he drew threaded reassurance through the room, syncing with the frantic tether of my pulse. His presence steadied the wild drum inside me.

Naomi's lips trembled. She blinked up at us, and for that sliver of a moment the cruel mask cracked to reveal something that was unmistakably Naomi, her fear, she was pleading, and a flicker of an apology. It cut through the air like a knife. The possibility that we could reach her, even as she hung between being fragile and terrifying.

"She's being used," I told them, my voice rough. "They most likely made her think it's her power. Which…clearly, it isn't."

The faint tear on Naomi's cheek glinted once more before she gasped, a small, raw sound, and for an instant the dark völva lost its edge. Mani's senses catalogued everything: the slump of her shoulders, the little tremor in her hands, the way the magic around her stuttered. It might have been enough. Then the leashed tightened again. The brief surrender snapped shut like a trap.

Naomi's expression slammed back into cruelty so fast the air itself seemed to crack. Her lip twitched; her eyes flipped between hunger and terror. She whispered Andrew's name and the sound came wrong, warped and desperate, then swung to me in a glassy, pleading stare that dissolved the instant it formed. The change was a fissure in a mirror: startling and brief, then gone.

Mani pressed forward, a sharpened vibration of warning threaded through sympathy. '*She's breaking,*' she breathed. '*If she shatters, what do we do?*'

Andrew's shadow moved over us like a shield. He brushed my wrist and murmured, "Stay with me." His voice was rough with the same fierce protectiveness. I clung to that steadiness because the thought of the dark völva waiting beyond that crack, eager and patient, made the room tilt.

Then the house groaned as if finally exhaling. The walls shuddered and darkness peeled itself free from the corners and seams of the room, crawling upward in pulsing, vein-like strands that throbbed with a life of their own.

Naomi dragged herself up onto her knees, and then jerked violently backward, her fingers clawing into her scalp as if trying to tear something out of her skull. A sound ripped from her throat, guttural and wrong, too deep and too fractured to be her own, echoing through the room like a voice forced through broken stone.

The floor pitched beneath my feet, reality lurching sideways as if the house itself recoiled. Heat and cold collided in the air. The stench of smoke and iron flooded my lungs, sharp and metallic, burning my eyes and coating my tongue with the taste of blood. Magic pressed in from every direction, heavy and suffocating, and I knew, without a doubt, that the dark völva had just tightened his grip.

Mani lunged inside me, her growl rolling through my bones as the runes seared to life and the air thickened with the stench of raw, unbound magic. Naomi's cry warped into something unrecognizable before cutting off entirely. Her body crumpled back to the floor, while that broken laughter lingered at the edges of the room, sharp as glass caught in the walls.

Andrew moved instantly, turning to call for help, for anyone, but I slowly and cautiously walked over to her and crouched by her still shape. We both had seen the same thing: a woman wearing my face, a puppet with stolen skin… and then, for a single breath, the girl beneath the mask, terrified, shame-faced, and reaching for a hand to pull her back.

'Killing her would be clean,' Mani rumbled, teeth bright in my mind. *'Quick. Merciful.'*

"No." The word left me before I could stop it. My hands clenched until my palms ached. *'She's being used. She thinks—or thought—she owned her power. If we kill her, we let whoever holds the leash win. If we save her, she could lead us to the dark völva... and whoever he works for.'*

Mani's growl shifted, rolling through anger and hunger before catching on something else—a spark of reluctant respect. *'You'd rather play rescuer than executioner? Fine... But if she so much as breathes a lie, I will chew her throat out myself.'*

I exhaled, the breath tasting like surrender. *'She can't know that we will use her to get to the dark völva. We pry the tether off and twist it back on whoever put it on.'*

A soft, almost amused huff brushed the back of my thoughts. *'Look at you.'* Mani's tone sharpened. *'All right. We save a puppet. We find the puppeteer...most likely the dark völva. And if the puppet snaps at us? I eat first, ask questions later.'*

Even as the room settled into an uneasy quiet, Naomi's broken laughter seemed to linger, sharp and impossible to forget. A promise that the darkness would not be silenced by one small victory.

Chapter 15

The early-morning fog lay low over the training grounds like a wet shroud, swallowing the tree line and muting the world to a gray whisper. The air tasted like sweat and the first bite of coming winter, mixed with churned dirt, still damp from last night's rain. The steady thud of fists striking dummies, layered with the sharp grunts of sparring pairs, gave the yard a slow, relentless heartbeat.

Naomi had been taken to the hospital hours ago. They carried her out stiff and silent while I stood frozen, my hands clenched so tightly I lost feeling in my fingers. I'd wanted to follow, to stay at her side, to make sure she didn't vanish into whatever darkness had taken her, but I knew I couldn't. The hospital walls reeked of memories I didn't want to revisit. Lying in that bed would have only let the dark völva's laughter creep back into my skull, feeding on the cracks in my resolve.

So, I came here instead, to the training hall, because continuous motion steadied me. I moved along the edge of the ring like a ghost, every step heavy, every face blurred by exhaustion. My limbs ached with the weight of too many sleepless hours, too many fights stacked back-to-back, adrenaline long since soured into bone-deep fatigue. The runes on my skin pulsed faintly beneath the numbness, a stubborn rhythm that refused to let me forget.

Bo was at the center of it all, his arms crossed as he barked corrections at a pair of recruits. Solid as stone, as he

always was, his shoulders squared, jaw set, the kind of presence that anchors a place simply by just existing in it.

I stopped at the edge of the ring and let the noise of training wash over me. The thud of fists, the scrape of boots in the dirt, and the harsh exhale of effort. For a moment, it all patched the crack in my chest, dulling the questions that gnawed like rats in the dark. But exhaustion sat heavy in my bones, a hollow weight that no amount of movement could shake.

Bo noticed me lingering. His gaze was sharpened, then it softened. With a clap to the recruits' shoulders, he dismissed them and crossed the ring towards me.

"Astrid," he said, concern edging his voice. "You look like you've been through a war."

"Feels like I have," I murmured, my throat too tight. I met his eyes, unwilling to circle around what I needed. "Bo… I need to know about my mother. Anything. Whatever you can tell me."

The firmness in his stance faltered. He exhaled, rubbing the back of his neck as his eyes drifted toward the weapon racks lining the wall—axes, spears, swords, all worn bright with use.

"Edna was… secretive," he said slowly. "Too secretive. My wife and her dabbled in things most would never dare. Old rites. Ancient magic. Things people whispered about in the dark."

I stepped closer, searching his face. "Did she ever say why she left? Where she would go?"

Bo shook his head, the lines of worry deepening around his eyes. "No. Only that she was afraid. Said she had to protect you. Told everyone else to keep clear of it."

My pulse thudded harder in my ears. “The Odinsráð,” I pressed. “Naomi… mentioned them. Did she ever talk about them? About who they are?”

A shadow crossed his expression. He shook his head again, but hesitation lingered in the silence that followed. “Never heard the name. But Edna… she trusted no one after Laura, my wife...” He trailed off. “She always said the world was darker than we wanted to believe. More dangerous than any story could capture.”

“Did she leave anything behind?” My voice frayed. “A letter, a clue…anything?”

Bo’s silence stretched. Finally, he spread his hands helplessly. “If she did, she buried it deep. She was clever like that. Too clever. She wouldn’t have made it easy for anyone…not even you.”

The weight of his words pressed cold against my ribs, heavy as the fog rolling over the grounds. I nodded stiffly. “Thank you, Bo.”

He looked as if he wanted to say more, then thought better of it. Instead, he clapped a calloused hand on my shoulder, firm and gentle, and then turned back toward the recruits who waited for his command.

I left the ring with the clang of steel and the barking of orders chasing me out into the mist. The morning air felt sharper, each breath stinging my lungs as though the world itself was warning me to stop digging. But I couldn’t, I refused. Not when the shadows of my mother’s secrets pressed so heavily against my chest, cold and insistent.

By the time late morning crept overhead, I found myself wandering through the streets without direction, my feet moving on instinct alone. The cold wrapped around me like a

shroud, every exhale curling into white smoke, and my heart thumped too fast, not from the winter's bite, but from the restless pull gnawing inside me. Something unseen tugging at me, a thread woven through memory and fear, pulling me forward.

When I finally lifted my head, I found myself standing before Trovi's house. Its weathered stone and darkened windows gave it the hollow look of something abandoned, drained of breath. The stillness around it felt unnatural, stretched too tight.

I hadn't meant to come here. But some quiet, stubborn part of me had led me back all the same.

I lingered at the gate, the frost-stiffened grass crunching under my boots. A part of me wanted to turn back, to leave the past buried where it belonged. But the house loomed before me with answers to my unanswered question, and I was tired of not knowing the truth.

My hand brushed the wood of the gate, worn smooth by years of touch. It yielded beneath the lightest push, groaning faintly on its hinges. Only my footprints led to the front door. When I opened it the scent hit me first, old wood and dried herbs, familiar and fading. The air seemed colder inside, stagnant, as if the rooms had been holding their breath all this time. Dust drifted in pale shafts of light that cut through frost-veined windows, shimmering like ash.

My body sagged under the weight of it all, the days of training, the fight, and the gnawing worry for Naomi, every muscle raw, and my bones heavy. For a heartbeat, I almost saw her—Trovi seated by the hearth where her shawl still hung neatly on the chair, eyes lifted as if she had been expecting me all along. The vision dissolved, leaving only the empty room and the lingering press of her presence.

I moved deeper inside. Papers lay stacked on the small desk, some yellowed and brittle, others freshly marked with ink. A teacup sat abandoned beside them, a faint ring of dried herbs clinging to its rim. When I brushed my fingers over the table, the air shifted. A voice rose, not sound but vibration, threading through the stillness.

'Your mother walked through that door many times. Andrew's did too.'

The words thrummed through me, familiar and strange. I sank into the chair opposite Trovi's empty one, my cloak curling around my legs.

'They thought I didn't notice how heavy their secrets had become... But I did.'

The echo settled deep in my bones. My chest tightened. My mother. Andrew's mother. Trovi had seen them, and guarded them, carrying a weight that no one ever knew about.

I swallowed hard, whispering to the silence, "Tell me." Only the silence answered. But in it, I felt the truth press down on me, heavy and undeniable.

'She isn't really here,' Mani snapped. *'You're just chasing shadows.'*

'I don't think so,' I murmured, my gaze searching the dim corners. *'Her words feel alive... like they're meant for us.'*

'Or meant to distract you,' Mani growled. *'The dead have nothing to give but riddles. We should just leave.'*

'No.' I shook my head, though my pulse thrummed hard in my ears. *'There's something here, something I'm meant to know. My mother, Andrew's mother, they trusted Trovi. If she left her voice here, maybe it's because we're meant to listen.'*

'Or because she wanted to bind you to grief that isn't yours,' Mani countered, her tone colder now, tired. *'Every secret you dig up drags us further under. When will you learn that not all truths are safe?'*

"Maybe not," I whispered, brushing the arm of Trovi's chair as though the woman herself might solidify beneath my touch. *'But some truths change everything. And I can't turn away...not from her. Not from Andrew. Not from what ties us together.'*

Mani sighed. *'You always chase the flame, even if it burns you. Just remember...that I'm here too,'*

I closed my eyes, steadying myself. *'I know... Just a little longer. We must know.'*

The air stirred, faint but undeniable, as though Trovi's voice brushed my ear like breath. *'What they were trying to hold back... it wasn't just for themselves. It was for you. For him. For what the two of you could become.'*

The words lingered in the air, soft and insistent, like a faint exhalation brushing against my skin. A shiver rippled down my spine, not from cold but from the press of unseen presence. Then the air softened around me, and the shadows bled together like ink in water. Small specks of dust ignited and began to shimmer in strange and twisting shapes. My breath caught… there it was, magic, alive, and shifting into memory.

And then I saw them. My mother, Edna, and beside her a woman that must have been Andrew's mother, Laura. They moved through Trovi's archives with purpose, their forms glowing faintly, hands brushing over drawers and shelves. A small ornate chest appeared between them, along with folded papers, their movements precise, and deliberate. The air shimmered with their magic as if protecting their actions from prying eyes.

But there was Trovi, she was silent, unseen by the women, her eyes sharp and watchful. She didn't interfere, but her presence hummed through the room like a tether, ready to intervene if anything went wrong. A soft, almost imperceptible pulse radiated from her, connecting the past to me, letting me sense that I was being shown the truth for a reason.

The vision shifted, the magic bending, guiding my attention to the corner where Andrew's mother and mine had hidden their burden behind stacks of books and loose scrolls. A soft memory of Trovi's protective watch pressed against my senses: '*They were never alone, even when they thought they were,*' Trovi's memory murmured. *'Neither are you.'*

My heartbeat thundered and my hands trembled as I crossed the room. The air hummed, guiding me. I started removing books, papers, scrolls and setting them down carefully piece by piece until the chest emerged, it was heavy, sealed with runes that pulsed faintly as if waiting for me.

I felt it, a connection to the past, to the mother I barely knew, to Trovi's quiet guardianship. The echo of their intentions, the magic they had woven, hummed against my skin like a heartbeat. What they had hidden wasn't just objects or papers, it was power and knowledge that would shape the world, and it was now mine to uncover.

I carried the chest to the coffee table in the room. My fingers brushed the lid. *"Protect, learn, choose wisely."* My mother's voice lingered faintly in the back of my mind. And I knew then that this was the beginning of everything: the path forward, the choice to embrace the power that our mothers had hidden from us.

I tried to lift the lid, but it wouldn't budge. The magic seemed to resist my touch, cold and firm, humming faintly when I touched it. The runes on the chest flared, resisting me. It was like the chest knew me and rejected me.

"It won't open," I whispered, my frustration rising.

A voice stirred in the air, soft as a breath. '*You're meant to be together.*'

My hand brushed the top of the chest. *'I can feel it, like the chest…it's alive somehow.'*

'It's not alive. It's guarded… or protected. It's bound to more than just wood and runes.'

'What do you mean?' I asked.

'It's tied to him… To Andrew. It must be. Your mothers…they forged it together. Maybe only the two of you together can open it.'

'Together?' I echoed. The word steadied me. *'That makes sense. But he's not here. I…'*

'Exactly. You're one half of the key. The chest senses the missing half. Without him… it won't yield…clearly.' Mani said.

'Then let's go get him and bring him here,' I said.

'Good. Look at you using that brain of yours,' she says making me roll my eyes.

'Ok…ok,' I said, standing up. *'Let's put it back for now,'*

'Why? It's not like…' Mani starts to say.

'We don't know who else comes in. It's not like her house is locked.' I say

'I get it… put it back and let's get Andrew here as soon as possible.' Mani says with excitement.

This legacy, or whatever all this was, it wasn't just mine alone. I need him, more than I understood.

The house was silent except for the soft creak of the floorboards under my boots as I moved toward the door. Outside, the wind curled cold around me, sharp with frost and damp leaves.

'Andrew...' I say in my mind link to him.

A warm pulse answered, steady and alive. *'Astrid? Where are you?'* His voice, though silent to the world, filled me completely.

'Trovi's house,' I murmured, glancing back. *'I saw... something... My mom, your mom... hiding something in Trovi's bookshelves. Trovi was watching them, protecting them.'*

'You saw them?' His voice vibrated with awe and caution.

'I did; they hid a chest. It's waiting for you. For both of us. I...' I start.

'Trovi... she's awake.' Andrew cuts in, making me take a sharp intake of breath echoing through our link.

'She's awake?' Concern, laced with urgency, tightened the space between us. *'Are you there? Is she—?'*

'I don't know fully yet,' he admitted. *'But she's conscious and alert. We need to go. She might have answers. I'm leaving Dad's office now.'*

'Then I'll meet you there.' My tone was steady, but the urgency threaded through every thought.

I closed the link, feeling Mani's low rumble vibrating through my chest.

Mani's voice thrummed with urgency. *'Food. We're running on fumes, Astrid. You'll drop dead before you find answers if we don't get some food.'*

My stomach clenched sharp in agreement, the emptiness sudden and undeniable now that she'd named it. I lifted my

nose to the cold air, catching the faint tang of deer in the distance.

The sharp tang of blood humming just beneath the skin, threaded with the green bitterness of crushed leaves and sap clinging to its coat. Underneath all that was a musk, earthy, ripe, and unmistakably alive. Sweat and fear mingling in a way that makes my jaw tighten and my throat ache. The scent carries the ghost of movement: churned soil, snapped stems, and the faint sweetness of grass still on its breath. To a predator it was a promise of strength, marrow, and survival, so vivid that it floods the senses and drowns out everything else.

"We move together," I whispered, the words an anchor as much as a vow.

I stripped slowly, the chill biting hard against my skin, then I let the shift take me. My muscles stretched and elongated, as fur spread in a rush of heat as the world sharpened into edges and sounds. Every vibration, a living thread. Every scent, a map. The transformation was instinctual, familiar, yet still electric, like stepping into the truest shape of myself.

Once fully shifted, Mani picked up my clothes and shoes into her jaws, tucking them neatly behind Trovi's fence before we launched ourselves into the frost-lit trees. Leaves crunched beneath our paws, each step crisp in the stillness. The forest opened its arms around us, the damp earth breathing mist into the cold air. My senses stretched wide, every detail a living thread: the snap of a branch somewhere deeper in the trees, the restless rustle of sparrows lifting from their roosts, the musk of rabbit trails winding through the underbrush, every detail alive, every signal pulling us forward.

'I don't want to waste time,' I murmured, though our jaw tightened with need, my fangs pressing sharp and insistent against my lip.

'Survival isn't wasted. Besides,' Mani's tone curled sly and amused, *'you know you love the chase.'*

She was right. The thought of it sparked something almost feral in me, a flint-strike of instinct that, for one suspended heartbeat, shoved aside Naomi's pallid face, the dark völva's laughter, even the cold, ghost-pull of my chest.

We slipped deeper into the trees, our bodies low, paws whispering against damp leaves. The deer's scent thickened, carried on the frost-edged wind, rich and intoxicating. Anticipation thrummed through Mani, braided so tightly with my own hunger that I couldn't tell where hers ended and mine began.

Then, there, movement ahead. A doe lifted her head, ears flicking, and her breath clouding in the cold.

Mani surged. Muscles coiled and released, our paws tearing into the earth as the world narrowed to a single, pounding rhythm. The doe bolted, her tail flashing white, but Mani was already on her, silent and with merciless speed. She lunged, fangs sinking deep into the throat, the struggle ending in moments beneath her weight.

The forest went still. Only the ragged sound of our breath and the metallic tang of blood remained.

Mani lifted her head, our muzzle wet and gleaming, eyes burning with fierce satisfaction. *'Now this,'* she rumbled, voice thick with primal delight, *'this is what keeps us alive.'*

And despite everything, the exhaustion, the ache, the relentless pull of my chest, I felt it too.

I turned from the kill, our breath misting in the air, the weight of it all settling back deep in my chest. Behind me, bones cracked softly as Mani tore into her prize, the wet sounds of survival grounding her in ways I couldn't afford to let myself dwell on.

Not when destiny was waiting to be claimed—or changed.

Even with the copper tang of blood thick on the wind, even with strength flooding our veins, it waited, silent, patient, and unyielding. The echo of Trovi's home stirred within me, the magic woven by our mothers pressing insistently at the edges of my mind. A ghostly tug, insistent and unyielding, pulled me toward answers I could almost grasp.

Chapter 16

By the time we returned to Trovi's house, the fog had long since lifted away, leaving behind only a pale-gold haze clinging to the edges of the horizon. Shadows stretched long across the pavement, the hospital not far away, looming sterile and sharp in the waning light. Mani was still restless from the hunt, flexing her claws once before retracting them, her tension easing only slightly as we slowed.

The run had steadied us but now came a harder part.

'It's time,' I murmured, the words tasting heavier than they should have.

The change came slow. Muscles softened, fur receded, and then Mani's power drew inward, fading until only the quickened pulse of human blood remained. My fingers flexed as the claws retracted, and the subtle echo of wolf senses lingered like a phantom against my skin. I gasped softly as the world contracted back to my human scale. The cold air a little more crip now; the hospital lights not as harsh, the scents and sounds no longer magnified, but the loss still ached.

Once I was dressed, we moved again, leaving Trovi's quiet house behind. The run toward the hospital was shorter, but no less urgent. The late afternoon light washed the streets in muted gold, shadows stretching long as the hospital rose ahead, clean lines, sharp edges, and utterly indifferent. Mani shifted inside my mind, a restless curl of energy pacing. I felt the echo of her claws flex, not against flesh, but along the edges of my consciousness, before she drew them back. The sharpness of

her tension dulled slightly as we slowed, though it never fully disappeared.

"Hey, love," Andrew called as we turned the corner.

His green-orange gaze caught the lingering tension in my shoulders, the way I carried myself, the faint shimmer of the wolf still woven into my stance.

"You shifted?" he said softly, awe and something warmer threading his tone.

I nodded, brushing a strand of hair from my face, trying to smooth the remaining edges of the transformation. "We had to. She...we needed to relieve some stress... and grab a quick bite."

He stepped closer, his gaze scanning me like he could read the memory of every motion, every heartbeat. Then he gave me a smile. "I'm glad you got to relieve some stress," he said, before pulling me into a soft, passionate kiss.

For a moment, the world narrowed to warmth and breath and the steady reassurance of him. Then remembering where we were.

"I'm ready," I whispered as I pulled back. "Let's go see her." Andrew took a step back taking my hand in his, as he grinned.

"Let's go," he murmured.

I tightened my grip on his fingers, the spark of longing grounding me, and together we moved forward. Every footfall on the frost-stiffened path felt like a heartbeat. Every breath a drum counting us closer to Trovi, to answers, to the truth waiting just beyond the doors.

'Should we bombard her with questions as soon as she is awake?' Mani chimed in.

I stopped in my tracks.

Andrew glanced over at me. “Everything ok?”

“Mani just asked if we should ask her all our questions as soon as she’s awake?” I repeat, and the guilt I feel curled tight in my chest.

Andrew smiled gently. “Then let’s not ask her those questions yet,” he said. “Let’s just see our friend.” I nodded in return as relief loosened the guilt inside me.

We rushed to Trovi’s bedside. My hands trembling slightly as I grasped Trovi’s frail hand. “Trovi... you’re awake.” Tears pricked my eyes.

Trovi’s voice rasped faintly, but sharp with urgency. “Astrid... listen carefully. The man in my vision... he is no savior…but he is also no villain. He has a völva, but they are consumed by power, willing to restore corrupted gods at any cost.”

A shudder passed through her fragile frame. “You must flee. Before he comes for you too.” Trovi pleaded.

My gaze hardened, determination flaring “No.” I gripped Trovi’s hand tighter. “I’m not running. Not anymore.”

Trovi’s eyes searched mine, pleading with a quiet desperation. “Please... Astrid. End this before it’s too late.”

“I will.” I said, swallowing hard, the fire of resolve burning fierce in my chest. “For you. For my mother. For all of us.”

The room seemed to darken around us, shadows pooling like something alive. This was no longer merely survival—it was the fight for everything I held dear, a war.

I leaned closer, still holding her hand, as if letting go might undo the fragile truth of her being awake. For a moment, the words lodged in my throat, sharp and heavy. Relief burned behind my eyes, raw, almost painful as I tried to hold myself

together. She wasn't gone, she was here. Then suddenly, I couldn't keep any of it inside anymore.

"Trovi…" My voice wavered despite my effort to steady it. "So much has happened since that night." The words cracked something open. I squeezed her hand, grounding myself in the warmth of her skin. "I've been fighting ever since, fighting the nightmares, Naomi, fighting what's wrapped around her, the dark völva wearing her like borrowed skin. The glamour. The golem. The darkness she lets speak for her."

My breath shuddered out of me. "It wasn't just an attack." I shook my head, tears blurring the edges of the room, my grip tightening around Trovi's. "There was an offer of power, control, and certainty. Naomi and the dark völva kept pushing it at me, whispering how easy it would be to stop resisting. To let the rage take over. To let go and let the rage rise and *end* everything in one clean, brutal sweep."

Mani stirred uneasily, a low growl at the memories, but she didn't stop me.

"There was a moment," I whispered, my voice breaking, "where I almost did it. Where giving in felt… easier. Like relief instead of ruin." My grip tightened until my knuckles ached. "I felt it pushing into every crack I've ever tried to hide—every scar, every fear, every part of me that's so tired of bleeding."

A sob caught in my chest before I could stop it. "I didn't understand it at first, but that's how they break you. Not by force. By convincing you that surrender is strength."

I lifted my gaze to Trovi, tears slipping free now, unashamed. "I'm still standing because I said no. Because I didn't take what they offered." My voice dropped to a rasp. "But it cost me. They nearly drowned out Mani. Nearly drowned me."

Trovi's fingers twitched in mine, her grip faint but real. Her gaze was glassy but hooked on to every word. The simple proof of her presence shattered what little composure I had left.

"I thought that was the end of it," I went on, words spilling faster now. "But it wasn't. Ever since, I've felt these threads pulling at me—toward something bigger. Something buried. I was terrified of it. I tried to ignore it." I let out a broken laugh. "And then… somehow… I met my father."

Trovi blinked slowly. "Your father?" Her voice was no more than a rasp, but it carried weight, as if the word itself was dangerous.

"Yes." I nodded, as my chest heaved. "When I was standing before him, I felt… tethered… Like he wasn't just part of the past, but part of this… this unraveling that's swallowing me whole."

Trovi's hand tightened, just barely. A faint squeeze that made my throat close. "Astrid… "Trovi murmured, her voice thin but steady. "You carry more than blood. You carry a story that was meant to be buried."

"I know." The admission tore out of me. "And it terrifies me. Every step closer to the truth feels like standing at the edge of a cliff… I don't know if I'll fly… or shatter when I fall."

"Then you must learn to choose which voices to trust…" Trovi's eyes gleamed faintly, her voice threaded with both sorrow and urgency. "Before they choose for you."

I swallowed, clutching her hand like a lifeline. "That's why I can't run anymore. I won't. I'll face all of it, him, the chest, the gods, whatever's coming. Mani and I… we won't turn away... not anymore."

I hesitated, my breath hitching slightly. "So then, when I returned to your house... I saw them. My mother, and Andrew's. Shapes woven of magic, fragile but fierce. They were together, Trovi. They left something behind, something they hid in your archives. A chest bound by both their power." My voice broke. "I found it, but I couldn't open it. Not alone. It needs Andrew. Whatever's inside... it's meant for both of us…" I searched her face. "Why… why didn't you tell me? You saw them."

Her lips parted in a shallow gasp, the sound of air scraping through dry lungs. But her eyes burned with resolve. I straightened, steel creeping into my voice through the grief. "This is bigger than survival now. I can't run. I won't. This, Ewan may have his völva, but we have something stronger. A legacy. A bond. I'll find what our mothers hid, and I'll use it to end this, before it's too late."

"Please." Trovi whispered, her eyes brimmed with a quiet desperation. "Astrid... finish what we couldn't...we only meant to protect you." Trovi's breaths rattled faintly, but her grip on my hand was steady. Her eyes, half-lidded yet burning with unseen visions, locked onto mine.

"You carry something you don't understand, Astrid. You will take hold of something, but command is not the same as understanding. And without understanding… even mastery can become a blade turned inward, and it will consume you…unless you face it where it was forged."

Mani's voice echoed low in my mind, her tone sharp but protective. '*Does she mean the Garmr?*'

I felt Andrew shift closer, his hand brushing against my arm. "Hel gave it to you, didn't she?" he said quietly. "Her beast... But it's not tearing you apart anymore, is it?"

I shook my head, taking a slow and deliberate breath. “No. It listens now. It *answers*.” I swallowed. “I can feel it, coiled and waiting. Not to break free… but to be used. And that’s what scares me.”

Mani rumbled beneath my skin, not a warning this time, but acknowledgment. ‘*A power like that doesn’t rebel once it’s claimed; It waits to see what kind of ruler you’ll be.*’

Trovi coughed, pain wracking her frame, but her voice cut through with startling clarity. “That’s why you’re standing at a crossroads,” she said softly. “You’ve crossed the first threshold already. The Garmr answers you now, there is no ritual left to grant you command.”

Her fingers tightened faintly around mine. “But there is more coming,” Trovi continued, eyes darkening as if she were staring through me instead of at me. “Something older. The shadow... A power that doesn’t roar, it *waits*.”

A chill crept along my spine.

Mani stirred uneasily beneath my skin.

“You don’t understand it yet,” Trovi said. “And when it wakes, it will offer you more than strength. More than survival.”

Her gaze locked onto mine, unblinking. “If you shape it, it will remake the world around you. But if it consumes you, if you let it decide who you are, then everything you’re fighting for will be lost. Not broken… *Lost*.”

Silence fell heavy and absolute.

“What you lack isn’t power,” Trovi finished quietly. “It’s direction. And without that… everything becomes a catastrophe.”

My chest tightened. “So, what do we do?”

Trovi's fingers curled more tightly around mine. "There is a way. Not the same path you took before…but the crossing ritual. But this time, it must be forged in unity, not desperation. You'll need Mani, Andrew, your friends, and… me."

I shook my head sharp. "No…you just woke up; you can't just leave here…"

"I can sit," she interrupted gently. "I can guide. I'll ask for a wheelchair, a nurse. I won't be a burden." Her eyes held mine, fierce despite the weakness in her body. "But you don't walk forward blind, Astrid. Not after everything."

Suddenly, the room felt smaller, charged, but not with fear, but with the weight of choice.

Andrew's jaw clenched. "Last time you nearly stayed dead," he said quietly, eyes locked on mine. "Why risk crossing back at all?"

Trovi answered before I could, her voice soft but unyielding. "Because this isn't about control anymore." Her gaze burned into me, sharp and knowing. "Astrid has taken the Garmr under her will. Hel saw to that."

Silence stretched heavy until I swallowed it down. "So, another ritual."

Mani's voice reassured me. *'If it's what it takes to keep us whole, I'll walk with you again.'*

Andrew tightened his grip on my hand, his eyes fierce, protective. "Then I'm coming with you. No matter where it leads. Even if it's Hel's doorstep again. I'm not letting you face what comes next alone."

Trovi gave a faint, broken smile. "Good. Then you may stand a chance." Her eyes darkened. "Command may have bound the Garmr—but the path ahead will test whether you can wield what follows it."

Her words lingered sharp like broken glass. And for the first time, I felt the weight of it settle, this wasn't about surviving anymore. It was about carrying something immense forward without letting it hollow me out.

I released Trovi's hand gently and straightened. "Andrew, talk to a nurse, see what support Trovi needs. I'll call Red and get everyone moving." As I walked out towards the door.

Stepping into the hallway, I pulled out my phone, it felt cold and heavy in my hand as I pressed it to my ear. Each ring echoed like a drumbeat. On the third, Red answered.

"Astrid? What's wrong?"

I swallowed, glancing toward Trovi's fragile form on the bed, Andrew hovering close, Mani restless just beneath my skin. "We need you. All of you. At Trovi's house. Now.

Red paused. "It's that bad?"

"I'm not going back to Hel for answers about control. I already have that. I'm going because there's more coming. I need to do another ritual."

Silence. Then a sharp exhale on the other end. "You're serious."

"I don't get to be anything else," I said. "If I stop now, the Garmr won't fail—it'll just be claimed by something worse."

Red didn't answer right away. I could hear her moving, the shuffle of boots, the creak of a door. Then her voice dropped. "Astrid… have you looked at the sky tonight?"

I frowned, glancing out the window. Only a yawning void stared back. No silver glow. No sliver of pale light to cling to. Just a depthless black swallowing the stars. "It's a new moon," I whispered.

"No," Red said grimly. "It's worse. A black moon. The second new moon this month. It's the weakest night for wolves, for any ritual tied to the lunar pull. You'll be stepping into Hel half-blind."

"Then we won't rely on the sky," I said. The words scraped raw against me, but I forced myself to stand taller. "Then we'll just have to burn brighter in the dark."

"Astrid—"

"No." My voice cracked but I didn't falter. "We've run out of time. Bring them, please. I'll be ready."

Behind me on the bed, Trovi stirred weakly, eyes barely slitting open. "The black moon… doesn't weaken what's already claimed," she whispered. "It tests whether you can carry it without being seen."

Andrew met my gaze, his hand brushing mine like a silent promise. Mani pressed close, steady as a heartbeat. Red sighed hard on the line, defeat laced with reluctant respect. "Fine. hen if the sky's gone dark, I'm making damn sure you don't walk into it alone. I'll get everyone moving."

Then the call ended. The silence that followed wasn't empty but was filled with the sound of something enormous beginning to move.

Chapter 17

The air in Trovi's house was heavy with herbs and smoke, juniper and sage clinging to every stone as if the walls themselves had begun to breathe. Runes scrawled in chalk lined the garden floor, old sigils that seemed to flicker in and out of existence, no longer meant to bind but to witness. There was a slight breeze that stirred the fallen leaves, carrying a chill that slipped beneath skin and bone and settled there, patient and waiting.

Everyone had gathered—Red, Luca, Darcy, Damien, Andrew, even Bo, leaning silently against the far wall, just watching us all. They formed a loose ring around the room, as if instinctively bracing for something that might break loose anyway. Every face etched with some form of doubt.

Red broke the silence first. "This is madness." She snapped, slamming her palms against the table where Trovi's ritual texts lay open. "You want to send her tonight… under a black moon? Do you know what that means? No tether. No guidance. No pull from the sky to anchor her spirit. You're talking about throwing her in practically blind."

"I don't have a choice," I said, sitting on Trovi's couch, my runes faintly glowing as if impatient. "That's not what this is," I said. "I'm not chasing control. I already have it." the room went quiet again.

"I command the Garmr," I continued, meeting Red's stare without flinching. "It answers me. What's eating at me isn't chaos—it's what comes after." My gaze flicked briefly to

Andrew. "And whatever's waiting there… it's starting to stir. In me. In him."

Luca leaned back in his chair, sharp-eyed, arms crossed. "She's right. This isn't about sealing a beast. It's about crossing a threshold that's already been opened. Waiting won't close it. The black moon is the last moment of stillness before the next tide."

"Or it's the night that swallows her whole," Red snapped back. "Power doesn't mean immunity. I won't gamble her soul just because she's learned to hold a blade."

"Then don't," Trovi's voice cut through the room, thin but hard as steel. She sat rigid in her wheelchair, every word carrying weight that silenced the room. "It isn't your soul to risk… or save. Astrid's path isn't yours to steer."

Darcy shifted uncomfortably, her gaze flicking between me and the runes etched onto my hands. "Even if Garmr answers to you… are you certain this is the end of it?" she asked carefully. "Helheim's guardians were never meant to stand alone. They guard something. Or someone."

"I know," I said quietly.

Andrew sat beside me, hands clenched tight in his lap, his green-orange eyes tracked every movement in the room, alert and protective. Even though he tried to hide it, he was afraid of what was to come.

"Are you sure you want to do this now?" Andrew asked, his voice low but edged with concern. "To step past the line?"

"I don't have a choice." I said as I flex my fingers, the runes flaring brighter in response, like fire beneath my skin. "I can feel it." I said. "Something else is pressing in." My voice dropped. "Something that knows my name...our names."

Trovi inhaled sharply. "Then you already understand the danger. That power isn't yours to cage, Astrid. But it's also not something you should hand over freely. Magic like this…shadow-forged, runed in blood…it takes more than it gives."

"I know," I whispered, my throat dry. "I won't let it. I just… I need to understand it."

Andrew's hand brushed mine. "You're not alone in this," he said softly. "I've felt it too. The way your magic stirs something in me… like it's calling to mine. But whatever you face in there, I'm going with you."

I searched his face. "What if I don't just survive it?" I asked softly. "What if I become something I don't recognize?"

"Then I'll remind you who you are," he said without hesitation. "Even if I have to fight every piece of you to do it."

Trovi studied him for a long moment. "If you step into this circle, understand this, you accept the same risk. Death or worse. Hel doesn't return all who come knocking."

"I know." Andrew didn't flinch. "I'm still going."

The room bristled with tension. Red cursed under her breath. Luca muttered a prayer. Darcy's hands twisted the hem of her shirt. And in the corner, quiet as a shadow, the nurse who had been tending Trovi stepped forward, her eyes oddly flat. Her voice was smooth when she spoke, too smooth. "Then let us begin. The sooner she enters, the sooner this ends." Something in the way she said it made Mani stir uneasy. A ripple of warning rolled through my chest.

'Something is watching,' Mani warned.

The circle was drawn, the candles were lit, and the elements gathered. There was no turning back.

"Stay outside the circle…I know you want to come with me, but like Trovi said…we don't know what she will do,"

I could see he wanted to argue, but he didn't. He let out a hard sigh and gave me a nod. I kissed him, hoping this wouldn't be the last time.

'*We will fight our way through,* 'Mani said. Not back, but through, and I wanted to believe her.

Trovi began chanting, guiding the others in the circle to weave the spell. The air thickened as smoke and light twining until the world itself seemed to hold its breath. I turned from Andrew and stepped into the circle. My runes flared white-hot. I felt my power extend, time suspended. The energy shimmered in the air, thickening like fog. A luminous bubble snapped into place around me, the rest of the world gone still.

I could still see everyone outside, and they had small smiles on their faces, hope strained thin with dread. Then I saw the nurse move to the edge of the circle, her hands raised as though to strengthen the barrier…

But I saw the light in her eyes shift. Black bled across her irises, swallowing the whites whole. Her lips curled in a smile that wasn't hers.

Trovi's chant faltered. "No…"

The nurse slammed both palms against the runes, twisting them. The sigils screamed, bending, breaking, and rewriting themselves under her touch.

The bubble I was in collapsed. The circle warped and then pain detonated through my chest as the world tore open, ice and shadow ripping wide, reeking of rot and soggy earth. Instead of pulling me toward Hel, it dragged me sideways…

"ASTRID!" Andrew's voice cracked, his hand clawing at mine…but it was too late.

The last thing I saw was his green-orange eyes, wide with terror, before the shadows swallowed me whole.

There was complete and total silence.

Then came the visions.

It started with fire, raging across endless galaxies, entire constellations consumed in a slow, merciless burn. Stars collapsing into ash, whole constellations screaming themselves out of existence. At the center stood a figure cloaked in shadows, his expression serene, unmistakably the dark völva. And beside him a second figure came into view, veiled but unmistakably familiar. My breath caught.

Naomi?

Before I could reach the truth, the vision shifted, violent and cold.

Then I was dropped into darkness on a cold stone floor. I gasped, my lungs burning, and my palms scraped against a frozen floor. Darkness pressed in on all sides. A cavern, vast and wet, the air sharp with mineral rot.

Then I realized I wasn't alone in the darkness.

"What are you?" I demanded, my voice echoing thinly. "Where am I?"

'Mani?' I asked, my panic flaring.

'I'm here,' she said but it was faint. *'But I don't feel right.'*

The shadows stirred, folding inward before shapes emerged, cloaked and half-formed. Their eyes glowed in the darkness, a vivid amethyst burn against the void, smooth and polished as cut stone, lit from within by a seething current of chaos… just like Naomi's. They surrounded me in a loose, deliberate circle.

"We are…what you call Elves," one rasped. Then their voices layered together, a chorus reverberating through my skull. *"Child of the wolf. Blood of the traitor. You were always meant for this."*

I pushed myself back as far as I could until I was up against a wall. "I'm not yours."

They laughed softly. *"But you have already tasted it, haven't you? The hunger. The power. You will bleed and bend shadows."*

The mist thickened and from it, a mirror rose. My reflection staring back at me, but it was cracked, my eyes were darkened, my runes glowing. Not me, not entirely. A version of me…untethered and unforgiving. I had seen her before…in the silver lake with my father.

Then the reflection smiled. *"This is who you become; you just need to let go."* Her voice was velvety soft, but there was malice underneath. *"And you will, because you already are."*

Then the mirror fell and shattered against the ground.

"Astrid" I heard another voice. *My father.*

The world wrenched sideways and silver flooded my vision. I was on the beachside again, the lake of silver stretching far. The wolf spirits circled me again, then from the trees came the ragged, wild-eyed, limping figure of a man, my father.

"You're stronger than me, Astrid," he rasped, his voice broken from disuse. "Don't make my mistake."

"What was that place?" I gasped.

"Svartalfheim." He whispered, shame threading his tone. "I won't be able to keep you here long. They will pull you back…they will torture you…

My breath came ragged, fury surged up my throat. "Why?" I shouted. "Why me?"

"Because that was their charge," he said hoarsely. "To carve and twist you… See what you become when all that's left is the darkest version of yourself…."

I swallowed hard. "I knew I remembered that version…one of the three that's within me...right?"

"Yes." He responded. "But don't lose hope…you have endured so much and will continue to do so."

"I shouldn't have to endure more shit like this!" I screamed.

"I know…" he said, his voice breaking. "But now you have something to fight for. To not lose control of this power or yourself…your found family you created."

'How does he know?' Mani whispered weakly.

"You've been…watching me?" I asked him. "All this time?"

He choked back a sob, nodding. "I'm sorry I wasn't there…I'm sorry there was nothing that I could be to stop him."

"I stopped blaming you a long time ago," I said quietly. "Now...like you said I endure."

He reached for me. When our hands clasped, his other covered mine, trembling. His eyes closed, whispering in a language I didn't know. The wolves around us dissolved, drifting into blue dust that swirled on a windless current.

The silver lake rippled violently. His eyes darted past me, and I felt the shift in the air.

His eyes snapped to mine. "Run."

Then it came. A shape too vast for one form, too jagged for a single beast. It was the wolf-dragon shadow stitched from Hati's hunger and Níðhögg's rot, crawling from the dark like a

nightmare given form. Its body dragged against the ground, almost slithering. Its claws like hooked scythes, gouging the earth. Its eyes two voids gnawing holes in the sky. Its breath steaming with rot.

"RUN!" my father roared.

I stumbled backward, legs already burning. Mani's voice roared in my skull. *'Astrid, don't stop. Don't let it catch you.'*

We ran. The black frosted earth fractured beneath our feet, the ground splitting into glass shards that bled with light. The beast thundered behind me, its body shifting, reshaping itself with every stride, getting closer. Its howls rattled my bones, every wingbeat sent me sprawling.

'We have to fight!' Mani snarled.

I tried, but every wound only bled more shadow. Every strike seemed to feed it. The beast reforming itself, it was vast and endless.

It leapt and I turned too slow. Its jaws unhinged wider than the sky, and then, impact.

I hit the ground hard, my ribs shattering with pain. The creature's body collapsed, not flesh but smoke, shadow, and fire, on top of my body. Its mouth opened wide and it started dissolving, seeping into me. Into my eyes. My ears. My nose. My mouth.

I gagged as darkness forced its way down my throat, flooding my lungs like I was drowning in ash. My body convulsed, every vein igniting as the shadow slithered through me, invading, claiming space that wasn't empty enough to resist. I tried to scream. It gagged me, shoving deeper, writhing through all of me.

"NO!" Mani howled.

I clawed at my neck frantically, trying to rip the shadow back out, but it only sank deeper.

My father's voice echoed, like static. "Astrid! Reconcile them, or you will be lost!"

My back arched until I thought my spine would snap. My ribs popped audibly. My nails split bloody as claws pushed through them. My mouth stretched wide, too wide, tearing at the corners as black smoke poured down my throat. I couldn't breathe. Couldn't scream.

The frosted black earth cracked completely apart beneath me, and I fell.

Then…nothing.

The next thing I knew, I was slammed back into the ritual circle. Stone scraped my skin as I collapsed, gasping, blood-slick and shaking. My chest rattled with every broken breath. My hands shook, runes scorched into my skin, and beneath it all… something pulsed.

"I've got you," Andrew whispered fierce and desperate. "You're back. I've got you."

I clung to him, burying my face against his shoulder, as though I could anchor myself inside his warmth. His heartbeat thundered against my ear, but it was too fast, too wild, like he felt something in me he didn't recognize.

He helped me stand, though my knees trembled beneath me. Defiance stiffened my spine, but my body quaked like something fragile, as if my bones hadn't decided whether to hold me or split apart.

Around us the circle erupted with voices full of fear, questions, and panic all crashing together, but they blurred into static. My eyes swept desperately for the nurse and found

nothing. Instead, I found Trovi. Her stare pierced through the chaos, wide and hollow, as though she saw something festering inside me that no one else could. She saw what happened to me.

Beneath my feet, the runes stuttered, once, twice, before the circle split with a sound like flesh tearing from bone. The shriek that tore through the air was piercing and unbearable. Everyone clamped their hands over ears as blood spilled from ruptured ear. They were thrown back as the ground convulsed.

The ground opened like a gaping wound in the earth that oozed shadow instead of blood. From its depths, black hands clawed upward, searing cold as they latched onto my arms and legs. My scream curdled in my throat before it could escape.

"Astrid!" Andrew shouted, his grip locked around my arm. I clung to him with everything left in me, forcing my gaze to his. Those wonderful green-orange eyes, the ones I trusted more than my own heartbeat, were wide with terror.

I wanted to tell him not to let go. I wanted to fight. But the pull was absolute, a tide that wanted me…only me. The darkness tore through me with the certainty of death.

And then I was ripped from his grasp.

Chapter 18

The tear split with a crack like bone shearing beneath ice, as I was dragged through it screaming.

Stone met me again, hard and quick. I hit with a wet crack, my body folding wrong, my skin seared raw where the shadow-hands touched me, leaving frost burns that felt like fire. Smoke clung to me, forcing its way into my lungs until every breath tasted like rust.

The air was stagnant… but beneath it lurked something fouler, as though the earth itself had started to rot and decay.

The runes carved into my hands flickered wildly. Some sputtering like dying embers, while others seared too hot, blistering my flesh from the inside out. My limbs jerked uncontrollably as muscles spasmed and locked. Then the shadows slithered toward me and swallowed me whole.

When I opened my eyes, I was suspended in a cavern carved deep into a mountainside. The walls pulsed faintly and were slick with veins of sickly light that throbbed like a diseased artery. Chains didn't hold me. Pure darkness did. It coiled around my wrists and ankles, alive with malice, tight as a living noose. It crept across my skin like parasites, burrowing beneath my flesh, cold enough to burn as it whispered in my own voice. My fears. My failures. My desires—spoken back to me in broken, mocking tongues.

They cut me slowly, deliberately, letting the wounds open just enough for the blood to spill. Shadows moved with

careful precision, parting my skin as though they were carving something sacred rather than harming me. My blood spilled into obsidian bowls etched with runes that pulsed like living mouths that were hungry and waiting.

Each drop shimmered as it fell, catching the darkness with a strange, unnatural light—as if the blood itself carried something they desired.

They didn't bother to bind me beyond the shadows that held me in place. They didn't need to.

And when the pain tore a scream from my throat, the sound didn't echo with horror.

It echoed like a chant.

Like an offering they had been waiting for.

"You're feeding it…just let it consume you," voices crooned, like oil-slick, crawling into my ears. "The one who waits beyond... It will rise through you."

They starved me. Kept me awake for days…weeks maybe. Time broke apart and lost meaning. Their whispers tangled until I couldn't tell what was theirs and what was mine. They showed me visions of Andrew's body, twisted and ashen. My mother was bound beneath a dead tree, sobbing. My father in a feral state, blood-drunk, and gnawing on the bones of the world.

Then came the worst visions. The ones that made my heart lurch not with horror but hunger. Naomi choking in my hands, her throat collapsing under my grip. The dark völva drowning in pools of blood I commanded. Wolves kneeling at my feet as I tore the gods down and took their place.

Then, someone I could only assume was their priestess came, her face inches from mine. Her breath froze against my cheek as one of her long, disgusting nails traced my jaw.

"This is your legacy," She whispered. "You were born to end things."

I spat in her face, my voice cracking like torn paper. "You're delusional... I wasn't made for that."

Her smile gutted me deeper than any blade. "Then tell me," she murmured. "Why does it feel so good when you stop fighting?"

Gods help me…she was right. There were moments when the hunger drowned everything. Moments I wanted to let go. To let the shadows guide me. To stop being afraid. To tear. To kill. To be what they swore I was.

But it was Mani. Her presence ripped through the fog like a wolf's howl splitting night. '*You are not theirs. WE are not theirs!*' Her voice thundered through my bones, her claws raking the shadows that gnawed at me. '*You are mine. And I am yours.*'

That's when *it* stirred.

Not Mani. Not Garmr. But that...thing. The wolf-dragon that had forced itself into me. It unspooled from my marrow, vast and starving. Its growl a vibration in my skull, its scales scraping down along my spine, not tearing but aligning, clicking into place like armor I had been holding at bay. My ribs ached, but not from invasion, but expansion.

My jaw cracked wide, teeth lengthening too sharp, too many. Claws punched through my fingertips, they were blackened and dripping shadow, and I welcomed the pain. My body was no longer only mine—it wasn't a cage, it was a threshold, and the beast wanted out.

The priestess laughed, her triumph slick and eager. "Yes. Yes! You see it now. You are the maw. You are the ending."

She thought this was surrender. She didn't understand the difference between losing control and letting go of restraint.

But then, through the fog of rage, I heard another voice. Not theirs. Not the beast's.

Andrew's.

"You're still in there." His eyes met mine across ash and blood, storm-lit and steady. He didn't flinch. He didn't fear me. He mourned me.

"I.. don't…" I whispered. My voice cracked, torn between a snarl and a plea.

"Yes, you do." He said, quietly. "You never left." Then something inside me clicked into place.

My scream turned into a roar, and it tore the vision apart. The cavern rang with it, as stone started to crack. The shadows peeled back, the bindings dissolving into smoke as the runes ignited, not in chaos, not in rage, but with pure willpower. And in that moment, I knew I wasn't theirs to carve. I wasn't theirs to command. They would realize that too late.

Power surged through me, controlled and balanced, as wolf and shadow braided tight beneath my skin. I merged with Mani, letting her fury sync with my own. The Garmr didn't strain against chains, and I loosened my grip.

The wolf-dragon roared, not in defiance, but in recognition, as I opened myself fully to the rage, the hunger, the violence I had kept leashed for so long. Not to lose myself to it, but to use it.

Once the power, the hunger, the rage flooded through me and I held firm with them, I moved. Not as prey. Not as victim. As something feral and deliberate, claws and shadow, healer and executioner.

Their shrieks rattled the cavern as they lunged, twisting, and pulling weapons from shadows, hooks, blades, things that writhed like they were still alive. They never reached me.

I hit the priestess first.

My claws went through her throat with a wet, resistant *drag*, not a clean slice but a tearing plunge that collapsed cartilage and muscle alike. Her scream cut off mid-sound as I ripped downward, splitting her chest open to the spine. What spilled out wasn't blood the way it should have been… it oozed, thick and sluggish, black-red sludge that slapped against the stone like mud thrown from a ditch. It steamed where it touched my skin, reeking of rot and iron.

I didn't stop. I just shoved her body aside as she was still twitching, her jaw working soundlessly, and waded straight into the others.

One reached for me, too close. I caught her wrist and crushed it in my grip. Bone burst through skin with a brittle snap, fingers folding backward at impossible angles. She screamed until I drove my elbow into her face, collapsing her skull inward like wet clay. Sludge-blood sprayed the cavern wall in a thick arc, sliding down in slow, obscene rivulets.

Another tried to flee, but I caught him by the spine. My claws hooked between vertebrae, and when I pulled, his back *unzipped.* His flesh tore. Bones popped. He came apart in my hands, his lower half dropping with a dull, meaty thud as the rest of him spasmed, empty-mouthed, before going still. The blood pooled beneath me, viscous and heavy, sucking at my paws as I shifted my weight. It clung to the pads and fur of my massive wolf form, dragging like swamp muck, streaking my pure coat and catching against the ridged obsidian dragon scales that armored my legs. Each step tore wet sounds from the

stone, claws biting through sludge and gore as I loomed over the ruin I'd made.

They struck me in panic, their shadow-blades skidding off my skin, dissolving the moment they touched. Every attack unraveled in my wake. Everyone fell apart wrong.

I moved through them like a god's punishment given shape, monstrous and precise. Claws severing tendons, my jaws crushing throats, the shadows peeling their skin away in strips, revealing muscle beneath that sloughed off my fingers like spoiled meat. Their screams layered over one another until they became noise…until even that stopped.

The hunger I pushed down for so long drank it all in, but I didn't let it own me.

Their blood coated the stone, thick as sludge, filling the grooves of the cavern floor, steaming and stinking as it settled. What was left of them lay scattered in pieces, broken, hollowed, and unrecognizable.

I stood among the remains, slick with gore and shadow, breathing steadily.

When I roared again, the cavern answered. Stone split completely and reality shifted as a portal tore open before me. I staggered toward it, my massive form unraveling with every step. Bone cracked and shrank, fur receding, scales tearing free and dissolving into shadow as the beast folded back into human flesh. Pain flared white-hot as I forced myself upright, bleeding, scorched, trembling—but still standing. I was not broken.

I was not lost.

Chapter 19

When I stepped through, Svartalfheim howled behind me. And when my feet hit Midgard again, my eyes were no longer soft. They had carved and twisted me, tried to strip me down to something unrecognizable, but something else had survived that cave in Svartalfheim. Something completely feral and monstrous, but that something was completely mine now. Andrew was the first to move.

"Astrid!" He dropped beside me, his voice ragged with panic as he pulled my limp body into his arms. My skin was ice-cold, and my pulse thready beneath his fingers. My hair hung damp with sweat and soot, streaked dark against my face. I opened my eyes and looked at Andrew. He caught his breath. The sound tore out of him like a wound.

"Astrid?" he asked, soft as if saying my name too loud might break what was left.

I didn't blink at the sound of his voice. Didn't sink into him the way I always had. My lips parted, and the words that came out weren't mine, not entirely. "Let go of me," I murmured, my voice low and void of warmth. Sounding flat and almost foreign.

Andrew recoiled as if I struck him. "Astrid, it's me. It's Andrew. You're safe now."

A bitter laugh ripped from my throat, jagged, humorless, and not wholly mine. "Safe?" My mouth curled into a smile too sharp for my own face. "There's no such thing."

My hand twitched. The runes carved into my arms ignited, searing white-hot as power lashed outward. The

shockwave split the air, hurling Andrew back. The ground split beneath him as he hit hard, dust and blood streaking his lip.

The others, Bo, Red, even Trovi, waited frozen at the perimeter of the circle. The air vibrated violently, shadows coiling like living smoke, too thick and charged to cross.

Andrew staggered upright to his feet, his chest heaving. Beneath his skin, light stirred, molten and golden, trickling like veins of lava across his skin. His jaw tightened, but his eyes never left mine.

"I care what they did to you…and I'm sorry," he said, his voice steady even through the crack in it. "I don't care how deep they buried you. I know that you're still in there."

Something inside me snapped. My head tilted at an angle too sharp, too predatory. My voice came in a hiss, layered and doubled, as though something spoke beneath my tongue.

"Am I?" I yelled. "Because I felt myself disappear piece by piece. Do you have any idea what that feels like? To scream… and hear nothing? To beg yourself not to give in, and lose anyway?"

The shadows surged in answer, slick tendrils crawling up my legs and arms. They cinched tight around my throat, stealing my breath.

Andrew's breath faltered, but he didn't retreat.

"I didn't just walk through a portal," I spat, voice breaking, body shuddering as the shadows distorted my shape. "I crawled out of a goddamn grave."

"I know," Andrew said softly, sinking to his knees before me, unflinching in the storm I have created. "And you don't have to fight it alone."

"If I didn't stop this, I would become exactly what they wanted me to be!" I shout

And then… I made a choice. I don't know whether it was me, Andrew, or the shadow.

But I slammed my palm to the earth, my runes igniting as another shock wave ripped through Trovi's garden. The air around us warped, the sound dying, the world outside slowing to a complete stop. A bubble of frozen time sealed Andrew and me inside the circle, cutting us off from Bo, Red, Trovi…everyone. Their shouts froze in their throats, and their faces locked in horror.

It was just us.

The shadow inside me shifted, then it started to pour out of me and fill our bubble.

Darkness surged from my chest like a breaking tide and slammed into Andrew. He staggered back as if struck by a battering ram, but the darkness didn't stop at his skin. It poured into him, forcing its way through his mouth, his eyes, his pores, threading itself into the seams of his being. He choked on it as I did, his body convulsing as if drowning on air that had turned to tar.

For a heartbeat, I saw it *inside* him, the skeletal outline of a dragon's skull pressing against his flesh from within, its jaws opening wide enough to split him in two. His back arched, and his bones cracked like old wood under pressure.

His scream never fully formed. It was strangled, shredded, torn into something less than human, a half-roar, half-death rattle. The sound made the circle tremble around us. The whites of his eyes turned black, only this time they seemed to almost ooze flame-dark shadows, his pupils blown wide until they couldn't focus on anything. His chest heaved violently, each breath cracking louder than the last as something massive tried to force its way through his ribs.

For an instant, he looked at me, really looked, like Andrew was still there, fighting to stay. But his jaw spasmed, his teeth grinding sharp against one another until blood streaked down his chin, and I realized the dragon wasn't waiting. It was *claiming him*, piece by piece, like a parasite wearing its host from the inside out.

His back arched again, violently, before he hunched over. His arms wrapped around himself tearing at his back, there was a crack that sounded like shattering stone, darkness unfurled. Great wings erupted from his shoulders, not flesh and feather, but vast and terrible shadows given weight. They stretched impossibly wide, the edges ragged as torn storm clouds, yet shimmering faintly with a cruel, moonlit gleam. When they snapped open, the air screamed, torn apart by violent gusts that drove me to my knees.

Then he seized me, gentle in intent, but claws had replaced his fingers, cold as iron around my waist. His eyes burned like embers caught between two worlds, Andrew's grief and the dragon's hunger mingling in their glow.

"Hold on," he rasped, though I couldn't tell if it was Atius, Andrew, or an older voice.

He was all threat and devastation, a creature built to destroy. Yet in his arms, I was at peace, like we were no longer divided by fear or power, but standing as equals at last.

Then his wings snapped down. The wind didn't just howl, it *sang*, vibrating through my bones and blood as the world fell away beneath us. The earth peeled away, and he carried me upward through a veil of cold and shadow. Below, the ground dissolved into darkness, while above us the air shimmered, trembling with power. Each beat of his wings rippled through the sky like a spell being cast, thunder rolling not from clouds, but from him.

The mountains rose to meet us, jagged and patient, their peaks catching moon light like broken glass. They loomed ahead, like ancient teeth waiting to close around the storm we had become.

I pressed my face against his chest, heat radiating from him like a living forge, the rattle of bone and sinew shifting beneath skin. Magic bled from him in waves, curling around us as we flew. Every breath felt stolen. Every wingbeat shattered another piece of the man I knew, reforging him into something vast, terrible, and sacred.

And as the mountains swallowed us whole, I understood this wasn't an escape, but an ascension.

We hit the mountainside with a thunderous impact that should have shattered bone, but he absorbed it, his massive form shifting, twisting mid-fall as though gravity itself bent to his will. Rocks splintered beneath his claws; snow and stone sprayed into the wind like sparks. I clung to him, pressed against his scorching chest, every heartbeat pounding through my own body like a drum of war.

His wings beat again, slower now this time, pinning me against the jagged ridge. The air crackled and shuddered around him, a living vibration of power that tugged at my chest and made my blood hum.

He set me on a rock, and I sank into it, watching him move. Then he pulled his shirt free, letting it fall to the ground, and turned to stride further up the hill. I stayed rooted, eyes fixed on him, every movement carved into my mind.

Then the fire in him surged. Beneath his skin, molten veins ruptured like rivers of living gold, churning and coiling

through his chest and limbs. Then jagged obsidian scales burst from his flesh, snaking across his jaw, down his shoulders, and his spine like shards of night forged in a sunless furnace. The heat radiated in rolling waves, bending the mountain air, warping it with a shimmer that made my eyes sting. Bones rattled, sinew tore and reformed with harsh, resonant cracks, and his muscles stretched impossibly, as if the world itself had no choice but to reshape around him.

For a heartbeat, he was barely human. Atius had emerged, but he was larger, more immense, a creature of fire and shadow, grief and hunger. His eyes had turned to his obsidian, flame spilling from the corner of his eyes, and glowing red irises. Every breath, every movement radiated power, and the very air seemed to recoil, trembling under the weight of the dragon within.

Then he arched his back, the shadow-lindworm within him surfaced. Darkness erupted from the seams of his body: from his eyes, mouth, elbows, even the folds of his wings, smoke-like shadows spilling in ragged torrents, twisting and writhing around him. His wings, solid shadow, with vast membranes stretching impossibly, snapped outward, scattering ice and debris like a storm breaking over the peaks.

I pressed closer, gripping his scaled shoulders as the first roar tore from his throat. It wasn't a roar of flame or fire it was *gravity itself*, a soundless pull that made the snow tremble and the mountain quiver. The blackness of his shadow seemed to absorb all light, drawing it in and spinning it into the coils of his shadow, the lindworm incarnate.

And then… it happened.

The smoke-like shadow tore free—not from his body, but from his will. Darkness poured outward, spilling from him in great, rolling waves, coalescing in the air behind his towering form. The gold veins of fire beneath his skin dimmed, retreating inward, while the shadow gathered mass and shape of its own.

The lindworm was born from smoke and void.

It unfurled above and around him, a vast serpentine body forming from roiling blackness—spine lengthening where there was no flesh, muscles suggested by shifting currents of shadow rather than bone. Claws carved themselves from darkness and slammed into the rock, gouging deep furrows as if the mountain itself could feel pain. Its head emerged last, immense and crowned with curling horns of smoke, jaws yawning wide enough to swallow light.

Andrew stood at its heart, untouched, anchoring it.

The lindworm rose higher, coiling around the jagged peaks like a living eclipse, its vast form blotting out the sky as it moved. Each motion dragged the air inward, each exhalation spilling black smoke from its jaws and eyes, from the joints of its massive shadow-limbs, trailing behind it in writhing tendrils of nightmare.

It was not wearing him.

It was answering him.

And as the shadow-lindworm reared at his silent command, the truth settled into my bones—this was no transformation of flesh, no loss of self. He hadn't become the monster.

He had accepted it. And it had accepted him in return.

I clutched my shirt tighter as my own shadow stirred in response. Mani shifted and I felt her instincts flaring. And as the lindworm settled its full weight onto the ridge, the mountains below seemed insignificant, a mere backdrop to the colossal dark majesty he commanded.

He looked down at me, and somehow, impossibly, he was still him. Still my Andrew. Even as he became more than any mortal could ever survive to see.

"Astrid," he said, my name vibrating through the air as much as through me.

I didn't answer with words. I stepped forward.

My hand lifted, trembling, not with fear, but with recognition. I felt him before I touched him: the pulse of the shadow-lindworm thrumming beneath his skin like a second heart, vast and ancient. When my fingers brushed his scales, they weren't merely solid, they were living void, writhing and curling, feeding on the air, the stone, the mountain itself.

Then Mani stirred, claws dragging along my ribs as if scraping chains from bone. The bloodlust hunger pulsed beneath my skin, a living furnace that rattled the marrow in my chest. I exhaled, low and sharp, and let the shadow flow through me, let it bleed out along my veins. It wasn't just a shadow, it was *mine*, darkness, blood hunger, and wolf-fury, threaded through with my pulse, sharp, alive, and mine.

Then I stepped closer, not toward him, but *into* him, into the storm that was Andrew, into the living darkness that obeyed him. My hands pressed against his scales, and I didn't feel resistance. I felt response.

The moment our powers touched, the air tore apart. My shadow coiled over his midnight scales like smoke climbing fire. His body shivered violently, an earthquake of muscle, but I pushed deeper, letting power bleed outward until it braided with his shadow.

My scream fractured into a roar.

It wasn't born of fear or pain, but of declaration. The sound became weight, force, rippling through the void of his form. Atius arched, spine bowing as the shadow-lindworm convulsed in response. Black smoke burst from every seam of him in violent torrents, pouring from his wings, his jaw, the fissures between scales.

My own transformation answered in kind. My shadows flared along my body as claws tore free from my hands, lengthening and blackening. My ribs shifted with grinding pops, vertebrae rasping as my spine thickened and stretched. Teeth elongated, fangs scraping sharp, and a growl rose from my chest that was both mine and not mine.

Our bond tightened in a single heartbeat. My wolf-shadow fanged through him. His roar answered mine, not echoing, but *melding*. A soundless vibration that clawed at the mountainside and shook the air like storm and earthquake fused.

Then something shifted. The smoke that had been spilling from Atius slowed, before reversing. Tendrils of shadow curled inward, drawn back into him, reabsorbed scale by scale, seam by seam. The chaos folded into order. The lindworm did not rage.

It obeyed.

I could see him then, through all the endless black—his eyes flickering with Andrew's grief and recognition, still fighting, still present beneath the vastness of the shadow-lindworm. And I knew he could feel me too: the wolf, the hunger, the fire-thread of Garmr pulsing through every black scale, every coil of shadow.

Atius arched again, wings spreading wide. Shadow-membranes rippled, but the smoke no longer spilled uncontrolled. What remained curled inward, wrapping around us both like armor, protective and deliberate.

The mountains trembled beneath us. Snow, rock, and ash skittered helplessly in the violent updraft of his wings. I held my ground, claws dug into stone, shadows entwined with his, fangs bared in instinctive fury.

At ten feet tall, my berserker form mirrored his new shape, wolf and dragon, fang and scale, shadow answering shadow. We were equal in height, equal in presence, twin titans locked in the same storm.

For the first time since this nightmare began, I didn't feel small. I didn't feel hunted. We were no longer two. Not Andrew, not Astrid.

We were a duet of shadow and hunger, wolf and lindworm, fire-threaded and night-wrapped. Standing side by side like a living storm carved into the mountainside.

And in that awful, beautiful bond, I knew the truth: We were unstoppable.

Chapter 20

The mountains were still trembling when the world began to sharpen back into focus. The dust thinned first, curling from my claws in fading ribbons before dissolving into the cold like breath in winter. The scent of stone and frost clung to the back of my throat, sharp and crisp.

I stepped back, just a fraction, and felt the pulse of everything inside me. Mani, her light of the moon, the bloodlust that was a relentless predator, the wolf-shadow. The darkness that gnawed at the edges of my mind. It all screamed and bled together in a chorus that was just mine.

Every part of me, once I had spent so long resisting, the feral rage, the bloodlust, the shadow, but they all no longer fought for dominance. They *belonged* to one another, and they all belonged to me.

My breath tore from me in uneven gasps as my spine arched beneath the weight of it, power flooding every vertebra, every nerve, until my body felt too small to hold what was waking inside of it. Muscles and tendons drew tight, coiling and reforging themselves, strength layering over strength as if my bones were being taught a new language.

My claws extended farther than they ever had before, curving with lethal precision, their edges catching the moonlight in faint silver flashes that could cut through the jagged peaks. I flexed my hands and felt the world differently, the stone, the air, the distance, all of it suddenly measurable. My teeth lengthened with a sharp, breath-stealing pull, serrated

and predatory, my jaw stretching beyond its old limits until my mouth ached with the promise of violence and hunger.

Beneath my skin, veins of pale light and shadow braided together, pulsing in slow, deliberate rhythms, a living lattice of moonlight and shadow that mapped every part of me. It didn't burn. It *belonged.*

Mani pressed close, steady and unyielding, her presence a powerful calm beneath the surge. Her awareness beat in time with my heart, grounding me in the surge of power, reminding me that this strength was not something that was going to overtake me.

'Who would have thought?' She murmured as we both leaned into the power together. *'We will not break.'*

'I know,' I whispered back. *'I'm holding it.'*

'No.' Mani corrected gently. *'We are becoming something more.'*

The ground beneath me caught a fractured sliver of moonlight, a stone polished smooth by ice and time, its surface dark and glassy. I glanced down without meaning to and I froze.

The eyes that stared back at me were mine. But they gleamed like a shard of fractured moonlight, pale blue at the center, rimmed with silver moonlight and by shadows. The whites were blackened, the darkness pressing close, not consuming, but framing.

A memory surged, the silver lake, still as a held breath. My father's presence beside me. Three of my reflections staring back at me from the lake, not the monster, not a saint, certainly not the human, but something in between.

'You remember,' Mani said softly.

'I do,' I breathed.

The truth settled into my bones with a quiet, unshakable certainty. I was not the light, untouched by darkness, and I was not the dark that learned mercy was a weakness. I was both, moon and night bound together, hunger braided with restraint, fury held in the grip of my own will.

Shadow did not diminish the light within me, and the light did not weaken the darkness I carried. Together, they made something stronger, something whole.

I was the balance.

And the choice of what that balance became… was mine.

The monstrous wolf in the reflection held my gaze without flinching. And for the first time in a long time, I didn't look away.

I let the power flow through every part of me. The shadows twisted around me, and instead of recoiling, I leaned into them. My claws tore through the air as my ribs stretched with predation and power. Mani's strength sang through my bones, harmonizing with hunger and the shadow, weaving everything into one unbroken whole.

My body contorted and expanded, muscles lengthening, spine stretching, as shadow flowed over me like a second skin. My claws scraped against the rock beneath my feet without leaving a mark.

I was the ultimate predator. The hunter and the hunted. Moonlight and beast-fire. Shadow and flesh. All of it coiled through me, a living lattice wrapped around bone and muscle.

And then I exhaled.

The sound wasn't just a breath; it was a declaration. A roar, a howl, a pulse of life and death released all at once. The mountains shuddered again. Shadows bent towards me, drawn

by gravity that had nothing to do with weight. Moonlight fractured across the peaks like silver lightning, gilding the darkness that cloaked my body.

I stepped forward in my new wolf self. My eyes burned with wolf, shadow, and light, a kaleidoscope of power. I didn't hesitate. I didn't fear myself.

I could feel Atius's gaze on me, his immense form looming, larger than before. Black fire spilling from his eyes, mouth, and his elbows. His wings, wrought of pure shadow, stretching impossibly wide, pulling and pushing the air like an ocean tide.

But he didn't rush to me.

He stayed still, his eyes fixed on me as if seeing something he'd always known but never witnessed. Me, untethered and unanchored, standing wholly in my own power.

Through our bond, I felt him. Not his fear, and not his hesitation, but pure awe. A raw and wordless acknowledgment that wasn't submission but respect. Atius watched me with curiosity. But Andrew was still there, they had merged together. His presence pressed at the edges of my mind, not demanding, not claiming, but waiting.

I raised my hand slowly, and my shadow and wolf-fire unfurled from me, not as weapons, but as an invitation. Tendrils of dark warmth threaded through the air, winding gently through the smoke spilling from his form.

"Andrew," I whispered through our mind link. *"Meet me. All of me."*

He didn't move at first. His eyes, radiant red in an abyssal black, flickered as something vulnerable broke through the vastness of him. Then, carefully, as though afraid to shatter the moment, he reached out. His black fire curled around my own, fitting against it like it had always belonged there.

My shadow poured like liquid night, my wolf-fire igniting in tandem. It slid along his scales, braided with the black fire that escaped from him.

I felt him tremble. His massive form pulsed, scales rippling as the smoke writhed, caught between escape and surrender. I mingled within his darkness, letting my essence flow into him and his into me, without restraint.

Our magic collided, but it didn't clash this time, it interlocked. The mountains quaked as tendrils of shadow and streaks of wolf-fire lanced into the sky, black smoke spiraling around pale-blue fire energy. The air was etched briefly in light before dissolving back into night. My body arched, every nerve aflame as his darkness threaded into mine, a communion of predator and predator, shadow and fire, wolf and dragon.

I felt Andrew beneath the scales and smoke, the steady truth of him hidden inside. I reached for that place, not with force, but with loving trust. The wolf within me bared our teeth, not in challenge, but in recognition, sinking into the raw edges of his shadow. Mani brushed along his obsidian veins, gentle and sure, a wordless *I see you. I will always choose you.* Then we folded into one another.

Our power threaded together, breath, pulse and hunger, aligning until there was no clear edge between his darkness and mine. We roared, not in fury, but in release, one sound carried by two minds, predators and shadows entwined in a communion both terrible and beautiful.

And in that moment, I no longer feared what I was, or what I might become. I was whole and complete.

And in meeting me there was Andrew.

When the roar finally faded, it wasn't silence that remained, but understanding, a quiet, steady, and irrevocable.

He didn't reach to steady me. He didn't need to. Instead, he bowed his head and nuzzled into my neck, his massive body curling low around me, and that was enough.

My shadow and wolf-fire started to subside slowly. The violence of it softened first, the roar of power lowering into a steady hum as the lattice of energy threading my body began to fold inward. Heat bled from my limbs in slow waves, leaving my muscles trembling, overworked, aching, as though they were relearning their proper shape. The pressure along my spine loosened, vertebra-by-vertebra, and I shuddered as the force that had held me monstrous drew itself back into my core.

The darkness unspooled next. Shadows peeled away from my arms and ribs in slow, deliberate threads, lifting from my skin like smoke caught by a tide. They did not vanish; they retreated, sliding across the ground and into the waiting hollows of the forest, pooling at the roots of trees, slipping between stone and bark as if the land itself were drawing a breath around me. When the last of them left, only a faint dusk-sheen remained along my skin, a memory of night rather than its grip.

My claws shortened with a dull, dragging pull, silver glints fading as fingers reshaped themselves, joints cracking softly as they remembered how to be human. My jaw tightened, teeth shrinking with sharp, breath-stealing pressure, and I gasped as my lungs expanded fully again, drawing air like I hadn't needed to before.

Wolf-fire dimmed last. The pale blaze along my veins guttered, not extinguished but banked, folding inward with aching slowness until it sank into my heartbeat. It settled there, burning but contained, braided with shadow in a way that no longer fought me. When the change finally slowed, I stood naked and shaking, skin raw with sensation, the power humming beneath it like a sleeping storm.

Andrew moved then. He rose and took a single step back as the last traces of smoke drew into him, reabsorbing scale by scale until only the man remained. His eyes burned, a red radiance rimmed in black, yet they were achingly familiar, clear and present, *my Andrew*. He looked at me the way a man looks at something sacred and dangerous all at once.

The bond between us pulsed, strong and pure, no longer roaring, but a steady current between two beings who had seen each other fully and remained.

"You've accepted yourself," he said softly, voice rough as stones. "All of you."

I nodded, my claws still glinting faintly in the fractured moonlight. "And you didn't pull me back."

His jaw worked, a muscle ticking. "I wanted to."

"But you didn't."

"No." His wings were the last to dissipate into smoke, leaving only the man, the shadows burning faint in his veins. He reached for me slowly and carefully. "I never wanted to hold you back." He said quietly, "I just… wanted to protect you. And wanted to be beside you when you rose."

I stepped into him. "Then walk beside me," I whispered.

His hand found mine, not to steady, not to lead, but to match my step. And in that simple, deliberate choice, we became what we were always meant to be, not halves, not each other's saviors, but two whole forces moving forward together.

He lowered his head, his eyes burning with both longing and devotion. For a heartbeat, the sheer gravity of him stole my

breath, yet when his breath curled over my skin it was gentle, coaxing, a tide of smoke laced with warmth.

"Take me home," I whispered.

Andrew's eyes flared with mischief, catching the moonlight, and the shadows behind him rippled like water. Then, his wings burst from his back. They unfurled in silence, darker than night yet edged with a faint glimmer of starlight, their span so great they blotted out the peaks behind him.

Before I could move, his arms swept under me, one firm under my knees, the other bracing my shoulders, lifting me with effortless strength. We were both bare now, stripped of scale and smoke and every last remnant of transformation, skin to skin beneath the open sky, and yet the cold never touched us. He cradled me against his chest as though I weighed nothing at all.

His heat wrapped around me, while his heartbeat a deep thunder beneath my cheek. Above us, his wings arched wide, immense cathedrals of night and edged with starlight. For a single breath, they folded around us, enclosing us in warmth, as if the world itself paused to let us pass.

Then he crouched low and leapt. The mountains vanished beneath us, swallowed by the darkness of the night. My vision sharpened, as though another gaze slid seamlessly over my own. Mani leaned forward, I felt her looking through my eyes, drinking in the sweep of forest and mountain peaks, the dark veins of rivers flashing moonlit silver below. Every movement of air, every shift of shadow, registered with quiet, predatory delight.

'See how far it stretches,' Mani said in pure awe. *'How open it is.'*

Wind tore at my hair, sharp and clean, but it couldn't steal the warmth between us. I felt Mani's pleasure ripple through me, wordless and fierce. She did not howl. She did not need to. This was running of another kind. His wings cut through the night with impossible grace. Each beat was thunder; each rise pulling us higher into the star-drenched sky. Mani rode the currents with him, with me, with Atius, silent but fully present, cataloging the land below, and savoring the height, and the freedom.

I clung tighter, but not from fear, but from the wild exhilaration surging through all three of us. A laugh tore free of my throat, feral and unrestrained, and Mani shared it with me.

Below, the forest rolled endlessly, a dark, living sea. From here, the world seemed smaller, yes, but not unknown. And yet, I had never felt more alive.

Mani watched it all with me, just simply *being.*

And in that shared silence, carried between wings and stars, we flew home together.

Andrew glanced down at me, his gaze locking with mine, his eyes fully human again, green and orange and burning with something wordless. Not just protection or possession, but something more like gratitude and absolute trust.

We descended only when the glow of Trovi's house appeared below, warm lantern-light steady and waiting. His wings flared wide, slowing our fall until the ground rose gently to meet us. His wings dissolving into drifting smoke as our bare feet touched earth and frost-kissed stone.

There he stood, human, unguarded, wrapped only in the remnants of night, looking at me as though the flight itself had bound us tighter than any vow ever could.

Chapter 21

The air still trembled with the echo of what we'd become. We stood at the center of what remained of Trovi's ritual circle. Chalk lines lay scoured and broken, symbols burned into the stone as if something inside had clawed its way free. Mist curled from my skin as my breath steadied, the power beneath it, restless but contained.

Andrew set me gently on my feet. I turned to face him, the world narrowing to the space between us. For a long moment, he only stared, as though the shape of me had rewritten everything he thought he knew. Awe and disbelief warred across his face before settling into something reverent. As though he were seeing me not as I had been, but as I was.

I flexed my fingers, feeling the power spill through me in rolling waves. I should have felt fear, but instead, exhilaration tore through my chest, bright and feral. '*I can hold it all. I can command it.*'

The house around us did not share my confidence. The beams groaned overhead as shadows slithered unnaturally across walls that should have been still. Ash sifted down from the rafters in slow drifts, and even the stone beneath my feet trembled, as though it remembered what had been unleashed here.

"Well," a voice said dryly, making me jump, the world snapping back in place. I looked over Andrew's shoulder to see Bo pushing Trovi towards us in her wheelchair. Bo deliberately refused to make eye contact with me. Trovi, on the other hand, looked us over with calm precision, her gaze dropped once, then lingered a little further. The corner of her mouth twitched.

She folded her arms as she took us in, naked, the steam rising faintly from our bare skin, the winter air wreathing us like something dragged straight from a half-forgotten myth. "That's one way to make an entrance."

Heat rushed to my face as I crossed my arms instinctively, which helped very little. Andrew shifted closer, angling himself to shield me without thinking.

Belated awareness crashed over his face. He stiffened. "I…"

Trovi lifted a hand. "No. Don't." Her eyes flicked pointedly between us. "I have lived a very long time, boy. I have seen visions of gods born, beasts crowned, and bloodlines ruin themselves in spectacular fashion." She sighed. "I did NOT need to add *full-frontal wolf and dragon* to that list tonight."

With a sharp flick of her wrist, Trovi hurled two thick towels at us with surprising accuracy. One smacked Andrew square in the back of his head. The other hit me directly in the face.

"Wrap yourselves," she snapped. "Before the house decides to collapse out of modesty."

I fumbled the towel around myself, my heart still hammering. Andrew did the same, his jaw tight and his ears burning red.

As Bo turned Trovi towards the house, she added over her shoulder. "Bo and Red had the foresight to go and grab you clothes. Which tells me two things: one, they know you both far too well." She glanced back, eyes sharp with dark amusement, "and two, what they didn't plan for is how many things are paying attention now."

She paused at the doorway, something knowing curling at the corner of her mouth.

"Come inside," she said. "Get dressed. Then we'll talk about what you just became… and your new markings."

The door creaked open, spilling warm light across the wreckage around us.

"New markings?" Andrew muttered, stepping back as his gaze dropped to my bare skin that was not covered by the towel, his brow furrowing as he began to examine himself.

That was when I noticed the others were gone. Red, Darcy, Damian, and Luca. Only smudged footprints and the lingering scent of smoke remained.

'No,' Mani's voice rumbled, low and sharp. *'This isn't right. They wouldn't just leave.'*

'Maybe they're inside… waiting for us to come back.' I murmured, though the words felt thin even to me.

Mani's growl carried a thread of dark amusement. *'Waiting? Or hiding from what they fear. And we're walking straight into it.'*

A chill slid down my spine.

'It's a possibility,' Mani replied.

I clenched my fists, letting the heat of her words mingle with the fire still thrumming inside me.

Andrew's voice broke through the tension, low and rough. "Astrid… you've done it."

Pride flickered in his gaze, but caution followed close behind. His eyes swept the ruined circle, then to the glow beyond the windows. "Everyone must be inside."

I nodded, as a strange prickle traced my skin, as if unseen eyes pressed through cracks in the world itself.

Whispers clung to the scorched runes at my feet, half-formed and elusive.

A raven landed on the back fence. It looked directly at us then started shrieking, sharp and discordant. It made me freeze.

'What is that?' Mani hissed, low and uncertain. *'Do you hear them?'*

I nodded, my heart hammering. *'It sounds like... voices... but I can't... I don't know what they're saying.'*

The air shifted, carrying faint, fractured syllables through the soft breeze. A name slithered through the murmur: *"Ewan... Owen..."*

'Ewan?' Mani growled softly, confusion rolling through her. *'Or Owen? Which fucking name is it?'*

I shook my head, trying to catch the sound, to make sense of it, but it slipped like smoke. *'It doesn't matter yet,'* I whispered. *'But... it feels familiar... like a warning.'*

'We can worry about that in the future.' Mani replied.

The weight of inevitability settling over me. We had revealed ourselves, and in doing so, drawn attention. Fear gnawed at the edges of my mind.

'We can endure.' Mani said firmly. *'Together we can meet whatever comes.'*

I drew in a slow breath and met Andrew's eyes. "Let's find the others."

He nodded once, and together we stepped beyond the broken circle, the night air cool against our skin. As we crossed the back deck toward Trovi's house, the world seemed to hold its breath. No voices. No movement. Only the faint creak of the boards beneath our feet.

Inside, the house was unnervingly still as well. By the back door, a neat pile of clothes and boots waited for us. Andrew's jacket draped over the rail like someone had thought ahead.

"Dad," Andrew murmured, recognition softening his voice.

I reached for the sweater first. The fabric was warm from the house, comforting against my skin that was still humming with power. Pulling it on felt strange, like fitting myself back into something smaller than I'd been moments ago. My fingers trembled as I tugged on leggings, the scrape of cloth against hypersensitive skin sending shivers through me.

Andrew turned slightly away as he dressed, giving me privacy, or maybe taking it for himself. As he lifted his shirt, the warm light caught his bare back, and I froze.

There were the markings… It ran straight down his spine, inked deep and dark, as though it had been carved into him. At its center sat a rune I didn't recognize but *felt*. It was sharp with severe lines forming something ancient and deliberate. An arrowhead pointed upward at the top, angular strokes beneath it like a command etched in shadow.

Lower, two elongated diamond shapes intersected, bound together at their narrow points. A meeting point.

From the lowest point, a single line descended, ending in a downward-pointing arrow, perfectly mirrored, above and below, balanced and intentional.

The edges weren't clean. They blurred and feathered, black ink bleeding outward in faint wisps, like smoke seeping from beneath his skin, softly drifting away, as if *breathing*.

I reached out and touched his marking, and my own back prickled in response, heat blooming between my shoulders, and I knew, without seeing it, that the same mark burned into me.

"Andrew," I whispered, stepping closer. "There's…"

He turned his head. "I know… I can feel it."

"It's not just a mark," I breathed. "It's some…"

Trovi's voice cut through the dark, calm and unyielding. "Are you decent yet?"

Andrew pulled his shirt down, the marking vanishing from sight, but the weight of it remained, pressed between us, unfinished. Andrew's gaze flicked to me, not hungry, not startled, just steady and present. His hand brushed mine with a silent promise.

We walked hand in hand to where Trovi sat alone at her dining table, a cup steaming gently between her hands. The scent of herbs and something faintly sweet, chamomile, perhaps, hung in the air.

Her face held a lot of emotions. I'm sure we will get through them all tonight. Her eyes lifted briefly, unreadable in the dim light. She said nothing, simply gestured toward the circle of candles already burning on the table. Their glow was soft and steady, casting shifting patterns across her lined face.

We took our seats in silence. Andrew moved slowly, deliberately, as though afraid even the air might splinter beneath his touch. I mirrored him, folding my hands in my lap, forcing my breathing to match the quiet rhythm of the room.

The air smelled of smoke, steeped tea, and something older, magic still humming faintly in the wood and stone. Trovi's house was alive with it, every shadow holding its breath. It was a pause, the breath the world takes after a storm passes, but before the next begins.

The quiet stretched long enough to become its own kind of pressure. Trovi's eyes flicked from me to Andrew, her gaze sharp despite the exhaustion etched into her features. The candlelight deepened the lines of her face, turning her into something older.

Finally, she spoke. "The others have gone home. When you were pulled under… what did you see?" Her tone was soft, but it carried an edge. "Where did you go, Astrid?"

The question coiled through the room, and the silence that followed felt heavy enough to crush breath.

My fingers curled against my knees. "I was told that it was Svartalfheim," I began. "It was like I was in a cave. There was no light, only… movement. Like being swallowed whole by a living shadow." I hesitated, glancing at Andrew. His hand brushed mine beneath the table. "There was something there...they shared Naomi's features."

Trovi's eyes narrowed slightly. "Silver hair and ebony skin? That would make sense."

I nodded. "Their…priestess" The name seemed to weigh down the air itself. "She showed me things. Memories that weren't mine. Visions of what they want me to become. And when I came back…" I exhaled the words tasting of iron and smoke. "Everything was different."

Trovi didn't blink. "Different how?"

Before I could answer, Andrew stared. "When she came back," he said, "she didn't just return. Something else came with her. Astrid's power called to mine… it felt like the world itself shifted to make room for it."

Trovi's eyes flicked toward me, sharp as flint in the dim light. "The wolf, the dragon, and the shadow," she murmured.

"Two bloodlines that should never have converged. And yet, here you sit…alive and bonded no less."

The chair creaked as she leaned back, studying me the way one might study an omen rather than a person. "Your mother's legacy runs deep, Astrid. Too deep, perhaps. You carry the wild from your wolf kin, and you," she gestured to Andrew. "The hunger from the dragon, and something older still, the darkness that bound them together."

My breath hitched. "Do you know anything about my father?"

Trovi's gaze softened only slightly. "I have studied the old bloodlines of your mother, and I know that your father was human, but now he's the one who walked between forms. Wolf by curse and shadow." She set her cup down, the faint clink of porcelain loud in the silence. "He sought to kill it. Most believed it killed him."

A chill rippled through me, the candlelight dimming as if the house itself listened. Mani stirred faintly in my chest, her voice low and uncertain. *'We know that he didn't die. Not entirely.'*

I swallowed hard. "He's the reason I am what I am…why we are…"

Andrew's hand brushed mine beneath the table, steadying me. "And the reason they'll come for her," he said quietly, his gaze still locked on Trovi. "Those who wanted her before will see her as the result. What they couldn't use as a weapon."

Trovi nodded once, slowly. "Now they will come for both of you. The night stirs with old names again. The eyes that watched him will not ignore you." Her attention flicked toward

Andrew. "Nor you, dragon born. The shadow remembers its kin."

Outside, a branch scraped across the windowpane, a harsh whisper against the glass. The air thickened, pressing down like the weight of prophecy.

I met Trovi's gaze, my voice steady despite the tremor in my chest. "Then they'll learn what my blood is truly capable of."

Mani's growl hummed low, dark and sure. *'Let them come.'*

Trovi's lips pressed thin and unreadable. "Then the night will not stay silent for long."

Andrew's shadow flickered against the wall, alive and restless. I felt the same pulse within me, twin storms tethered by something far greater than either of us could name.

I drew in a slow breath and met her eyes. "Then neither will we."

The candles guttered low, their flames shrinking into thin, wavering threads of gold.

"Hmmm," She said not fully in agreement.

The house had gone quiet by the time Trovi spoke again.

"Get up and turn around," Trovi said.

I did and Andrew followed suit, standing beside me, close enough that our shoulders brushed.

"Lift your shirts." As we did Trovi's breath caught, slightly.

The candlelight revealed the marks in full, identical glory.

Trovi wheeled over to get a closer look, reverent now despite herself. "And it isn't a blessing." she said softly.

Her fingers hovered near the rune but did not touch it. "It's a shadow-binding sigil. Old. Older than the runes we teach. Designed to bind what should not coexist."

She traced the air along the shape. "The upward arrow, awakening. The downward, descent. Above and below, seen and unseen." Her gaze lingered on the intersecting diamonds. "This is the dangerous part. A sealed convergence. A place where realms touch and are *forced* to agree. But with you two… you did this together…willingly. Sort of."

The candle flame guttered.

"And the smoke?" Andrew asked quietly. As we turned to face her.

She looked between us then, eyes sharp with something that wasn't quite fear, but close. "This mark doesn't represent just shadow," she said. "It *houses* it. A vessel etched into living flesh."

My throat tightened. "What does that mean for us?"

Trovi exhaled slowly. "It means the shadow recognizes you as its keepers." Her gaze softened, just a fraction. "And that frightens me more than almost anything."

She met my eyes. "This mark means the shadow will *call* to you. When it does, it will not ask."

My stomach tightened. "And if we refuse?"

Her gaze sharpened. "Then it will take."

Silence pressed in.

Finally, she added, quieter still, "Because vessels are never meant to remain empty. Or obedient… Forever."

The candle hissed.

The rune on my back pulsed, once as if answering.

Trovi wheeled back without a word, and we replaced our shirts, before we turned to face her, her expression was unreadable as she gathered the remnants of the ritual, the ashes, shards of chalk, and a burned fragment of earthbound grass between her fingers.

"Bo arrested the nurse… I assume he is holding her until there are answers." Trovi turned her back to us. "The others will remember enough to be wary, but not enough to be in danger. That's the best I can offer." she said quietly.

"And us?" Andrew asked.

Her gaze lingered on me, tired but fierce. "Rest if you can. Because tonight was not an ending."

When Trovi finally disappeared down the hall, the silence she left behind was heavier than before. Magic still clung to the air, a pulse beneath the heartbeat of the house.

We sat there for a long time, neither of us speaking. The night deepened outside, and the last candle hissed out, leaving only the soft glow of moonlight through the curtains.

It should have been peaceful.

But peace doesn't hum.

Peace doesn't whisper.

The echo of power still coiled beneath my skin, and I understood something with startling clarity.

This wasn't about surviving what came next.

It was about the choices I would have to make and the edge of the blade I would walk now, balancing light and shadow.

Chapter 22

The morning arrived gray and unhurried, pale light slipping through the edges of Trovi's curtains as though the dawn itself hesitated to enter. The scent of smoke still clung to everything, our skin, the walls, the old floorboards. It was drifting in from the garden where the ritual had finally burned itself out the night before.

Andrew and I said very little before we tried getting some sleep. He sat near the window, head bowed, hands clasped, his eyes unfocused, as if he could see a world beyond the veil, right where he sat.

I wanted to reach for him, but something in me hesitated. The quiet between us was fragile, and I was afraid to break it. I got up and moved toward the cold hearth, running a hand along the soot-darkened stone. It pulsed faintly under my palm. Then, beneath my skin, something shifted, an echo of another voice, another fear.

The residue of magic was thick here, familiar, but wrong. My pulse stuttered. A whisper slid through my thoughts, barely a sound at all.

'Don't leave me here.'

I froze. The voice wasn't Andrew's. It wasn't Mani's.

Naomi.

Her tone was fractured as it echoed, like a broken reflection. I swallowed hard and tried to focus, grounding myself in the physical world, the rough stone beneath my

fingers, the faint rhythm of Andrew's breathing behind me. But the voice came again, stronger now and edged in panic.

'I can't find the door. It's dark. Help me...please...I'm still here.'

A flicker of a figure weeping on the floor, surrounded by darkness, tugged at the edges of my mind. Naomi's face flashed before me, pale and wide-eyed, she was like a ghost behind glass.

"Astrid?" Andrew's voice was low and cautious.

The room tilted, shadows stretching too long. For an instant, the scent of smoke deepened into something colder, like ash and rot. Another presence pressed against my mind, slick and invasive, threading through my thoughts where it didn't belong. The dark völva. Anchored inside Naomi, using her as a vessel.

"Andrew…" My voice cracked.

He was moving before I finished, crossing the space between us. "What is it?"

"She's still here," I whispered, swallowing hard. "Not here, here. But in my head... I can feel her."

His expression darkened. "Naomi?"

I nodded once, my pulse quickening. "The dark völva locked her away in her own mind. She's fighting... but she's losing hope."

Mani's growl resonated in my chest. '*It has to be a trap. The dark völva is just using her.'*

"I know," I murmured. "But I can't ignore her. Not when I could hear her breaking."

Andrew took my hand, his grip steady and comforting. His eyes darkened, that dragon-fire flicker waking beneath the surface. "Then we need to end it. Cut the connection so she can find her way back."

The morning light flickered across his face, glinting off the faint scales still ghosting his throat. For a moment, the air felt heavy with unspoken promises and gathering worries.

Outside, a raven called once, low and distant, and then everything was utterly still.

A floorboard creaked from the adjoining room.
The scent of coffee beans being ground stirred a moment later, followed by the faint, steady hiss of a kettle.

Andrew turned first, shoulders tensing. "She shouldn't be up."

We hurried to the doorway and found Trovi standing there, shawl hanging loosely around her narrow shoulders, her white hair escaping its braid in fine, wayward strands. She moved with the slow precision of someone who hadn't slept, and every motion deliberate, every ache present. Steam curled around her as she poured water into an old clay pot, the scent of coffee grounding the room in something almost ordinary, except nothing about this morning felt ordinary.

"You need rest," I said. "You shouldn't even be on your feet yet. You were already drained before the ritual. You shouldn't…"

Trovi waved a hand, dismissing my concern. "Sleep won't help me if things are already shifting." Her voice was rough but steady. "Besides, I've been listening."

She turned slightly toward the window, as though she could still hear the echo of the raven's cry. "The air hums differently today. You feel it, don't you?"

Andrew frowned. "You mean the residue from the circle?"

"No," she said, setting the pot down with a soft clink. "Something else."

My stomach tightened. "Is that why I …hear Naomi?"

Trovi's eyes flicked toward me, sharp and knowing. "So, you've heard her?"

I nodded.

"Then we can't wait," Trovi said. Her tone left no room for hesitation. "You might be able to reach her now, before the dark völva seals her completely."

Andrew stepped in front of me so abruptly his shoulder brushed mine, placing himself between me and the suggestion like a shield.

"You're asking her to astral project again?" His voice cracked with disbelief, anger rising fast beneath it. "After last night? She barely made it back!"

His jaw tightened, eyes flashing as he looked between us. "You almost didn't either, because of the dark volva," he added, the words sharper now, edged with something closer to fear than fury. "And you want her to walk right back into that?"

Trovi turned to face him fully, the steam from her cup curling between them like a veil. "The longer we wait, the stronger the corruption becomes. The dark völva will consume what's left of Naomi and use her as a puppet. If Astrid can sense her now, she has a chance to close that door or at least pull Naomi back through before it locks."

I swallowed hard. "And if I fail?"

Trovi met my gaze and her eyes softened. "Then you'll learn where your limits truly lie."

Andrew's hand found mine, his grip tight and steady. "You're not doing this alone."

The coffee in Trovi's cup rippled once, as if something unseen had brushed the air.

Trovi's gaze flicked toward me again. "Astrid, if you're going to reach her, it has to be now."

Outside, the raven called a second time, sharper this time, almost urgent.

And beneath my skin, I felt it again. The connection. Naomi's heartbeat, or maybe something pretending to be.

Trovi set her cup down with a decisive clink and pushed herself off the counter she was leaning on. The movement was slow but certain, the way an old tree bends with the wind but never breaks.

"Then we prepare," she said. "Now."

"Prepare how?" Andrew asked, already on alert.

Trovi moved quickly to the shelf in the living room, pulling down a weathered box bound with silver clasps. "You'll need a boundary, something to hold your mind in one place." She glanced toward Andrew. "You, fetch the iron bowl from the hearth. Three candles from the bookshelf. And the salt. Not the kitchen salt… the black one."

Andrew hesitated. "Does that really matter?"

Trovi gave him a look so sharp that it could've cut through stone. "If you want her soul to stay *inside* her body, yes, it matters."

He blinked. "Right. Black salt. Got it."

Then he moved, muttering under his breath as glass jars clinked and metal scraped in the small space, the sound of reluctant obedience filling the room.

"Astrid, take this." Trovi said, her sharp gaze flicking toward me as she handed me the kettle. "Out there, by the old

circle. Sit on the ground. You'll draw from what's left of the night."

I did as she asked, stepping into the garden's cool air with her kettle in hand. The dirt was frosted and slightly damp beneath my knees, and the faint scent of ash and herbs still lingered, remnants of the last working.

Trovi followed, pulling a small pouch from her belt. The contents glimmered faintly in the candlelight: coarse salt, ash, and crushed rowan berries. Her fingers trembled slightly, though her expression never faltered as she began to trace runes of warding in slow, deliberate arcs around me—ᚠ (Fehu), ᚨ (Ansuz), ᚦ (Thurisaz)—each murmured under her breath in the old tongue. The salt hissed faintly as it met the earth, a whisper like breath against the veil.

"This will hold your *hugr*, your spirit's shape, if the dark völva tries to unmake you," she said, her tone all command and gravity.

Andrew returned then, setting a small iron bowl beside her with a soft clink. "What's this for?" he asked.

Trovi took the black salt and poured it into the bowl with deliberate care, murmuring a protective blessing over it. She lifted the kettle from my hands, letting the steaming water flow in, the vapor spiraling upward like smoke from a sacred offering. "Reflection," she said softly, her voice reverent. "This will guard you, Astrid, keep you steady in the in between, and ward off ill intent. Every soul sends ripples through the web of worlds. This will show the way…and mark the line if we need to pull you back."

Her voice softened, just barely. "Naomi is still tethered by blood and memory. The dark völva is probably using her fear to anchor himself. Astrid… if you reach her, do not chase the dark past her. Do you understand?"

"I understand," I said, though the words sat heavy on my tongue.

Trovi held my gaze, the lines around her eyes deepening. "You may see things that are not hers, echoes of what the dark völva twisted. Ignore them. They're bait."

Andrew crouched beside me, close enough that I felt the brush of his hand before he pulled away. "If anything goes wrong…you get out of there."

Trovi nodded once, approving. "Good. Then let's begin."

She lit three candles and set two on either side of me at my knees and one at my back. Their flames guttered in unison, then steadied as she began to chant in a low, resonant hum that made the air feel thicker, denser, as though the garden itself held its breath.

"Follow the pulse," she murmured. "But don't chase it."

The world dimmed. The raven outside screamed again, long and sharp.

And then…

My body stayed seated in the garden, but my awareness slipped sideways, pressed through something thin and resistant. At first, I thought I had been dragged back to Svartalfheim, to that endless black expanse with no sound, no end, no form. But this wasn't another world. It was *Naomi's mind.*

A vast, empty void stretched around me, softly glowing black, like standing inside nothingness, suspended between worlds. The emptiness trembled with something faint and fragile, a pulse. Slow, unsteady, like a heart trying to remember how to beat after too long in the dark.

My body jerked as if struck. The pain wasn't just in my head, it rippled down my spine, clawing through every nerve. Somewhere far away, I thought I could faintly hear Andrew's voice. It was muffled and desperate, but I had already been swallowed whole into this nightmare.

Naomi's scream echoed through the void, warped and jagged. I stumbled forward, forcing my breath steady, forcing my heart to slow, even as the shadows moved with intent. The air felt thick and alive, like it was watching. I could feel the dark völva pressed into the space with me, spreading like oil across water, slick and choking, smothering what little light remained.

And then I heard it.

Naomi's voice, thin and trembling, wove through the darkness. "Astrid…?"
It carried none of the venom from before, only fear, raw and fragile.

The darkness around her rippled like water, and I realized these weren't shadows, they were fragments. Shattered memories drifting through the black. A flicker of laughter. The edge of a mirror. Silver hair tangled in someone's hands. Naomi's mind had been cracked open, and the dark völva was the rot inside, and it was spreading.

"Naomi, it's me," I said, stepping forward. My voice echoed. "You have to fight him. You're stronger than this."

Light flickered, weak and uncertain. Threads of gold shimmered between them, trembling as she reached toward them. The moment her fingertips brushed one, pain seared through her skull.

His laughter followed, low and cold, rippling through the dark.

"Little wolf," the dark völva whispered. "You keep trying to fix what I want broken."

Naomi screamed.

The sound wasn't human, it was ear-*splitting*. The black space convulsed, and images bled through: Naomi standing in a field of white flowers that withered into ash; her reflection melting into shadow. The völva was feeding on her fear, rebuilding this prison out of Naomi's own twisted memories.

"Let her go!" I shouted. "She doesn't belong to you!"

The laughter deepened, curling like smoke through the dark. "She called to me. All I did was answer."

A flicker of movement, Naomi appeared again, half-hidden, chains of shadow wound around her wrists and throat. They tightened, pulsing in time with her heart. Her violet eyes found mine, wide and pleading.

"I can't…he's in my head," Naomi whispered.

"Then take my hand," I said, stepping closer. "Before he takes everything."

"Little wolf…you are not following your fate…I was to…it doesn't matter. What will be, I will make it happen."

The pulse between us surged. For a heartbeat, the light flared, one of the chains holding Naomi snapped. The dark völva screamed, his voice splitting the void, and the world began to crumble inward, the dark swallowing everything.

I lunged for her, desperation tearing through me. "Naomi, hold on, just hold on!"

Her fingers slipped away before I could grasp them, she was torn from me, swallowed by the dark, the remaining light extinguished in a single, merciless breath.

My body arched as if struck, every nerve screaming. My knees hit the ground inside that collapsing void…and then, with

a final jolt, I was thrown back outward and back into my own mind.

I gasped awake into Andrew's grip, sweat clinging to my skin as he held my shoulders and searched my eyes. His wings unfurled halfway, a silent reflex born of fear and protection.

Trovi stood a few steps away, her posture still, her gaze sharp with wary understanding—as though she'd already guessed the shape of the answer.

"What happened?" Andrew demanded.

My breath came ragged, my pulse still echoing in my ears. "She's alive," I said, forcing the words past the tightness in my chest. "But she's trapped. Inside her own mind. And the dark völva is using it against her."

Trovi's expression hardened, the lines of her face deepening. "Then we find a way to break through," she said quietly, "before Naomi forgets how to wake herself."

I swallowed, the memory of that place still clinging to me. "She tried to reach me," I said softly. "But it was like moving through syrup. Every step, every thought, slow, heavy. The darkness clung to her, pulling her back."

Outside, the raven cried out again.

I looked at Andrew. His gaze locked with mine. Beneath my ribs, my heart stuttered once, then it fell into sync with that faint, distant rhythm.

Naomi answered us.

And this time, I understood the cost.

Chapter 23

The raven's cry hadn't finished echoing before Trovi was already moving again.

"Inside," she said sharply, reaching for her satchel of herbs. "Now. We don't have much time."

Andrew helped me to my feet. My legs felt hollow and unsteady, the echo of the void clinging to my bones. The morning light crept over the mountains, thin and cold, catching on the mist that rose from the ward circle like breath leaving a dying body.

Trovi shoved open the back door and waved us inside. The lights flickered as we crossed the threshold, as if something unseen followed close on our heels.

"We can only hope she gets stronger," Trovi muttered. "Or angrier."

"Both," I said. My voice came out rough. "The dark völva… he said something… something about *fate.* Like he'd been given a version of what was supposed to happen… and I wasn't following it."

Andrew stiffened. "Like a script? From who?"

I shook my head. "I don't know."

Trovi froze mid-motion, the pouch of herbs and the bowl of black salt suspended in her hands. "That's not possible," she murmured, almost to herself. "The dark völva doesn't receive guidance."

"Then who wrote him a future?" I said quietly. "And he didn't like that I refused to play my part."

Andrew's jaw tightened, his arms crossing. The tension in the room thickened until Mani whispered, sharp as lightning. '*What about that name...?*'

My breath hitched. I looked up before the thought had fully formed. "Ewan," I said aloud.

The word left my mouth, the lights overhead flickered, a faint stutter like a skipped heartbeat. My fingers tingled, heat blooming in my palm as if I'd brushed too close to a flame. The name hung between us, heavy and acrid, like smoke before a storm.

Trovi's mouth tightened. "Ewan?"

I nodded slowly, the memory prickling down my spine. "When Andrew and I came back last night... that name was whispered." I hesitated, the echo still clear in my mind. "When the raven shrieked, it was like... like the wind itself said it... not spoken, but insisted"

Trovi's eyes snapped to the window, then back to me, unease flashing across her face.

Andrew frowned. "Who is that?"

I looked at Andrew, unsure, but Trovi went still. Her expression sharpened, that familiar flicker of calculation lighting her eyes. "Ewan," she repeated quietly. "Do you know his full name?"

"Ewan... Owen?" I said. "I think...why?"

Trovi didn't answer. She crossed the room in three brisk strides, dragging a cracked leather tome from the shelf hard enough to send dust spiraling into the air. The pages whispered as she flipped them, thin as pressed leaves.

“Because names remember what people forget,” she said. Her fingers flipped rapidly through the yellowed parchment until she stopped on a page dense with runic symbols. As she traced the first symbol, something *answered her*.

A low thrum vibrated through my bones, echoing in my palms, my brow, the same place my magic always stirred before it burned free. A flash cut across my mind: yew branches twisting skyward, bare and ancient, their roots tangled around a skull half-buried in snow.

“Ewan,” Trovi said quietly. “From the old tongue *Eòghann*… born of the yew tree.” Her voice lowered. “A symbol of death and rebirth.” The pressure in my chest deepened. Mani stirred uneasily.

“And Owen,” Trovi continued, her finger sliding to the next marking, “derived from *Owain*. A name once bound to the Allfather himself.”

The room seemed to tilt.

My pulse stuttered. “You’re saying…”

“I’m saying,” Trovi cut in, turning the book toward us. “That this… isn’t a name the wind chose at random.”

Ink bled across the page — a one-eyed god, ravens poised on his shoulders, spear raised.

Heat flared in my palm, sharp enough to sting.

“If he is reborn,” Trovi went on, “and the dark völva is working with him…” Her gaze lifted to mine. “Then this boy may be what remains of Odin.”

Andrew’s jaw clenched. “You mean …like… reincarnated?”

Trovi nodded once. “Awakened slowly. Testing the world. Seeking what was lost, power, order, dominion. If he’s

waking now, maybe it's because he wants the realms to be restored to the way it was before Ragnarök."

A shiver ran through me, unbidden. "He wants to rebuild it?"

Trovi's gaze was grim. "No… He wants to *rule* them."

Silence settled, heavy as stone.

Mani stirred, her voice low. '*He will bring chains with him,'* she whispered. '*The old ones never rise without taking what they believe is theirs.'*

Her words tasted like iron and ash.

Naomi's faint pulse flickered again inside me, uneven and fragile, like a candle struggling in the wind. She must have crossed paths with Ewan before the dark völva had reached her. Something vast and deliberate had brushed her mind then, not to break it, but to *test* it, pressing gently and patiently, searching for weaknesses. That first touch hadn't shattered her. It had marked her. And once she was marked, the darkness didn't need to force its way in, because it was already welcome.

Andrew's voice cut through my thoughts, low and taut. "So, the dark völva is serving him?"

"Or being used by him," I murmured. "Either way, this… Ewan or Odin, has found himself reborn again and is creating havoc."

Andrew's jaw flexed. "That doesn't mean he's fully awake."

"No," I agreed, unease curling in my stomach. "But it means he's *stirring*, whispering on the wind, and touching minds."

Trovi exhaled slowly, her fingers tightening around the edge of the table. "Awakenings rarely begin with fire and thunder," she said. "More often, they begin with influence."

"With fractures," Andrew added.

I nodded. "Naomi had fractures. A perfect vessel, someone he could test the world through. If she called to him, and he answered… then this isn't random chaos. It's reconnaissance."

Andrew's gaze darkened. "So, the question isn't *if* he's awakening."

I met his eyes. "It's how long he's been planning."

Trovi met my eyes and held my gaze. "Then perhaps it's time you stop running from all this," she said quietly. "and start rewriting it."

Her words landed like cold iron, their weight settling beneath my skin. For the first time, my fear twisted into something sharper, with calculated purpose.

"I have already rewritten my path… according to the dark völva …" I said, the words fading out.

'Odin, reborn?' The thought rippled through me like a storm tide.

The Allfather, the one who had helped shape the world itself, walking the realms again. If it was true, then maybe the Norns had woven the threads long before I was born. But threads weren't chains… and I had never been very good at following the path laid out for me.

A god's pattern, winding us toward another war. The realization hollowed me. What was choice, if even rebellion had been foretold? What was freedom if the loom had never stopped spinning?

That thought burned in my mind. I'd lived long enough in other people's designs. I wouldn't live in this one either. Fate had always been a noose made of stories, and I had nearly died

more than once with it tight around my throat. I refused to wear its collar again.

My gaze dropped to the bowl of black salt and water Trovi had set aside. The surface quivered, as though stirred by an unseen wind. Runes etched along its rim began to smolder, the lines of light breathing, then fracturing, one by one.

My reflection wavered, as if something unseen followed close on our heels, then blurred until my face was no longer mine. Something vast and shadowed, eyes like twin eclipses, my new wolf's eyes. For a heartbeat, it felt as if the world itself was holding its breath.

My hands curled into fists, my nails biting into my palms as I whispered, "I won't let my fate be written by the gods anymore."

Mani's voice rippled through me, a growl laced with amusement. *'Let him rise. I've been itching to teach a god what happens when you pick fights with things that bite.'*

Despite everything, a laugh slipped from me, half disbelief and half defiance. *'You'd bite Odin?'*

'Please,' she scoffed, *'I'm sure all Gods taste like arrogance and old mead. I've bitten worse.'*

I let out a small laugh and looked up at Trovi. Her gaze was locked onto the bowl. The runes had gone dark, cracked and faintly smoking, as if burned from the inside out.

Her breath caught. "By the Norns…" she whispered, her eyes wide, and awe and dread warring in her voice. "She's broken her thread."

For a long moment, none of us moved. The air was still, yet the world itself felt subtly altered, nudged just off its axis.

Outside, the raven cried again harsh and echoing through the mist as it took flight.

It didn't sound like a warning anymore.
It sounded like a challenge.

Chapter 24

The sun had climbed above the mountains, a pale gold disk muted by thinning clouds, its light weak and wintry. The air held that brittle cold of early winter—the kind that came before the first heavy snowfall, when the world seemed to pause and listen. Morning mist clung stubbornly to Trovi's garden, drifting low around the half-buried stones and the charred edges of the ritual circle. The air was sharp with salt and smoke, carrying the charged stillness of rain held back by ice, like the moment just before the sky broke open.

Andrew stood a few paces from the table, his brows furrowed, his eyes flicking between the bowl and Trovi's drawn face. "What just happened?" he asked quietly. He hadn't seen what I'd seen, hadn't felt the reflection twist or the runes split open beneath my gaze.

Trovi didn't answer right away. Her eyes were fixed on the fractured markings etched along the bowl's rim, where faint smoke still hissed. "I saw it," she murmured, almost to herself. "And the bowl saw *her.*"

Andrew frowned, still glancing between us. "Saw her? What does that mean?" But even as he spoke, his voice faltered.

Before she could answer, the mist over the garden shifted, rolling inward toward the circle as if drawn by an unseen tide. The air seemed to bend, not violently, but with a strange reverence, as though the world itself hovered on the edge of a breath.

I felt Mani smirk. *'Another day, another near apocalypse. Standard procedure.'*

My skin prickled with the memory of those splintered reflections, of every version of myself staring back from the silver lake.

Trovi finally tore her gaze from the bowl and looked at me. "You felt it," she said. "The break."

I swallowed. "I think…I did."

Andrew's confusion deepened. "You're both acting like something in that bowl just woke up." He stepped closer, cautiously, and leaned over the table. The water inside had stilled, just black and depthless, reflecting only the faint gray light of morning. He frowned and glanced back at me. "Astrid… none of this makes sense."

I could feel Andrew's uncertainty like a tremor through our bond, his mind searching for logic in a moment that had none.

Trovi's expression softened, but her voice remained grave. "That's because Astrid changed her fate… and in doing so, likely altered yours as well. Fate doesn't reveal itself to those who stand outside its thread." Her eyes cut back to me, steady and intent. "But it recognized you."

The words settled between us like smoke. Andrew's jaw tightened, and his eyes locked on mine with a sharp worry that made my chest tighten. His hand brushed mine, just a flicker of contact, but it set a current through me, pulling, warning, and intimate all at once. It also warned me how thin the ground beneath us had become.

Then the sound broke the silence. A harsh, rasping chorus, wings beating against the morning haze. Ravens, dozens, maybe hundreds, descended from the mist, settling on

the edges of the circle, on gnarled branches, the roof, the stones. The fog swirled low over Trovi's garden. Their eyes glinted like scattered ink drops in the pale sunlight, and the air seemed to tremble under the weight of their wings.

Andrew's hand tightened around mine. "Visitors?" he murmured, voice uneasy, looking to Trovi.

Trovi's face hardened. "Not the kind that knock."

As she finished, Trovi's eyes narrowed. She said nothing as she turned from the kitchen and headed towards the front door, her steps slow and deliberate, each one falling with the certainty of a woman who knew exactly where the threshold lay. The floor seemed to hush beneath her feet. Andrew and I followed close behind, tension winding through us like drawn wire.

She reached the door and pulled it open, the cool air brushing her face. The mist from the garden drifted inward, curling along the threshold, but she didn't hesitate. With one fluid motion, she stepped onto the porch, shoulders squared, eyes fixed on the approaching shapes.

Her fingers brushed against the railing, tracing the carved runes etched into the wood. "Not past here," she said, voice calm but sharp, cutting through the fog like steel. The air seemed to pulse around her, as if the porch itself had become a barrier no one could cross.

Shapes emerged from the swirling gray, elongated shadows, moving with unnatural grace. For a heartbeat, they looked human, then wavered, edges flickering like smoke caught on a breeze.

The shadows solidified into figures clad in dark gray cloaks, faces veiled, eyes faintly glowing like dying embers.

Between them stepped a man, tall, sharp-featured, and utterly calm.

"Völundr," Trovi hissed. The name landed heavy, full of old anger.

"Völundr?" Andrew repeated as we looked at each other.

'Who is that?' Mani asked.

The man smiled faintly. "Still breathing, I see," he said, his voice smooth as oil. "You always did have a knack for surviving the forge." His gaze slid to me, sharp and curious. "And this must be the girl who cracks runes without touching them." He paused, then added, almost theatrically, "Please, my name is Verrik. Völundr is only my title."

For a moment, the world seemed to warp around him. He was broad-shouldered, and heat radiated from him, not blazing, but relentless, like a forge banked too long. His skin gleamed like dark bronze, patterned, as if metal itself had cooled into flesh. His amber eyes caught the light, smoldering even in the shadow, bright enough to burn, yet cold and assessing, as if the forge itself had tempered his gaze.

His hair was a wild sweep of black streaked hair with copper, curling like smoke caught mid-rise, and the faint haze drifting from him smelled of hot metal and ash, tangling in my senses. I felt it even from this distance, the warmth radiating from him.

Every motion he made carried weight, deliberate and precise. Power didn't cling to him; it had been forged into his bones. When he tilted his head back in Trovi's direction, that intensity, that appraisal, settled over my chest like a hand pressing down, equal parts command and challenge. I realized then, with a shiver that wasn't entirely fear, that this wasn't

merely a man but a force: born of fire and iron, beautiful and terrifying in equal measure.

Verrik embodied the essence of creation and destruction in the same breath. He drew the eye the way a flame does, magnetic, dangerous, and beautiful. There was an inevitability about him. Like fire, he could never be contained, only survived.

Trovi's stance didn't waver. She raised one hand slowly, palmed out, as if the very space before her could be molded into a barrier. The wind stirred, rustling the mist, lifting leaves, and feathers into a slow spiral around her like a protective cage.

"You step any closer," she warned, "and you'll find this threshold doesn't forgive trespassers."

Even the shadows standing behind him hesitated, edges quivering as if unsure whether to advance. Andrew moved with me as we stepped closer to Trovi, his shoulder nearly brushing mine, tension tightening every line of his posture.

Trovi's eyes met mine briefly, a flash of warning, and something fiercer, older, born of years spent defending what could not be taken lightly.

Mani bristled inside me, claws scraping against my ribs. *'He reeks of the forge…of bound souls.'*

"You know him?" Andrew asked Trovi under his breath.

"He's from a lineage of smiths of the old realm," Trovi said. "Maker of weapons, the Völundr's are known for their exceptional skills."

Verrik's smile didn't reach his eyes. "And now, perhaps, a collector of rarities. You two shine too brightly to be left unsupervised."

The shadows flanking him began to spread, seeping through the ground like oil. Their movements were wrong, silent and slow, yet everywhere at once.

Andrew's wings flickered into existence, shadows unfurling across his shoulders. I felt the pulse of our bond surge in answer. Power calling to power, raw, unsteady, and dangerous.

"Careful," Trovi warned, stepping back toward her doorway. "If you break what remains of the wards, this place won't hold."

But it was already too late. One of the shadows lunged. Andrew moved without hesitation. His hand snapped out, fingers closing around the shifting dark mid-strike. It fought him immediately, slick and freezing, twisting like living smoke, but he held fast, his muscles locking as if he'd seized something solid and furious. The shadow recoiled, straining against his grip, its edges tearing and reforming as it tried to escape.

I didn't think. I reacted.

My hand plunged into the smoke-thin edge of another shadow. The cold bit deep, seeping into my bones as it writhed against me, resisting, pulling back like a living thing that knew it was being claimed.

The instant I connected with the darkness, everything *stopped.*

The shadows froze mid-lunge, their forms shuddering as if caught between moments. Panic rippled through them, raw and instinctive, surprised to be seized, to be *answered* by forces they hadn't anticipated. The runes etched into my palms flared, pale-blue light blazing to life. I pressed my hands deeper into the shadow and willed it to dissipate.

It screamed, if it could be called that It wasn't a sound so much as a sensation, but a grinding, tearing howl like molten metal being stretched past its breaking point. The shadow buckled under my touch, unraveling, its edges burning away in streaks of light and smoke.

'They...they didn't expect this,' Mani grinned excitedly, exhilaration sharp in her voice. *'Did you feel that? You're not fighting them... you're commanding them.'*

"I…I think I am," I whispered, as I stared at my palm in awe of the runes etched into my skin.

The runes blazed brighter, their pale-blue lines crawling from my skin into the shadows themselves, binding, reshaping, *searing*. The darkness shrieked again, thrashing wildly—but it couldn't break free. It bent. It listened.

"I never thought…" My breath shook with awe and disbelief. "I never thought we could control them like this."

'They're ours,' Mani growled, fierce and protective. *'Every shadow that comes near you answers us now. Every. Last. One.'*

Trovi stood frozen, her eyes wide, and her jaw tight. She couldn't speak, she could only watch as Andrew and I twist the shadows like wet clay, our power reshaping it in real time. Shock warred with fear across her face… and beneath it, something close to wonder.

"They didn't see that coming," Andrew muttered, a sharp grin breaking through the tension.

Across the garden Verrik tilted his head, amused. "You see?" he said smoothly. "You wield your power like children. So afraid of what might happen when you stop holding back."

Something inside me snapped.

"We're just getting started," I said, and the words left my mouth like a command.

Power surged through me, raw and hungry, flooding through my veins and into the shadows. Andrew's energy flared beside mine, his dark wings rippling as his power tangled with mine—shadow and light spiraling together in a violent, beautiful storm. The darkness obeyed instantly, coiling tighter, pulsing beneath our combined grip.

For one suspended heartbeat, the world *bent around us*.

The shadows locked in place, their forms shimmering, trapped between light and void. My pulse thundered. I could feel it then—the terrible, intoxicating ease of letting go. Of ending this. Of erasing them completely.

Then Andrew's hand caught my arm. "Astrid, stop."

His voice cut clean through the chaos of my thoughts, pulling me back. His touch reminded me what control meant, not weakness, but a choice. The bond between us steadied, the chaos thinning into breath.

The remaining shadows hesitated, as if suddenly unsure of their own existence.

Verrik's smirk faded. "Interesting." He tilted his head slightly. "You're learning… quickly. That makes you dangerous."

He retreated, the mist folded in on itself, swallowing him whole. And just like that, he was gone. The shadows dissolved into nothing, leaving behind only the faint scent of smoke and hot metal, the echo of power still humming in the air.

For a long moment, none of us moved. The garden felt hollow without the pressure of his presence.

Trovi swayed where she stood, one hand gripping the porch railing. The faint glow of her wards flickered once… twice… then guttered out completely.

"Trovi," I murmured, crossing the distance before she could protest.

Her skin was clammy beneath my fingers, color leeched from her face. Holding the threshold had clearly cost her more than she let on. I slipped an arm beneath hers and guided her inside.

She didn't resist, just sank into the nearest chair by the hearth, with a shaky exhale. "I'll be fine," she said, though the tremor in her voice betrayed her. "Just… gods, I haven't gained as much of my strength back like I had hoped…"

Andrew emerged from the kitchen without a word, a mug of water in hand. He pressed it gently into Trovi's grasp. Her fingers shook as she lifted it, the surface rippling faintly with each unsteady breath.

After a long sip, she let out a sharp exhale, eyes half-lidded beneath the exhaustion. "Tell me," she said softly, "what did you feel when you touched them… the shadows?"

The question stole the air from my lungs. I swallowed, the memory raw and vivid. "Like they knew me," I murmured.

Andrew leaned against the wall, his jaw tight. "They tried to fight back, but instead they listened. That's what surprised me the most."

Trovi's mouth curved faintly, caught somewhere between pride and worry. "Then you've learned something most don't until it's far too late," she said. "The shadows don't answer to fear. They answer to intent."

Her gaze moved between us, me kneeling beside her with worry all over my face, Andrew leaning back on the wall with his arms crossed, and she sighed. “Just be certain whose intent they’re listening to.”

A flicker of warmth passed over her face, quickly overtaken by weariness. Then she murmured, almost to herself, “That is how you learn.” Then her eyes sharpened as they lifted to ours again. “But this Völundr… Verrik… doesn’t come without reason. Whatever happened in that bowl… it isn’t just fate that’s shifting now.” Her voice lowered. “It’s who’s watching.”

Mani rolled her eyes, her voice dry as ever. *‘Someone is always watching,’* I couldn’t help but agree with her.

Andrew’s gaze drifted toward the fog beyond the window, where the last trace of Völundr had vanished. His voice was tight. “Well, we just sent a message that we’re not afraid to fight.”

Trovi shook her head slowly, a ghost of a smile tugging at her lips. “No,” she said quietly. “You just showed them you’re learning… and quickly”

I moved closer to her as she put the mug down on the coffee table, brushing a strand of hair from her face. “Rest now, Trovi. We’ll get some food and come back.” I helped her lie on her small couch and I placed a blanket over her.

She nodded tiredly, eyes slipping closed. A faint shiver ran through her, the effort of holding the threshold evident in the slump of her shoulders, but for the first time in hours, she looked like she might actually let herself breathe.

I exchanged a glance with Andrew. “Pack house?”

He nodded, offering a small, fleeting smile. “Pack house.”

We left her there, resting, and stepped out into the early afternoon light. The tension of the morning lingered, heavy and unresolved.

Outside, the mist thickened around the garden's edge, listening still. Somewhere beyond it, a raven cried, no longer in warning, but in quiet, unmistakable satisfaction.

Chapter 25

The Pack house smelled of roasted meat and fresh bread. It was warm and inviting, offering a fragile tether to normalcy. Conversation hummed around us, laughter spilling from the kitchen, the clatter of plates, the sounds nearly made me forget what was waiting outside these walls. Almost.

Andrew moved ahead of me, balancing two trays as we looked for a table. I followed close behind, but my mind kept drifting. Being pulled by something beyond the chatter and clinking dishes, a ripple in the air, a signature I'd felt briefly before.

Naomi.

The moment we sat down, I closed my eyes and drew a slow breath.

'*Focus,*' Mani said trying to help.

The room softened at the edges. This shadow energy that coiled around me, it was elusive, like trying to catch smoke, not to use as a weapon, but as a conduit. My hand twitched instinctively as my runes sparked briefly across my palm. I forced them to dim binding threads of light. I wasn't here to destroy. I just wanted to reach her, if I could.

'You're trembling again,' Mani murmured, low and steady.

'I can feel her,' I whispered, fighting the shake in my hands. *'Can't you feel it? Like she's close… but just out of reach.'*

'I feel a pull,' Mani said warily. '*It's faint, but it's there.*'

'I know she wants our help,' I whispered. *'We've seen it... she's trapped.'*

'Careful, Astrid,' Mani warned, *'If you reach too far, the dark völva might snare you before we even get close to her again.'*

I swallowed hard, letting the words settle.

'Remember what Trovi said,' Mani continued, softer now. *'Intent. The shadows don't just obey... they listen. If you let them, they might help you find her... even if she's buried deep.'*

'Then maybe I can help her find her way out,' I said, though the tremor in my voice betrayed me.

'Start with trust,' Mani replied. *'Yourself first. Then I'm sure that hers will follow.'*

The shadows seemed to breathe with me, curling and uncoiling through the hollow space of my thoughts. I closed my eyes and drew a slow breath, centering on that fragile thread tightening in my chest.

'I will find her.' The vow struck hard and true. I wanted to reach through that invisible tether, to *grab hold* of the thread I felt, and refuse the distance that separated us.

In my mind's eye, I reached for it, the faint shimmer of connection, thin as spider silk, trembling but intact.

The instant my fingers met it, the world shifted beneath me. The connection snapped into place at once, fine and fragile as a thread.

I wasn't sitting anymore, I was standing.

When I opened my eyes, I was in a vast, glowing black of nothingness that stretched in every direction. It was empty but something was *watching*, its darkness alive with a low, pulsing sheen, like obsidian warmed from within. There was no floor and no sky, only the sensation of movement, of being carried forward by intent alone.

Suspended within the void was a structure of glass and light, or what remained of one.

Fragments drifted in slow orbit around me, each shard glowing faintly against the black, memories caught mid-shatter. There were different faces, voices, and laughter that fractured into sharp, silent echoes. Anger split clean down the center. Longing warped and bent, its edges jagged and dangerous to touch.

I moved carefully between them, each step deliberate, as though this place itself would punish carelessness.

This place had once been whole.

A house built of memory, of identity… of Naomi.

Now it hung in ruin, suspended in the dark like a broken constellation.

The damage wasn't random. Impact points scarred what remained of the walls, concentric fractures radiating outward, spiderwebbing through the glass. I could *feel* the intent behind them. Stones thrown with patience. With purpose. The dark völva hadn't rushed this destruction.

He had tested her, over and over.

Naomi flickered at the center of the wreckage, her form dim but defiant, barely holding herself together. Her energy trembled, scattered among the drifting shards, but beneath the ruin, the spark that had always made her, *her,* still burned stubborn and bright.

"Naomi…" My voice carried strangely, as if it was swallowed and returned to me altered, thinner. "It's me, Astrid. I'm here."

For a single breath, everything stilled. The drifting shards slowed, their fractured edges hanging motionless in the dark. Even the void dimmed, as if the nothingness itself had leaned in to listen. Naomi's amethyst eyes lifted, blinking as though surfacing from deep water.

Recognition sparked.

Then the void *reacted.*

A crushing pressure slammed through the space. The black glow flared harsh and blinding as an unseen force tore through the suspended fragments. The shards exploded outward, screaming without sound, and pain ripped through me, white-hot, absolute. I gasped and staggered, knowing with sick certainty that I was feeling only a fraction of what Naomi endured.

This place was no longer hers alone.

The dark völva surged into the ruins like a thrown storm, his presence violent and deliberate. He twisted the fragments as he passed, corrupting their light, wrenching control away with ruthless precision.

Naomi screamed, her presence splintering further. And in that moment I understood, with chilling clarity, that I wasn't just walking through what was left of her memories. I had stepped into a ruin the dark völva was still actively breaking.

The glowing black void convulsed as his presence poured in, a pressure like a fist closing around the broken glass of Naomi's mind. The drifting shards twisted, their light sickening, bending inward as if dragged by an unseen gravity. Cracks sealed themselves—not repaired, but *reordered*, forced into a new, cruel symmetry.

I watched Naomi at the center of it. Her form buckled, the light folding in on itself as something *else* slid beneath her skin. Her posture straightened unnaturally, jerking upright like a marionette pulled upright by invisible strings. The defiant spark in her eyes flared once, bright and desperate, and then it was smothered.

Her body became a threshold.

The dark völva moved through her, wearing her like a borrowed shape. Her memories warped around him, reshaping to fit his will. Her expressions hollowed as his presence pressed outward, settling into bone and breath and thought with practiced precision.

Her mouth opened. But the voice that emerged was not Naomi's. His presence lashed through the link between us like a whip, venomous and intimate, twisting her intentions, her thoughts until they were unrecognizable. Agony detonated through me, white-hot and blinding. My lungs seized and my vision tore apart into static.

But I still felt her there inside him, trapped and screaming.

The world tilted violently. I would have fallen if not for the steady weight of Andrew's hands anchoring my shoulders, holding me upright as the connection burned through every nerve.

And with sickening clarity, I understood—

I wasn't walking through the remnants of Naomi's memories. I was standing inside a body that had been taken.

"Astrid!" Andrew hissed, careful not to draw attention. "What are you doing? What's wrong?"

I clenched my jaw and forced the pain down, gathering myself around a single point of control. The shadows surged

instinctively, tendrils flaring, eager and dangerous—but I didn't meet their hunger with fear.

I *guided* them, whispering to them. *Not as chains, but as shelter.*

The shadow threads hesitated, pulsing in response to my intent, then shifted, stretching toward Naomi in soft, protective ribbons of both light and shadow intertwined. I wove them around her carefully, not to bind, not to cage, but to shield her. To give her choice where the dark völva had stolen it.

Something in her shifted. Her presence flickered, the suffocating darkness thinning just enough for a single thought to slip through, raw, shaking, and unmistakably her:
'I didn't know it would be like this.'

I exhaled, relief crashing through me even as dread followed close behind. The dark pressure struck again, hammering at the edges of my control, but I held. My hands glowed faintly, my veins humming with restrained energy. This was new, dangerous territory, unfamiliar ground, and one wrong step would cost us both. My will had to hold steady. I would not let the dark völva pull me into her abyss.

Andrew leaned close, whispering, "Astrid..."

I swallowed hard, forcing my breath steady, keeping the fragile thread between us from snapping completely. "I… I reached her," I whispered. "She's still in there."

Trovi's warning echoed through my mind: *Be certain whose intent they're listening to.* I tightened my focus, letting the words ground me. The shadows weren't my chains, they were my voice, my will. They answered intent. If I lost that clarity, even for a heartbeat, Naomi would slip beneath the dark völva's grasp forever.

The connection shuddered once, then it steadied, weak and flickering, but alive. Naomi's presence hovered at the edge of the dark, her thoughts fluttering like moth wings against a storm. Slowly and carefully, I withdrew, drawing the link back until it dimmed to a soft pulse. Leaving behind a faint echo. A door not fully closed, but a choice she could reach for.

When the link finally broke, the silence that followed was deafening. My strength gave out all at once. I sagged forward, collapsing against the table, the cool surface pressing against my forehead as my chest heaved for air.

'How did you know what to do?' Mani murmured, her voice full of quiet awe. *'You... like... guided them.'*

I let out a shaky breath, the shadows still curled faintly around my thoughts, pulsing in time with my heart. *'They... just listened.'* I replied, still half in disbelief.

Mani was quiet for a moment, then softer still. *'You didn't reach for power to fight, you reached to protect.'* A pause, soft and wondering. *'I didn't even know the shadows could respond...at all... let alone like that,'*

A shiver ran through me, not from fear but from the truth. Naomi's fractured presence lingered in my thoughts, along with the certainty that intent mattered more than strength. For the first time in a long while, I felt it—not mastery, not yet—but the beginning of something real. Something mine. Something where the gods have no say in my fate.

"You're quiet," he said, drawing me back.

"Just thinking," I muttered, nudging a piece of bread around my plate. "About what Trovi said... about intent."

He gave a low hum, somewhere between agreement and unease. "I don't think she's wrong. I could feel them... the shadows. Like they're waiting for something."

I met his gaze. "It didn't feel wrong," I admitted softly. "Just… awake."

Before he could respond, we both felt the air in the room shift. It was subtle at first, like the pressure before a storm. Then came the heat, thick and heavy with the scent of hot iron. The room's easy chatter faltered. Laughter thinned. The hum of the Pack house dulled to an uneasy hush as a figure crossed the cafeteria threshold, his presence warping the air like heat over stone.

Verrik stepped through the doorway. The light warped around him, as though the sun itself couldn't decide whether to touch him or retreat. His body seemed to drink the brightness of the day, sending it back in distorted waves. His boots struck the floor with measured weight, and behind him followed familiar figures from Trovi's house, each radiating that same muted, unnatural energy.

My fork froze midair. Andrew froze beside me. The space between us felt electric.

Verrik didn't look our way at first. He and his companions moved with the casual ease of predators who already owned the room. They claimed a table across the dining hall, still far too close for comfort, and too deliberate to be a coincidence. As he sat in his chair, his head turned and our eyes met immediately.

His amber eyes cut across the cafeteria like molten fire, locking onto me with a weight that pinned me in place. A slow, mocking smirk curved his mouth, before his gaze slid to Andrew, tipping his chin in a silent challenge.

Andrew's hand found mine under the table, steady but tense. I could feel the power coiling beneath his skin, the urge to rise, and protect what was his. I met his eyes and gave the smallest shake of my head.

"Not here." I murmured. "Not with this many people."

He didn't like it, but he understood.

We stayed seated, forcing ourselves to breathe, to finish eating, and to act as though everything was fine. Around us, conversation flickered back into life in uneven, uneasy ripples, unaware that something dangerous now sat only a few tables away.

Mani's voice came low and certain: *'He's not done.'*

I swallowed against the tightness in my throat, power buzzing beneath my skin, aching to be unleashed. Andrew's hand squeezed mine under the table, but even that couldn't ease the knot of tension coiling in my chest.

The moment my eyes met Verrik's again, the sound hit me, not outside, not distant, but *heard*. The measured clang of a hammer on steel ringing through my skull, slow and deliberate, as if some unseen forge had flared to life the instant he saw me.

A cold certainty settled into my bones. Whatever came next wasn't chaos or chance. It was being shaped and measured, to be forged with intent.

I drew in a slow, steady breath, holding his gaze. '*We're not done either.*'

Chapter 26

Across the room, Verrik leaned back, one arm draped lazily over the chair beside him, exuding a calm so sharp it cut. His allies mirrored his ease, too deliberate and synchronized. For a fleeting heartbeat, the cafeteria itself seemed to hold its breath, laughter thinning to a meaningless hum against the gravity of the power gathering in that corner.

The shadows reacted before I did, slipping beneath the tables, quiet and unseen, as they reached for Verrik. Smoke-like tendrils unfurled, uncertain yet wanting.

Mani's voice followed, low and almost lost beneath the noise. *'You just said there were too many people. Let's just be ready.'*

I blinked, my pulse quickening, only then sensing the faint hum of power still rippling from my fingertips. I hadn't meant to reach for him; the shadows had acted on their own, but following my intent, not a command.

I forced my shoulders to loosen and drew in a slow breath, letting the energy coil tighter beneath my skin. Verrik hadn't moved, but every second he sat there, every glance, every smirk, felt like a warning. He was assessing, testing, and marking the battlefield, even if that battlefield looked like an ordinary cafeteria full of clattering trays and oblivious laughter.

I could *feel* the invisible tension between us stretching taut.

Beneath the table, my thumb anxiously drew small circles on Andrew's hand, and he squeezed once in response, no words were needed. One glance between us was enough to understand.

Then I heard it again.

The faint, rhythmic clang of hammer on steel, louder this time. Like a countdown.

Then a shrill wail split the air. The fire alarm screamed to life, piercing and chaotic, red lights strobing across every surface. Chairs scraped, trays clattered, and the once-placid room dissolved into motion. Students shouted, some laughing nervously, while others ran for the exits.

Even with the blaring chaos, Verrik didn't move. His allies remained seated, statues carved from arrogance. Through the flashing red lights, his gaze locked on mine, unyielding, daring me to look away, but I refused.

Andrew rose, scanning the crowd. "Red?"

She was across the room, one hand on the alarm lever. The other already glowing faintly, her fingers haloed in the soft flare of controlled flame. Her eyes met mine, and she was calm and fierce.

'She wouldn't have done this without a reason.'

The last stragglers cleared out, doors slamming shut behind them. The shriek of the alarm cut off mid-wail, leaving behind a silence so thick it felt alive. Then, the lights flickered.

Verrik's group rose in unison, slowly almost bored, their chairs scraping in eerie harmony as shadows bled off them, slow at first, then faster. Like black ink spilled across the floor, swallowing the linoleum, the tables, the walls. The air itself seemed to warp around them. Faces distorted, melting into the dark that pooled beneath their feet until only silhouettes remained.

Everything disappeared into the darkness, everything except us.

Mani growled, reverberating through my bones. *'Now.'*

Red moved first. Not with a charge, but with a breath. She lifted her palms, her fingers unfurling like a dancer finding her opening note, and the light in her hands bloomed. It was controlled. Fire answered her the way silk answers motion. Gold and crimson ribbons spilled from her wrists, coiling around her arms in smooth, spiraling arcs.

She stepped forward and the flames followed.

Red turned, pivoting on the ball of her foot. The fire swept with her in long fluid streams cutting elegant paths through the air. Each movement was precise, practiced, and graceful, as if she were ribbon dancing across the floor. Except her ribbons burned.

She slashed her arm downward, and the fire cracked like thunder. The ribbons snapped outward, colliding with the oncoming shadows in a blinding surge of heat and light. The impact tore through the room, static and flame rattling my bones as a shockwave skidded chairs across the floor and sent ash spiraling toward the ceiling.

Red didn't stop.

She spun again, fire tracing her silhouette, carving through the dark forms with lethal beauty. Where the ribbons passed, shadows peeled apart, unraveling like scorched cloth. For a heartbeat, I saw them, humanoid and reaching. But they just broke.

The Odin agents screamed without mouths as their outlines twisted and scattered, hurled backward into nothing, burned down to vapor by controlled fury.

Red slowed, drawing her arms inward and the fire obeyed, curling back toward her wrists, dimming to a steady, molten glow. Smoke drifted upward, the room still sizzling in her wake.

I just stood there frozen, my breath caught in my throat. My skin prickled with the energy that lingered in the air, every molecule charged, every ember still burning bright in the air between us.

'Gods,' I thought. '*She's stronger than before.'*

Mani went still, her growl fading into stunned silence. '*She's learned control,'* Mani murmured, half in awe, half in disbelief. 'P*ower with purpose.'*

Then suddenly the awe I felt twisted sharply into guilt. I'd spent so long buried in the library, chasing runes, dissecting old prophecies, losing myself in histories and ghosts, that I had forgotten to notice her, and help that she might have needed, her training, turning into this…a complete badass.

We used to spar together. Laugh until we couldn't breathe. Now I barely remember the last time we'd shared a meal. My throat tightened. I hadn't meant to drift away, but obsession and fear had consumed everything.

Mani's voice softened, more thoughtful. *'She's still our friend, Astrid. She never stopped being our pack. Some bonds don't fade. They just wait for you to look up again.'*

Now, watching her command that inferno like it was always a part of her soul, I realized I hadn't just lost time. I'd missed the moment she became who she was meant to be.

Andrew stepped forward, wings unfurling halfway with a low, resonant hum. Shadowed light traced the edges, sharp and dangerous, as if they could cut the air itself. His eyes

burned red, rimmed in black, tracking every breath Verrik took, every micro-shift of muscle and intent. Atius.

I moved to Andrews and Atius's side instinctively, our energies slipping together like they'd always belonged. Power threaded between us, dark and light interweaving in a rhythm that felt predatory and protective all at once.

Verrik smiled slow, bones cracking softly, as if warming up before something he'd waited far too long for. "Finally," he said, voice edged with relish.

He struck first. For his massive size, he was terrifyingly fast. A burst of heat that was razor-sharp, as he cut across the room. Andrew deflected with a sweep of his arm, shadows curling into a shield that absorbed the blow. The impact rang out like steel grinding on steel.

Andrew reacted on instinct. He swept his arm up, shadows surging to meet the blow, folding into a dense shield just in time. The impact detonated with a shockwave rattling windows and shuddering through the floor. Verrik let out a satisfied laugh that was hungry. He came again, his fists crashing down like hammer strikes, each blow carrying enough force to shatter bone. Andrew caught the first, blocked the second, but the third slammed into his chest with brutal precision. Sending him sprawling into a table and shattering it. Dust and magic burst outward in a violent wave as Andrew was thrown back, skidding across the floor in a spray of debris.

"NO!" I shouted.

The shadows answered before I finished the thought. Like living smoke tore across the floor, snapping through the air with a crack of dark light as they lunged for Verrik.

He twisted away at the last second, fast but heavy, each motion dense and deliberate, like iron dragged into motion.

Then his fist struck Andrew again. I felt it through our bond, a flash of pain, a spike of fear that stole my breath. Andrew staggered, his vision blurring, his wings twitching as he struggled to stay upright.

Verrik's grin widened. He was enjoying it, he was living for it. For the impact. For the sound of breath forced from lungs. For the way Andrew's power flared in defiance.

Verrik's laughter deepened, vibrating through the floor. "There it is," he said, eyes alight with predatory delight. "That spark beneath your ribs. That hunger for Power."

His voice slithered through the air, rich and coaxing, threading itself into me, into the shadows that trembled beneath my skin. "You could end this, Astrid. You could end me." Each word pressing closer, heavier. "You've felt it, haven't you? That dark pulse under your skin. The thing that makes you stronger." His gaze burned into mine. "The light won't save you here."

The words sank deep, too deep. Threading into something inside me aching to be acknowledged. The shadows within me quivered, no longer passive, no longer waiting. They were listening.

"Step into it," Verrik whispered, his tone turning intimate and cruelly tender. "The dark knows you. It's been waiting for you to stop pretending you're not one of us."

Mani's snarl cut through. '*Don't listen.*' But gods, it was *tempting.*

The air pulsed with Verrik's power, thick and intoxicating, and it *answered* something in me. A vast, terrible presence stirred beneath my ribs, coiling, stretching, eager to rise. The shadows leaned toward him, yearning, reaching for release.

"Do it," he murmured, madness flashing behind his eyes as his grin widened. "Embrace it. Let the dark claim you."

For a heartbeat… I almost did. It felt like standing on the edge of a storm, where surrender promised flight and ruin in equal measure. One step, and I could drown the world in shadow. One breath, and everything would burn.

It would be so easy, too easy.

Mani's voice cut through the haze, fierce and unyielding. *'If you take that step, the dark völva wins. That's the path they want you to take.'*

My breath shuddered out, sharp and uneven. The decision struck like lightning. "No."

Verrik lunged again and Andrew met him mid-strike, their collision exploding through the room like thunder. Darkness and light scattered outward, sparks skittering across the walls in violent streaks of color. I felt every impact through the bond, every jolt of force, every strained breath, every frantic heartbeat, and I matched him instinctively, my power rising to meet his.

"No…!" The word tore from me, raw and desperate.

The world buckled. Sound warped and stretched thin, then vanished altogether. The air shimmered, and the motes of dust hanging midair froze. Light fractured and hung suspended, brittle and unreal. Time itself held its breath. Everything stilled, everything, except me.

Verrik's fist hovered inches from Andrew's jaw. A thin line of blood arced between them, caught in motion like a ruby suspended in glass. My chest heaved. I hadn't meant to do it, hadn't even thought about this power in months. But instinct had taken the reins, and all I could think, all I could *feel*, was the need to stop it. To stop *him.*

I stepped forward. Each movement sending ripples through the frozen world, the air shimmered, resisting me like thick water. Light bent around my body, warping as I passed. I reached for Andrew, brushing my fingers against his cheek. His skin was cold, but beneath it his pulse was steady and strong. Relief hit me so hard my knees almost buckled.

Mani's voice cut through the silence, calm but urgent. *'Easy, Astrid. Don't get ahead of yourself.'*

I forced my breathing to slow, scanning the still world around us. Verrik's suspended fist hung inches from Andrew's jaw. The blood in the air gleaming like scattered rubies. Shards of light hung suspended midair, the shockwave of their last clash caught between moments.

Then I saw it…threads. Thin, snaking lines bleeding from Verrik's body, pulsing faintly with corrupted magic. They twisted and converged, all of them anchored deep within his chest.

Mani's voice was steady and deliberate. *'See where it flows. The threads power is anchored in his chest… there, near the heart. Do you think that if we sever that, and the rest collapses?'*

I swallowed hard, a fear threatening to break my focus. *'Guess we'll find out.'*

Power surged through me, wild and electric, thrumming just shy of breaking loose. The runes on my palms flared to life, hot and hungry, drinking in the storm gathering beneath my skin. Light and shadow twisted together, coiling through my veins until every heartbeat burned.

I forced everything, my fear, my fury, and my resolve into my hands, then placed one hand over Verrik's heart. The markings blazed brighter, veins of molten light threading up my

arms. Verrik's frozen grin taunted me still, cruel and confident, daring me to falter.

'Now,' Mani whispered. *'Release it.'*

I exhaled.

The world snapped back into motion.

The blast detonated like a thunderclap. Raw power tore through the runes and slammed into Verrik's chest. The impact sent him hurling backward, slamming into the far wall with a sound that cracked both tile and bone.

Andrew was already moving. He grabbed Verrik by his collar and hauled him upright. The grin was gone now, stripped away, replaced by disbelief trembling at the edges of his mouth.

As Verrik's weight sagged and the last of his awareness slipped away, the shadows slithered back like serpents.

They didn't vanish all at once, they just began to withdraw, sliding back along the walls, draining from the ceiling like spilled ink being pulled into unseen cracks. The oppressive pressure that had twisted the air loosened, the magic unraveling thread by thread. The cafeteria reasserted itself in fragments: scattered tables, overturned chairs, and shattered light fixtures flickering weakly overhead.

What remained was devastation. Tile was cracked and scorched, tables splintered or reduced to twisted frames. Glass glittered across the floor like frost. Burn marks and shadow scars stained the walls, refusing to fade completely, as if the room itself remembered what had passed through it.

Red stepped through the thinning haze, her fire dimmed to a shimmer. Her eyes gleamed with fierce satisfaction as she tossed something toward me. A pair of arm bracers etched with runes that pulsed faintly yellow.

"Trovi said you'd need this," she rasped, her voice raw but steady. "For Bo. She saw…something coming." Her gaze flicking to Verrik. "Said this will keep him human, long enough to matter."

I caught them easily. The bracers vibrated against my palms, alive with residual magic.

Mani's voice was threaded with pride and inevitability. *"One down. Many more to come."*

Outside, silence pressed against the windows, heavy, almost sacred in its stillness even in the sunlight. Inside, the air still shimmered with leftover magic, thick with ozone and ash. The cafeteria looked like itself again in shape only, a familiar place hollowed out and broken, its normalcy an illusion stretched thin over wreckage.

This wasn't victory.

It was survival, stolen time in a war that had already begun. I could feel it in my bones, in the pulse beneath my skin, the quiet before something vast and merciless took notice. Threads I couldn't see were already tightening, drawn taut by hands far beyond my reach.

And somewhere beyond that silence, a force stirred, displeased with how the pieces had fallen.

Chapter 27

The silence didn't last. At first, the air only quivered—so faint I mistook it for the aftershock of magic still humming in my bones. Then it deepened, the vibration settling into something heavier, a pressure that rolled through the room like an approaching tide.

I blinked and looked toward the cafeteria doors. Bo was already there, one hand steady at Trovi's elbow as he guided her up the short flight of steps. Her green cloak whispered over the concrete, each movement deliberate and measured. She leaned into him more than I'd ever seen before, and for the first time, her age showed, in wear. Bo held the door open, letting her enter first.

The words escaped me before I could stop them. "Trovi… how did you know?" My voice caught. "And why…why come here? This could've gone so wrong. Anything could've happened."

Her gaze met mine, calm but unyielding. There was steel there, buried behind gentleness. "Because I saw it would," she said softly. "Because it had to happen now. Because waiting…" Her voice dipped, just slightly. "Waiting would have been worse." She didn't elaborate. She didn't need to.

Bo shot a glance at me, tension sharp in his expression, but I pressed on anyway. "Still, it wasn't safe."

Trovi's expression softened, only a fraction. "Danger isn't always a choice," she said. "Sometimes it's a necessity."

Bo didn't answer. His attention drifted instead to the wreckage around us, tables splintered like kindling, chairs overturned and twisted, scorch marks gouged deep into the tiles. Smoke curled lazily through the ruins. Every detail told the story of the chaos that had erupted here, and he absorbed it all in tense silence, his shoulders tight and jaw set. Then his gaze landed on Verrik.

He lay broken and unmoving, shadow still clinging to him in faint, twitching tendrils, like the last breaths of something dying. For a long moment, Bo simply stood there, taking in the scene. Then he exhaled through his nose, a short, bitter sound, and muttered, "Damn it…" The words carried more sorrow than anger.

His eyes lifted, flicking first to Trovi, and then to me, measuring and searching.

Trovi crossed the room and knelt beside Verrik, her fingers hovering above his chest. The runes on my hands flared softly, answering the corrupted magic that seeped from him the closer I drew.

"He's alive," she said, her voice flat, but edged with certainty. "Barely. Whatever this was, it was meant to kill him outright. It was meant to hollow him out, control him entirely."

Andrew shifted nearby, rolling his shoulder with a sharp hiss as fresh blood soaked into his sleeve. "Then take him," Andrew said hoarsely. "Before something else decides to finish the job."

Bo's eyes flicked to the bracers in my hand. "Trovi said she sent those," he said quietly. "Guess I owe her."

"I think you do," I replied, my voice rough but steady.

Trovi nodded once and extended her hand. "We'll contain him until we know whether he can be saved… or if he's already too far gone."

Something tugged at the edges of my mind, a persistent pull that refused to be ignored. My eyes narrowed, unease tightening my chest. "Why," I whispered, "does it look like he's… leaking?"

Threads bled from Verrik's body, thin, twisting strands of shadow and light, spilling from him like exposed veins. They curled into the air, alive, shimmering faintly in a way no one else seemed to notice. They writhed just beyond the edge of my perception. Visible only if you knew how to look. My breath caught as the pull sharpened, undeniable and intimate, yet completely invisible to everyone around me.

"I… I can see them," I breathed. "The threads… they're coming from him."

For the first time, surprise flicked across Trovi's face. It vanished almost immediately, replaced by something like approval. Then her expression softened, pleased, but grave. "Good," she said quietly. "Follow them, Astrid. Let them guide you. If there's a way to pull him free, these threads will show you the path."

My instincts bristled, nerves sparking with equal parts fear and exhilaration. I stepped toward Verrik, feeling invisible currents snake through the air, tugging insistently at my core. My hand twitched toward the nearest filament, the one pulsing faintly from his chest, as though it recognized me.

"You're sure about this?" I asked, glancing back at Trovi.

"I've never been more certain," Trovi replied. "The threads will lead you."

I exhaled slowly, surrendering to instinct. The pull drew me forward through smoke and scorched tile until I stood over Verrik. The first thread quivered, tightening like it had been waiting for me. When I reached for it, my runes flared soft at first, then searing hot.

The threads weren't just magic. They were veins of corruption, sinewy and alive. I could *feel* where they anchored themselves, tangled deep around his mind and his heart. Each pulse carrying a rhythm that wasn't his own.

They whispered as they shifted. Voices like breath in my ear. "*Come closer… you can feel it too. The dark knows your name.*"

The words slithered through my thoughts, sweet and heavy, pulling me toward something vast and hungry.

'Easy now,' Mani murmured, her voice a low murmur. *'They'll fight you, like they always do.'*

'Doesn't surprise me,' I muttered, sweat breaking along my temple. *'Let's see if we can even…do whatever we're trying to do.'*

I dropped to my knees in front of Verrik and closed my eyes, trying to reach deeper into the unseen threads binding him. The air thickened, vibrating with resistance as I began to pull. The thread in my grip writhed violently, twisting and snarling, fighting to stay buried.

It tightened around my fingers like wire.

Pain flared as the thread bit into my skin. Thin red lines opened across my palms and fingers where it dragged, sharp and hot, but I didn't release it.

One by one, I tore the infected strands free. Each one hissing as it left his body, unraveling into curls of shadowy smoke that evaporated before they could touch the floor.

Verrik convulsed in Bo's grasp, a low, broken sound ripping from his throat, pain, maybe, or relief. Bo held him steady as Trovi's chant rose and fell, steady and ancient. The runes on the bracers blazed to life, their light spilling outward and wrapping around Verrik like a living ward, sealing him off as the retreating darkness tried to clawed for a way back in.

'That's it,' Mani murmured, her presence pressing close, warm and fierce.

The last thread fought harder than the rest. It was coiled tight around Verrik's heart, a living snare buried deep into his flesh and spirit alike. My fingers trembled as I reached for it. The moment I touched it, it twisted, slick and cold as oil, then it snapped taut.

It sliced across my palm.

I gasped as it dragged against my skin, carving thin cuts along my fingers as if the thread itself had teeth. Blood welled instantly, slicking my grip, but I held on.

The thing writhed once, violently, and a surge of frost shot up my arm, biting deep into the bone.

"I can't…" The words tore out of me, thin and shaking.

'Yes, you can.' Mani's voice cut through the panic like steel. *'Just fucking pull.'*

So, I did.

I pulled past the trembling in my limbs, past the sting of blood running down my hands, past the burning ache in my chest, until something deep inside me tore open and answered. The thread screamed as it unraveled. Not a sound heard, but one that vibrated through my bones, my marrow, and my memory. Darkness peeled away in shuddering ribbons before scattering into nothing. And then there was only silence.

When it was done, Verrik sagged fully against Bo. He was pale and trembling; his breath was shallow, but he was alive. The shadows that had infested him were gone. What remained was fragile, barely tethered to the world, but his own once more.

"You did well," Trovi murmured, her voice softer now. "Not all wounds are meant to be healed. Let's see when he wakes."

I swallowed hard, the glow fading from my hands as I looked down at Verrik's still form. "Then let's hope he remembers how all this happened." I let out a small, uneasy breath.

Trovi's gaze found mine again, steady and certain. "One saved," she said. "Now, see where the others lead."

'Great,' Mani muttered. *'More riddles,'* I could feel her rolling her eyes.

Before I could answer, a chill rippled through the air. The space where the last thread had vanished shimmered faintly, reality warping just enough to make my skin prickle. A voice slid through the silence, low and smooth like oil.

"You would unmake what I have bound?" it hissed. *"Your mercy will not go unpunished, little wolf."*

The air curdled. The words crawled over my skin and sank deep, lingering long after the voice faded. I knew that voice. The dark völva had lost a toy, and he was pissed.

Trovi's attention snapped to me. She'd felt it too. Behind us, Bo and the others lifted Verrik carefully.

"All that stirred today," she said softly, "The one causing all this, wasn't done watching us."

I watched as Trovi followed Bo out.

Outside, the clouds above the shattered cafeteria shifted, tearing just enough to reveal a streak of pale gold on the horizon.

'The gods are moving their pieces,' Mani said softly.

'Do you think they are scrambling?' I asked, a tired smirk tugging at my mouth.

'Don't get cocky,' Mani snapped. *'We still have other things to deal with, you know,'*

Her meaning hit me a heartbeat later, Andrew! I turned and found him slumped against an overturned table, one hand pressed to his shoulder. Blood soaked his sleeve, dark and tacky, the edges crusted with soot and debris. The fabric torn where Verrik's blow had landed.

"Hey," I said softly, crouching beside him. His eyes flicked up, tired, but steady. "You're bleeding."

He gave a weak grin. "Not my best day."

I tore a strip from the hem of my shirt and reached for him. "Hold still."

Andrew's protest was soft, frayed at the edges. "You shouldn't be doing that."

"Too late," I said softly, pressing my palms against the wound. My hands trembled, not from fear, but from the power humming beneath my skin. The runes etched across my fingers shimmered, faint at first, then brighter, as if responding to the pull of his pain.

Warmth bloomed in my palms, spreading through torn fabric and flesh alike. Beneath my touch, the blood's heat changed, its rhythm syncing with my own. A soft light began to glow where my hands met his skin. Gold threaded with silver, humming in time with my heartbeat.

Andrew sucked in a sharp breath. "Astrid…"

"I know," I whispered, eyes fixed on the light as it pulsed once, then began to fade. The torn edges of the wound knit together, the angry red tissue, softening to pink. It wasn't perfect, he still looked pale and exhausted, but the bleeding stopped, and it looked like his pain eased.

When the glow finally dimmed, I sat back on my heels, my breath shallow, and my hands still tingling. The runes flickered one last time before settling. For a moment, the only sound was our breathing and the distant drip of water through the broken ceiling.

"I'll find Red later," I said finally, breaking the silence. "I want to talk to her, about… everything. And… I need to talk to her about this." My gaze drifted across the cafeteria.

Andrew nodded, his expression softening. "Yeah. You should."

I stood and offered him my hand. "Come on," I said, glancing at the cracked ceiling above us. "Before this place decides to finish falling apart."

He took it, leaning into me when his balance wavered. His weight leaned into me just enough to remind me how much we'd both been through.

"Let's just get to bed," Andrew muttered, a tired laugh escaping him. "I don't know about you, but I'm fucking wiped."

That drew a quiet laugh from me, half relief, half disbelief that we were both still standing. "Yeah," I breathed, "No arguments here."

As we moved through the wreckage, the air was still thick with the scent of smoke and ozone. For one fragile heartbeat, it almost felt peaceful. But I knew better. Whatever had started here, it wasn't over. Not even close.

Chapter 28

The dream came first, if it was a dream at all.

A whisper slipped through the dark, soft as silk, edged like broken glass. I was back in the void between realms, weightless and suspended in a place that was neither night nor dawn. Shadows folded and unfolded like breath, the air too still to be real. Then, out of the endless quiet, a voice broke the silence, fragile and trembling, but unmistakable.

"Astrid…?"

I turned sharply, my body cutting through a liquid darkness that was thick as oil and alive with shimmer. Each movement stirred clouds of black silver that curled and flowed around me, catching unseen light as they slid along my skin before drifting away in slow, luminous spirals. Metallic ripples radiated outward from me, flashing briefly before sinking back into the void.

"Hello?" The word echoed back, warped and empty, stripped of warmth, as though the void itself had borrowed my voice. There was no answer, only the slow, soundless drift of silver light, curling away from me.

I twisted again, searching. "Naomi?" The name escaped before I could stop it, fragile and exposed, as if speaking it had thinned the dark.

Something flickered at the edge of my vision, a glint of violet, beating like a heart in the dark, faint but rhythmic, pulsing like a living heart buried deep in the void. For a terrible moment, I wondered if I was drifting the wrong way, if this place even *had* directions, but my instincts stayed eerily silent. No warning. No resistance. Only a quiet, inevitable pull. I let myself drift toward it.

With every inch I closed, the void reacted. Shadows bowed inward, folding like wounded things. The darkness shuddered, recoiling as if my presence disturbed something dormant. Whispers bled through the silence, syllables too old to belong to any living tongue, brushing against my thoughts rather than my ears.

The violet light brightened. The air thickened. The space around me tightened, stretching thin, like skin pulled over a fracture.

Then the world cracked.

When I opened my eyes again, I was in the hospital hallway. The lights flared too bright before collapsing into a weak, uneven pulse. The sterile white walls seemed to soften, their edges bleeding and unraveling back into darkness. The sharp scent of antiseptic soured, turning bitter, like ash caught in the back of my throat. For one disorienting moment, I couldn't tell if I'd woken at all, or if the between had followed me here—but I felt her.

I pushed myself upright, heart slamming against my ribs. "Naomi?"

The shadows along the far wall thickened, pooling unnaturally before drawing themselves into shape. What emerged was not entirely her. She looked torn, unfinished, as if reality had failed to agree on where she belonged. Her skin shimmered with a faint violet sheen, translucent in places, veins lit from within by runes that crawled beneath her flesh like living script. Her amethyst eyes burned too bright in her

hollowed face, filled with exhaustion, terror, and something dangerously close to regret.

"I didn't think I'd reach you," she whispered. Her voice wavered, thin and brittle, like glass stretched to its breaking point. "He doesn't let me… speak."

My throat tightened painfully. "The dark völva?"

Her expression fractured, pain and fear rippling across her features as if through something unseen had tugged on invisible strings. "The one behind Verrik," she said, a hollow laugh slipping free. "The one pulling the strings." Her eyes flicked nervously to the shadows. "Odinsráð only serve *him*."

"Because this…Ewan… gave the order." I said.

The air dropped several degrees, turning sharp and metallic in my lungs. Static crawled over my skin as the wrongness of her presence pressed in, an off-beat rhythm, like a second heart thudding out of rhythm with my own. The space around us wavered, walls stretching too long, corners bending inward as if listening.

Then I wasn't alone anymore.

Mani stood at my side. She hadn't been there a heartbeat ago—she *manifested*, dragged here by instinct and danger. Her massive white form resolved from shadow and frost, her paws landing soundlessly against the warped floor. Her hackles raised and teeth bared. Her body angled subtly in front of mine, a living barrier, her presence anchoring me to something feral and real.

A low growl vibrated through the space, I felt it more than I heard. The space recoiled in response.

Even from across the room, I could see Naomi's shadow-chains wrapped tight around her limbs and torso, biting deep, dragging her backward inch by inch as she fought to stay upright. The chains didn't clink or scrape. They moved with a slow, unsettling life of their own, writhing and tightening like dark tentacles coiling around prey.

"No," Naomi said sharply. "He alone doesn't control them… not anymore."

The shadows tightened as if punishing her, for her defiance.

Before I could ask anything further, Mani stepped closer, her shoulder brushing my hip. Heat radiated from her despite the cold, solid and unmistakably physical. Her eyes burned silver-blue, locked on Naomi—and on something behind her, something I couldn't see but could *feel* pressing through the dream like fingers testing thin ice.

"Naomi," I said carefully, my voice sounding too loud, too fragile in the warped space. "You need to tell us about Ewan Owen."

Naomi shook her head sharply, panic splintering through her exhaustion. "I can't." Her breath hitched. "He's listening. They are always listening."

Mani's growl deepened, reverberating through my bones. The shadows along the walls flinched.

"Astrid, you don't understand," Naomi whispered, desperation cracking her voice. "He's already inside their minds. Odin's order—it's hollow. Every high-ranking member, every operative…" Her eyes shone with something raw and terrified. "They're puppets. Controlled from within."

Ice spread through my veins. "Through what?" I asked. "Magic? Blood?"

"Both," she hissed. "He's not just wielding power, he's being used to rewriting loyalty itself. They *believe* they're

chosen. They don't even know they're enslaved." The shadows surged violently around her, swallowing half her face.

Mani lunged forward, a snarl ripping from her chest, teeth snapping at empty air as if she could tear the bindings free by sheer will. The dream *buckled.* Naomi convulsed, choking on a scream that never fully escaped, smothered by power that was not her own.

For a split second, the bindings revealed themselves fully, runes carved deep into her skin, burning red with command sigils that pulsed in time with her heartbeat.

"Naomi!" I cried, reaching for her without thinking.

Mani snapped her jaws shut around my sleeve, not biting, but stopping me, holding me back with unyielding certainty. Her presence warned. *Not yet.*

Naomi's gaze snapped to mine, wild and stripped bare of every mask she'd ever worn. "Astrid..." her voice shook with urgency clawing through the fear. "He's coming for you. He *needs* your blood to finish what he started."

The room lurched. Power slammed outward in a violent pulse, rattling the walls. The floor rippled. Loose papers tore free from the counter that hadn't existed a moment before, spiraling upwards like birds fleeing a fire. The lights flickered erratically, casting fractured shadows that twisted and crawled along the floor.

Mani planted herself fully in front of me, her fur bristled with her faint blue hue, teeth flashing as she threw her head back and *howled.*

It wasn't sound, it was command. The surge broke around us, bending away from Mani like a wave striking stone.

Naomi staggered forward, her form glitching, flickering like a broken signal fighting to stay connected. "You have to find the Heartstone," she gasped, each word dragged from her like it cost blood. "Before he does. It's hidden… if he gets it…" The rune at her throat flared blindingly bright. The light cut her off mid-breath.

"Naomi!" I shouted.

She collapsed to her knees, clutching her chest as if trying to hold herself together. Cracks of violet light split across her body, spreading rapidly as her form began to unravel. She broke apart into motes of glowing violet, each one drifting upward like embers carried on an unseen current.

Mani whined, low, frustrated, helpless, as the last of Naomi slipped away.

But her voice reached me one last time, thin and completely broken.

"Please, Astrid," she whispered. "Don't leave me here." And then she was gone.

The silence that followed pressed down, hard and suffocating, until everything stilled. As if stunned by its own violence. Even Mani went rigid, her breath steaming in the cold air, ears swiveling as she listened for something that had withdrawn but not vanished.

The glow in her eyes dimmed slightly as she turned back to me, pressing her massive head into my chest. The contact was solid, her fur warm beneath my fingers, her breath steady against my ribs.

'She's still fighting him,' she says, her voice edged with tension and restrained fury.

"But for how long?" I murmured, staring at the empty space where she'd knelt, my pulse roaring in my ears.

Naomi had been jealous, sharp-tongued, and manipulative. She was so easy to hate. But what I'd seen just

now wasn't that Naomi. It was pure *fear.* It was someone drowning, desperately thrashing toward the surface with the last of their strength.

"If I leave her to him…" my voice dropped to a whisper. "I'm no better than he is."

Mani shifted closer, her voice certain. '*You already know what that choice costs.*'

The dream seemed to hush around us, shadows pulling back instinctively.

I swallowed and nodded, the weight of the decision settling deep in my chest. "I already did it with Verrik. I have to try again… for her."

Mani exhaled, a long breath. Not resignation but of acceptance. Her tail flicked once, decisive. '*Then we hunt to find this Heartstone,*' she said, fierce and unyielding. '*And we tear her free before he finishes breaking her.*'

I huffed weakly, exhaustion and dread knotting together. "Great," I muttered. "Let's go see our favorite oracle. I'm sure she'll be thrilled to help us."

I felt Mani's mouth curve into, not quite a smile, but it was close. A low, darkly amused huff rumbled from her chest as the edges of the dream began to thin, shadows pulling apart like smoke in a sudden wind.

'*Wake up*,' she urged gently.

The world snapped.

I gasped and bolted upright, lungs dragging in air as if I'd been underwater. My heart slammed against my ribs. The dim light of the room swam into focus, walls solid, unmoving, and painfully real. No void. No shimmering darkness. No chains. But the echo of Naomi's fear still clung to me like frost.

Andrew was already there, sitting up beside me, his hand gripping my wrist as if he'd felt the moment I tore free of the dream. "Astrid," he said urgently. "You're shaking."

"I saw her," I whispered, my throat raw. "Naomi. She reached me… or I reached out to her?"

The look in his eyes sharpened instantly. "Then we don't wait."

Andrew didn't bother with explanations or caution. We got up, got ready and left. Minutes later, we were moving through the hospital corridors. The air hung thick and electric, heavy with the charge of the approaching storm. Every shadow along the corridor seemed to vibrate with Naomi's last words, echoing faintly at the edge of my mind.

When we finally found Trovi, she didn't look surprised when we entered. Her sharp eyes swept from Andrew to me, pausing on the tension in my jaw, the way my hands still hadn't stopped shaking.

"You've seen her, haven't you?" she asked quietly. "Naomi."

I froze. "You know?"

She nodded slowly, rubbing her hands together as if to warm them. "Only fragments. Whispers through the wards. Dreams bleeding where they shouldn't." Her gaze met mine, steady and searching. "But if she reached *you*…"

Her voice softened, threaded with something like reluctant hope. "Then she's still fighting," Trovi said. "And she wants to be free."

I stepped forward, keeping my tone low but steady. "She said we need to find the Heartstone… before they do. Do you know what that is?"

Trovi's expression shifted, a flicker of fear just beneath awe. She glanced toward the far wall, her posture tightening as if she could feel some hidden weight closing in on us. "Your mothers did," she murmured. "Both of them hid it here. Said it wasn't safe anywhere else."

My breath caught.

"Our mothers?" Andrew asked, surprised.

Trovi nodded once, then met my gaze. "I believe you've already found it," she said quietly. "That's why the chest responded to you… but it needs you *together*."

The hallway fell silent. Her words pressed against my chest, a pulse I couldn't ignore. Andrew and I exchanged a look—one that carried the same silent understanding that had guided us through every impossible thing so far.

"Then we need to go," I said.

Trovi's expression darkened. "It's still where you hid it, isn't it?"

I hesitated, then nodded. "In your house. I didn't know what it was then… only that it felt… alive."

Her mouth tightened. "Then let's not waste time."

The walk to Trovi's house passed in uneasy silence, except for our hurried footsteps. The streets gleamed wet from the rain, headlights smearing into rivers of gold on slick asphalt. The storm had rolled east, but its presence lingered, low thunder rumbling like a warning across the horizon. Andrew's hand brushed mine, a silent reassurance that we were headed exactly where we needed to be.

When we arrived, the air inside her home carried the familiar scent of dust, dried herbs, and something faintly metallic, that old magic sleeping beneath the floorboards. Books crowded every surface, their spines cracked and worn.

The moment I stepped inside, I felt it again, that same hum I'd felt the first time I'd found the chest. As if it was a call to me.

Trovi walked over to the old shelves, her fingers trailing across the worn wood before she pushed aside a stack of ancient tomes. Dust spiraled upward like ghosts disturbed. There, behind them sat the box, its small, rune-etched, with ironwood surface darkened with age. Faint light bled from where the symbols met, as though it had been waiting.

Trovi hesitated before lifting it free, reverence and dread warring across her face. "I wanted to keep it buried among my books, in plain sight," she murmured. "I knew one day their children would come for it."

My throat tightened. "You knew this would happen?" Andrew and I followed Trovi as she set the box on the coffee table. The runes shimmered faintly under his touch, reacting to the energy that pulsed through us both. Trovi sat in her usual chair and Andrew, and I sat on her couch.

"It's sealed," Trovi warned. "Only blood tied to its origin can open it."

I pressed my palm against the lid. The wood was warm, almost breathing beneath my fingers, as if it recognized life itself. A sharp, electric sting lanced through my skin. Blood welled along my palm, sinking into the rune-carved grain, and the box let out a single, resonant click.

"Your turn Romero," Trovi said, her eyes flicking to Andrew.

He rolled his eyes then glanced at me, and I gave a small nod, steadying him, letting him know that whatever happens we were ready. He placed his hand on the lid. The same sting shot through him. Another click echoed in the quiet room, and slowly, the box creaked open.

Inside lay a stone, it was roughly the size of a clenched fist, though its jagged, asymmetrical shape made it seem larger, like a fragment torn from some ancient, cosmic root. Its surface was a paradox of textures: smooth in places where unseen energies had worn it down over millennia, yet sharp, branching ridges jutted out like veins of gnarled tree roots.

Its base glowed with a deep amber-gold, translucent in spots where light seemed to pass straight through, revealing swirling veins of silver, obsidian black, and rich crimson, like it was frozen mid-flow. When the light shifted, fleeting glimmers of green and violet danced across its surface, reflections of a boundless energy captured within the stone itself.

When I touched it, warmth seeped into my palm, alive with a quiet, insistent hum.

"That's a piece of the World Tree itself, thrumming beneath your skin." Trovi said in awe of the stone.

It was heavier than it looked, as if the weight of all creation had been pressed into its core. Yet it radiated raw vitality, as though it waited for the right hands to wield it.

Andrew inhaled sharply. "That's it."

Trovi's voice dropped to a whisper. "The Heartstone of Yggdrasil," she said. "Born from the sap of the World Tree itself, where divine blood once spilled into its roots. The gods called it *Hjartsteinn*, the living ember of creation. It carries the breath of the Nine Realms, binding oath to spirit, truth to consequence. Those who wield it do not command it…" her eyes flicked up, "…they are judged by it."

The air thickened, heavy and ancient, as if the world itself had paused to listen. The Heartstone pulsed faintly between my hands, its rhythm syncing with my own.

Andrew glanced at me. "If he gets this…"

"He won't," I said, placing the stone back and closing the box with trembling hands. "We find a way… to use it first, to free Naomi."

Trovi looked between us, worry etched deep into her lined face. "Then be careful. That stone doesn't just bind… it remembers. It was never meant to be wielded by mortals."

'She's right,' Mani whispered, her presence warm but taut with warning. *'That relic bears judgment older than gods. We don't know what it will do to us if we use it.'*

'Then what do we do?' I thought back. *'Let him take her? Let him win?'*

For a moment, there was only silence, the kind that stretches too long. Then Mani huffed softly, a familiar edge of dark humor threading through her resolve. *'What do wolves do, Astrid?'* she said. *'We hunt. We protect our own. We tear apart whatever dares threaten the pack.'* Her presence pressed closer, fierce and unwavering. *'And all the while look fabulous. We can sort out the consequences after breakfast.'*

I smiled despite everything. The fear didn't vanish, but it shifted, reshaping itself into something harder. I looked at Andrew. Exhaustion carved shadows beneath his eyes, but the fire in him still burned, bright and stubborn.

"Then it's a good thing he's a dragon," I said, "and I'm a reincarnation of an ancient wolf."

The lights overhead flickered before steadying again. In the distance, thunder rolled low and slow, like the world itself drawing a long breath. The storm wasn't over, not by a long shot. But neither were we.

Outside, lightning split the sky, its echo crawling across the horizon, no longer just as a warning, but a challenge.

Chapter 29

Trovi had already hidden the Heartstone again, wrapped tight in a cloth, sealed back in the chest, and buried behind her wall of forgotten tomes. Even now, I swore I could still feel its pulse beneath my skin, faint and ancient, like the echo of something that didn't want to stay asleep.

Andrew had helped her return it to its hiding place, both of them moving with the kind of care reserved for handling relics, or curses. I replaced the tomes myself, one by one, until the shelf looked untouched. But looks meant nothing; that box *remembered* us.

By the time we made it back to our room, the storm had dulled to a soft, steady rain, the kind that whispered against the windows instead of howling through them. The scent of rain and vanilla candlewax hung heavy in the room. Our boots left dark, uneven wet prints across the worn floorboards. Neither of us spoke for a long time; we didn't need to. The silence wrapped around us, thick and comforting, alive with everything we'd survived and everything that still waited beyond these walls.

'If we're lucky,' Mani muttered, *'It stays asleep until we need it." Though luck never seems to be on our side.'*

I smiled faintly, running a towel through my damp hair. *'Then we'd better rely on our stubbornness instead.'*

'Our best trait,' she purred, sounding smug.

Andrew let out a low, exhausted laugh as he sank onto the edge of the bed. His shoulders slumped, head bowed, the lamplight spilling over him in soft gold, gentle enough to make even his weariness look beautiful. “Let’s get some sleep…” he murmured. “I’m beyond beat.”

But when I really looked at him, the words caught in my throat. Faint bruises that bloomed along his face and arms, shadows of violence from Verrik that hadn’t fully faded. Half-healed cuts traced his skin like careless signatures. Something tight pulled through my chest.

“Wait,” I said softly, stepping closer. I knelt beside him and brushed my fingers just above his wounds on his arm. “You should let me check these.”

He glanced down at my hand, then back at me, amusement flickering through his exhaustion. “Just my arm?” he asked mildly. “That seems… inefficient.”

I frowned. “Andrew.”

“What?” His lips curved into a grin. “If you’re already in healer mode, you might as well be thorough.” He tilted his head, feigning innocence. “Wouldn’t want you missing anything important.”

Before I could respond, he reached for the hem of his shirt and pulled it over his head, the fabric clinging briefly before coming free. He dropped it to the floor like the matter was settled. “There,” he said. “Full inspection access granted.”

I let out a short laugh and rolled my eyes. “You are unbelievable.”

“Yet remarkably cooperative,” he replied, clearly pleased with himself.

I shook my head, still smiling despite myself, and shifted closer, this time letting my hands move more deliberately, along his ribs, his shoulder, the faint cuts and deep bruises I’d missed before.

"Sit still," I warned. "This isn't an excuse to show off."

He teasing softened then, as he watched me with quiet attention as I checked each injury.

"I know," he said gently. "I trust you. Figured I might as well make it easy."

My touch lightened as I traced the edges, barely touching them, my fingers hovering over them like a ghost. His skin was warm, the steady rhythm of his heart thrumming against them. The air between us thickened, charged like the moment before lightning.

Andrew's breath hitched. "Astrid…" My name was a warning and a plea all at once.

I lifted my gaze and his gaze met mine, steady and burning with something deeper than pain. He slowly reached out, brushing a damp strand of hair from my cheek, his thumb tracing the edge of my jaw. The touch was gentle, his hand lingered, warm and certain. His thumb drifted upward, brushing across my lips in a slow, unconscious motion that stole the air from my lungs.

"You shouldn't worry so much," he murmured.

"Someone has to," I whispered back, my voice catching in the quiet.

He smiled, that crooked, tired smile that always unraveled me, and his hand slid to the back of my neck, drawing me forward until our foreheads rested together. The space between us pulsed, alive, the bond humming low and electric beneath my skin.

Mani stirred, purring. *'Finally,'* she sighed. *'You two are worse than a soap opera.'*

A soft laugh trembled in my chest, fragile and fleeting, dissolving the moment Andrew tilted his head and kissed me.

The world blurred at the edges. His lips met mine slowly. It tasted of warmth and familiarity, of home and all the things we never needed to say aloud. Then our kiss deepened, heat rising like a spark catching dry tinder. His hand settled at my waist, his fingers tightening with quiet possession, while mine curled instinctively against his bare shoulder.

The bond sang under my skin, alive and waiting, tugging at something deep and wordless. His touch traced my spine with reverent care, as though memorizing every inch of me. Outside, thunder rolled low and distant, echoing the rhythm of our hearts.

When we finally drew apart, the world felt softer. The lamplight flickered across his face, and when his thumb brushed my lower lip again, the look in his eyes was fierce and gentle. My heart raced, wild beneath his touch, and yet something inside me settled, tucked safely into the steady shelter of him.

The room was quiet except for the uneven rhythm of our breathing and the slow drift of shadows along the walls. I felt the pull of him, steady and magnetic, our bond tugging at me with a quiet insistence.

My hands moved over his shoulders, tracing the shape of them as if committing every line to memory, feeling the warmth and restrained strength beneath his skin. My fingers lingered at the center of his chest before sliding lower, unhurried, brushing over the firm planes of his stomach.

When they reached the edge of his waistband, I paused, my touch feather light.

Slowly, I rose from his lap and stepped back. The distance between us was only a breath, but it felt charged, humming with anticipation. I let my clothes fall away piece by

piece, slow and unhurried, the cool air whispering across my skin. Andrew didn't speak. His breath caught softly, his gaze fixed on me, drinking me in with awe and hunger flickering through his gaze.

I started to turn away from him, teasing. I never made it more than a step.

He was on me in an instant, closing the distance with a quiet, predatory grace that sent my pulse racing. His hands slid over my sides, warm and certain, drawing me back against him until our bodies aligned perfectly, heat meeting heat.

The contact sent a shiver straight through me.

Then, with effortless strength, he lifted me. A startled laugh escaped me as we tumbled together onto the sheets, limbs tangling, breathless and warm.

Already wrapped up in each other before we even settled, a current sparked through me. His chest pressed against mine, the solid strength of him grounding me even as the warmth of his skin seeped deeper, melting me from the inside out. My hands wandered over him instinctively, tracing the firm lines of muscle, the small scars and faint bruises that spoke of battles fought and survived. He felt real beneath my palms, strong and alive in a way that made my chest ache.

His fingers followed the curve of my spine, slipping into the hollow of my back as he drew me closer, until there was no space left between us.

Our lips met in a kiss that was slow at first, soft and tender.

Then it deepened.

The warmth of his mouth, the quiet intensity behind it, sent sparks racing beneath my skin. When I gasped, he caught the sound with a quiet smile against my lips, a low rumble of amusement vibrating through his chest.

The sheets twisted and tangled around us as we shifted together, our bodies finding a rhythm that felt instinctive, inevitable. Every brush of skin sent another ripple of warmth through me, every touch sending a ripple of need straight to my core. I could feel him everywhere, the strength in his arms, the curve of his hip, the protective weight of him holding me close, and it drew me deeper, tethering me to him with an urgency I couldn't resist.

He whispered my name against my neck, "Astrid," low and teasing, sending shivers down my spine. I arched into him instinctively, hungry for more of the warmth and pressure, the slow, consuming closeness that made the world outside fade to nothing. Every touch, every shiver, every quiet gasp was a promise, an unspoken vow that we were a single fire now, relentless, uncontainable, and burning brighter than anything else.

After hours tangled together, the edges of wakefulness softened. I let myself drift, my head resting against his chest, fingers laced with his, the warmth of him seeping into every inch of me. Outside, the rain fell steady and gentle, a muted hymn against the windows. Inside, for tonight at least, the world felt safe, and fiercely ours.

For a few precious hours, the world felt quiet, it was soft and let us be at peace. The heat of our closeness, the quiet rhythm of our hearts, and the unspoken promise of safety between us, it was enough.

But nothing would ever stay gentle for long. Before the sun even rose, the storm clouds returned. Not with rain this time, but with a powerful presence that a storm brings. It didn't strike. It invaded.

A pulse tore through the world, deep and wrong, like something ancient had woken beneath the earth. The town groaned beneath it, windows shuddering, walls flexing as though they were breathing. The air itself twisted, thick with the metallic scent of iron and ozone, until each inhale scraped my throat raw.

Shadows stopped behaving. They stretched where they shouldn't, warped around corners, *moved* when nothing else did. The lamplight flickered once… twice… then bent sideways, as if gravity itself had forgotten its purpose.

From deep beneath the floorboards came a knock. It was slow and deliberate.

The room pulsed with every heartbeat. The walls seemed to narrow, and the ceiling pressing lower. My reflection in the dark window blinked a moment too late, the mouth curving into a smile that wasn't mine.

Through it all, I could *feel* him… the dark völva, moving through the early morning night like a storm made of whispers.

I woke with a jolt, my heart hammering, limbs tense, and my breath sharp. The thread that had once hummed faintly between Naomi and myself was now a white-hot coil beneath my skin, thrumming with violence. A ripple of wrongness slithered through the air. It was cold and predatory while it watched, calculating.

Lightning flashed through the window, stark and blinding. The calm of last night was gone.

Andrew was already awake. He stood by the window, his shoulders tense, and his wings were half-unfurled in the dim light coming from the fireplace. The faint crimson in his eyes flickered like embers on the verge of ignition.

"Do you think he's retaliating?" he asked, his voice low and rough. "Naomi's message didn't go unnoticed."

'Not to mention...whatever you did to Verrik,' Mani murmured, her tone sharp but laced with grim amusement.

I winced as the memory flashed, the way I'd unraveled the dark völva's hold on Verrik like a loose thread. *'We'll see what sticks in that skull of his.'* I muttered, swinging my legs off the bed and beginning to dress.

Andrew turned toward me, the storm light painting jagged shadows across his face. "You still feel it, don't you?"

"The pull to Naomi?"

He nodded.

"Yeah," I admitted. "It's different now… angrier." My hand pressed instinctively to my chest, where the thread coiled beneath my skin like a live wire.

Lightning flared again. For a heartbeat, the room warped, the walls stretched, and the window rippled. Andrew's reflection didn't move in sync with him. My stomach dropped.

"He's close," I whispered.

Andrew's jaw tightened. He reached for me, his fingers brushing my wrist. "Then we move now," he said. "Before he takes her over completely."

Thunder rattled the glass. The metallic scent thickened, charging the air. Somewhere beyond the walls, something howled, a sound too deep, and too wrong to be human… or wolf.

Mani growled low. *'He's not waiting anymore. This is a hunt.'*

Andrew's wings flexed wide, scattering shadow across the room. "Then let's make sure he remembers what happens when wolves and dragons are cornered."

I nodded, and together we stepped into the hall.

The Pack house was half-lit, still feeling like a dream. The storm outside clawed at the windows, light and shadow flickering like a heartbeat. We moved fast, down the corridor, past sleeping rooms. The air itself felt wrong, too still, too thick, like we were walking through syrup.

Another low roar split the wind outside, making the building shudder.

Red appeared near the front door, her hair falling around her shoulders, and a small fire burning in her palms. "You hear that too?" she asked, her voice tight.

"Yeah," I said. "He's coming."

We barely had time to brace before the doors blew open. The world *bent*. The corridor rippled like liquid glass, and the walls folded in on themselves. The scent of rain and wood vanished, replaced by something old and cold. In a blink, and the Pack house was gone.

We were standing in a forest with completely black trees, their twisted branches hissing like dry whispers in a language I couldn't understand. Shadows clung to the roots like spilled ink, thick and viscous. Amid the dark thicket, one tree towered above the rest, enormous and impossibly black. Its shape identical to the tree where my father had lived. Around it, runic standing stones jutted from the cliffside, etched with symbols that seemed to pulse. The sky churned with storm light and smoke, jagged flashes illuminating the unnatural forest.

"Separate them," a voice hissed from the dark. "Break the bond."

I spun, my heart slamming against my ribs. The sound seemed to rise from everywhere at once, from every tree, from the wind, from the very air around me. The ground cracked like splintering bones, and from the fissures rose the Odinsain, people carved from shadow and sorrow. Their forms flickered, shadows imitating human shape, some echoing ancient warriors, others twisting into wolves or serpents, edges unraveling into mist. Darkness bled from them, thick and metallic, carrying the stench of rot and old blood.

Andrew's power flared, deep and resonant, a wave that pushed against the dark. "We're not going anywhere!" he shouted.

The first beast lunged. The runes on my hand surged, tinged with shadows, I extended my hand and touched the first shadow creature, it was slammed back midair with a sound like tearing cloth. Its smoky form writhed, trying to consume my magic. I pushed deeper, then folded the attack inward. The creature shrieked once before imploding into nothing but smoke.

Behind me, Red's magic ignited the air. Ribbons of molten light lanced from her palms, slicing through another Odinsráð, scattering its form into ash and whispers.

The illusion twisted again. The forest shrieked. The ground dissolved into mist. My stomach dropped. I was falling into nothing, the void that wanted to swallow me whole.

"Focus!" Andrew's voice cut through the distortion. His hand found mine, heat and shadow grounding me. "This isn't real."

The dark völva's laughter shredded the air, cruel, and impossibly sharp. "Isn't it? Every fear you've buried, I can make it real."

Images slammed into me: Naomi's shattered face, Hel's cold gaze, Verrik's smirk before he fell, the touch of Alastor. Memory and reality trying to splinter. For a heartbeat, I couldn't tell what was true.

Then Mani's voice cut through, sharp and clear: '*Breathe…we know the truth. Breathe, listen, and focus.*'

I exhaled hard. The illusion shivered. I reached outward, not to fight, but to bend it. The void flickered, then buckled beneath my will. Shadows recoiled. The beasts faltered. The sky cracked.

The dark völva screamed, a sound that scraped against my bones. "You're learning too quickly," he spat. "But it won't save you. We're already moving."

And then he was gone.

The world shattered like glass. We were back in the front room of the Pack house. The hallways scorched, and smoke curling along the floor. Runes along the walls flickering like dying stars.

Red sagged against the wall, her chest heaving, light guttering out in her palms. "Okay," she said breathlessly. "Someone want to explain what the hell *that* was?"

Andrew's jaw was locked tight, his wings still half-visible, shuddering as the last traces of power bled off him. "He wasn't testing us," he said. "He went straight for the bond."

A chill slid down my spine as the truth clicked fully into place. The way the illusion had warped. The way the world had tried to fold around us, pull us in opposite directions.

"He tried to rip us apart," I said quietly. "Separate us before we could react."

Andrew turned to me then, his eyes burning crimson, fierce but steady. Ready for whatever comes next. "He underestimated us."

Mani huffed, sharp and unimpressed. '*He tried to scare you into breaking,*' she muttered. '*Congratulations to him, he's officially made to the top of "things we're going to tear apart slowly" list.*'

"This wasn't a warning," I continued. "It was a calculated strike. He wanted us off-balance."

Andrew nodded once. "Buying time."

"He said they were already moving." Red said. "We need to figure out how to break the control on Naomi before going after them, because their next move is already in play."

I straightened, resolve settling like armor over my ribs. "Then we stop playing defense. We break whatever's binding Naomi to him, *first*."

Thunder rolled like distant applause, slow and satisfied. The dark völva had made the first move on the board, smug enough to believe he could pull us apart with a whisper and a shadow.

I welcomed the attempt. Let him think this was his game. Let him believe we were something fragile.

Because when I reached him, it wouldn't be as prey. It would be as consequence.

Chapter 30

The world still hummed from the aftershock of the dark völva's magic. Smoke clung to the walls, the air heavy with scorch and the bitter tang of corrupted power. My hands wouldn't stop shaking, not from fear, but from the adrenaline still roaring through me. The illusion had been too real, the screams, the faces, the way it had *felt*.

Andrew was pacing near the front window, his wings gone but tension still radiating from every movement. Red still sat against the far wall, her hair streaked with ash. A thin cut along her temple, one she hadn't even noticed yet. No one spoke, each of us lost in their own thoughts. The silence pressed in, loud and raw, as if the house itself were holding its breath.

"They're already in motion," Andrew finally said, his voice low and held together by sheer will. "If what the dark völva said was true, then they've already begun moving their pieces."

'And we're behind,' Mani murmured, her voice coiled tight. *'Again.'*

I dragged a hand through my hair. "Then we don't have time to regroup. We moved. We get to Naomi and sever whatever's binding her to them before she becomes their weapon, or worse…"

Trovi's voice came from the doorway, calm but edged with steel. "Then you'll have to move fast."

I nodded, already turning. "Let's go to her hospital room… while she's still asleep…"

"She's gone." Trovi's words stopped me cold.

She stepped fully into the room, a satchel slung over her shoulder, far too small for the weight it carried. "Her trail's faint, but it should be enough to follow. If we can't reach through to her, there won't *be* anything left of her to save."

Bo followed her in, swearing under his breath. "What happened—" He stopped himself, jaw tightening. "Never mind…"

Trovi cut in. "I think she ran south into the thickest part of the forest."

Bo went pale. "That's suicide. The ley lines up there are unstable as hell. One wrong move and…" Bo started.

"She won't die," Trovi cut in coldly. "She'll be used." The word landed like a physical blow. "They're going to use her as a sacrifice," Trovi continued. "A living portal between realms. If they finish the work…" Her fingers tightened around the satchel strap. "If what I've seen comes to pass. There won't be a way to seal it."

Silence fell, heavy and suffocating.

The thought of Naomi, who was once sharp-tongued and smug, was now twisted by dark threads she couldn't escape, tightened something in my chest. She had never been innocent, but this… this wasn't justice. No one deserved to be hollowed out and used like a puppet. Not even her… even if she did bring it upon herself.

"She doesn't deserve to be their pawn," I said quietly. "No one does."

Andrew's eyes softened when they met mine, though the storm still burned behind them. "Then we bring her back," he said. "Whatever it takes."

For a moment, no one moved. Then Red stood, brushing ash and dust from her jacket and cracking her neck like a soldier about to march into fire. "Guess we're doing this," she said. "I'll grab the med-kits… and maybe a miracle."

Bo muttered something about needing a drink first, but he was already moving, checking his weapon I didn't realize he was carrying. Then everyone fell into motion, quiet efficiency replacing the earlier stillness. And yet, beneath the urgency, something else hung heavy in the air, a collective understanding that this time, they weren't just chasing an enemy. We were trying to save one of our own.

I lingered for a moment longer, my gaze drawn to the scorch marks on the floor where the illusion had collapsed. The scent of burnt cedar and old blood still clung to it. *A warning,* or maybe *a promise.*

Red appeared beside me and I was startled. "You want to talk about it?" she asked softly. "About what just happened… or about why you've been so distant lately?"

I almost told her no, that we didn't have time, that it didn't matter, but the words caught in my throat. The truth was, I didn't even know where to start. How could I explain the way the dark völva's magic had reached inside me, peeled back everything I thought I'd buried, and took a *look*?

"I'm fine," I said finally, but the lie sounded hollow even to me.

Red folded her arms, one brow arching. "You keep telling yourself that," she said, crossing her arms. "And every time I see you, you look a little more worn each time I see you."

A tired laugh escaped before I could stop it. "Guess I'm not as good at pretending as I thought."

Her expression softened, “You don’t have to be.” She hesitated, then added, “You scared the hell out of all of us back there. Andrew most of all. He’s trying to hold it together for you. Don’t forget… he needs you to do the same for him… we all do.”

That landed deeper than I expected. I glanced toward Andrew. He was still pacing near the window, tension etched into every part of him. The firelight caught the faint shimmer of his skin where his wings had vanished, the shadows that still clung to him like smoke.

“I know,” I whispered. “I just… every time I close my eyes, I see what the dark völva showed me. Naomi, Verrik, horrible visions, it all feels like it’s *waiting* for me to make one wrong move.”

Red reached out, resting a soot-streaked hand on my arm. “Then don’t do it alone.”

For a long moment, neither of us moved. The house creaked softly around us, the smoke thinning as the silence settled into something heavy but bearable.

Then I stepped forward and pulled Red into a hug.

She went rigid in surprise—clearly caught off guard. I had never been the one to reach for her first. For a heartbeat she just stood there, stunned, before her arms slowly came around me in return.

After a few minutes, I stepped back and looked at her.

I drew in a steady breath and nodded. “We find Naomi.” I said. “We break whatever hold they have on her. And then we burn down whatever’s fucking left.”

Red’s expression flickered, shock first, then something like awe, before settling into an impressed, almost reluctant

grin. "Who are you?" she said, then gestured at me. "Because this… is the Astrid I can get behind."

'Are you sure we're ready for this?' Mani asked.

'No,' I whispered. *'But we'll do it anyway.'*

Andrew's hand brushed my shoulder. "Then let's go get her."

I blinked at him. "Go where?"

Andrew stepped closer, lowering his voice, not out of doubt, but certainty. "The cave behind the waterfalls," he said, taking my hands into his. "Ours. The current there is steady, constant. No outside interference. Trovi's wards will hold."

His gaze locked on mine. "It's the only place she can set this up without the tether shredding you from the inside out."

Trovi nodded, drawing her satchel tighter against her side as if she could feel the magic stirring already. "He's right. I need clean, moving air and stable water flow. Anything stagnant and the tether will collapse." Her mouth thinned. "and take you with it."

A beat of silence.

I let out a sharp breath. "Wait…" I looked between Andrew and Trovi, disbelief flickering across my face. "I thought we were tracking her down, physically. Not…" my voice dropped. "Not diving back into her head again."

Trovi didn't hesitate. "If we chase her body, we lose her mind," she said quietly. "And if we lose that…"

"We lose her," I finished. I inhaled slowly, then straightened, resolve settling in my bones. "Well, let's not waste any more time."

By the time we reached the cave, dusk had begun to swallow the forest whole. The last threads of daylight bled between the trees, fading into shadow as mist crept low across the ground. It clung to the rocks in cold, silver veils, slick against my skin, soaking into fabric and breath alike, as if the forest itself was washing us clean before letting us pass.

The waterfall loomed ahead, its constant thunder cutting through the quiet. The air sharpened as we drew closer, stripped clean by the rushing water, heavy with the scent of wet stone and moss, touched by the faint, earthy bite of river algae. Each breath felt rinsed, as if something old and clinging was being pulled from my lungs and left behind.

When we stepped through the curtain of falling water, the roar swallowed the world. Sound collapsed into a steady, rhythmic pulse that echoed through our bones and blood. The spray drenched us, cold and cleansing.

Trovi moved with precise efficiency, her satchel swinging from her shoulder as she unpacked bundles of herbs, chalk, and glinting fragments of quartz. "I need space," she said, motioning toward a smooth stone where the roar of the falls softened into a steady heartbeat. "If we're going to do this safely, the wards have to anchor here. The flow of the water will help keep the tether stable."

Andrew set down a lantern beside her. Its flame flickered against the wet walls, reflecting off the mist in tiny shards of gold. "You're sure this will work?" he asked, his voice low but steady.

"It has to," Trovi said, her tone leaving no room for argument. "If Astrid's going to reach Naomi, she'll need to enter through the tether itself. It's not a simple projection. It's more. One misstep and…" Her words hung in the damp air, unfinished but heavy with warning.

I knelt beside the spot Trovi had cleared, brushing the slick stone with my fingers. It was cold. A faint drip from the ceiling landed on my hand. As if the cave was offering the little protection it could offer.

Andrew crouched beside me, his presence a quiet gravity I couldn't look away from. "You don't have to do this alone," he said softly.

I wanted to tell him I already knew that, that I could feel him even in the dark, but the words caught in my throat. "If I take too much energy, it could pull you in with me," I said instead. "And whatever is inside Naomi… it's feeding on connection, on bonds. That's exactly what the dark völva wants, to break our bond."

Trovi's hands stilled for a moment over the chalk lines, her sharp eyes narrowing. "She's right. The tether is alive and hungry. Don't underestimate it."

Andrew's jaw tightened. "Then come back," he said quietly. "No matter what it takes…even if it means…leaving her behind."

I met his gaze, the weight of his words anchoring me like the stone beneath my palms. "I will," I whispered.

Trovi lit the last of the candles. The circle flared to life in hues of violet and blue, runes shimmering across the stone and reflecting in the rippling water nearby. The hum of power grew, a subtle vibration that tickled my teeth, pulsing in time with my own heartbeat. Every breath tasted faintly of smoke and wet earth, grounding me while reminding me how fragile this crossing was. One wrong move, and I could become trapped in Naomi's mind, or worse, leave myself vulnerable to the darkness feeding there.

I stepped into the circle. The mist curled around my ankles like smoke, cold and teasing, smelling faintly of river and sage. I lay down, the stone pressing into my back, and for a heartbeat I closed my eyes. I listened: the waterfall's roar like a living drum, Andrew's steady breathing beside me, the faint, desperate echo of Naomi's cry somewhere deep in the dark. Then I let go. The world fell away, and I was on the threshold of something vast, broken, and alive.

Naomi's mind was a labyrinth of broken glass. I stood at some kind of threshold. Fragments of light and shadow floated in the air, each one catching a distorted reflection, memories that didn't belong to me: Naomi's smile twisting into terror, her laughter echoing in rooms full of strangers, the dark völva's hand resting on her shoulder like a brand.

The deeper I stepped, the thinner reality became. The void turned into floorboards that bent like water, and walls that breathed with whispers. Naomi's consciousness was splintered into pieces, some pleading for help, others snarling with hate. I could feel the strain in her own mind, the way Naomi's turmoil pressed against my own thoughts like a tide trying to drag me under.

'You really picked a hell of a time for a field trip, you know that?' Mani's voice murmured. *'She's still tied to the dark völva. Push too hard and that bond will drag you under faster than you can say "oops."'*

I clenched my jaw, a small smirk tugging at the corner of my lips despite the tension. *'I have to try.'*

The air trembled, and Naomi appeared ahead of me, a half-formed silhouette shimmering between light and shadow. Her eyes were wild, unfocused, and darting to things I couldn't see.

"You came back," Naomi whispered, her voice trembling. "I told you not to."

I took a step closer. "You're still in there… in here, Naomi. I can feel it."

Naomi laughed, a hollow, brittle sound that fractured the air. "Feeling me doesn't mean you can save me. Walls were built inside me, Astrid. Rooms I can't close, others I can't open…but if you…"

Her sentence broke off as the world shifted. The floor beneath us splintered into a thousand mirrors, each one flashing a different version of Naomi, cruel, sorrowful, frightened, and triumphant. My own reflection appeared among them too, but twisted, eyes burning with something that wasn't all me.

'This is her prison,' Mani warned. *'Stay centered.'*

I felt the pull, shadow turning on me, voices calling my name, showing me visions of failures, of Andrew bleeding, of Naomi laughing as I fell. It was too real, but I pushed past them all.

"Naomi!" I shouted, forcing my voice steady. "Look at me."

One reflection shifted. Naomi stood there, she was real, trembling, and clutching her arms around herself. "I didn't mean for this," she whispered. "He promised… I would be strong… That I could have him back."

My throat tightened. "Andrew?"

Naomi nodded, tears sliding down her cheeks. "He said… all I had to do was deliver you. But he never let go… how can I give you to him? He's inside every part of me now."

The darkness behind Naomi rippled, forming the faint outline of a man's face. The dark völva's voice slithered through the cracks: "*You cannot save what is already mine.*"

Pain split my skull, sharp and sudden. My mind filled with static, my thoughts unraveling. For a heartbeat, I couldn't tell where Naomi ended, and he began. Mani's growl cut through the noise, low, commanding, and protective.

Trovi's voice slid through my mind. *"If you get pulled too deep, there's a real chance you won't come back. The tether can hold you in there, or it can leave you exposed. Both end badly."*

The words landed like a stone. Failure wasn't just losing the fight—it was vanishing from the inside out.

'Just grab a shadow thingy and pull, like you did with Verrik,' Mani suggested, as if that simplified the metaphysical equivalent of brain surgery.

'We don't even know what it did to him,' I snapped, trying to keep the panic out of my voice. *'If I twist the wrong thread, I could scramble her brain.'*

'Then...do what feels natural,' Mani said, with a reluctant softness that steadied me. *'And don't you fucking die.'*

I drew a slow, shuddering breath, forcing my heart to remember how to beat steady, even as the tremor in my limbs refused to settle. The roar of the waterfall pounded in my ears, Andrew's steady breathing behind me, as a lifeline, a tether to the world outside the storm of Naomi's mind. I lifted my hands and cupped her face, my palms trembling, the runes flaring faintly, warm against her cold skin.

The first filament coiled around my fingers, black and slick, writhing with malevolence. It hissed, a sound that scraped at my skull, and tried to dig into my mind, seeking cracks.

A shock of ice-laced fire ripped up my arm and through my chest. Then Naomi's fear poured into me, jagged and cold, slicing along my nerves like shattered glass. Her panic

hammered against my ribs, her despair pressed against my lungs, and every breath felt jagged, sharp enough to cut. I bit down on the ache, forcing the runes' light along the corruption, tugging, twisting, and unspooling.

Each filament released left residue in my veins, a bitter, metallic taste that clung to my tongue and made my teeth ache. Memories clawed at me unbidden: Naomi laughing in a sunlit kitchen, then a hand I didn't recognize brushing her hair, the warmth of a life I'd never lived. They screamed for me to linger, to give in, and it nearly pulled me under. Staying too long and she would remain trapped there, shattered and unhealed. Give too much, and I would lose pieces of myself, threads of thought, fragments of memory, the edges of my own soul.

When a filament finally snapped free, it stabbed across my palm like a blade of ice, leaving a searing ache that spread up my arm and into my chest. I gasped, using the pain to anchor myself as the darkness hissed and writhed beneath the runes, until, for a split second, everything tore open inside my vision.

A massive image flashed through my mind: the Ouroboros, vast and ancient, coiling in on itself, endless, devouring its own tail, eyes like burning voids that seemed to recognize me.

Then it was gone.

I staggered, my breath breaking, as the coils around Naomi began to dissolve into the air. Slowly, agonizingly, the coils dissolved into the air, leaving only the faint pulse of light and the heavy, tremulous weight of the small tether between us.

"You're not his anymore," I whispered, voice cracking as the last coil twisted free and fell away. "Come back."

Naomi jolted, convulsing with a shudder that ran through us both. I felt the tremor in my own limbs, the thread between us contracting and then loosening like a held breath. For a single clear heartbeat her eyes cleared, wet and raw.

"I… I don't deserve this," she murmured, small and broken.

"Then earn it," I answered, my hands still warm on her skin, the light from the runes washing over her. "Live long enough to make it right."

I could feel the remnants clinging like dust, faint and stubborn, but the strangling grip was gone. I stayed standing there in the hush, our breath shaking, my fingers still humming with residual light, knowing the price had been paid, the balance had shifted, just enough for her to breathe.

Then the dark völva's scream tore through the edges of her mind, but I steadied myself, letting the remnants of his power roll off like waves dissipating against the shore. The mirrors around us shattered into nothing, shards vanishing into the void. Every pulse of light left us trembling, our bodies and hearts echoing the strain.

When it finally stilled, Naomi slumped to her knees, utterly limp yet breathing. I wrapped her in my arms, holding her close, feeling the shadows finally lift, her mind slowly stitching itself back together.

She cried into me hard, ragged sobs of soul-crushing relief and I let her. Naomi had been trapped for too long, and now, finally, she was free. The black threads were gone, fully unwound, but their echoes lingered: a faint pulse of fear, a ghost of shadow clinging like a memory. I could feel it brushing against my own heartbeat, a quiet, persistent reminder of the bond between us that was still tender, still dangerous.

Mani's voice broke through the hush, sardonic and approving. *'Congrats, tiny disaster magnet. You poked the darkness, gave it a wedgie, and somehow came out mostly in one piece.'*

I let out a strangled laugh, the sound ragged in my chest, still heaving from the effort, but lighter, somehow.

Chapter 31

The world slammed back into me with a soundless fracture.

Air burned in my lungs. Water roared in my ears. My body convulsed against cold stone as if I'd been thrown back into myself too violently. For a heartbeat, I didn't know who I was, only the sensation of falling, choking on light and shadow at once...again. Then hands gripped my shoulders, firm and steady, pulling me up until I was sitting in the circle's heart.

"Astrid!" Andrew's voice cut through the haze, hoarse and frayed at the edges. He hauled me upright, and I clutched at him without thinking, palms pressing to his chest as if I could anchor myself to the sound of his heart. It thundered beneath my hands—fast, alive, unmistakably *here*.

I gasped, shuddering. The air smelled of sage, mist, and blood…mine, maybe. The cave spun, the waterfall's constant roar collapsing into a deafening pulse inside my skull.

Trovi dropped to her knees beside us, fingers already at my throat and my wrist. "Her pulse is erratic," she muttered. "Her energy's still tangled with the tether. She's not fully back."

Andrew pressed his forehead to mine, his breath shaking. "Come on," he whispered, fierce and pleading all at once. "You said you'd come back."

"I…" My throat scraped raw, the word barely a whisper. "Naomi…"

Trovi shook her head. "She's most likely unconscious, we need to move quickly and find her."

I sagged against Andrew, as the runes on the ground dimmed, the glow faded from my skin. "The dark völva's thread is gone," I managed. "But the remnants…" My voice failed me. "They didn't vanish, they scattered."

Andrew cupped my chin gently, forcing me to meet his eyes. His expression was fierce—almost desperate. "You don't have to carry this," he said. "Not alone."

I wanted to believe him. Gods, I wanted to. But even as his warmth steadied me, I could feel it, the faint thrum of leftover corruption, like a bruise pressed too deep to fade.

Mani stirred, her voice rough with exhaustion and irritation. '*Next time, let's not play psychic tug-of-war with evil völva, yeah? Maybe try letting people deal with their own choices.*'

A weak, breathless laugh escaped me. "Maybe…next time," I murmured aloud.

Trovi pushed to her feet, already scanning the tree line beyond the ritual circle. "We don't have time," she said. "If Naomi's unconscious out there, exposed, and still marked by that bastard, anything could find her."

Something in my chest snapped into place.

"I can," I said, already pulling free of Andrew's hold. "I can find her."

Red opened her mouth to argue, but the words died when my knees buckled and instinct surged to compensate. Heat tore through my bones, sharp and violent, but familiar. I barely had time to gasp before my body answered the call.

The shift ripped through me. My skin gave way to fur, my spine folding and reforming as Mani surged forward. The world sharpened, colors and sounds snapping into brutal clarity.

I caught Andrew's nod through the haze of motion, then I was moving, sprinting for the waterfall.

Cold mist slapped against my muzzle as I burst through the curtain of falling water, stone slick beneath my paws. One misstep—then the world tipped. We slid, crashed, and plunged into the pond below, the shock of icy water stealing my breath and thought alike. I fought for purchase, claws scraping rock, hauling myself out as water streamed from my fur.

We climbed the slick jagged rocks until we reached the top of the waterfall. Then the faint but unmistakable scent hit me. Corruption. It rode the wind like a dying echo, old magic rotting at the edges, tangled with fear and blood. A residue that should have been gone, and the instant it touched my senses, I didn't wait.

The moment my paws hit the forest floor, I was gone.

I tore through the undergrowth, branches snapping against my flanks, breath ripping from my lungs as I chased the faintest trace of a scent that might—just might—have been Naomi. Deer scattered. Birds burst from the canopy. None of it mattered. Prey could wait. She could not.

The trail wavered, weak and inconsistent, but my desperation sharpened it. Corruption always lied, but fear never did. I followed the fear, my nose low and heart hammering, until the forest dipped into a shallow ravine choked with ferns and fallen limbs.

There she was. Naomi lay crumpled against the roots of an old cedar, body half-muddied, hair plastered to her face. Her chest rose, shallow and uneven, but it *rose*. The corruption clung to her like smoke after fire, thin strands drifting from her form, still carrying the lingering warmth of the darkness that spawned them.

Relief hit so hard my balance wavered.

'Andrew.' I pushed the word through our mind link, sharp and urgent, opening my mind without hesitation. *'I found her. She's alive. South ravine, cedar stand. She's fading.'*

He responded instantly. *"On our way.'*

I stayed near Naomi, pacing, we were too drained to lift her ourselves. The forest barely had time to settle before Andrew arrived, the air cracking as he skidded to a halt, power still humming beneath his skin. Bo followed a heartbeat later, his eyes bright, and his breath easy, like the distance had simply decided not to exist for him.

Andrew stepped toward Naomi without thinking, and a low growl rolled out of my chest. It wasn't loud, it wasn't violent, but it was territorial.

Andrew froze mid-step. Then, slowly, a grin spread across his face, unmistakable and entirely unrepentant. "Seriously?" he murmured, amused.

I moved between them on instinct, hackles lifting, body angling not toward Naomi, but toward *him*. A clear, feral line drawn. *'You are MINE. You don't touch other women. Ever!'* Mani said to Andrew through our link.

Bo barked out a laugh. "Well," he said, shaking his head, "that answers that."

Andrew's shoulders shook as he laughed quietly, hands lifting in surrender. "All right, all right. Message received." His voice dropped, fond and teasing. "Didn't realize I was the one in danger."

Andrew met my gaze, warm, unbothered, and deeply entertained. There was no confusion there at all.

Bo stepped in instead, calm as ever, carefully lifting Naomi as if she were made of glass. The moment she left the ground, the scent shifted, less volatile, and less sharp.

Andrew glanced back at me, smirking. "You know," he said mildly, "I like this version of you… jealous."

I huffed and turned away, pretending to ignore him—but my tail betrayed me, giving a sharp, irritated flick. His quiet laugh followed us as we moved.

We didn't linger. Bo took Naomi to the hospital. Bright lights replaced forest shadow, controlled hands replacing claws and instinct. Wards were laid with careful precision, thin, layered, meant to stabilize without disturbing what lay buried too deep to touch. Naomi was stabilized, cleansed as much as they dared. The rest would have to wait.

By the time we regrouped at Trovi's house, the rain had returned, draping the world in dreary gray. Red had pressed extra clothes into my hands, soft and warm, grounding in their ordinariness. We gathered around Trovi's table, exhaustion settling into our bones.

The air was thick with smoke from the hearth, melting candle wax, and unease. Thunder rolled overhead, distant but persistent, but the real storm brewed inside the room.

Maps were spread open, marked with sigils and hastily drawn circles. Candles burned low, their flames flickering as they cast long, uneasy shadows over all the gathered faces, Red, Luca, Darcy, Damien, Bo, Trovi, and Andrew. For a moment, no one spoke.

Trovi exhaled sharply and broke the silence. "She'll need rest. All of us do. Whatever link the dark völva forged… it's broken, but not harmless. We don't know what it left behind."

Andrew's arm tightened around me. "Then we keep watch." His voice softened. "Together."

I nodded faintly, the word *together* echoing somewhere deep in me, through the exhaustion, through the ache, through the fragile thread of hope still binding us.

And still, I couldn't shake the feeling that something… or *someone*… was watching from just beyond the edge of things, waiting.

Red spoke next, her voice rough. "We shouldn't have brought Naomi back. She's a risk. You've seen what she's capable of…"

"…and there's probably more that we don't know," Luca finished grimly.

Red shot him a glare, frustration flickering faintly in her eyes. "I'm not saying we leave her to rot. But Astrid nearly didn't make it back… again. If anything's still tethered between them…"

"It could drag her under for good," Bo finished, jaw clenched. "That's how gods work. Truth twisted with just enough mercy to make you trust it."

My pulse quickened. Manipulation woven into mercy, temptation disguised as trust.

Trovi's voice was soft, haunted. "Ewan's influence weaves through Odin's circles. I've seen it, minds clouded, loyalties bending. He's using divine residue like poison."

Red cursed under her breath. "This is fucking great… So… we're fighting gods and ghosts now?" Her gaze cut toward me. "Astrid… you barely got out of there, and that wasn't even a God."

"Then we fight smart," I said, pressing my hands flat against the table.

Red scoffed quietly, shaking her head. "Smart? You walked straight into a nightmare and almost didn't come back. You want to do that again?"

"If I don't," I said, meeting her gaze, "someone else will. And they won't have Mani. They won't have Andrew. They won't have all of you."

Her eyes narrowed, studying me.

"I'm not rushing in blind this time," I continued, softer but firm. "We know what we're facing now. We prepare. But hiding won't stop any of this. It'll just give them more time."

Red exhaled through her nose, tension pulling at her jaw. "You're really not going to back down from this, are you?" she muttered.

"No," I said simply.

For a long moment she just stared at me, then her mouth quirked faintly. "All right," she said, leaning back slightly. "So, there *is* a plan… right?"

Andrew shifted beside me, his shadow stretching long in the candlelight. "She always does," he said quietly.

Red gave a breathy laugh, half worried, half affection. "Yeah, that's what scares me. Because unless that plan includes recruiting a miracle or a god-killer, we're fucked."

I straightened, steadying my voice. "We don't need to kill them," I said. "We just need to cut their threads. The dark völva's power, Odin's reach, they're all connected through the same weave. If we can sever it at the root…"

"…then we take away their leverage," Trovi finished, her eyes widening slightly. "You'd be striking at the heart of the network itself."

Bo frowned. "That's assuming we can even *find* the root. If Odin's truly meddling, he could be anywhere."

The room fell quiet, the weight of it pressing in from all around. It felt like a ship caught in dying winds, with its sails hanging slack, the crew waiting in tense silence, each of us feeling the drag of uncertainty.

I met each of their gazes in turn, knowing we all felt it… and knowing none of us were ready to surrender to it.

"Then we start small," I said. "We find a thread…we start with Naomi's mind, the remnants of the tether, the symbols the dark völva left behind. If there's residue, I'll find it and burn it clean."

Red leaned forward, her elbows on her knees, the firelight dancing in her eyes. "You sound awfully sure of yourself," she said softly. "You nearly got lost in there. I just…" Her voice cracked. "I just don't want to lose you again, okay?"

"I didn't get lost," I said. "I…just…came back with something."

Trovi blinked. "What do you mean?"

I turned toward the window where the rain had begun to fall again, soft and steady against the glass. "When the threads snapped, I felt something, seen something? It was a pattern behind the dark völva's magic. A symbol burned into the void before it faded."

Andrew's voice was careful. "And what did it look like?"

My fingers brushed unconsciously against the runes on my hand. "It looked like a serpent devouring its own tail."

A silence fell over the room, sharp, heavy, and knowing.

"Ouroboros?" Bo muttered. "The cycle that feeds itself?"

Trovi went still, the color draining from her face. "Not just a symbol," she said quietly. "It's a lock, a seal and a boundary both. It keeps the balance. When it breaks… it doesn't just open. It *undoes.* Chaos follows. Transformation too, if anything survives it."

The words sank deep, colder than the storm outside. Lightning cracked like a warning, thunder rolling low through the house.

Red exhaled shakily, rubbing her face. "Well," she said, managing a small smile, "guess that answers my question. You *do* have a plan."

I met her eyes, lightning catching the edge of my reflection in the window. "Not a plan," I said quietly. "A guess at best."

And somewhere deep within, Mani stirred, a low growl that sounded dangerously like agreement.

Andrew brushed my hand, voice low enough for only me. "Don't stress about the details right now, we will get it figured out."

I exhaled slowly. "I'm just trying to keep us alive."

Red stepped next to us, her boots soft against the wood. Andrew pressed a kiss to the side of my head and went to see the others out.

Red lingered in the flickering light of the candles. The storm outside caught her face in flashes of silver and shadow. "You scared the hell out of me, you know that?"

I turned slightly, catching her faint, wry smile in the window's reflection. "You and everyone else."

She gave a soft snort, but her voice cracked when she spoke again. "Next time you decide to dive into the abyss, maybe let one of us hold the rope, yeah?"

A small, weary laugh escaped me. "Deal."

Red's expression softened. She bumped her shoulder lightly against mine, a quiet show of affection that said more than words. "Get some rest," she murmured. "You look like fucking hell."

"Yeah," I whispered, watching the rain snake down the glass, twisting in thin, silver rivers. "Rest."

But Mani's growl stirred faintly in my chest, low, restless, and ready. *'We'll sleep when the hunt's done.'*

Red's footsteps carried her toward the door, and as the wood creaked under her weight, I noticed Trovi lingering in the doorway. Her gaze was distant, unfocused, but sharp enough to pierce the quiet.

"Those who seem your enemy might not be," she murmured. "But those closest to us… they might be. They're watching Astrid. Testing which path you'll take."

I turned back to the window. Lightning cleaved the courtyard in stark flashes of white and shadow, painting my reflection across the glass, tired, scarred, but resolute.

"Then they'll have their answer soon enough," I whispered.

'And when they do?' Mani's voice rumbled low, more felt than heard. *'What happens when they realize what you've become?'*

Another flash lit the stormy sky, washing my reflection in sharp silver and deep shadow.

"Then they'll learn to fear it, or follow it," I said, voice steady despite the tremor in my chest.

'Careful,' Mani warned, pride threading beneath the growl. *'You sound more like me every day.'*

Chapter 32

The storm outside had begun to loosen its grip, thunder retreating, leaving only the soft hiss of rain remained, water whispering against stone and glass. Inside me, nothing had eased. Shadow and instinct pulsed beneath my skin, restless, coiled, unwilling to release their hold. I let my fingers trail along the windowsill, following the cold paths of rain as if they might anchor me to the world I had fought so hard not to slip from.

Every breath felt heavier than the last, burdened with what we'd uncovered, and with what still waited beyond the dark. Threads of power and deceit tangled far deeper than I'd imagined. Somewhere within that web lingered Naomi, her presence like a spark on dry brush, fragile, volatile, and far from extinguished.

I turned from the window, letting the storm's fading whispers fall away behind me, and stepped into the hall where the others were gathering. Red stood tightening her coat, and shoulders squared. Bo checked his phone, jaw locked tight as if distance itself might break under his grip. Trovi's wards shimmered faintly at her doorway, carved runes humming low, alive and watchful.

The air carried the sharp scent of wet asphalt and rich, fresh-turned earth from Trovi's garden, layered with candle smoke that clung to the vaulted ceiling in dark smudges. Soft light pooled along the walls, unsteady. Footsteps echoed

through the hall, careful, hesitant, as though even the house sensed what was coming.

Red met my gaze for a heartbeat, steady and fierce. "Don't do anything reckless," she said, though her tone carried more hope than command.

I managed a faint smile. "You'd hate me if I didn't."

She snorted softly, but her expression softened. "Just come back," she said, barely above a whisper.

I nodded, the weight of her words sinking in deeper than I let show. "Always," I murmured. She pulled me into a fierce, sudden hug, her arms tightened before releasing me just as quickly.

As I followed her toward the door, the hall seemed to narrow. The light dimmed, not all at once, but subtly, like a breath being held. The house itself felt watchful. I felt a whisper behind me. The maps rustled, the smell of damp stone and candle soot thickened. Then the world rippled before it broke.

At first, I thought I felt heat. The air shimmered, light warping across the walls. The hearth fire wavered, its glow bending like it was seen through water. Then the distortion deepened, peeling back like the surface of a mirror. The timbers overhead groaned. The runes carved into the beams began bleeding shadow, ink-black tendrils seeping out of the wood. The walls around us warped and rippled, their solid shapes hollowing out and stretching, until the room became something else, something wrong.

"Andrew…" I began, my voice barely steady.

He was next to me instantly, his hand already tightening around mine. "I see it," he said, voice taut. "What is this?"

The floorboards shivered beneath us, trembling as though the house itself had taken a sharp, fearful breath.

Shadows pooled and writhed in the gaps between the planks, thick and almost sentient, moving as if they breathed with a life of their own, a darkness that should never be. The air shifted, charged with the acrid tang of ash, damp earth, and something older, something metallic and electric that prickled my skin. Then the whisper came, silken and intimate, as it crawled across my senses as though it were spoken directly along my flesh.

"You've touched my dark völva's threads, little wolf."

My pulse spiked. "Is this…Ewan?" The name burned on my tongue, tasting like smoke and static, sharp enough to sting. My vision fluttered, colors snapping too bright, too vivid, edges blurring in the sudden intensity.

Around us Red, Bo, Luca, Darcy, Damien, and Trovi reacted instantly, summoning their power and striking at forms that weren't fully there.

They were just illusions, phantoms wearing familiar faces. One stepped forward, it was in my mother's likeness, smiling faintly, her eyes hollow and wrong. Another assumed Naomi's shape bloodied and pleading. "You left me," it whispered. "You always leave them."

"Don't listen!" Andrew shouted. Energy flared from him, scattering the figure like smoke, yet three more shadows slithered from the warped walls behind him, crawling with intent.

Red's hands ignited, flames licking out into the gray haze. "They're feeding on guilt!" she yelled. "Don't give them form!"

But it was already too late.

Then he appeared. Ewan's illusion took shape, tall and sharp-eyed, his presence pressing against the room itself,

bending space, warping the air. The ground beneath him oozed a dark, iron-rich red, like ink mixed with blood, veins seeping through the wood and stone, crawling outward in slow, deliberate tendrils.

"You cannot fight what you do not understand," his voice thundered, layered and immense, as though it rose from every shadow and every stone at once. "Every shadow you claim, every light you wield, it all belongs to the weave I built."

My shadows recoiled instinctively. Even Mani faltered in my head. *'He isn't truly here,'* she warned, unease threading her growl. *'But his power is. Be careful.'*

Andrew stepped forward anyway, jaw set, defiance burning brighter than fear. "Then we'll tear it down."

Ewan tilted his head, and the world detonated. The blast threw us all backward. The air itself burst apart in a concussive wave that hurled us backward. I slammed into the long oak table, the impact ripping the breath from my lungs in a sharp, brutal gasp. The solid wood didn't give, but something in me did. Pain flared through my ribs as I hit the floor, the table shuddering but holding firm.

Smoke and dust clouded my vision. Through the ringing in my ears, I saw Andrew on one knee, his wing twisted at an impossible angle, blood spreading dark and fast across his shoulder.

"Andrew!" I screamed, dragging myself toward him, every movement burning.

The illusion of Ewan watched us with quiet amusement, untouched, unbothered, an observer savoring the damage.

"You think this love protects you?" he said smoothly. "It only binds you tighter to the pain."

Rage tore through me, raw and unrestrained. My power surged without permission, shadows erupting outward in violent arcs, writhing and coiling as they fused with the storm still echoing beyond the walls. Lightning flashed through the windows, answering my pulse, my fury, my fear. For one breathless heartbeat, I felt unstoppable, lethal and almost divine.

But when I reached for Ewan's phantom, he slipped through my grasp like smoke unraveling into light, taking half my strength with him as he faded.

The backlash hit instantly.

I collapsed beside Andrew, gasping, hands shaking uncontrollably as power burned through me, overdrawn and unforgiving. The shadows recoiled at last, leaving only the ache, the exhaustion, and the knowledge that Ewan had never meant to finish us.

Only to measure us himself.

Red dropped to her knees beside us, her face ashen, fury flashing beneath the fear. "He's…" she said sharply "Astrid… you have to…"

"I know," I snapped, the word breaking apart as it left me. I pressed my hands to Andrew's chest, palms burning as I forced my energy inward, searching blindly for the fragile cadence of his heart. "*Don't you dare leave me.*" The whisper tore out of me, wild and desperate.

For the first time, Mani wavered. Her voice trembled in my mind, stripped of its usual iron certainty, as if she could feel him slipping through her claws.

'Don't fight the current,' she urged, urgent and afraid. *'Follow it. Find his rhythm... his breath... anything. Anchor yourself to him. Do not let him go.'*

I obeyed. I matched him, breath to breath, beat to beat, letting my own pulse bend and sync to his, forcing my magic to move with him instead of against him. The seconds stretched, agonizing and endless, until Andrew's chest finally jerked beneath my hands and he drew in a ragged, desperate gasp.

His eyes flew open, irises flaring molten red for a heartbeat before fading back to their familiar green-orange.

Relief hit me like a blow. I sagged forward, a broken laugh catching in my throat as tears burned hot behind my eyes. "You idiot," I whispered hoarsely. "You can't just take on a god."

His mouth twitched into a crooked, breathless smile. "I'm pretty sure," he rasped, "it won't be the last time."

Bo's voice echoed faintly from across the wrecked room. "They're gone! Illusions all fading!"

But the victory felt hollow. The scorched runes still marred the wood and stone, their lines burned deep, while veins of ink-dark red pulsed through the warped surfaces like a wound that refused to close. The marks throbbed faintly, as if whatever power had carved them there hadn't fully faded.

Ewan hadn't been trying to kill us. He'd been measuring us, probing, pressing, threatening to see how far he could push before we broke. Testing the limits of what we could endure.

I pushed myself to my feet, steadying Andrew as he rose beside me. My power still buzzed painfully beneath my skin, a low, warning hum I couldn't ignore. "We can't fight this alone," I said, voice low, resolute. "Not gods. Not like this."

Andrew nodded, his wings folding tight against his back, his expression dark with understanding. "Then what are we supposed to do?"

Outside, thunder rolled again, distant and hollow, like the fading echo of something vast moving beyond sight. The storm had passed, but the air inside the house still hummed with divine residue, a lingering charge that clung to the walls and floorboards like a scar the world had yet to close.

In that strained, uneasy silence, the truth settled into me with brutal clarity.

This was no longer a war fought in shadows or whispered spells.

It was a war against the shape of fate itself.

And I would meet it head-on—with every shred of resolve I possessed, every ounce of will still burning in my blood.

Chapter 33

The rain had stopped sometime before dawn, but the air still tasted like smoke and static. When the sun finally broke through thinning clouds, the house had fallen into an uneasy quiet. Trovi's wards sputtered across the splintered beams, runes still flickering where Ewan's illusion had torn through them. The scent of scorched oak clung to everything, sharp and bitter.

Red stayed behind to help piece Trovi's house back together. She moved through the wreckage with clipped efficiency, scooping up the scattered papers I'd left in my wake, muttering a steady stream of curses under her breath. Ash smeared her fingers; splintered wood crunched beneath her boots. "It's like the whole house got rewritten," she said at last, glancing toward the scarred beams overhead. "I can still *feel* him in the walls."

"He left a signature," Bo replied quietly. His gaze followed the faint red veins still pulsing beneath the floorboards, like half-healed wounds glowing through skin. "A warning, I'd say at the least."

I said nothing. My hands trembled despite my efforts to still them, the aftershock of overdrawn power lingering in my bones. Every time I blinked, I saw it again—brief flashes of red light beneath my skin, like embers trapped under ash. Ewan's influence hadn't fully released me. It clung, faint but persistent.

Andrew sat beside me on the step near the hearth, close enough that I could feel his warmth through the chill in the room. His breathing had evened out, slow and steady—but his silence pressed down on me harder than any visible wound.

I tried to help reinforce Trovi's wards, forcing myself to move, to *do* something. But the moment my fingers brushed a rune, it shuddered beneath my touch. The glow flickered and pulled away along the carved line, recoiling as if it sensed something wrong.

I froze.

The ward wasn't rejecting *me*.

It was the magic clinging to me—Ewan's residue still tangled in my aura from the clash. The rune shrank back from my hand like a living thing recognizing a familiar threat.

As if it remembered him.

I jerked my hand back, my breath catching.

My power was still too raw. Too close to his.

"He knew exactly where to strike," I murmured, the truth settling heavy in my chest. "Not just to test us, but to remind us how small we still are."

Andrew's gaze snapped to mine, exhaustion etched into his features, but fire still burning beneath it. "Then we don't stay small."

The words lingered dangerously. Around us, the others went still. Trovi's hand stilled mid-rune, and slowly she turned her head towards me. Her gaze locked onto me, not my face, but something *behind* it, almost *through* it. The wards along the beams flickered in response, their hum sharpening as if they'd sensed what she did.

"Astrid…" Trovi said quietly.

The way she said my name sent a chill skittering down my spine. She stepped closer, her eyes narrowing, pupils

dilating as her sight slipped past the physical. The air between us tightened, pressure building in my chest like a held breath.

"...there's a... residue... still on you," she said, taking it all in. "Not possession... Not corruption." Her jaw tightened. "Like a thumbprint."

Andrew straightened instantly. "What does that mean?"

Trovi nodded once, slow and grave. "He's threaded himself through you."

Cold crept up my spine, sharp and undeniable.

"That's how he found us," she continued, her voice low and precise. "Not by breaking my wards, but by *stepping around them*. Through the one mind, he's already touched." Her gaze sharpened.

The room seemed to tilt.

"He didn't force control," Bo murmured, realization dawning. "He listened and nudged them. Whispering into people's thoughts."

Trovi's eyes never left mine. "The dark völva taught him how or he's remembered how." A pause. Then, softly, "Odin never ruled by strength alone. He ruled by *knowing*."

Everything inside me went cold. "The voice," I said slowly, pulse roaring in my ears. "The first one I heard before everything else... long before the shadows ever moved."

Trovi inhaled sharply.

Silence crashed down around us.

"That was him," she finished. "Reaching through the crack you didn't know was there yet."

The truth landed with brutal weight. Every instinctive turn. Every moment of unease. Every step that had led us just a fraction too close, or too late.

Andrew's hand found mine. "He won't get her again."

Trovi finally looked away, expression dark and troubled. “No,” she said. “But now that you know how he moves… you’ll feel him before he speaks.”

My shadows stirred uneasily beneath my skin.

And suddenly, the house didn’t just feel violated anymore. It felt *watched*, I felt watched.

I turned toward the window as dawn crept slow and pale through the rain-streaked glass, painting the forest in silver and smoke. Somewhere far beyond those trees, Ewan was watching and waiting. And for the first time, I felt it, not just his reach, but something older beneath it.

The air still hummed, sharp with leftover charge. I was halfway down the hall when movement snagged the corner of my eye. A shadow, moving on its own. It slithered across the floor, thin and deliberate, clinging to the wall like smoke searching for a seam. It lingered by the warded door at the far end of the corridor, the one Trovi had resealed.

“Red?” I called softly. No answer. Only the rain, whispering against the windows and the fading pulse of runes.

The shadow flickered again, almost beckoning me. Then it slipped beneath the door and vanished into the morning.

My chest tightened. ‘*Mani?*’

Her voice stirred faintly, threaded with unease. *‘I don’t think that’s us.’*

I followed it outside, the world was slick and cold, the forest dripping from the night’s downpour. The shadow wove between the trees, its edges blurring with the mist, always just far enough to make me question whether I was chasing it or being led.

The closer I came to the main road, the more unstable the shadow grew. And the faster my pulse climbed. It wasn’t

just on the ground anymore, it was under my skin, syncing with my heartbeat.

The hospital loomed through the fog, its pale walls washed gray by morning light. One of Trovi's wards still glimmered faintly over the entrance, dim but intact. The shadow slipped through the cracked door and vanished inside.

Mani's voice stirred faintly, threaded with unease. *'Astrid. Don't.'*

But I already had. The halls were quiet, too quiet. The scent of antiseptic and cold metal hung in the air, that sterile sharpness only hospitals seemed to hold. My boots echoed off tile as I turned the corner toward the recovery wing. That was when Red's voice came from behind me, taut and urgent. "Something's wrong with her!"

Naomi? She'd been stable under Trovi's wards since she was brought to the hospital, contained and protected. But the air now felt wrong, like it was razor-sharp, humming like a live wire ready to snap.

I followed as Red ran past me through the open door, every instinct on edge.

Naomi lay motionless in the hospital bed, her face pale beneath the dim light. Monitors hummed softly beside her, their steady rhythm was the only sign of life in the sterile quiet. For one fragile moment, she looked peaceful, fragile even.

Then the shadow slipped beneath the door. It poured across the floor like spilled ink, climbing up the side of her bed and forcing its way in through her ear, with a soundless push. Then the monitors stuttered. Naomi's back arched then her eyes flew open.

A strangled gasp tore from her throat as runes flared to life along the walls, patterns I hadn't noticed before, light crawling across the floor in fractured veins. She bolted upright, her movements jerky and wrong, whispering to no one, half-words and fragments spilling out in a trembling rush.

"They said it would stop…he promised… it would stop…don't let her see… don't let her see…"

Her nails raked down her arms, tearing through skin until blood welled up in thin rivulets. Veins along her throat blackened, pulsing with threads of violet light as through it was alive and writhing, as though something buried deep inside was trying to claw its way free.

Trovi pushed past me to get into the room and was already at her bedside, knife flashing as she carved fresh sigils into the tile. "Her mind's destabilizing," she said sharply. "Whatever you pulled her from… she didn't come all the way back."

Then Andrew stepped beside me, tension rippling through his wings. "Can we stop it…stop her?"

"Not stop," Trovi said grimly. "Contain, maybe. But one wrong push, and we lose her completely."

The pulse beneath my skin deepened, then Mani stirred, uneasy. Her voice brushed through my mind, low and trembling with a fear she tried to hide. '*It's not anyone's fault, Astrid. But what's happening to her… if you touch it, he'll see you. The dark völva … Ewan… they will see us.*'

I stepped forward anyway. "Then he can watch."

Naomi's head snapped up, eyes blazing, her amethyst eyes fractured with shadow.

Before anyone could move, the sound came. A scream. A loud, but deep, scream that vibrated through the air and into my bones. The kind of sound no mortal lungs should make.

I flinched as Andrew moved without thinking, his presence coiling instinctively around me.

"What the hell is that?" Red shouted, clamping her hands over her ears. "Is she… is she fighting it?"

I nodded, my gaze locked on Naomi. She trembled against the sheets, her body bowed under invisible weight. The runes carved into the floor around the bed pulsed in a frantic, uneven rhythm, their light stuttering like a failing heartbeat. The shadows were thick, glistening strands of ancient völva craft, snaked around her limbs, binding her wrists and ankles in shimmering black chains. Old magic. Cruel magic. Each surge of power sent sparks skittering across the tile, sharp and violent, like oil striking open flame.

Mani whispered again, softer now. '*You feel it, don't you? The thread unraveling... not gone but loosening.*'

"I feel it," I murmured, sinking to my knees beside Naomi. "But if she slips…"

'Then you catch her,' Mani said simply. No fear. No anger. Just will. *'Well... what's left of her.'*

Naomi's head snapped up. Her eyes burning violet, pupils narrowing like a predator's. "He's still inside," she hissed through her teeth. "The dark völva… he's watching…"

My chest twisted painfully. Sweat slicked her skin, her hair plastered to her temples, her breath coming in shallow, ragged pulls. She looked suspended between moments, between selves, caught between worlds that were both trying to claim her.

"I know," I said quietly. "But you have to be stronger than him."

A broken laugh tore out of her. "You don't know what he made me do," she rasped. "You don't know what he's willing to do."

"I don't need to," I replied, my voice low as I reached toward her. Shadows flickered over my fingers, drawn to her pain. "I just know… you're still you."

For a single heartbeat, something flickered behind her eyes, then the chains reacted. Black flame surged up her arms, the shadows tightening, biting deeper. Naomi screamed.

Andrew stepped forward, tension snapping through him, but I barked. "I've got her!"

I dropped both palms to the floor, letting the rhythm of time bend beneath my hands. The air rippled outward from my hands, light fracturing as though submerged beneath water. Reality slowed to the pace of a single heartbeat. Each breath shimmered, distorted, and stretched thin, as though the world itself had turned liquid around me.

The runes flared white-blue, their glow caught in the current of suspended seconds. Shadows unfurled from my skin like ribbons of night, weaving through the fractures with purpose, patient and deliberate, seeking the rot that clung to every corner.

The darkness that bound Naomi hissed in protest, but I didn't fight it, I rewound it. Every pulse of corruption was met with an answering surge of healing light, shadows carrying fragments of time backward past the invasion, past the fracture, to before the wound was ever carved.

Naomi's body arched once, twice, then the chains dissolved into glittering ash, suspended in the slowed air like dying stars before scattering into nothing.

Then there was just silence.

Even time itself seemed to hold its breath.

Naomi sagged forward, trembling violently. When she finally lifted her head, the sharp edge in her eyes had softened, the shadows retreating as her breath evened out. "I can't hear him anymore," she whispered, disbelief trembling through the words.

Relief crashed through me like air after drowning. "Good," I breathed. "But it won't last unless we keep you anchored."

"Anchored?" she echoed weakly.

"To yourself," I said softly. "To the part of you that still remembers why you wanted out."

For once, she didn't argue. Just nodded, exhausted, trembling, a fragile spark of something still alive beneath the ruin.

Slowly, I released the tension in my hands. The distortion faltered, the rippling light smoothing out as time found its rhythm again. The room exhaled, lights flickering, dust motes drifting back into motion, as the last traces of the dark völva's presence were devoured by my shadows, leaving behind only the clean, sharp scent of antiseptic air.

I pressed my palms flat to Naomi's forehead, easing the flow of power from force to care. Healing energy rippled outward, not in blinding light but in warmth, steady and deliberate. I let it seep through Naomi's mind like a gentle tide, stitching torn edges, softening the violent rhythm of her pulse, and for the first time since stepping into that room, I felt her *steady*.

But the air was still wrong, residue clung to the corners—warped shadows twitching like wounded things, refusing to fade.

"Not anymore," I whispered.

My shadows stretched outward, fluid and knowing, sweeping across the walls and floor with quiet authority. Where they touched, the corruption hissed and burned away, leaving only faint traces of ozone and ash.

When the last of it faded, the room felt… lighter. Clean. The kind of silence that came *after* something had been set right. Naomi swayed, then collapsed to her knees, a trembling sigh escaping her as the last of her strength drained away. Her skin was pale, almost translucent beneath the dim light. "It's… quieter," she murmured—her voice frayed, but unmistakably her own.

Relief loosened something deep in my chest. "Good," I said softly. "Hold onto that quiet. It's yours."

A fragile, exhausted smile ghosted across her face. Behind me, Trovi let out a shaky breath, lowering her clenched hands from her chest. "You just cleansed the whole damn room," she whispered, awe and disbelief tangled in her voice.

"Not cleansed," I corrected, my voice hoarse.

Red stepped closer, her fire dimmed to an ember. "She seems stable…for now."

Across the room, Andrew exhaled, the tension finally easing from his frame. "That was…" he stopped, then shook his head. "What even happened?"

I looked at Naomi as my shadows slipped fully back beneath my skin. For the first time, she didn't look haunted. Fragile and free, for now.

As the seconds finally caught up to themselves and reality settled, I knew we'd bought her something rarer than survival.

We'd bought her time.

I wiped the sweat from my brow, my pulse still unsteady. "She still might be dangerous," I said quietly. "But she's not our enemy... not now anyway."

Mani's voice was low, sure, almost tender. '*Compassion can be a weapon too... if you know when to wield it.*'

My throat tightened. I looked at Naomi, the girl I once despised, now trembling in the fragile calm of her own redemption, and I knew Mani was right.

Fear only feeds the darkness. But empathy… empathy can bend even time.

Wind drifted through the open window, carrying the scent of rain and clean air. The storm still lingered on the horizon, waiting, but for this heartbeat, for this stolen moment, time bowed to peace.

Andrew stepped closer, his arms coming around me as the last tension drained from him. His breath brushed my ear when he spoke, low and reverent. "You didn't just buy us time," he murmured, resting his forehead against my shoulder. "Whatever you did… it drove the darkness back."

"Maybe," I said softly. "But it's not gone."

He glanced at Naomi, who was still trembling on the floor, and then back at me. "Then we keep watch."

The words settled between us like an oath. I rose slowly, flexing my fingers as the final echoes of the magic faded from my skin. The air still shimmered faintly where time had bent, reluctant to forget. For a moment, I could still *feel* the rhythm of it, the way the world's heartbeat aligned with mine, steady, fragile, but alive.

Then it passed.

Somewhere in the distance, thunder rolled again, low, deliberate, a reminder that peace was only ever borrowed. I turned toward the narrow window, watching the storm clouds drift apart just enough for a sliver of sunshine to spill across the city. In that golden glow, the air seemed to tremble, a ripple moving through the air, subtle but certain, as if time itself had exhaled.

Mani's voice was amused. '*I'm sure he felt that.*'

Chapter 34

Trovi's wards flickered one final time before guttering out completely, leaving the room washed in the cold, artificial glow of hospital lights. The shadows they left behind stretched unnaturally long across the floor and walls, warped and hesitant, like they hadn't decided whether to stay or flee.

Red paced near the door, her boots scuffing against tile. Her fingers twitched with restless energy, her body refusing the concept of stillness. Every few steps, she muttered something under her breath, half curses, half prayers. Andrew hadn't moved from my side, but his gaze tracked every shift in the room, alert and coiled.

"She's stable," Trovi said finally, her voice low and careful. "But the residue… what you pulled her out of…" She hesitated, then released a slow breath. "It wasn't just the dark völva *destroying* her. It was directional."

I frowned. "Meaning?"

But before Trovi could answer, Mani did.

'She was being guided,' Mani said. *'We know that he was using her.'*

I sighed. *'We assumed that.'*

'And it seems we were right,' Mani continued. *'He made her believe she could carry his power, made her hungry for it…then used that hunger to control her.'*

My throat went dry. "Naomi thought she was in control," I whispered under my breath, barely aware I'd spoken aloud.

'She never was,' Mani said. *'But she wanted to be. That's the weakness he needs. Wanting. Needing. He seems to thread himself through it.'*

The room seemed to tilt slightly, as if the floor itself had lost its certainty. The edges of the overhead light flickered, briefly dimming. The memory of Naomi's eyes, wild and glassy, flashed behind my closed eyes. "She looked at me like she knew what was in me." I said. "Like he was inside her, watching through her skin."

Andrew's head turned sharply at the sound of my voice, tension sharpening his features. Trovi was already studying me, a grim understanding in her expression.

"That's exactly it," Trovi said. "He wasn't just feeding on her mind. He was *focusing* her. Channeling through her and from her… to reach you."

She then uncorked a small vial and brushed her thumb across Naomi's forehead. An iridescent sheen bloomed beneath her touch, shimmering faintly. The liquid hissed where it touched her skin, like it was burning away the corruption that remained. "Meaning it wasn't random," Trovi continued. "That shadow didn't just *find* her…it was *sent.*"

Andrew's jaw tightened, muscle jumping as he clenched his teeth. "That's not surprising," he muttered, fury held just barely in check. "She asked for it. And he answered."

Red stopped pacing. The harsh fluorescent light caught a scar along her jaw, a pale line that deepened as she clenched it. "The dark völva," she said, almost spitting the name.

The words echoing against the walls. The lights above us flickered again. The air thickened, pressing in, like the sound alone had weight. For a breath, I could hear it: thin, patient

laughter crawling through the cracks in the wards, whispering beneath the hum of hospital machines.

Trovi's gaze snapped to me, sharp and knowing. "He wanted… us to see that," she said quietly. "Wanted *you* to see it."

A chill rippled through me.

'He's watching through the cracks,' Mani warned softly. *'Calling us back to where it began.'*

The words lodged deep in my chest. I met Trovi's eyes, my pulse spiking. "The house," I murmured.

Red's head snapped up, her eyes narrowing. "What house?"

Trovi's gaze darkened. "That's most likely where he still lives. If you felt him through Naomi, that's where he's feeding from."

But then Trovi hesitated, remembering what happened the last time we went there. Her hand went to the satchel slung across her chest, unfastening the clasp. "There's more," she said.

From the layers of protective cloth, she withdrew the Heartstone. Its light flared softly in her hands, soft, pulsing, and alive. The glow painted her face in rose-gold hues, but beneath that beauty, there was fear.

"I wasn't going to bring it," she admitted quietly. "It was hidden, sealed in the old chest beneath my wards. But when the wards broke, when he appeared, the chest nearly combusted. The stone was fighting to get out."

I felt then the deep thrum within my chest, answering the one in her hands.

"I couldn't leave it behind," Trovi continued. "It seems to be drawn to you, Astrid. There are layers of god and goddess essence woven into it. If the dark völva draws power through this… through *you*… given your lineage and Ewan's influence…" Her voice faltered for just a moment before she steadied it. "That connection could fracture the remaining realms. It would burn the Heartstone from the inside out." She took a breath. "And if the Heartstone is destroyed, there will be no mending what breaks."

Andrew's gaze flicked toward the glowing stone, tension pulling his features taut. His voice came out tight. "It reacted to him before? How can we keep it from him?"

"Yes, it did," Trovi said, her tone weighted with grim certainty. "And if the dark völva is at the house, then the stone may be the only thing that can help you, strong enough to keep you from being pulled apart by what waits there."

The low hum in the room deepened, vibrating through the floor and into my bones. I reached out, brushing my fingers across the Hearthstone's smooth surface. It pulsed once beneath my touch. It was warm, and its light flickered like it recognized me.

'It's remembering,' Mani whispered. *'It knows what's coming.'*

Static crackled through the air as I slid the stone into the inner pocket of my jacket and squared my shoulders. "Then let's end this son of a bitch."

Red didn't hesitate, she grabbed her coat and the silver-etched blade from the table. "Good," she said. "Because I've got a few words for our favorite pain in the ass."

'I doubt he will come here,' Mani warned. *'He'll make you follow. That's how I would hunt.'*

I turned toward Trovi. Exhaustion showed in the small tremor she tried to hide, the faint shadows beneath her eyes, the

way her hand lingered on the table for balance. "You don't have to come," I said quietly. "After what he did to you last time…"

"I remember," she cut in. Her hand pressed against her side, fingers tracing old scars beneath fabric. "I can still feel where his magic cut across me. But hiding from him won't undo it. And I'm the only one who can read the trail he left."

"Still," I said. "If you're not ready…"

"I'm not," she interrupted. "But I'm coming anyway." Her eyes met mine, fear flickering there, but beneath it, something unyielding "If we don't end this now, he'll keep spreading. Through wards, through minds, through people like Naomi. I won't let that happen again."

Red's hand twitched on the hilt of her blade, her voice low. "You sure about this, Trovi? Last time he nearly—"

"I know what he nearly did," Trovi interrupted again, softer now, but no less steady. "And I know what he *will* do if I stay behind."

The silence settled heavy between us. Only the hum of hospital machinery filled the room, the faint, rhythmic beep from Naomi's monitors blending with the low growl of thunder outside.

I reached out, resting a hand lightly on Trovi's arm. "Then we do this together," I said.

She gave a small nod, then inhaled slowly. The air around us shifted and bent as she whispered an incantation. Light gathered between her fingers, soft and golden at first before deepening into a peach-rose shimmer that spread like ripples through the room. The ward light hissed, sealing the space behind us.

"He knows you're coming," she said. Her voice was softer now, almost reverent. "He wants you..."

I stepped forward, the Hearthstone's warmth seeping through my jacket and into my chest. "Then let him think what he wants," I said. "Because this time, we're ending it on our terms."

Red cracked her neck, the sound sharp in the charged air. "About damn time," she muttered.

Andrew's gaze met mine, his expression grim but unflinching. "He called you back," he said quietly. "You sure you're ready to answer?"

I glanced down at the Heartstone resting in my pocket and pulled my jacket tighter around myself. It pulsed once, steady and certain. "I don't think we have a choice."

The fluorescent lights above us flickered once, twice… and then the entire room began to shimmer. We all stood frozen as we watched Trovi transform the hospital room, the air thickening until it felt like breathing through water.

The edges warped first, the corners bending and stretching, as the sterile white walls blurred into a peach-rose haze. Light folded inward on itself, collapsing until the floor beneath us softened, tile dissolving into damp grass beneath our boots, and the smell of salt filled the air. Somewhere beyond the tearing veil of magic, the sea roared, a hollow, endless sound that vibrated through bone and blood alike.

And when the distortion finally faded, we were standing on the cliffside once more, wind biting and wild, the ruins of the old house rising ahead of us, etched in shadow, patient, and waiting.

Chapter 35

The air shimmered, and the world folded. In an instant, Naomi's hospital room bled away, replaced by cold wind and mist. We stood at the bottom of a hill that led to a rugged cliff that stretching endlessly toward the sea. The landscape was both alien and achingly familiar, the cliffside from my memories.

A lonely house crouched in the fog behind us, half-swallowed by earth and wildflowers. Its roof bloomed with heather and moss, as though the land itself refused to let it die. The air smelled of salt, rain, and something earthy, but nothing like the pine of the forest back at Melmont.

Beyond the house, the cliffs rose jagged and black, the waves crashing far below in a rhythm that felt like the heartbeat of the world. Near the edge stood a gnarled, sacred tree I hadn't noticed before, its bark pale as bone, roots clutching the cliff like fingers. Beneath it, runic stones circled the base, glowing faintly against the storm-dark earth. And before the altar, the shadows moved.

A group of hooded figures, the remnants of Odin's devoted, chanted in low, reverent tones. Their voices rose and fell with the wind, weaving ancient syllables that made the air itself shudder. In the center of their ritual, an altar of black stone gleamed wetly. Upon it sat a bowl that reeked of iron and salt, filled with what looked like blood. Beside it, a blade etched with runes pulsed faintly in the moonlight.

And in my pocket I could feel the heat of the Heartstone, it was so hot it almost burned.

The moment stretched, heavy with knowing. The cliff itself seemed to hold its breath. Then the wind shifted, and the chanting stopped. Ewan stepped from the shadows.

Stormlight carved his face into something hard and unreal. Black light pulsed faintly through his veins; smoke curled from his skin like the ghost of something burned too long.

Andrew moved instantly to my side, wings half-flared, shadows restless around him. "He's… not himself," he murmured.

I didn't know how he was right, but I could feel it too. The air around Ewan was wrong, thick with something that didn't belong. Ewan stood in the middle, his eyes unfocused, his lips moving as if listening to a voice none of us could hear. His skin had the sickly pallor of candlewax, veins darkened beneath it like bruised ink.

"Astrid of Hati." His voice was layered, the voice intoned through him, hollow, as if it echoed from the bottom of a well. "You shouldn't have come."

My heart twisted. "Ewan," I said carefully, stepping forward through the wet grass. "I know… were enemies… but something doesn't seem right…"

His head jerked up sharply. His eyes were glazed over, clouded, pupils spreading like drops of oil over water. "You shouldn't have come," he repeated, his voice warping beneath the dark völva's tone, and another.

"Ewan, listen to me," I said, steady despite the tremor in my chest. "Whatever he's done to you, I don't think this is who you really are."

A flicker of confusion flashed behind his eyes, but then his lips twisted, and another voice spilled through his mouth, colder, smoother. "Who he is…was… doesn't matter anymore."

Andrew's shadows unfurled from his shoulders. "He's inside him," he muttered.

I saw it as we drew closer, a faint shimmer crowning his head, like heat rising off scorched stone. Threads glimmered there, black and silvery-gray, winding through his veins before unraveling into the air, thin and delicate as spider silk. Magic… but not his. The dark völva's magic?

'He's supposed to be the All-Father.' Mani's voice rippled through me, low and feral with laughter. *'Stronger? Look at him, Astrid.'* Her amusement sharpened, turning predatory. *'That's not a god, it's a god on strings. Let's see if his pride is the tether. Let's see what happens when we tug.*

For one reckless heartbeat, I imagined what it would mean to face the true All-Father, Odin whole, unbound, and unfractured. The answer landed cold and absolute. I wouldn't survive it. Not with my magic. Not with Mani. Not with everything Hel had carved into me.

Odin's power wasn't just strength, it was knowledge. Centuries of war, sacrifice, and bargains etched into the bones of the world. You don't outfight that. You don't outthink it.

'Not ever,' Mani agreed, her voice stripped of humor. *'A god whole is a storm you kneel through… or you break.'*

But this… this wasn't Odin. This was a man wearing a god's name while someone else pulled the strings.

The realization struck like lightning. I met Ewan's empty, glassy stare and let my tone turn sharp as a blade. "You're not Odin."

His head tilted just a fraction; I could see his anger flicker, exposing himself. “What?”

I stepped closer, the sea wind tugging at my hair, keeping my eyes on the threads around him. My words were deliberate and cruel. “All that talk about destiny, power, *Odin reborn*, and yet here you are, drooling and doing someone else’s bidding. The All-Father reduced to a ventriloquist’s dummy. Tell me, Ewan, how long have you been dancing to his tune?”

A muscle jumped in his jaw. “Careful, wolf,” he rasped, but the words didn’t sound fully like his.

‘Yes,’ Mani urged. *‘Dig deeper. Let him choke on it.’*

I tilted my head, feigning pity. “What happened to your divine wisdom now? Your mighty will? I thought Odin feared no one. And yet you…” I gestured at the trembling threads around him, “…you can’t even think without him whispering in your ear.”

His breath hitched. For a heartbeat, one of the threads recoiled from his skin. “I…”

“You used to sneer at weakness,” I pressed. “Said only cowards bowed to power they didn’t earn. Yet here you stand… *His hound,* collared and blind.” My voice dropped. “You’re not Odin reborn, Ewan. You’re what’s left when someone steals a god’s name and leaves the man behind.”

Andrew stayed silent behind me, but I could feel his approval like a steady pulse. “*Keep going,*” He said in our mind link.

Ewan’s hands clenched, veins flickering with light and shadow. The dark völva’s voice bled through him, distorted and furious. “You think you can turn him against me?”

“I don’t need to,” I said, stepping closer until I could see the flicker of Ewan’s real self behind the fog. “He’s already

ashamed. He chose you because you were easy. Predictable. Desperate enough to kneel for scraps."

The tremor in his body deepened, and then he screamed, a sound torn between fury and grief. The threads around his body wavered violently, the dark völva's hold faltering under the weight of his rage.

Before he could answer, darkness poured from Ewan in long, writhing ribbons that coalesced into skeletal shapes, jaws and claws that lunged with a smell like old blood. The metallic tang of blood and salt filled the air.

'He can't hold it,' Mani snarled. *'Not power like this. Not without breaking.'*

Andrew was a blade of motion, his wings snapped wide, meeting those shapes head-on. I could feel his heartbeat through our bond: furious restraint, the need to protect.

Mani surged within me. My hands shifted, claws of light and shadow flaring as the runes ignited on my hands. I struck through the dark, each blow scattering the dark völva's constructs into smoke, but for everyone that fell, two more rose.

"Ewan!" I shouted above the roar, my voice ragged. "Listen to me! Is this what you are? A puppet?!"

For a fraction of a breath his movements faltered; recognition, raw fury, flashed under the corruption. "NO ONE USES ME!" he roared. "YOU WERE TO SERVE ME! NO ONE ELSE!"

"He lies to you," I cried out. "He feeds you what you fear most."

Andrew lunged to sever the main shadow from Ewan; he grabbed it and pulled it apart until it shattered, the backlash hurled him across the ritual circle. He hit one of the runic stones hard, wings folding with a grunt.

"Andrew!" I yelled.

He coughed, blood bright on his lips, but his eyes stayed defiant. "Finish it," he rasped. "Break the hold."

'There,' Mani whispered, fierce and wild. *'Now tear him out.'*

The choice hung heavy. A single choice would free them from him. I thought of Naomi, of fragile minds and the price of mercy. Without thinking, I sprinted toward Ewan and I quickly pressed my palm to his chest.

"I won't kill you," I whispered, voice shaking but resolute. I closed my eyes and willed the runes on my hand to heal.

Mani answered with a fierce tide. *'Now. Hold him. Root him in himself.'*

Light burst from my palm, pouring into the fractures of his will. My shadows rushed out at the same time, not to consume but to comb, to unknot. They slid along the poisoned filaments, then I felt it… shame first, then the memory beneath it, then the man buried under both.

The spider-silk threads hissed and sizzled as the light struck them, unraveling them into smoke. The dark völva's voice tore through Ewan like glass breaking, high, furious, then muffled.

For one terrible second it fought, a howl that filled the night sky, but the pressure of his own rage and my light pressed harder. The dark völva's voice cracked and then fell away.

Ewan collapsed into my arms, gasping, drenched in sweat, and trembling as though the darkness had left ice in his veins. When he blinked, his eyes were his own, bloodshot and haunted.

Andrew staggered to his feet, the runic stones at the altar pulsed once and faded. The storm split wide overhead. I could see that he was torn between fury and relief.

I looked at Ewan and shook my head. "You're not our enemy," I said softly. "You're just another pawn..."

The wind screamed across the cliffs, carrying the last echo of the dark völva's rage, which was both a promise and a curse.

I retracted my claws, the runes cooling beneath my palm. "He's using your power against you, poisoning minds," I said softly. "Starting where they believe he's salvation."

Red ground a curse between her teeth. "So, what then?"

Thunder rolled like distant drums. We were left standing in the ruin, shaken, furious, but clarity burned through the exhaustion. He had seen us tear down another one of his hounds. He would not stop.

And neither would we.

Andrew's wings folded in. "He'll come harder next time," he said, voice low, steadying himself as the storm wind tore at his hair. "He knows what we're capable of now... and you're getting better at it."

"And what we're willing to risk," I murmured, glancing down at Ewan. He was barely conscious, trembling against the cold ground, his breath shallow. Whatever the dark völva had left behind in him wasn't completely gone, it lingered like oil under the skin, waiting for the right spark to flare again.

Trovi crouched beside him, her face drained of color, her jaw tight. "He's marked," she said quietly. "Even with the thread's cut, the stain remains. The dark völva can still find him."

I looked down at Ewan, at the way the power still clung to him like oil beneath the skin, and understanding settled heavy in my chest.

What I'd done here wasn't victory. It was survival.

'And only because the god was absent,' Mani said quietly.

I swallowed. Because if Odin ever stood before us whole, unbound and unfractured, no threads to cut, no shame to pry open. Only the cost of facing a god as he truly was, and we wouldn't survive it. No one would. And I wasn't foolish enough to believe I only could.

"Then we move him," Red said sharply, cutting through my thoughts. She was already scanning the horizon, her eyes caught the faint glimmer of lightning far out at sea. "Before he comes looking to reclaim what's his."

I turned toward the cliff's edge. Below us, the ocean was black glass, restless, whispering against the rocks as if it knew what had transpired here. The Heartstone pulsed faintly at my side, its rhythm syncing with mine… with the storm itself.

'I feel like he's still watching,' Mani warned, her voice low and certain.

"I know, I feel it too." I whispered back, though my throat tightened. The weight of an unseen gaze pressing against the veil of the world. A god's hunger. A dark völva's fury. A war yet to start.

Andrew came to stand beside me, eyes tracing the horizon where the sea met the sky. "This isn't the end of it."

"No," I said, taking Andrew's hand as he helped me to my feet. "It's the beginning of something worse… if Ewan was a pawn…is the dark völva really working alone?"

A rumble of thunder rolled overhead, deep and deliberate, as if the world itself answered.

Trovi rose with me, her cloak snapping in the wind. “Then we’d better be ready,” she said, voice quiet but fierce. “Because if the dark völva is indeed working with someone else… then the worst is yet to come.”

The wind howled harder, carrying with it the scent of rain and salt and blood. And as we turned away from the cliff’s edge, the Heartstone in my pocket flared once, warming me in the biting cold wind and rain.

Somewhere beyond the storm, something ancient stirred. And this time, it was calling my name.

Chapter 36

The storm was closing in fast, its weight pressing down on the air—thick, electric, and alive, as if the sea itself was crawling onto the land to hunt. Lightning split the horizon in brief, merciless flashes, illuminating the cliffs in stark white. We didn't have long before it hit.

The dark völva's house was crouched low against the hillside, half-swallowed by earth and grass, as if the land itself had tried to bury it. Above, bruised storm clouds pressed down, their edges churning with silver light. Wind tore over the cliffside, flattening the tall grass and howling around us.

I hesitated, my pulse thrumming as the first drops began to fall—cold, sharp, warning. Andrew stood at my side, his jaw tight, fist clenched, every muscle coiled like he was waiting for something to strike. Red lifted an arm to shield her face from the few droplets, scanning the horizon. Trovi's white hair whipped across her cheek, plastering to her skin as she stared at the turf-covered roof, unease flickering in her eyes, like she half-expected the house to finish the job from last time.

"We can't stay out here," I said, raising my voice over the gale. "The storm will tear us apart."

Andrew's gaze lingered on the house's doorway. "That's it? The dark völva's house? What if he's still in there…"

"Then we end him," I cut in. "But if we stay out here we're dead from the cold."

No one argued.

"Help me carry him," I gestured to Ewan, fully unconscious in the grass.

Andrew's jaw went hard. "We're not hauling a live grenade into the dark völva's den," he snapped. He glanced at Ewan, then back at me. "What if he wakes up with… whatever… still in him?" He gestured vaguely at Ewan.

Red rounded on me, voice low and sharp. "No. We're not dragging this… mess into the one place that MIGHT be safe... We leave him and burn the house after we're done."

I could see the logic in both of their arguments, they were sensible, mostly. But it tugged against something deeper.

Ewan wasn't a weapon to be lit and tossed away. He was a man folded into a web that could be traced back to the source. Abandoning him was handing the dark völva possibly the one thing he needed.

Trovi's tone was clipped but steady. "Killing him closes a door we might need open. If we want answers… or leverage… we keep him breathing. Mercy can be a weapon as well."

She crouched, checking Ewan's pulse with practiced fingers. "He's alive… barely. If we can get him inside and stabilize him, we can preserve an anchor instead of losing one to the storm."

Andrew's hands flexed at his sides. "Or we walk inside and he's there waiting with a knife at our throats the second we cross the threshold."

"He might be," I said, stepping between them. The wind tore at my coat, urging me forward. "Or he might expect us to run. Either way, leaving him here gives the dark völva the better play." I let my thumb brush the Heartstone in my jacket pocket; it thrummed against my finger, faint but present. The stone's reacting resolves me of any doubt. "Whatever it is, whatever he wants, it's tied to him. We can't ignore that."

Red tensed, and for a moment I thought she'd refuse. Then she let out a long, ragged breath and spat, "Fine. But he stays between us. One wrong twitch and I gutting him myself." She slung the silver-etched blade over her shoulder like a promise.

Andrew gave me one look, a warning, a question, a plea all at once, then moved without another word. He lifted Ewan carefully, like lifting someone who might break. Trovi leaned in and took his legs; I slid under Ewan's shoulders. The man was heavier than he looked, dead weight in my arms, still radiating a lingering warmth, the faint scent of fire and smoke clinging to his hair.

We rose together, awkward and careful, boots slipping on wet grass as a gust tugged at us. The house's black doorway yawned like a mouth. Behind it, the storm pressed closer, an abrasive roar that promised to swallow us whole if we hesitated.

"Watch for anything," Andrew said through gritted teeth. "If anything moves, cut it down."

"Duh," Red said, a hint of annoyance in her voice. The door hung broken on its hinges. The moment I stepped inside, the air shifted, colder, but thicker somehow, saturated with old magic and memory. The scent hit me first: iron, dust, and decay. The residue of rituals long finished but never truly gone.

Trovi hesitated at the threshold, as she dropped Ewan's legs, her hand brushing the doorframe. "He's not here," she murmured, her voice shaking with something I couldn't name.

"Are you sure?" Andrew asked, struggling to keep hold of Ewan.

She gave him a firm nod and then murmured the path-sealing wards under her breath as we crossed the threshold, the words anchoring like ropes in the wind.

Each footstep echoed like it didn't belong to us. The silence felt worse than presence. We carried Ewan further in, closer to the fireplace and set him gently on the warped floorboards. His chest rose and fell in shallow, uncertain breaths. For a breathless beat we all stared at him, the rain hammering the roof above like some furious gods.

Andrew finally said, voice rough. "He comes with us. But if he moves wrong, if the dark völva uses him as a leverage, we end it, and we end it fast."

I met his eyes and nodded. "Agreed."

Outside, thunder rolled and the incoming storm began to smudge the cliffside into gray. The house groaned around us, shaking dust loose from the ceiling. For a moment, I swore I saw runes flash faintly in the walls, like veins of dying light. The residue of the dark völva's power still clung to the space, whispering through the stone.

'He's gone,' Mani's murmured, low but guarded. '*But his presence lingers. This place remembers him.'*

'I can feel it,' I answered, tightening my grip on the front of my jacket. '*The magic's fading, but it's not dead.'*

'Be wary,' Mani warned.

I swallowed, pushing down the chill that crept up my spine.

Andrew brushed dust off his shoulder, glancing toward the open doorway where the wind howled like a living thing.

"Storm's on us. I guess we will stay here… let's make a plan on what we should do next."

I nodded absently, scanning the room. The dark völva's house didn't look like it had been abandoned, but every surface breathed a kind of memory. The walls hummed faintly, dust floating in currents that didn't match the wind.

Trovi was near the shelves, running her fingers along a row of warped spines. "These aren't random," she murmured. "They're arranged by rune order… like someone meant to hide something, not display it."

I joined her, brushing away a thick layer of soot. Most of the books were ruined, spines split, pages blackened, titles long lost to time. But one caught my eye. Its cover gleamed through the grime, the deep blue of dusk over a restless sea. Silverwork traced runes and sacred knots across its surface, symbols older than language, humming softly with restrained power. A dragon-shaped charm hung from its spine, tarnished by time yet faintly radiant. It moved of its own accord, swaying to some invisible rhythm, as if recognizing what watched it.

A cold certainty slid through me. "That one," I whispered.

Trovi shot me a wary glance but reached out. The instant her fingers brushed the cover, the room inhaled. Dust stirred without wind. The air grew sharp, alive with a low hum that crawled through the bones of the house itself.

She hesitated, then pulled the book free. The spine crackled like ice breaking. When she opened it, the scent of sea salt and burnt herbs drifted into the air, faint, like something preserved beyond its time. The pages were impossibly intact, their ink still dark, each rune carved with deliberate precision.

Trovi's breath caught, her voice trembling with awe as she turned the pages "Not Elder Futhark, its older… Proto-Norse… The tongue of the first rune singers." She was lost to the pages. "This…this is impossible," she murmured, almost to herself. "The script predates the sagas by centuries. Look at this…every line, every curve, perfectly preserved. No decay, no fading. The craftsmanship alone… gods, what this book *remembers*."

Her fingers hovered over a line of ink that shimmered faintly in the dim light. "Proto-Norse," she whispered, reverent. "It shouldn't have survived this long, not like this."

She kept talking as if no one else was there, her fascination carrying her voice like a prayer. "Someone didn't just write this, they perfectly preserved it. Protected it. It's more than a relic… it's an original grimoire… blessed by a god, Freya no doubt."

"Why are you so sure it's Freya?" Red asked from across the room.

"She is the mother of magic." Trovi said so softly I doubt that Red heard her.

Andrew walked over, his eyes narrowing. "Can you read it?"

"Barely." Her fingers traced a line of faded script, reverent and trembling. "It's... an invocation."

Her voice dropped as she began to read aloud:

"Ek kalla á þá er binda myrkrið undir rótum himins. Vakni sá sem var bundinn við blóð og stein."

(I call upon those who bind the darkness beneath the roots of heaven. Let the one bound by blood and shadow awaken.)

The sound of the words didn't belong in the air, it *pressed* against it, reshaping it. The house responded, a pulse deep within its frame like a second heartbeat.

"Trovi," I warned softly. But she didn't stop. She turned the page.

The ink shimmered, the runic lines twisting beneath her touch. A low vibration rolled through the floorboards. Somewhere behind us, a deep groan sounded, wood dragging against stone.

Red's voice cut through the tension. "Tell me that wasn't you."

Before I could answer, the shadows along the hearth began to stir. Shadows at the hearth curled inward, twisting against the stone, thickening into silvery-black liquid. They shimmered like oil and moonlight, until the void coalesced at the mouth of the fireplace.

Ash and mortar sifted to the floor as the hearth yawned open, revealing a hollow space behind it where no opening should exist. The air that poured out was stale, cold, metallic, and laced with salt. It whispered in a tongue I almost recognized but couldn't quite hear, like a prayer spoken underwater.

Andrew stepped forward, the light catching the tension in his jaw. "A passageway?" he said, voice low and wary. "Hidden… of course."

Trovi's expression darkened. "No… not hidden," she murmured. "Sealed. Whatever this is, it wasn't meant to be found. The wards weren't to keep us *out.*" Her gaze flicked toward the black maw of the fireplace. "They were meant to keep *something else in.*"

Mani's voice rippled through my mind, low and edged with unease. *"Whatever he built down there... you don't think it was meant for us, do you?"*

A chill rolled through me, sinking deeper than the cold air spilling from the fireplace. The shadows around the hearth pulsed, almost breathing. *"Most likely... we were practically invited,"* I murmured back, my eyes fixed on the black door.

Andrew took a step back, shoulders bunching like he was bracing for impact. He jabbed a finger at the yawning doorway where darkness pooled. "You can't be serious," he said, voice tight. "Clearly it's a trap!"

"I know what it is," I snapped, feeling the heat of the Heartstone on my chest like a pulse against my ribs. "That's exactly why we go in."

Andrew's face went hard. "Because you're stubborn? Because you want a scrap of revenge? It's a trap, Astrid. He'll use the house, the wards, whatever's left of Ewan, he'll turn it into a murder room."

"Or we wait," I shot back, stepping closer to him, "and he spreads. He threads himself through more minds. Naomi was baited, most likely not his first victim… if we don't cut him out now, we'll be pulling people from his maw for the rest of our lives."

Trovi's fingers traced a soft rune in the air, the ward light trembled along the threshold. "There's movement," she said, eyes narrowed. "Residual magic… old, but active. I don't sense life… yet."

Andrew's jaw clenched. He looked at Trovi, then at me. "And if he's planted something worse below?"

"Then we make sure he fears what's coming his way," I said. "We go now while we still have a trail and Trovi can still read it. We go prepared and together. We have to end it here."

I let out a frustrated sigh then look at everyone else in the room.

'He just wants us safe, you can't blame him,' Mani said, trying to keep us from escalating our disagreement.

"I know why you want to wait," I said softly, stepping into his arms, hearing his fast-paced heartbeat. "You're trying to keep me safe. You're trying to make sure I come back, that we all come back."

He closed his eyes for a flicker, then opened them and met me. "I can't lose you," he said, voice raw in a way I'd never before. "Not you, and you cannot lose Trovi or Red, not anyone."

"I know," I breathed, the truth of it folding into me. He dipped his head until our foreheads were touching, our breaths mixing with the air. "And I need you to keep being that… watchful, furious, and stubborn. But if we can't wait."

He searched my face as if memorizing it, as if weighing my answer. "There's a difference," he said finally, quieter than before. "Between risking ourselves and throwing ourselves away."

"There is," I agreed. "And we're not throwing ourselves. We're ending it. Now, while Trovi can still read the trail and while the Heartstone will answer to us." I curled my fingers around the stone in my jacket, it warmed beneath my hand like an answered promise.

Andrew's jaw eased, barely, a small surrender that spoke louder than words. The tension in him didn't fade so much as change, tempered into something fierce and achingly

tender. His gaze softened when he reached up to brush a strand of hair from my face, his fingers lingered, tracing the line of my cheek as though memorizing it.

Then he kissed me.

It wasn't rushed or careless, it was steady and consuming, a collision of restraint and raw need. His hand slid to the back of my neck, holding me close as though the world itself could split and he wouldn't let go.

When he finally pulled back, his breath trembled against my lips. "On one condition," he murmured, voice rough, eyes still locked on mine. "We do it my way. No lone runs. We move as one. We get Ewan out if we can. No heroics."

"Together," I said, and this time the word wasn't just agreement. It was a promise, a vow pressed between us.

He exhaled slowly, resting his forehead against mine for one lingering heartbeat. Around us, Trovi tightened her grip on the book, and Red folded her arms waiting for us to finish. Andrew's arm found my waist, strong, and grounding, and with one shared breath, we all turned to step into the dark as one.

Beyond the hearth, the stairs spiraled downward, slick with condensation, until stone gave way to something far older, walls that shimmered faintly, pulsing with a breath all their own. The deeper we descended, the denser and earthier the air became. Then came the shift, a moment so subtle it barely existed, and yet I knew, deep in my bones, we had crossed a threshold. A barrier, similar to the one around Melmont.

The walls rippled like dark water, as if mocking every step we took. I could feel the magic pressing against my thoughts, an intimate cold that crawled under the skin and settled in the mind.

"This isn't real," Trovi murmured behind me. "He's twisting the space."

I nodded, not taking my eyes off the path in front of me. The dark völva's sanctum wasn't a place, it was as if it was a living memory, a labyrinth built from nightmares. Even the torches flickered with black flame, casting light that devoured instead of revealed.

Behind us, Trovi moved cautiously, her presence sharp and deliberate. The ward light shimmered faintly around her fingers, casting peach-rose arcs that danced like veins of lightning along the walls. Shadows clung to her like dust to glass, but her eyes, bright and fevered with focus, cut through the dark.

"He's close," Trovi murmured. "Just beneath the surface. Watching… listening."

Andrew's gaze flicked back, wary and protective. "Then maybe he'll hear this, if anything happens, I'll end it fast."

Trovi didn't flinch. "If anything happens," she said evenly, "it won't be fast."

"Enough," I said quietly. "No one is dying tonight… except him. Stay focused."

The path forked ahead, two identical tunnels spiraling into shadow.

Mani stirred. *'Here, let me help.'* she whispered, and the world sharpened. The air thickened with scent and sound, old stone, blood that has long dried, the faint electric hum of magic buried deep. Every heartbeat, every shift of dust, sang in my ears.

The psychic noise didn't vanish, but it changed, less like chaos, more like a current I could swim through. Voices still murmured from the dark, laughter that didn't sound real.

"Left," Trovi said suddenly, her voice cutting through the silence like a blade. "It's a lure, but it leads closer to the source. I can *feel* the runes pulling."

Andrew's eyes narrowed. "How can you tell?"

Her fingers traced the air, runic symbols flaring and fading like embers. "These sigils don't just mark space," she said softly. "They bend *intention.* The more afraid you are, the stronger they twist the path. But this one…" she pointed toward the left-hand tunnel. "…it's feeding on expectation. It wants us to avoid it, so that must be where the heart lies."

For a heartbeat, I saw the strain behind her control, the slight tremor in her fingers, the pale shimmer of sweat at her temple, and I nodded. "Then lead."

We followed closely behind Trovi. The air grew heavier, saturated with the scent of smoke and ash. The walls pulsed with oily reflections.

Every illusion was a weapon. Every memory, a snare. At one point, I stumbled, my hand brushing a wall that rippled into the visage of Hel. Her split face smiled, half divine, half decay.

"You've learned much," the illusion whispered. *"But will it save you when your soul is the key he seeks?"* I tore my hand away. The image dissolved into mist.

Trovi slowed, pressing a trembling palm to a rune-marked pillar. "We're close," she breathed. "The magic is folding in on itself, the runes are repeating, devouring their own meaning. That only happens when a spell reaches its anchor point." She glanced back at us, eyes bright with both awe and dread. "But be ready. The wards here don't test strength, they test resolve. They have a *taste* for fear."

Andrew moved closer to me. "Be ready." He whispered.

I reached for his hand, "Together," I said.

The maze pulsed once, as if it had heard. The path ahead widened into a vast chamber, dark, glimmering, and familiar. Smoke drifted from the floor, shaping into silhouettes that wore our faces, our fears.

"Illusions," I said, though my voice felt far away. "They… look like us."

Trovi stepped forward, eyes glinting with grim understanding. "No," she whispered. "They're what he believe we are, but reflections of his intent. The maze mirrors his perception… and that's what makes it dangerous."
The chamber's shadows stirred.

And as we reached the center, the dark narrow passageway we walked out of sealed itself behind us with a sound like a heartbeat.

"No turning back now," Andrew said quietly.

The Heartstone in my pocket pulsed once, like it agreed.

And as the smoke shifted, whispering with the cadence of our own voices, I knew the maze was *listening.*

Chapter 37

The chamber was alive, every surface pulsing with a rhythm that felt wrong, too deliberate to be natural. Shadows crawled along the walls, stretching and splitting until they formed grotesque, half-familiar mockeries of ourselves. My pulse stuttered to match the beat beneath my feet, and every step forward felt weighted, as if I were walking through solid stone and something imagined but no less real.

And yet, something about this place called me. The rhythm, the faint shimmer breathing through the walls, the way the air moved in time with my heartbeat, as though it recognized me. A chill slid into my bones, carrying with it the certainty that I had been here before. Not in this life, perhaps not in any life that was truly mine, but the memory stirred anyway, an echo rising from somewhere deep and buried.

The air reeked of smoke and iron, of old blood and burned feathers. The ground was carved with runes, blackened and scarred so deep they throbbed faintly, like a heart trapped between life and death. Circles of bone and jagged shards of obsidian ringed the ritual space, their edges catching the firelight like rows of broken teeth.

This time, it wasn't just a dream.

This place, it was older, was something pressed into the marrow of the world itself, a memory that did not belong to me… and yet, somehow, remembered me.

Trovi moved beside me, calm but coiled tight. "The traps aren't just physical," she said, her voice low and analytical. “Remember, they bend intent. The runes feed on fear and memory, twisting them into form until the illusion feels real enough to kill.”

Andrew’s hand brushed my arm. “Then we don’t give it what it wants,” he murmured. His voice was low and steady, the kind of calm that slowed my pulse just enough to think instead of react.

Red stood right beside me, rigid, shoulders squared, her fingers twitching as firelight gathered in her palms. “Not gonna lie,” she said, forcing a grin that didn’t quite reach her eyes, “This place feels like it’s breathing. If it starts talking, I’m out.”

Despite the tension, a laugh ghosted from my throat. It sounded strange in this place, alive in a room made of death. “You’re not going anywhere,” I said softly. “Not yet.”

My gaze swept across the cavern. The air shimmered, thick with whispers I almost recognized, like names spoken just beyond hearing. “This place…” My voice faltered. “It feels familiar. Like I’ve walked this path before.”

Trovi’s eyes snapped to me, sharp and searching, but she didn’t press. Instead, she lifted her hand and began tracing slow, deliberate patterns through the air, following threads only she could see. “Some of this might be mutable,” she murmured. “If I can alter the flow, the maze won’t feed on what we feel. But if I can’t…” Her jaw tightened. “You won’t see the danger until it’s already inside your mind.”

The ground shuddered before I could respond. Shadows erupted from the floor, tendrils surging upward like living chains. Trovi tensed beside me, her hands flaring with that peach-rose light, but instinct moved me first. I stepped forward, reaching into the dark, willing it to bend… to *listen.*

It did… but not the way I thought.

My shadow lunged to meet them, snapping outward with violent force. They collided with a crack like thunder, a shockwave tearing through the chamber. Pain lanced across my back, sharp and electric, like the lash of a whip, but I held my ground, teeth clenched, forcing the darkness to obey.

The tendrils shattered, splintering into black mist that bled back into the floor. The silence that followed pressed close, heavy as a held breath.

My chest tightened. I saw Trovi's falter, the strain biting at her focus. "Trovi…"

"I'm fine," she cut in, too quickly, her voice tight, but steady. "I can feel its rhythm. It's studying us… trying to understand what we are."

The cavern seemed to react at her words as if it was insulted. The stone shuddered. The floor rippled beneath our feet, warping into the illusion of a bottomless pit. The walls stretched and curved inward like the ribs of something vast, rising and falling with a slow, unnatural breath. Runes slithered across the surface of the stone, rearranging themselves into serpentine patterns that hummed low and hungry.

"Nobody move!" I shouted.

Without having to think, Mani was already there. Her power coiled through me, fierce and bright. With Mani's eyesight, the world illuminated the dark, the illusions gained weight and scent and pulse.

Mani didn't need to speak for me to feel her grin. *'You really know how to pick your vacation spots,'* she muttered.

"Next time," I breathed, steadying myself, *"I'm booking a beach."*

'You'd still find a fuckin sea monster to fight,' she said dryly.

I scanned the shifting chamber, and now I could see it all, the shimmer of illusion translated into scent, vibration, and pulse. The maze couldn't hide anymore. Not from Mani's wolf-eyes. Not from me.

Trovi moved closer beside me, her fingers tracing invisible sigils as she murmured under her breath. The air shivered where her hands passed. "The runes seem to have reacted to emotion," she said quietly. "Fear feeds them. Doubt strengthens them. But intent, pure, unwavering intent, disrupts their pattern."

"Then let's show them resolve," I said, forcing steadiness into my voice.

Andrew's voice cut through the dark. "We've faced worse." Power thrummed beneath his words, a low, resonant hum that pressed into the air, turning it heavy and charged, as if the space around him recognized.

Red snorted. "Yeah, but the last time, the floor didn't *move.*" Still, she squared her shoulders, blade steady. "Let's end this, before I get seasick."

We moved together. Andrew channeling his power, black fire coiling around his now dragon-scaled hands, flames burning like living shadow. Red carved through illusions with fire cupped in her palms, each strike sharp, precise, and merciless. All guided by Mani's heightened senses, I wove my shadow into theirs, shaping it into a living current that caught, redirected, and amplified each strike until our magic flowed as one seamless rhythm.

Then came the cruelest illusion yet.

The ground heaved. The cavern groaned. Then the ceiling split with a sound like stone screaming, a jagged seam tearing across it as dust poured down in choking clouds. With a

crack like the sky being ripped open, something broke through. Silver spilled through the fracture in a slow, glimmering cascade. It fell slowly.

Not water—something thicker. It cascaded in a slow, glimmering fall, each drop catching the light before twisting midair, sliding sideways… then rising, as if gravity had simply lost its hold. The liquid bent and curled through the space, pooling where no pool should exist, casting warped reflections that shivered across the walls.

It seemed to move with intent.

It flowed and gathered between us, tightening, spinning faster. The shimmer dulled as it thickened, the motion slowing, compressing in on itself until the surface smoothed—until the liquid stilled.

And then it hardened.

Cutting us apart, sealing Trovi on the other side.

What remained was a mirror.

It was semi-transparent and coldly luminous, as if moonlight itself had been poured into glass. Shapes bled through its surface, warped and doubled, reflections lagging just a heartbeat behind reality.

Through the glassy divide, I saw her silhouette. Her reflection moved out of sync, eyes gone hollow, her lips forming silent words I couldn't hear. Runes crawled across her mirrored skin, igniting like fresh brands.

"Trovi!" I shouted, slamming my fists against the surface. It rippled under my touch but didn't yield. My own reflection stared back, warped and fractured by fear, and for a heartbeat, I couldn't tell which side of the mirror I was really on.

The air thickened, the silver water pulsed, and shadows writhed within it, whispering in my own voice. Panic clawed at my mind, sharp and relentless. My chest tightened, my breath shallow and uneven, like I was drowning in air. Thoughts collided and spiraled, each one louder than the last. *I can't. What if. I can't.* My hands trembled, my vision blurred at the edges. Every heartbeat thundered against my ribs, accusing me, mocking me, dragging me deeper into the chaos. A scream lodged in my throat, trapped and burning.

'Breathe, Astrid,' Mani murmured, low and insistent. *'Focus on me. I'm here. Always.'*

I swallowed hard, my chest tight. *'I… I can't. It's too much…'*

'Stop,' Mani cut in, firm as steel. *'No what-ifs. You're not alone. Feel me. Let me steady you.'*

It wasn't just her voice… it was her presence, wrapping around me, threading through the fractures in my mind. I reached for it, shaking. *'I… I'm trying…'*

'That's all you need,' she said, softer now, though the steel beneath her voice never wavered. *'One breath at a time. Let the panic burn away into purpose. You've got this… because we've got this.*

I closed my eyes and leaned into her presence, letting it steady me, anchoring me, like roots driven into stone.

'Always,' Mani promised. *'You and I, we're one. Trust that. Trust me.'*

I drew a shuddering breath as her presence coiled around me tighter, fierce and unyielding, a lifeline drawn tight against the dark. The panic that had been clawing at my mind loosened its grip, dissolving into something sharper, focused determination. My thoughts slowed, my trembling hands

steadied, even the thudding of my heart fell into rhythm beneath her strength.

Then I reached for the darkness. I let my shadow slip free, gliding forward to thread through the mirror's liquid edge like smoke searching for open air. The surface resisted, shuddering beneath the contact, then, slowly, it gave. As if it answered, letting me find her.

Trovi's magic flared through the connection, cold and precise as a blade. For one suspended heartbeat, we were a single force, my wild instinct fused with her unwavering control, and the mirror shattered under a violent surge of pressure, sound rippling outward as its surface collapsed.

The world snapped back into place. The silver shards turned back to their liquid form and rained upward, unraveling into nothing, leaving the chamber hushed and breathless.

Trovi staggered, her breath coming in sharp pulls as she lowered her hand, the glow at her fingertips fading. "It's adapting slower now," she murmured, her voice trembling but sure. "It's beginning to understand that we're… aligned."

I stepped to her side, placing a steadying hand on her shoulder. "Not aligned," I said softly. "United."

The cavern responded with a low, resonant hum, the vibration rolling through the stone beneath my feet. Shadows peeled away from the walls, curling back like retreating smoke, and the chamber began to transform again.

Stone pillars rose from the floor, forming a perfect circle around us, each etched with runes that pulsed faintly in the dim light. Dark feathers and streaks of dried blood littered the ground, the remnants of rituals long abandoned, but also long remembered. Flames kindled along the edges of the circle, their light throwing jagged shadows across the walls and ceiling.

My breath caught. The air was thick with the weight of memory and anticipation. Then I realized why I recognized this place. This was the place from my dream, the one I hadn't allowed myself to think about. Here, where truth bled raw, where endings and beginnings collided.

Then I noticed a figure standing near what resembled a stone podium, his back to us. I didn't need to see his face to know who it was. Slowly and deliberately, he turned to face us. The ground heaved, the cavern groaned, and the ceiling sealed shut with a sound like stone screaming in protest. Firelight kissed his features, illuminating the sharp angles of his face and the cold precision in his gaze. Everything about him radiated command, the same ruthless authority that had shaped this labyrinth and the circle around us.

"You were born for Ragnarök," the dark völva said, his voice sliding into my bones like a blade. "And you will be the reason it is released… to finish what it started."

The flames surged higher, silver, white, and black entwining as the runes beneath my feet throbbed with power. I drew a steadying breath, my pulse syncing with the slow, deliberate heartbeat of the chamber.

"Let's finish this," I said.

Everyone drew closer, determination burning in their eyes, ready for whatever awaited. We stood in the center of the ritual circle, when suddenly the circle itself was surrounded by flames.

'That can't be good,' Mani muttered.

"Understatement of the century," I whispered, forcing my voice steady as I felt all eyes turn toward me.

'Oh, I just fucking love understatements,' she replied dryly, though I felt the strength in her words coil around me, steadying my panic.

I exhaled and muttered, "Perfect. Just a casual stroll into a screaming magical death trap. Totally normal day."

'Wouldn't want it any other way,' Mani said, a flicker of dark amusement threading through her words.

Chapter 38

The ground throbbed beneath my boots, a deep, rhythmic pulse that traveled straight up my spine, as though the stone itself had a heartbeat. Flames surged along the ritual circle, spilling light across the stone as if the cavern itself were breathing. And we stood dead center.

"Perfect," I muttered, blinking against the glare.

The walls, what I *thought* were walls, shimmered and warped like heat mirages, distorting into twisted roots, drifting smoke, and whispering shapes that refused to settle into anything solid. Even the air smelled wrong, sweet and metallic, like iron dipped in honey.

'*Don't move. Not yet.*' Mani's voice was low, her tone sharp as a blade.

'Wasn't planning on it,' I snapped back, even though my knees felt unsteady.

The power in the air pressed against my chest, intimate and invasive, like it already knew my name. Then I heard it, a heartbeat that wasn't mine, deep and slow, echoing through the stone. Each pulse sent the runes flaring brighter, their glow crawling across the stone in hungry lines. Somewhere beyond the smoke, someone laughed softly.

"Well," I murmured under my breath, "This doesn't scream 'safety' at all."

'Stay focused,' Mani snapped.

'Trying,' I breathed, straining to see past the flames.

The laughter came again, closer this time. Smoke twisted, drawn by unseen fingers. A shape stepped forward, pale hands weaving the air itself into form. Yellow eyes emerged first, burning through the haze. The dark völva smiled, a curve that promised ruin.

"Welcome, Astrid," he said, his voice like velvet dragged over broken glass. "Shall we begin?"

The air split open before I could answer. Runes ignited across the cavern walls, spiraling upward in searing lines of fire. The ground buckled violently, throwing me to my knees as the völva lifted his arms.

Andrew moved instantly, Shadows tore free behind him, unfurling into vast wings edged with silver shimmer, like moonlight caught in smoke. "You're not touching her," he snarled as Atius surged beneath his skin, sharpening his voice into something feral.

The dark völva's smile widened, slow and venomous, but certain. "Oh, but it's you who will start this."

The ground convulsed beneath us. Power detonated from the circle's center, ripping us from our footing and flinging me backward through a blinding flare of light. I heard Red shout my name, Trovi's voice dissolve into static, as the world blurred past.

I slammed into the stone wall, the impact knocking the air from my lungs in a brutal rush. For a moment, there was nothing, no breath, no sound, just a high, sharp ringing, like a bell struck too hard, echoing through my skull.

The world spun. When my vision finally cleared, it snapped back into jagged focus.

Red and Trovi lay sprawled motionless across the floor, too still.

My pulse spiked, panic surging up fast and cold, clawing at my throat before I could get a handle on it.

'They're breathing,' Mani said quickly, too quickly, like she was forcing the certainty. *'They're unconscious, but alive.'*

I dragged in a shaky breath, trying to steady the spiral before it took hold.

"Andrew," I breathed, scanning the chamber. "Where…?"

Then I saw him.

He stood alone within the circle as flames coiled inward, tightening like serpents closing around their prey. With a hiss like snapping jaws, the barrier sealed behind him. Runes beneath his feet ignited, crimson lines spreading through the stone like veins, feeding on the air until even smoke seemed to burn.

The dark völva turned toward him, his smile razor-thin and merciless. "The dragon will be first," he murmured, lifting his staff that I hadn't seen before. "Break the bond… and the wolf will follow."

Andrew didn't hesitate. He became motion, a blur of moonlit shadow. The chamber erupted in sound and violence. Obsidian scales tore across his skin in a rippling cascade, catching the fractured light like shards of night, the unmistakable mark of Atius rising within him. Shadow-forged wings tore free from his back, vast and jagged, their edges glowing faintly with silver moonlight.

Living darkness lashed out in writhing tendrils, coiling around his limbs, dragging, constricting, trying to smother both his fire and his will. Andrew roared against them, the sound raw and ancient, no longer entirely human, as Nidhogg's black fire ignited along his arms in a devastating surge.

The shadows recoiled as both flames, crimson and abyssal heat climbed up his limbs and tore through the darkness, scattering them like ash. His wings snapped open in a thunderous sweep. The air trembled, stone groaning beneath the weight of their clash. Andrew stood, as man and dragon, a living shadow all at once.

I staggered upright, my vision tilting. My palms scraped against the slick cavern wall as I tried to stay standing. The air between me and the ritual circle burned and froze simultaneously, light and shadow colliding in blinding bursts that made my eyes sting.

At the center of it all stood Andrew, my Andrew. His wings flared wide and sank slightly as he met the dark völva's strike head-on.

"Andrew!" I screamed, but my voice vanished, devoured by the roar of colliding power.

The next strike didn't come as a blast, it came as intent.

The dark völva moved, and his staff drove forward with brutal precision, punching straight through Andrew's torso, through flesh and through bone, knowing exactly where to end him.

Then time shattered.

For one endless, suspended moment, Andrew hung there, impaled, his body lifted by the force of it. His eyes found mine, shock and confusion, light flickering behind them like dying stars.

Then the staff tore free.

He dropped.

His knees hit the stone first, the sound cracking through the air like something sacred breaking. His body followed, folding in on itself as if the strings holding him upright had been cut.

And my whole world collapsed. The silence that followed swallowed everything, it was thick, suffocating, and wrong.

The scent of pine and blood filled my lungs, sharp and inescapable, anchoring me to a reality I refused to accept.

"No…!" The word tore from me, raw and ragged, echoing as I lunged forward. The fire and frost clawed at my skin, the chaos of the circle's energy ripping at me, but it was nothing. Nothing compared to the agony tearing through my chest.

I dropped to my knees beside him, my hands shaking as I pulled him into my lap. His body was heavy, and too still.

Shallow breaths. A faint pulse flickered beneath my fingers, weak as dying embers.

He looked… asleep. Peaceful in a way that twisted something deep inside me, that made the floor tilt beneath the crushing weight of helplessness. But I knew better… I knew he wasn't sleeping.

'Astrid.' Mani's voice cut through the haze, trembling in a way I had never heard, fear laced with anguish, sharp as a warning bell. *'We can't let him go.'*

"I won't," I choked, pressing my hand over his heart, as if I could will it to beat.

The dark völva's laughter slithered across the cavern. "You can't save what the Norns have already claimed," he hissed, venom dripping from every syllable.

I clenched my teeth, ignoring the heat searing through my veins, and the icy bite clawing deep into my bones.

"FUCK THE NORNS!" I roared.

Every shred of fear, pain, desperation, all of it threatening to tear me apart and collapse inward, crushing into a single, immovable truth: *Andrew is not lost.*

What surged through me wasn't panic but resolve. The moment I released it, the cavern shuddered and bowed beneath the force of my will. Silver warmth exploded outward from my body, flooding the cavern.

Time fractured, and everything slowed. Each heartbeat stretched into eternity, each falling ember frozen in the air like trapped stars. The flames, the runes, the walls themselves dissolved into a whirl of silver radiance, my power devouring the cavern until all that remained was the shimmering tunnel of light binding me to him.

His pulse, faint but steady, echoed through my veins. *"Hold on. I'm here. I'm coming."*

The dark völva's smirk faltered, carved clean away by the sudden flicker of doubt in his predatory eyes. And I understood then, I had nothing left to fear.

Everything I was. Everything I could become. It would all belong to Andrew now. That's why he went after him first.

I clawed through the chaos, searching for *anything*, something to hold onto him. My hands trembled, fingertips grasping at shadows, at the flames, at the air itself. I screamed out in panic as it clawed at me, a tide I couldn't stop, tears streaming down my face, and yet I forced myself to keep moving. *Find him. Don't let him go.*

Then a familiar voice cut through me, sharp and impossible to ignore. "*Search for your bond.*"

Bo. His words echoed inside my mind, threading through the fear and despair like a blade of clarity. "*The bond. It's the bridge.*"

I saw it.

The bond, our bond. A fragile light tangled with shadow, trembling like it might vanish. I closed my eyes and reached for it. It burned, sharp and searing, as if every thread of our connection demanded my all.

It was a fluid shimmering thread, like molten light caught between worlds, stretching and flowing. It was the Bifröst, alive, pulsating, a bridge of light I had walked to reach Hel's domain. It arched between me and him, threads tangling like liquid silver and pale blue fire, mapping the constellation of everything we were, everything we shared.

I reached for it again.

It moved like water in my hands, flowing between my fingers, responsive to my heartbeat, bending around me. I could feel it twisting into him, into Andrew, filling the empty spaces in his chest, wrapping him in the pulse of our connection.

The realization struck like a blade of fire and frost all at once, searing and absolute. This bond wasn't just a tether. Like Hel had said, *it was a bridge*. A lifeline. *Our* lifeline. My path to him. And if I could walk it fully… I might be able to bring him back.

I drew in a shaking breath, letting my mind flow with the threads. The instant I surrendered, the bond flared to life, liquid light spilling from my palms, from my chest, streaming into Andrew. It wasn't just light, it *sang*, alive with power, with memory, with *us*. The Bifröst threads pulsed in perfect rhythm with our hearts, weaving between our souls like a cosmic heartbeat, and the moment the light touched him, the memories flooded through.

Not in order. Not with logic or reason. But the way love remembers.

Laughter came first, bright and breathless, echoing against the walls of my mind. Andrew's crooked grin. The way he'd shoved his hair back, only for it to fall right back into his face again. The warmth of his hands on my hips. The soft, surprised huff of a laugh when he held me close, tangled together in the quiet of shared sleep.

Then sorrow, sharp and raw.

My body slowly healing itself after Niflheim.

His whispered apologies pressed into my hair.

The helplessness tightening in my throat every time I thought I wasn't enough.

Pain followed, ours, shared.

My near-permanent death.

His screams tearing through the dark.

The hollow, ringing silence of the world when he thought he'd lost me.

And my own agony watching him fight himself, the shadow-dragon I put inside him, battling the fear that he wasn't worthy of the power that lived in his blood.

But beneath it all, woven through every memory, every word, every breath, was love. Our relentless, feral, and unyielding love for each other.

The way our souls wrapped around each other the first time we kissed. The way my heart steadied in his hands the first time he said my name like it mattered. The way everything, even the broken pieces, somehow fit when we were together.

The bond didn't just show us these moments to say goodbye. It *dragged* us through them, every survival, every emotion we'd bled, every truth we'd been too afraid to voice—stripped bare and burning with impossible clarity.

My power surged again, the memories looping and amplifying, becoming a current that neither of us could have stopped even if we tried. The cavern, the runes, the battle itself unraveled, dissolving into the bright, relentless infinity of *us*.

As the Bifröst threads tightened around our souls, I felt him stir, not just his body, but Andrew and Atius. He was the dragon and man both, reaching back towards the light, through the memories, through the storm of everything that we were.

The threads drew us closer, binding our breaths, our hearts, our histories into one singular truth:

We had never been alone.

Not for one moment.

And not in any lifetime.

Then suddenly pain tore through me, white-hot and absolute. A scream ripped from my throat, it twisted into a howl as Mani rose with it, but I didn't stop, I couldn't. I poured myself into him: every ounce of magic, every spark of will, every memory that made us… *us*.

Through the tears and blinding light, the memories flared again in fractured flashes. Andrew's crooked grin beneath moonlight. The brush of his hand against mine as we trained together. His laugh, soft and startled, like he never quite believed he deserved happiness. The way his eyes always found mine in a crowd, making the world falling away in an instant. The warmth of his breath when he whispered my name.

Each memory became a heartbeat, a surge of *iridescent light,* like molten glass catching every color of dawn, racing through us, through bone, breath, and soul. The air grew thick with the scent of pine and the dark sweetness of moss and soil, wrapping around me like the memory of home I hadn't realized I'd been searching for. Beneath us, the ground trembled as the

Bifröst sang, its resonance echoing with the heartbeat of creation itself.

'He's slipping!' Mani's voice broke, ragged and rising, panic clawing through every word. *'We're losing him... we're losing him, we can't... don't let him go!'*

"I won't lose him!" I forced out, my voice breaking under the weight of it. "Stay with me, Andrew, please! Don't you dare leave me!"

Light exploded from us, pure, blinding, and divine. My pulse synced with his, once, twice, and then it faltered. I felt my strength bleed into him, my soul unraveling thread by thread as the Bifröst seared white-hot across my skin, burning through flesh and bone, carving its path through me without mercy.

The dark völva's snarl cut through the roar. "You'll kill yourself!"

"Then I'll die keeping him alive!" The words ripped out of me before I could think. There was no hesitation left in me, no room for fear or doubt. I gave everything, every drop of magic, every breath that still clung to my lungs, every piece of my soul that hadn't already been burned to ash.

My runes blazed so bright they devoured the shadows entirely. Color and sound collided, gold bleeding into violet, violet collapsing into green-blues, until the world itself seemed to unravel around us.

And then the world shattered.

For one unbearable heartbeat, the bond snapped, going cold and empty.... completely severed.

My scream rips out of me before I can stop it, raw and shattered, tearing my throat open as I lurch forward on my knees. The stone grinds beneath me, biting into my skin, but I barely feel it.

"Don't take him… please…!"

My voice breaks, dissolving into sobs I can't control. It feels like my chest is caving in, like something inside me is being *ripped away*, piece by piece, and I can't… I can't…

"He can't go… he can't…"

The words choke off into nothing. I'm shaking so hard I can barely breathe, my hands useless where they clutch at him, at the fading warmth, at the slipping *thread* I can feel unraveling beneath my fingers.

Something cracks above me.

I don't react, I can't. The sound barely reaches me through the roar of my own sobs, through the way my chest heaves and breaks and refuses to breathe right. Everything hurts too much, too loud, too *empty*.

I don't notice anything changing, or the darkness shifting.

Only when something soft brushes my skin, faintly, almost unreal, do I flinch, like I've been pulled back from somewhere I was drowning in.

Theres nothing but light.

I lift my head, tears blurring everything, and see it. Moonlight.

It spills through the fractured ceiling in thin, trembling streams, like the sky itself is breaking open. It shouldn't be here. It *can't* be here.

But it is.

It finds me. And it's calling to me.

A sob tears through me again, quieter this time, fragile and aching as the silver glow spills over my hands, over him, over *us*. It feels warm, impossibly warm, like it's alive, like it's *reaching*.

"Please…" I whisper, my voice barely there. "Please…"

The light pulses.

I freeze.

It *pulses* again.

Not distant. Not silent. Not empty.

Alive.

It wraps around me, sinking into my skin, threading through me. My breath stutters as Mani surges, not beside me, not separate, but *within* me, vast, overwhelming, and *awake*.

And then I feel it.

A presence so deep, so old, it makes my bones ache with recognition.

Mine.

It isn't just a word. It's a truth. A claim. A promise that settles into the very core of me.

I gasp, my back arching as the light burns brighter, pouring into my veins like liquid silver fire. It hurts, Gods, it hurts, a searing, unbearable ache that threatens to split me apart. But I don't pull away. I *lean into it*, clinging to the pain like it's the only thing keeping me from shattering completely.

Then, something *snaps* into place. Energy surges through me, like something is building, slow and relentless, filling every hollow space, until I don't know where I end and it begins, until I'm brimming with more than I think I can possibly hold. My breath catches, my body locking as something deep within me shifts.

Suddenly power explodes through me, wild and uncontrollable, ripping a cry from my throat that is no longer just grief, it's something bigger, something deeper.

The cavern shakes as light bursts from me in a blinding surge, spiraling upward toward the shattered ceiling, toward the moon that is watching, and *answering*. The air trembles, thick and charged, like the world itself is holding its breath.

I feel it.

The edge of him.

That fragile, fading thread.

And I *grab it*.

"No!" I sob, clutching tighter, pouring everything I am into it. "You don't get to take him… you don't…!"

The light surges in response.

Through me.

From me.

With me.

Death falters, it cold and reaching. Pausing at the edge of him.

And then…

Breath slams back into him in a sharp, desperate gasp beneath my hands. I choke on a sob as warmth floods after it, chasing away the cold, filling what had been empty. The thread I held was fraying and breaking, snaps back into something whole, something *unbreakable*.

I collapse forward, a shattered sound leaving me, half sob, half something I don't even recognize, as my body trembles uncontrollably. My hands won't stop shaking where they clutch at him, afraid to let go, terrified this will all disappear if I do.

But it is.

It's real.

The silver light fades slowly, sinking back into my skin, then deeper, further into my bones, leaving something behind, something vast, quiet, and *eternal*.

The moon heard me.

It *answered* me.

Not with mercy.

But with power.

With life.

With *rebirth.*

The dark völva's spell shattered under it, his scream swallowed by collapsing stone and dying flame.

Andrew gasped. The sound was small and broken, but he was alive. His chest rises beneath my hands, uneven but real, and then, his fingers move. Weak and trembling, but certain as they find mine where they press against him.

"Astrid…"

A laugh broke from me, sharp and soaked with tears. "You tried dying on me," I whispered, my voice cracking under the weight of it.

Around us, the cavern shudders as everything begins to move again—time snapping back into place like a breath finally released. Runes fracture along the stone, their glow splintering as flames flicker out one by one, leaving only darkness and dust in their wake.

Mani's voice was soft and steady now. '*You did it,*'

I feel… hollow. Drained down to nothing, like the power that filled me burned everything else away. But Andrew was breathing. He was alive. That was enough.

As the las of the light dimmed and darkness settles back around us, his grip tightened around my fingers. His voice is rough, but there's something fierce in it now.

"Astrid… what happened? What did you do?"

I looked at him, really looked. Faint traces of light still shimmer beneath his skin, threading through him in soft violets, golds, and silver, like something divine hasn't quite let go. My vision blurs with tears, but I smile anyway, small, fragile, and real.

"I brought you back," I whispered. "I wasn't going to lose you."

When I finally let go, it wasn't surrender. It was relief. It crashed through me all at once, stealing what little strength I had left as I fold forward, collapsing against his chest. The warmth of him, solid and real, is the only thing keeping me upright.

His heartbeat pounds beneath my ear, stronger with every second, and I cling to it like it's everything. My breath shuddered, breaking apart as exhaustion dragged me down to the bone.

Alive.

He was alive.

The truth of it breaks something open inside of me, something I didn't realize I'd been holding together—

And I sob.

Hard.

Between us, the bond shimmered faintly, threads of iridescent light weaving through the air, alive, soft, and steady now. No longer burning. No longer strained.

It was just *there*.

Proof that even death itself hadn't been enough to tear us apart.

Chapter 39

By the time my breathing finally steadied, and the tears burned themselves dry, exhaustion settled deep into my bones. My body wanted nothing more than to collapse. But I refused to let the dark völva live. The darkness pressed back in, thick and suffocating, like a living thing. Voices brushed at the edges of my awareness, too muffled to understand, but too loud to ignore. Concern, fear, and urgency scraped against my mind, trying to break through—but none of it quite reached me. My eyelids felt impossibly heavy, as though the very air conspired to drag them shut.

Beyond the muffled voices, there was movement through the haze, shuffling feet, the low, strained moans of someone forcing themselves upright. A jagged memory tore through me, sharp and icy. The dark völva.

Something ignited beneath the exhaustion and burned—a pulse. *My pulse. Mani's.* And we were furious. The world rushed back in violent fragments, smoke and shadow, blood and shattered stone. My eyes snapped open and everything bled red. Everything warped and dulled, distant and distorted, as if I were submerged beneath dark water.

Across the ruined ritual circle, the dark völva staggered, struggling to steady himself. His staff dragged through the ash, spitting sparks with every uneven step. Magic slithered from him in oily, venomous threads, reaching for Andrew, for Red, for Trovi.

Not again. Not them.

Heat rose inside me, slow and unrelenting. It spread through my veins like wildfire, consuming weakness, burning away restraint. Mani surged forward, teeth bared and claws eager. The Garmr's rage swelled, and this time, I didn't fight it. I let it take me.

The change tore through me. Bones snapped and ruptured like brittle branches under sudden weight. Flesh split along my spine, heat and agony racing together as my scream twisted into a growl, a war cry that thundered through the cavern as I hunched forward. Limbs stretched grotesquely past human limits, joints grinding and reforming, reshaping themselves into something vast, powerful, and lethal.

I felt every second of it. I was becoming my wolf, past Mani, massive and terrible. Muscles surged beneath thick white fur, rippling with raw, animalistic power. A bristling mane ran along my shoulders and spine, crowning me in a silhouette both regal and monstrous, a creature born for battle and blood.

My face reshaped into a snarling mask of fury. Bone elongated, features sharpening into a muzzle, fangs gleaming as they slid into place. My eyes ignited an electric blue, so pale they nearly burned white, light spilling from them like frozen flame. I stood upright but hunched beneath the strain of instinct

warring with thought, beast pressing against mind. My claws unfurled, long and curved like sickles, each one promising death. I was no longer just Astrid. I was a predator forged from darkness and pain, from unyielding rage and iron resolve.

My massive, clawed hand lashed out, slicing through empty air where the dark völva's throat had been a moment earlier. Too slow. Without hesitation, Mani and I merged, heartbeat and rage entwined, a living force that roared through the cavern.

"You've taken enough!" I bellowed, my voice splitting into a growl, half-human, half-wolf, pure, unrelenting wrath. The sound shook stone from the ceiling, rattling dust and echoing like a drum of war.

The dark völva staggered back, shadows flaring from him in writhing coils, serpents of darkness twisting into jagged spikes and hurling themselves toward me. I lunged first, my massive limbs coiling and released with predatory precision. Claws shredded through his darkness, tearing magic apart like rotted thread. He barely dodged the first strike, stumbling as he recovered, and I saw it then, the falter. Every movement carried a hint of hesitation. A flash of pain. Even the smallest weakness was enough. Hope cut through the fury like a blade.

Then I felt it, a pulse inside me, bright and undeniable. My bond. Andrew was moving. My heart stuttered, relief and rage crashing together in my chest. The sight of him, bloodied, broken, but breathing, ignited something deeper than berserker fury. This wasn't just rage anymore.

It was protection.

It was love.

I turned back just as the dark völva struck. A whip of shadow snapping towards me, crackling with venom. I was faster. Mani's instincts and my own controlled fury sharpened every reflex. I twisted aside and raked my claws across his chest, tearing through his robes, shredding the last illusion of invincibility he clung to.

He screamed. Spells erupted from him in wild desperation, black fire exploding against stone, shockwaves shattering the cavern walls. Flames clawed at me, but I walked through them, my muscles coiled, my body massive and unyielding, feeling utterly unstoppable.

Every heartbeat thundered through my awareness, mine, Mani's, Andrew's, Atius's, four rhythms bound together. The Bifröst bridge pulsed between us, a living tether of light and will, alive and burning. Each beat of Andrew's heart fed my control, keeping the berserker fury leashed, even as my rage strained to devour everything in its path. My vision exploded in silver, violet, and icy blue as I surged forward again, slashing and roaring, a force of fury guided by love.

A hammer-blow of black fire slammed into me head-on. hard enough to shatter bone, to send shock ripping through my entire body, but I don't move.

I *catch it*.

My claws close around the spell mid-strike, runes igniting along my hands in a violent flare. The magic fights me, writhing and screaming as it tries to tear free, but I crush it and it detonates in my grip.

The cavern convulses with the force of it. Stone groans. Dust and shards of rock rain from above. Smoke and iron choke the air, thick and suffocating, filling my lungs with every breath I don't realize I'm dragging in.

Something slices across my side. I see it happen, seeing the flash of steel, the spray of crimson as it opens me up, but I don't *feel* it.

There's no pain.

Not yet.

Only heat.

Only rage.

It floods me, drowns everything else out, until the world narrows into something sharp and violent and *red*. My blood hits the stone, and it doesn't matter. None of it matters.

Not the wound. Not the damage. Not even the way my body should be screaming at me to stop.

Because all I can see is *him, the dark volva, still breathing*.

And then…

Andrew.

Through the chaos, through the smoke and falling debris, I catch him, Andrew, his eyes wide, locked on me. I feel him, too. His pulse through our bond, racing, shattered fear and desperate relief and love so sharp it nearly knocks the breath out of me.

It hits something already breaking loose inside my chest.

And my power erupts.

Wild. Feral. Uncontainable.

The air around me distorts with it, my runes blazing brighter and hotter, feeding off the fury coiling in my chest.

The world narrows. The smoke. The stone. The blood.

And him.

The dark völva.

I move.

I don't remember crossing the distance, only the impact of my arrival as I come down on him like a falling verdict. My claws tear through shadow as I strike, raking across him with enough force to split flesh and unravel the magic stitched beneath it.

He staggers, but doesn't fall yet… Not yet.

"I will end this!" I roar.

The sound isn't entirely mine anymore. It's something deeper, older. Something that shakes the cavern floor as it rips out of my throat.

He twists, trying to retreat, trying to melt back into whatever darkness spawned him.

I don't let him.

I drive forward and *take him.*

My hand locks onto him mid-escape, dragging him back into the open before he can disappear, slamming him down into the stone hard enough that the ground *cracks* beneath the impact. The sound that leaves him is raw, choked, and for a moment I feel the resistance of his power buckling under mine.

Not gone.

Not dead.

Just… *breaking.*

I don't hesitate.

With a final surge of everything burning inside me, rage, grief, love, and loss, I bring my claws down again.

They tear through him.

Not clean, not merciful, but final.

The force of it drives him deep into the stone, pinning him there as his body goes still, limp and unmoving, his magic flickering like a dying flame trapped beneath rubble.

But he's not getting up. His eyes are open.

Not yet.

I stand over him, my chest heaving, every breath shaking with power I can't fully contain. The runes along my hands still burn like they want more, like they're begging for permission to finish it.

His scream fractures into rage, pain, and disbelief, before cutting off entirely as his body went limp. The shadows around him unravel. Smoke curls off me like burned parchment, but it was his magic dying, not mine. The cavern fell into stunned silence, broken only by the steady pulse of my bond with Andrew, bright and alive.

My berserker form shudders violently as fur rippling and receding, my claws retracting as the rage and fury that had fueled them finally burnt itself out. Bone and muscle screamed as the massive limbs shrank, my spine and shoulders cracking and snapping back into their human shape. My face shortened, the muzzle retracting, fangs receding, and the electric-blue blaze in my eyes dimmed.

And then… it was gone.

Strength leaves me all at once, like the world finally decides I'm allowed to fall. My knees buckled, and the world tilted. Hands caught me before I hit the ground. I sag into them, shaking, barely conscious, fully human again, raw and trembling, every muscle screaming from what I've done. My lungs drag in air like they're relearning how to exist, my chest heaving as each breath burns its way back into me. Muscles still thrummed faintly with the fading echo of the wolf I had been, but the weight of my human form pressed down on me, reminding me that I was utterly spent.

Voices called my name, distant, distorted, and urgent, blurred shapes moving through the smoke. Around us, the cavern lay in ruin, shattered runes, smoldering shadows, ash curling along the floor. Then I realized whose arms held me, Andrew. He was safe and he was alive.

He coughed softly and smiled, then managed a crooked grin, lifting a trembling hand to my face. "You… saved me."

"No," I gasped, curling my fingers around his, as he cupped my cheek. "We saved each other."

I pressed against him, burying my face into the curve of his neck, inhaling the sharp, grounding scent of him, wet pine after a storm, earthy and alive, a forest reborn in rain. His warmth seeped into me, his heartbeat steady beneath my ear. My tears fell unchecked, hot and endless, tracing streaks down my cheeks and soaking into his shirt, but I didn't care. Relief, love, and exhaustion crashed through me like a tidal wave, leaving me trembling, raw, and achingly whole.

Andrew removed his shirt and eased it over me, his movements careful and steady. Then he held me tighter, pulling me close, one arm wrapped around my shoulders, his other hand entwined with mine. "I'm here," he murmured, voice low but firm. "I'm not going anywhere."

I closed my eyes against the sting of tears and the acrid tang of smoke, letting it all wash over me, the cavern, the chaos, the echoes of our battle fading into memory. The runes on the stone dimmed and smoldered. The flames guttered, and the air itself seemed to exhale, heavy with soot and relief. For the first time since we had stepped into this cursed place, I allowed myself to truly rest, sinking fully into Andrew's arms. I breathed in the faint metallic tang of blood mingling with the wet, earthy tang of stone and scorched pine. Every breath grounding me. Every exhale carried away fragments of the rage, the terror, the desperate need to save him.

And in that fragile, luminous quiet, something fierce and undeniable unfurled inside me, a fire tempered by love and trust. I knew that no matter what came next, no matter what the storms still waiting, we would face them together. I opened my eyes slowly, still wet with tears, and saw him, alive, breathing, and whole. His dark and silver wings folding slightly behind him, his gaze locked on mine. In that gaze, I found every promise, every anchor, every reason I would keep fighting, to keep holding on.

Chapter 40

The tunnels seemed to exhale as we stepped away from the cavern's heart, damp air brushing against my skin like the sigh of something ancient finally laid to rest. Residual magic still hummed softly, persistent and refusing to fade. The air carried the acrid tang of spent power—burned herbs and blood clinging stubbornly to the stones. The dark völva's presence lingered like a stain, a part of him that refused to truly die.

My hands trembled. Faint threads of shadow still flickered at my fingertips, obedient but restless, pulsing in time with my heartbeat, as if the storm inside me hadn't stilled so much as fallen into uneasy silence. Andrew's arm stayed firm around me, holding me steady.

He shifted as my knees threatened to give out, steadying me without breaking stride. "Easy," he murmured, his voice low and rough, his breath warm against my ear.

I leaned into him, letting his strength carry what mine no longer could. We moved together, one slow step, then another, unsteady but determined. One of his hands anchored at my waist, firm and grounding, while the other braced us both against the wall, keeping us upright as the world threatened to tilt beneath my feet.

Every step echoed hollow and uneven against the stone, as though the world itself hadn't yet recovered from the violence done to it. We moved in quiet rhythm together.

'You're walking like a newborn deer,' Mani muttered weakly, her voice rasped but still carried dry humor. *'All legs and no grace.'*

'You try walking after being ripped apart and reshaped.' I shot back, too tired to even roll my eyes.

'I did,' she replied smugly, exhaustion threading her words. *'I was there. And we looked fucking amazing.'*

A breathless laugh escaped me before I could stop it.

Andrew glanced down, concern softening into something warmer. "What's funny?"

"Nothing," I breathed, shifting more of my weight against him. "Just arguing with Mani. She thinks she's hilarious."

Andrew's mouth curved into a tired grin. "But is she wrong?"

Mani purred faintly at that, smug as ever.

I groaned aloud. "Great. Now you're both being insufferable."

Even through the ache, through the smoke and ruin, the moment felt absurdly normal, like laughter clawing its way out of the wreckage. And somehow, that small, ridiculous exchange made the pain easier to bear.

The cavern lay eerily quiet, save for the faint hum of spent magic still lingering in the air. I lifted my head and scanned the rubble. Then I saw Red.

"Red?" My voice still rough, raw from screaming.

Her eyes fluttered open, unfocused at first. "Astrid…?" she murmured, blinking hard. Then she saw us, Andrew's arm around me, both of us bloodied but standing, and relief broke across her face like sunlight through clouds.

But it didn't last. Her gaze drifted past us, toward the dark völva's still body, and something in her expression faltered. Disappointment flickered there, sharp and aching.

"I should've done more," she whispered hoarsely. "I…I froze."

I shook my head. "There wasn't anything more you could've done… we all did what we could." My voice wavered, but I meant it. "He's gone, Red."

Red exhaled shakily, her shoulders sagging as the tension finally cracked. Her eyes glistened. "You did it, Astrid," she said softly. "You stopped him."

I swallowed hard and glanced toward the corpse that still smoked faintly, shadows unraveling from it like ash carried on a dying wind. "We might have stopped him," I said quietly. "But it's not over."

Andrew's arm tightened around my waist, silent and steady, a wordless promise that I wasn't facing this alone.

Red frowned. "What do you mean?"

I let out a slow breath, the taste of ash still heavy on my tongue. "Killing him freed us," I said. "But it didn't fix what he broke. That… doesn't just disappear."

For a moment, none of us spoke. The cavern's silence pressed in, thick and heavy, broken only by the distant drip of water and the whisper of rain filtering through the cracks above.

Finally, Red nodded, resolve settling over her features. Her voice was barely more than a breath. "Then we start rebuilding."

I managed a tired, crooked smile. "Yeah," I murmured. "But maybe let's start with getting out of this gods-forsaken hellhole first."

A soft, wet cough cut through the quiet. I turned sharply. Trovi stirred, her fingers twitching against the blood-slick stone before a shallow, shuddering breath escaped her lips.

"Trovi?" I whispered, trying to move closer as every muscle protested.

Her eyelids fluttered, heavy and unfocused. "D–did we win?" she croaked, voice raw.

Relief cracked through me like lightning. "Yeah," I said, smiling through tears I hadn't realized were still there. "We did. You're safe now."

She gave a faint, crooked grin. "Good… because I really hate caves."

A choked laugh escaped me, half sob, half disbelief. I glanced back at Andrew and Red, both battered and exhausted, but alive.

"They're all alive," I whispered, to Mani, to myself. My hands trembled as the truth finally sank in. "We're all still here."

Andrew reached for me, his voice low but steady. "Then let's go."

As we made our way toward the tunnel we'd come through, I looked back at the cavern, the place that had nearly become our grave. The shadows that had once crawled along its

walls were gone, leaving only ash and the faint scars of scorched runes burned into the stone. It felt wrong to leave, like walking away from a battlefield that still remembered you. But there was nothing left to fight.

The tunnels wound upward, twisting through darkness that slowly gave way to thin shafts of gray light. The air grew cooler, cleaner. I could taste rain on the wind ahead. My body screamed with every movement, muscles trembling under the weight of exhaustion. The remnants of my berserker form still lingered under my skin, raw and aching. I felt too human now, fragile in a body that had known too much power. Every breath reminded me of how close I'd come to the edge between strength and destruction.

Andrew's grip tightened around me as I stumbled. "Easy," he murmured, his voice rough but gentle. "Almost there."

When we finally stepped out into the dark völva's house, I froze, really taking in the small house. The air was sharp and cold, rain seeping through the cracked windows, and broken stone scattered across the floor. Wind howled through the gaps in the walls, carrying the scent of storm, ash, and something hollow, like the house itself knew it had been abandoned, stripped of whatever dark purpose once anchored it.

And there…Ewan. He lay exactly where we'd left him, sprawled across the floor, his skin gone ashen, his chest still rising, but barely, each breath thinner than the last.

Red was already at his side. Kneeling over him, her face streaked with soot and sweat, she worked with quiet urgency, focused and unshakable. Her hands hovered over his wounds, and they *glowed*, her light shifting between green and gold as it poured from her palms and sank into his flesh.

The air around her vibrated with it, a low, living hum that sank into my bones. Not just light, not just power, *healing*, woven into the space itself, thick and tangible like the world was quietly mending around her.

Despite the exhaustion etched into every line of her face, her movements never faltered, they were precise, practiced, and controlled, like a nurse who had seen the edge of death too many times to hesitate now.

Red let out a breath and glanced up as we approached. Her voice cracked, caught halfway between a laugh and tears. "You two really look like Hel chewed you up and spit you back out."

I managed a weak smile. "Feels about right."

Andrew's arm stayed firm around me, warm against the cold.

Mani stirred faintly, tired but present. '*Still breathing,*' she murmured. '*Still fighting.*'

We had survived, even if it was barely, but we were alive.

The world tilted. I stumbled forward and dropped to my knees beside Red, the impact sending a dull shock through my already screaming body. My arms trembled as I pressed my palms over hers, reaching instinctively for the thin, flickering thread of life inside Ewan. Power kindled weakly beneath my skin, answering before I could think.

"Astrid, don't," Andrew said sharply, panic edging his voice.

Red's head snapped up, her eyes wide. "You've burned too much already," she said firmly, though fear trembled beneath her words.

But I couldn't stop. Not yet. The thread between life and death thrummed beneath my hands, thin and fraying, begging to be mended.

"He's slipping," I rasped. "I can feel it… I have to try."

Iridescent light spilled from my palms, weaving across Ewan's chest, stitching torn edges of flesh and spirit together in fragile, shimmering patterns. For a moment, it held.

Then it flickered, sputtering like a dying flame. Dark spots bled across my sight as the glow guttered and faded, leaving a hollow ache in its wake. Ewan's breath hitched. It was a shallow gasp, but stronger than before. His chest rose again, barely perceptible, but steady. Relief slammed into me, sharp and dizzying.

And then my strength gave out completely. The magic slipped from my fingers like water. My body turned heavy, leaden, as every remaining thread of power had been torn free, leaving me to burn out in the dark. I slumped forward, too drained to even catch myself. Andrew caught me before I hit the floor, his arms locking around me, solid and sure.

"Astrid…" Andrew's voice was raw with fear. Up close, he could see it, the faint shimmer still threading through my veins, the soft light flickering beneath my skin. Power, not broken, not gone, just quieter now, settled into something deeper, something still very much alive.

His breath hitched. "Gods," he whispered, more to himself than to me. "What did you do?"

I tried to answer, but only a rasp escaped my throat. "You… you were dying…" I managed, the words breaking apart. "I had to…"

Andrew shook his head slowly, disbelief and fear warring in his eyes. His thumb brushing a streak of ash from my cheek, the touch impossibly gentle. "You could have killed yourself in the process," he said, awe and terror threading his voice. "And you still gave what you didn't have left to give."

Rain tapped softly against the shattered windows. Nearby, Red and Trovi worked on stabilizing Ewan, their voices low and urgent, drifting in and out through the ringing in my ears.

I looked at them, Andrew, Red, Trovi, Ewan, battered, bruised, but breathing. Alive. And in this rain-soaked ruin of the dark völva's lair, something settled deep in my chest. Survival wasn't a means to an end, but the start of a new beginning.

Chapter 41

I woke slowly to the sound of rain, keeping my eyes closed as I listened. It fell softly now—not the furious deluge that had shaken the earth when we arrived, but a steady, mournful drizzle. Each drop tapping softly against the cracked windows, a fragile rhythm filling the silence.

The house creaked faintly, its old bones settling beneath the weight of the storm. Somewhere, a loose shutter banged against the siding, hollow and irregular. The air smelled of damp earth and smoke, layered with the musty sweetness of dust long undisturbed, now stirred by our presence. Beneath it all lingered a faint trace of herbs and ash, the last remnants of the dark völva's magic seeping into the walls like a stain that would never fully fade.

When I finally blinked my eyes open, the world swam into focus in shades of gray and amber. Pale light filtered through the rain-streaked windows, washing over splintered beams, shards of glass, and the dim orange pulse of dying embers in the hearth. Dust drifted lazily through the air, catching the firelight in slow, glowing halos.

Andrew lay beside me, his arm wrapped around my shoulders even in sleep. His breathing was slow and even, a tranquil rhythm that quieted the noise in my mind. His skin was cool from the air, his weight against me felt solid, real in a way hope never had been.

Across the room, Red had fallen asleep sitting upright, her back leaning against the far wall, her head tilted to one side. The exhaustion of the night etched into every line of her face. Her hands were still streaked with dried blood and soot, Ewan's, maybe mine, and a small medical kit lay open at her feet, tools scattered in quiet disarray.

Trovi had dozed off in a chair next to Red and Ewan, a blanket draped over her shoulders. One arm wrapped in a rough bandage, a small cut still red on her temple from where she'd struck the cavern wall. Her body slumped with exhaustion, the weight of the fight and the journey pressing down on her. Even in sleep, the lines of age and battle carved deep across her face softened, her hand still resting close to the dagger at her hip. Ewan lay between them, pale but breathing. His chest rising in a shallow, steady rhythm beneath the makeshift bandages Red had wrapped him in.

I lay still, letting the sound of rain and the quiet weight of survival fill the space around me. My body ached in ways I couldn't name. Every breath sent a dull ache through my ribs, every shift felt foreign, as though my skin was still struggling to contain something far greater than it was ever meant to hold. My runes flicker faintly on my hands, like a dying ember, but not gone. I was still here.

'You're awake,' Mani murmured, her voice thick with fatigue. *'About damn time.'*

'How long was I out?' I asked.

'Long enough that I started to enjoy the peace,' she replied dryly, though her tone softened after a beat. *'You scared me.'*

A faint smile tugged at my lips despite the ache. *'Glad to know I was missed.'*

'Always,' she whispered, fading out again into the steady rhythm of the rain.

I turned my head toward Andrew. The dim light traced across his face, highlighting the bruising along his jaw and the dark sweep of his lashes resting against pale skin. His arm still held me, even in sleep. Seeing him like this, so unguarded, shook me more than the battle ever had.

My throat tightened. "We made it," I breathed, barely louder than the rain's gentle patter, as hot tears slid down my cheeks and pooled against his arm.

After a while, I pulled myself together, blinking as I tried to piece the night back into order. The last thing I remembered was Ewan's breathing finally beginning to steady, my magic faltering, and then… nothing. Just the hollow ache lingered, like power drained from my veins, leaving an emptiness in its wake.

Carefully, I shifted, my muscles protested, but Andrew only stirred, his grip tightening slightly before settling again. I studied his face, softened by sleep, the familiar tension smoothed away. He looked younger somehow, more at peace.

"We made it," I whispered.

'Barely,' Mani's muttered, her voice drowsy and sardonic. *'You really know how to make an exit, you know that?'*

A faint laugh escaped me. *'You're one to talk. You've been napping too since I passed out.'*

'I earned it,' she grumbled, a yawn threading through her words. *'Try not to set yourself on fire if you're going to feed the hearth, would you? I'm too tired for that kind of drama.'*

"Not making promises," I murmured, the corner of my mouth twitching.

Outside, the rain softened further. The air smelled clean and renewed, even if the house around us felt hollow and abandoned. Cold wind sighed through the rafters, slipping through the cracks like a ghost the refused to move on.

I watched the faint rise and fall of the people who had become my world. Every one of them bruised and worn thin, but alive. The fire in the hearth had dwindled to glowing embers. I rose quietly, careful not to wake anyone, and crossed the room. The floorboards moaned softly under my boots as I added small pieces of wood, coaxing the flames back to life. The orange light licked the walls, warm and steady, painting shifting shadows across everyone's sleeping faces. Ewan's fragile form, and across Trovi, still curled near the door. Each deliberate motion of stoking the fire carried a quiet serenity, a small offering to the fragile peace that had taken hold of the space.

The soft crackle of the fire stirred Trovi. She stretched stiffly, her eyes scanning the space as if half-afraid we might all vanish. "You're awake," she said, disbelief roughening her voice.

"Barely," I rasped, my throat dry.

She gave a slow nod, her gaze scanning the others before meeting mine again. "Then we should move soon. The storm's letting up. I'll get things ready for our transport."

"Are you sure you're up for that?" Concern threaded my voice. "We're all pretty battered."

Trovi's lips curved into a wry smirk. "Yes, dear. I can manage. Especially since the dark völva was well-stocked, it should make things easier." She rose and began cataloging the ingredients we had at our disposal, methodical and precise. I made a mental note to gather as much as we could carry when we headed back.

I glanced toward the cracked window, where pale dawn light was beginning to bleed into the sky. My bones screamed for more rest, but she was right. We couldn't stay here, not in this place that still reeked of magic and death.

Hours passed in a quiet blur. The rain thinned into pale gray light as thunder rolled farther and farther away. Trovi moved through the house, arranging transport back to Melmont, while Ewan drifted in and out of consciousness, his pale skin glowing in the firelight.

Red's voice rose softly through the room, threading through smoke and silence with a low, haunting melody. An old shanty, but changed, reshaped into something that belonged to *this night*. It wasn't polished or pretty. It was for the broken, for the ones still breathing when they shouldn't be.

Her voice carried steady despite the exhaustion dragging at it.

"Ooh-oh, we fought the night, aye, we fought the night...

With blood on our hands and fire in our sight...
Ooh-oh, the flames burn bright, aye, the flames burn bright...
Kept the dark at bay till the coming of light..."

The sound settled into the room, into the cracks in the stone, into the hollow spaces inside my chest. Ewan's breathing slipped between the lines, thin, fragile.

Andrew's hand tightened around mine.

Red didn't look up.

She just kept going.

"*Through shattered stone, and blood-stained hall,*
We stumble, we fall, yet we rise through all...
The wind may howl, the seas may rage,
But still, we stand upon this stage.

Her voice dipped but never broke.

The fire answered her, crackling low, shadows shifting along the walls like ghosts listening in.

Then the chorus returned, stronger now, like something refusing to die.

"Ooh-oh, we fought the night... aye, we fought the night...
With blood on our hands and fire in our sight...
Ooh-oh, the flames burn bright... aye, the flames burn bright...
Kept the dark at bay till the coming of light..."

I swallowed hard, my chest tightening.

Because we had.

Gods… we had.

"For those who fell and those who remain,
For every loss carved deep in pain.
The shadows loom, but we press on,
Through every dusk, towards every dawn."

My gaze dropped, my fingers curling tighter in Andrew's as the words settled too deep, too close.

Not everyone made it.

Not everyone would.

But we were still here.

And somehow… that had to mean something.

The rhythm shifted again—quieter now, heavier.

"Ooh-oh, we hold on strong... aye, we hold on strong...
We're not yet lost—we still belong...
Ooh-oh, the night is long... aye, the night is long...
But still we stood when the hope was gone..."

My breath hitched.

Something inside me cracked open at that—not sharp, not violent, but slow and aching.

Because hope had been gone.

And we stood anyway.

Red's voice softened further, like it was being carried away on something unseen.

"The waves may break, and the storm may cry,
But hear the song as it drifts on high.
For every heart that trembles, worn,
We sing the tune of the battle-torn."

The fire burned lower.
The room quieter.
Even the air felt like it was holding still.
Then—one last time.
Soft. Fading.
Like smoke unraveling into nothing.

"Ooh-oh, we fought the night... aye, we fought the night...
With blood on our hands and fire in our sight...
Ooh-oh, the flames burn bright... aye, the flames burn bright...
Kept the dark at bay till the coming of light..."

The last notes drifted into silence, the melody lingering like smoke, half-lullaby, half-mourning, wrapping the room in fragile, unsettling calm. Every movement in the room felt heavier than the last. Bones aching, muscles trembling, and hearts still racing from battles fought and narrowly survived.

The song had been for the broken and the weary, a quiet tribute to the night we'd endured… and a promise, to the uncertain path that still lay ahead.

The house itself felt different now, broken, scorched, still reeking of battle… and yet no longer only ruin. It felt like the song had settled over it, stitching something invisible back together in its wake.

I leaned into Andrew, his warmth solid against me, his heartbeat steady beneath my ear.

He was alive, and around us, it no longer felt like the end of something.

It felt like survival.

Like a promise we hadn't said out loud yet.

That no matter what came next…
We would fight it.
Together.

Chapter 42

Trovi had finished gathering the remaining supplies, stacking them neatly for transport while Ewan rested as best he could. I rose slowly, brushing dust from my palms, letting the lingering warmth of the fire seep into my frozen limbs, easing the ache in my bones.

"Ready?" Trovi asked. Her voice was quiet, but it carried the calm authority it always did.

I nodded, swallowing back the fatigue pressing heavy against my chest. Outside, the storm had passed. The air smelled of wet earth and salt, clean and sharp, as pale daylight bled through the cracked windows. It caught on smoke still curling lazily from the burning hearth.

Behind me, a low groan stirred the quiet. Andrew blinked awake first, rubbing the stiffness from his neck. Red followed soon after, stretching gingerly and glancing around the room as if surfacing from a long, fractured dream.

Trovi straightened from where she'd been packing the last of the supplies. "It's ready," she said softly. Her voice carried through the stillness. "Everyone, gather close."

We moved toward the hearth, where Ewan still laid. The fire burned low, its light flickering over faces drawn tight with exhaustion, but still breathing, still here. For a moment, none of us spoke. We simply stood shoulder to shoulder, bound by the unspoken understanding of what we'd survived together.

I bent down and picked up a tin pail from beside the hearth and poured the water over the flames. The hiss filled the room as smoke and steam rose in a brief, swirling rush upward before fading into silence.

We were leaving this beautiful, hollowed place, returning to the world we had once known, our home, carrying with us the ghosts of what had happened here, the weight of everything that was still unresolved.

And yet, as we turned toward the waiting transport, a fragile thread of hope wove through the exhaustion. We were together, and for now, that was enough.

Smoke still lingered in thin, curling ribbons, the scent of ash and damp earth mingling with the sharper tang of herbs. We huddled close around Ewan's still form on the floor, his breathing shallow, a faint tremor rising with each exhale. The dim light caught the sheen of sweat on his brow.

Trovi knelt beside him, a wide bowl balanced between her knees. Steam curled from its surface, carrying the scent of sage, crushed yarrow, and something bitter and metallic that stung the back of my throat. Her sleeves were rolled to the elbow, her hands steady as she stirred the mixture with the tip of a bone-handled spoon.

"This isn't a jump," she murmured, not looking up. "It will be just like last time. Space collapses inward, guided by rune and breath."

Her fingers traced the air. Runes flared briefly, then dissolved into gold dust.

"Stay close," she added, her voice a thin thread of calm through the silence. "The transport will hold better this time with this in place." she said, still stirring the bowl, not looking at anyone.

Andrew stood beside me, blinking groggily, while Red crouched near Trovi and Ewan. Trovi inhaled slowly, her eyes half-closed as she whispered the incantation. The air thickened at once, bending and shifting around her words. Light gathered between her palms, peach-rose and soft gold, rippling outward like the surface of a disturbed pond. The scent of her herbs deepened, filling the air with a strange, electric sweetness that prickled along my skin.

The ground shivered. Then, with a low hum that settled into our bones, the room began to dissolve. Color folded inward, the walls bleeding into light, the floor rippling beneath our boots as the shimmer wrapped around us. The groan of the ruined house faded away, replaced by a steady vibration that merged into a low, living thrum.

Red's voice broke the hush first, a soft hum, unsteady at first, then slowly finding its rhythm. The same melody she'd sung by the fire, quieter now, threaded with both grief and relief. The sound wove through the glowing bubble we seemed to be in, filling the space between heartbeats.

I leaned into Andrew as the ruined house dissolved around us, stone and shadow giving way to the familiar silhouettes of Melmont's trees. The air shifted, cool and alive, carrying with it the familiar rich, damp scent of pine and earth. Around us, the world blazed in gold and violet, the last light of sunset spilling through the branches like embers fading into night.

We all stood there for a long moment, just breathing. The air in Melmont felt different, warmer, softer somehow. Hearth smoke drifted on the early winter breeze, pine needles whispering overhead. The fading light gilded the treetops in bronze and fire, and for a heartbeat, the world felt still. Real.

After everything that had happened, it was strange to stand in a place that *didn't* hum with danger. It felt… safe. The hush of the forest settling around us, the whisper of leaves brushing against one another as though the world itself was exhaling.

Andrew's hand tightened briefly around mine. Red let out a slow, shaky breath beside us. Even Trovi, who was usually so composed, took a moment to tilt her face toward the light, her eyes closed, as if letting the last warmth of the sun touch her, as proof we'd made it back.

Then Ewan groaned, a raw, pained sound that cut clean through the fragile calm. The spell of stillness broke instantly.

"Easy," Red murmured, already kneeling beside him as she checked his pulse. He tried to sit up and failed, another groan tearing free as his breath hitched. In the dying light, his skin looked ghost-pale, sweat beading along his hairline.

Andrew and I moved at once, one on each side, easing him upright with careful hands. His weight sagged against us, heavy and unsteady, his breathing shallow but steady.

Trovi was already striding ahead of us, her skirt snapping behind her as she turned. "I'll get help from the

hospital," she said briskly, relief threading her voice. "Keep him steady. Don't move too fast."

She didn't wait for a reply. Within seconds, she was disappearing down the path, her figure swallowed by the deepening gold that led toward town.

Red glanced over her shoulder toward me as she lifted Ewan's feet up. "Feels strange, doesn't it?" she said quietly. "Coming home."

I nodded, though my throat felt tight. Through the thinning trees, Melmont's familiar rooftops came into view, small, steadfast, and impossibly ordinary. Chimneys, stone walls, quiet windows. A place untouched by what we'd just survived. And yet it all felt… altered. Or maybe it was us who had changed, carrying too much of the dark back with us.

"Let's just focus on getting him to the hospital," Andrew said, his voice rough with strain. We shifted our grip and started down the path together.

The walk was slow and brutal. Ewan's weight dragged at our arms, every step a careful negotiation between haste and pain. By the time the hospital steps loomed ahead, my legs were shaking. The doors burst open before we reached them.

Trovi stood framed in the light, two nurses at her side as they rushed forward with a gurney. Disbelief flashed across their faces as they took in the state of us, bloodied, soot-streaked, clothes shredded, and still faintly humming with magic.

"Gods," one of them breathed as they lifted Ewan from our arms, golden-green light already blooming in her palms. "You made it."

Andrew sagged against the doorframe, sweat and soot streaking his skin. "Barely."

The other nurse looked between us, really looked at us, at our torn clothes, the blood, the faint shimmer of lingering magic, and swallowed hard. "Get them all inside. Now."

The next hour passed in a blur of movement and murmured orders. White light flooded the small hospital room, casting long, wavering shadows across the beds as the nurses worked with steady hands and furrowed brows. Ewan was rushed into the emergency treatment room first, the soft glow of healing runes pulsing through the half-closed door. Nearby, Red and Andrew sank onto nearby cots, nurses already tending to burns and cuts, the air thick with antiseptic and crushed herbs. I perched on the edge of a bed while a healer pressed cool salve into the bruises along my arms and offered a faint, tired smile.

"Nothing broken," she said gently. "You're lucky."

Lucky. The word landed strangely, hollow and unfamiliar.

When Trovi finally emerged, her sleeves were smeared with dried herbs, and the faint residue of magic still clung to her hands. "He'll live," she said, her voice hoarse but firm. "But he needs rest. We all do."

'She must have helped them with Ewan,' Mani murmured, the suddenness of her voice making me flinch.

Andrew dragged a hand through his hair and glanced toward the nurse. "We don't have to stay overnight, do we?"

The nurse shook her head. "You're stable. There are no signs of internal bleeding, binding, or spell shock. But you should rest somewhere quiet. No more magic for a while."

Relief rippled through us, tired smiles, sagging shoulders, the kind of exhaustion that ran deeper than muscle or bone and straight into the soul.

Trovi, however, was already looking elsewhere. Her gaze sharpened with purpose as she wiped her palms against her apron. “Before we go,” she said softly, “I want to see Naomi.”

I slid off the bed and nodded. “I’ll go with you.” I turned to Andrew. “I’ll meet you…”

“I’m coming too,” he said, cutting me off. His tone left no room for debate. I met his eyes, then nodded.

Red stretched with a groan, every movement weighted with fatigue. “Well,” she said, smirking faintly, “I’m going home…to live in my bed forever. See you when I rise from the dead.” She pulled me into a quick, fierce hug before heading for the door.

The hallway was hushed as we followed Trovi towards Naomi’s room, the ward lights humming softly overhead. Naomi stirred as we entered, her eyes glassy and unfocused, darting from corner to corner as if chasing whispers only she could hear.

“The sky would split,” Naomi murmured, voice trembling as if the words themselves hurt to speak. “The roots will burn… the branches bleed gold… and he is lost between worlds.” Her words tangled, unraveling into prophecy and grief. Her gaze drifted toward the ceiling, unfocused, as if watching something far above them. “He’s forgotten the way home.” She whispered, “The ravens call, but he does not answer. He cannot answer.”

A chill threaded through the room, sharp and sudden.

“Naomi,” Trovi said gently. She didn’t react. Her fingers twisted in the sheets, her knuckles pale, trembling as if trying to anchor herself to the present. “The gates are closing,” Naomi went on, a thin, fractured laugh slipping free. “The light is dimming. He has to find his way back before the last ember dies…or the nine will fall with him."

Her voice faltered, the words unraveling into whispers. "He's where the stars drown… he waits to remember…"

Even the air seemed to tighten, as if the room itself were listening. Andrew's eyes narrowed, but there was nothing left to fight here, only the echo of the dark völva speaking through Naomi's fractured mind.

"Naomi," I said softly, stepping closer. I took her hands and sat on the side of her bed. "It's over. You're safe now."

Her gaze flicked toward me, and for a fleeting second, clarity shone through, sorrowful and haunted. Then it slipped away. She turned her face from me, muttering something about wolves and fire-light, about names written in ash.

Trovi's hand brushed my arm, a silent signal. "Come," she whispered. "There's nothing more to do tonight."

I nodded, but as I turned away, there was a scent. It was faint, but unmistakable floral. Warm in a way that didn't belong to antiseptic or crushed herbs. It brushed the back of my throat, hovering right at the edge of recognition, like a name half-remembered, a dream slipping away on waking. My breath caught as the scent bloomed and faded in the same heartbeat, familiar and unsettling all at once.

'Smell that?' Mani murmured, quiet and alert.

I frowned, the sensation lingering just long enough to feel almost tangible, almost known. It was right there, on the tip of my tongue, just beyond reach…

"Astrid," Trovi said softly.

The moment broke. The scent thinned, dissolving into nothing but the clean sterility of the ward. I blinked, my head

swimming, the weight of exhaustion crashing back down around me.

'Probably nothing,' I told myself. *'Just fatigue. Too much magic. Too little sleep.'*

Mani didn't answer, but I felt her withdraw slightly, watchful.

I glanced once more at Naomi, her eyes vacant as she whispered to ghosts only she could see, then followed Trovi and Andrew into the hall. The air outside her room was lighter, cleaner, the faint scent of antiseptic and herbs replacing the heavy breath of madness we left behind.

A nurse stood waiting just a few steps away, exhaustion etched into her features, but relief flickering in her eyes. "He's stirring awake," she said quietly to Trovi. "He's weak, but stable."

Trovi exhaled slowly, then her jaw tightened, but there was a glint of warmth in her expression, the fragile kind born from relief braided with lingering worry. "Then I'll check on him," she said, her voice softer now, slipping back into her natural maternal tone.

Andrew and I fell into step behind her as we turned down the corridor, the floor cool beneath my bare feet, the dim lights guiding the way toward Ewan's room.

Chapter 43

The busy hum of the hospital corridor faded as we stepped into Ewan's room. The air hit me first, it was thick and heavy, with crushed herbs and sharp healing oils clung to every surface, their bitterness colliding with the sterile bite of modern antiseptic. It pressed into my lungs with every breath, almost suffocating, a reminder of what we had been through. Even in our exhaustion, the smell was impossible to ignore, that left me lightheaded.

The pale evening light filtered through the blinds, painting thin stripes across the floor and the edge of the bed. For a moment, I swayed. Then, my gaze snapped to the bed. Ewan.

He lay propped against the pillows, pale, and drawn tight with exhaustion. Sweat clung to his brow, his chest rising

in shallow, uneven breaths. Fresh bandages wrapped his shoulder, stark and unforgiving against his skin.

But that wasn't what held me. It was the *pull* that was sharp and sudden. Something in me *recognized* him. Not his face, or his voice, but something older.

Something buried so deep it felt foreign yet familiar. It curled low in my chest, quiet but insistent, like a thread tightening between us.

I took an unconscious step forward but then stiffened.

'What was that?' Mani asked, but I didn't have an answer. *'Why are drawn to him?'*

"Astrid?" Andrew's voice cutting through my growing panic, but distant.

I blinked, forcing the feeling down, shoving it into the same dark place as everything else I didn't understand yet.

Trovi moved first, her usual composure softening into something more maternal as she approached Ewan. In the way she checked the runes etched along his arm, murmuring under her breath, steady and controlled, as her fingers traced the carved lines. Slowly, the glow steadied, settling into a calm, consistent light.

"You should be resting," she said, quietly but firm.

Ewan let out a rough, breathless huff that might have been a laugh. "You don't know me," he rasped. "I don't rest well when there's work unfinished." His voice was raw, worn thin by pain and spell residue. "How's…the girl…?"

'Naomi?' Mani chimed in.

"She's stable," I said carefully. My voice slower than I intended. "But she's… not herself."

His eyes closed briefly, pain flickering crossing his face. "She won't be. Not for a while... maybe not ever." He swallowed hard. "The dark völva took too much from her."

Trovi's jaw tightened. "She's lucky to have survived at all." Then, softer, almost to herself, "We all are."

The silence that followed wasn't empty. It was crowded and heavy with unspoken truths. Pressing against my ribs, against my thoughts, and beneath it, that *pull* returned, quieter this time, but no less insistent. I stepped closer before I could stop myself.

"What did you mean by 'work unfinished'?" The question slipped out, sharper than I meant. "What aren't you telling us?"

Ewan opened his eyes slowly, his gaze drifting toward the ceiling like he was searching for something just out of reach.

"There's more coming," he said, his voice low and uneven. The way he said it made my chest tighten.

"The dark völva… he wasn't acting alone." His breathing hitched. "His hand was guided… loosely. There are forces still out there, pulling at the edges. If we're not careful…" His words stumbled, fraying under the weight of what he was trying to say. Fear shadowed every syllable.

"She's not happy." he murmured. "You were… meant… to kill me."

My stomach dropped.

"She?" I snapped, frustration cutting through the unease. "Who…"

But the words died as his head tipped back, his body going slack as the medicine dragged him under. His body slumped back against the pillows, his breathing evening out as

unconsciousness took hold. The weight of his confession, however, pressed down on the room like a physical force.

Andrew shifted beside the doorframe, his arms crossed, and his gaze distant. "Melmont feels different," he said quietly. "Like it knows what we brought back."

He was right. The air outside this room, outside the walls, was off, almost unnaturally so.

Trovi adjusted Ewan's blankets, then straightened. "Let's go," she said softly. "Let him rest."

She paused as she passed me, her gaze lingering, sharp, but thoughtful.

"Astrid," she said, low enough that only I heard. "When you're ready… come with me. The archives. There's something you need to see."

A shiver traced its way up my spine, not from fear, but recognition. This wasn't over, not even close.

As we made our way outside, twilight bled across the sky, gray dissolving into deep indigo.

The truth began to unravel slowly, like frost creeping across glass. We knew now that the dark völva had not acted alone. That a thread of another's will had been woven through his actions, invisible but undeniable. A puppeteer's touch, guiding each movement from the shadows. My chest tightened as the realization settled: someone had been guiding it, steering chaos into purpose, shaping our suffering into a weapon, sharpened for their own design. And whatever that design was… we'd only just glimpsed the edge of it.

My thoughts sharpened, like a knife cutting cleanly through the fog. Every manipulation, every chaos we'd faced—it had all been this 'she's' design. The pieces on the board sliding into place. The hidden hand behind Ewan's actions, the shadow threads that had followed us from the start. He hadn't been a true enemy. He had been a puppet too.

The anger burned hot, but not because of Ewan, who had been as trapped as Naomi, but because of the invisible architect orchestrating the entire nightmare. The one who had reduced lives to pieces, pain to leverage.

Fury coiled through my veins. "All of it…" My voice barely carried. "He was never even in control."

Andrew's hand closed around mine. "Then who?" he asked. "Who is she? Who's been really pulling the strings?"

The space around us seemed to be tightening. Magic stirred uneasily, shadows flickering at the edges of my vision, reminders that lingering magic remained unstable and volatile. I was starting to see it now, all the threads, they were everywhere and connected to everything. Stretching beyond sight, a ripple of cosmic force stretched across layers of reality, threads of energy twisting into a vast, unseen web. And still, the weaver remained hidden.

My fingers curled into fists. Shadows stirred faintly along my skin, restless but restrained. Rage flared, hot and sharp, but it was tempered by the cold clarity of understanding. Strategy, not impulse, had to guide us. One reckless move could ripple outward, unraveling far beyond these walls, far beyond Ewan's partial manipulation or Verrik's defiance.

The path forward had changed. We had to anticipate, to move with precision, to confront this unseen architect rather than simply react.

Trovi's voice whispered in memory, a calm thread through the storm: "Intent first, Astrid. Know the board before you strike."

I let her words settle, feeling the shadows pulse gently in response. Mani, my Garmr power, and even the lingering echoes of darkness, all aligned in quiet rhythm, attuned to the next move.

"I see it now," I said finally, my voice steady despite the fire beneath it. "Every chaos, every völva, every twisted ally… someone has been orchestrating all of it." I exhaled. "But…just wish we knew who."

Andrew's gaze met mine, full of trust, patience, and resolve reflected there. "Then we plan," he said. "We take control. And we protect everyone caught in this."

My pulse steadied. The shadows curled loosely around my fingers, obedient and calm. I would no longer be caught unprepared. I understood the board, even if the player remained hidden.

My jaw tightened, as determination settled over me, heavy and sure. A small, resolute smile tugged at my lips. "Then we need to start moving," I said. "Carefully and with calculation."

"Not before we all get some much-needed rest," Trovi interjected, sharp and unwavering. Andrew and I both nodded, too exhausted to argue. We gave her a quiet wave as she disappeared into her house, the door shutting softly behind her. Then we turned toward our own, toward the room that had become our fragile sanctuary.

The first move had been revealed. Now it was our turn. We walked in silence, the weight of everything settling around us—heavy, watchful. Fully aware of the lingering threat, even as the shadow behind it remained unseen… for now.

The puppeteer's hand remained hidden, but our resolve burned brighter. And for the first time in what felt like an endless chain of battles, I felt it, not certainty and not peace.

But readiness. Enough to stand and enough to face whatever came next. Maybe not fully prepared, but no longer afraid.

And then, it hit me again.

That pull.

It was sharp and sudden, tightening low in my chest like an invisible thread had been yanked taut. Making my step falter, just slightly. It was Ewan again.

His name wasn't just a thought. It was as if I know him.

A quiet, insistent presence that hadn't stayed behind in that room, it had followed me. Or maybe… it had always been there, just waiting.

My fingers curled at my sides as the feeling deepened, not pain or fear, but something else entirely, something older. It settled beneath my ribs, steady and unyielding, like it belonged there.

I swallowed, forcing myself to keep walking, even as that unseen thread stretched between us.

It didn't weaken.

It didn't fade.

If anything, it was growing stronger.

More certain.

I didn't understand it.

Not yet.

But I could feel it taking root, weaving itself into something I wouldn't be able to ignore for long.

And deep in my bones, beneath the exhaustion and the fading echoes of everything we'd survived, a quiet truth began to form.

This wasn't just fate. It was something far older, something long set in motion.

And this was far from over.

The board had been set, and the players were already in motion.

And whatever had just awakened between us…

was only just beginning to stir.

Acknowledgments

To my husband—

This story, like every heartbeat between us, exists because of you. From the first flicker of *Timebound* to the deeper pulse of *Soulbound,* your quiet strength and unwavering belief have carried me through every doubt and dark night.

You've been my anchor and my light—my chosen in every realm, my constant across all threads of fate. My tether through every shadow, and my proof that Soulbound are real.

This book is as much a reflection of that truth as it is of us.

To my friend, Cami—

Thank you for pushing me to be better and to keep going, whether you knew it or not. You've been my steady ground and quiet strength, the voice that reminded me I could do this—even when I doubted myself. Your faith in me means more than words can ever hold.

To my incredible Beta and ARC readers—
Your honesty and heart breathed truth into these pages. Your sharp eyes caught what mine could not, and your faith carried me through every twist and revelation. This story is better because you were part of it.

And to everyone who's believed in this series—
Every moment you've given this story helped it come alive. *Soulbound* exists because you believe—in stories, in hope, and in rising again.

With all my love and gratitude,
A.J. Hanna

COMING SOON

UNBOUND

The truth will finally come to light, the hand behind every shadow, every betrayal, every loss, every thread of chaos has led to this moment.

Ewan is more of a friend now, than a fallen ally, he is more than meets the eye. And Astrid was always meant to be his end to start his beginning...

But fate is never simple. To kill him might save the realms—or it could destroy them entirely. To spare him risks unleashing the very chaos this veiled mastermind has been orchestrating, waiting for the perfect moment to strike.

As realms fracture, alliances shatter, and loyalties waver, Astrid stands at the crossroads of light and shadow, love and sacrifice.

Every choice carries unimaginable weight; every step could ripple across worlds. To stop the architect behind this nightmare, to save the ones she loves, Astrid must uncover the hidden truths that have bound her to this destiny—and decide what kind of demi-god she is willing to become.

The storm is rising. Darkness waits. And when the first move is made, the balance of all realms will hang by a thread. Will she rise in the light… or fall into the bloodied shadows?

About the Author

A.J. Hanna is a storyteller with a heart attuned to magic, connection, and the threads that bind us to each other. In *Soulbound*, she weaves a tale of love, sacrifice, and the fierce power of bonds that transcend worlds. Her stories explore the resilience of the heart, the weight of destiny, and what it truly means to fight for those we cannot bear to lose.

When she's not writing, Alexis is a devoted wife and mother, finding inspiration in quiet moments, deep conversations, and the extraordinary in everyday life. Her imagination thrives on the intersection of emotion and adventure, crafting worlds where love—fierce, tender, and unbreakable—changes everything.

Soulbound is her story of connection and courage, written with heart, shaped by dreams, and offered with gratitude.

Follow A.J. Hanna online:
Instagram: a.j.hannaauthor
TikTok: @a.j.hannaauthor
Facebook: A.J. Hanna Author

www.ingramcontent.com/pod-product-compliance
Lightning Source LLC
LaVergne TN
LVHW100503110826
845146LV00002B/500

* 9 7 9 8 9 9 9 6 3 1 6 4 0 *